PRAISE FOR BOO WALKER

"In this beautifully written story of an old crime, a secret has shaped a family for generations, until one woman goes in search of the truth that will allow her to reconcile the inherited traumas in her life. Celebrated author Boo Walker deftly explores the curious power of genetic memory in a modern American family . . . *An Echo in Time* vibrates at the sweetest frequency and pulls gently at just the right heartstrings."
—Kimberly Brock, bestselling author of *The Lost Book of Eleanor Dare*

"*An Echo in Time* is a beautifully written, emotionally powerful story of a young woman's journey to break the cycle of generational trauma . . . I found myself cheering for Charli at every turn and smiling at the deeply satisfying and nuanced ending."
—Yvette Manessis Corporon, international bestselling author of *When the Cypress Whispers*

"*An Echo in Time* is a captivating novel about the generational legacy of secrets and shame and one woman's journey to love herself by righting the wrongs of the past. Walker has crafted a beautiful and moving tale of loss and healing that is part love story, part mystery, and all green lights."
—Melissa Payne, bestselling author of *A Light in the Forest*

"Walker dazzles . . . The characters all earn the reader's emotional investment, and the pacing is perfect. Readers will fall in love."
—*Publishers Weekly* (starred review)

"Walker's attention-grabbing and surprising plot highlights the engaging characters in this tale of second chances. For fans of women's fiction such as Nicholas Sparks's and Kristin Hannah's work."
—*Library Journal*

BEFORE WE SAY GOODBYE

ALSO BY
BOO WALKER

The Secrets of Good People (with Peggy Shainberg)
An Echo in Time
The Stars Don't Lie
A Spanish Sunrise
The Singing Trees
An Unfinished Story
Red Mountain
Red Mountain Rising
Red Mountain Burning
A Marriage Well Done

Writing as Benjamin Blackmore

Lowcountry Punch
Once a Soldier
Off You Go: A Mystery Novella

BEFORE WE SAY GOODBYE

A RED MOUNTAIN NOVEL

BOO WALKER

LAKE UNION
PUBLISHING

Published by Lake Union Publishing, Seattle

www.apub.com

Amazon, the Amazon logo, and Lake Union Publishing are trademarks of Amazon.com, Inc., or its affiliates.

EU product safety contact:
Amazon Media EU S. à r.l.
38, avenue John F. Kennedy, L-1855 Luxembourg
amazonpublishing-gpsr@amazon.com

ISBN-13: 9781662523748 (hardcover)
ISBN-13: 9781662523755 (paperback)
ISBN-13: 9781662523762 (digital)

Cover design by Caroline Teagle Johnson
Cover image: © Timothy S. Allen, © pixdeluxe / Getty;
© VISUALSPECTRUM / Stocksy

Printed in the United States of America

First edition

For everyone at Hedges Family Estate, including Anne-Marie, Tom, Pete, Enrique, Sarah, Brent, Maggie, and Christophe, who gave me such a warm welcome to Red Mountain and a proper education in wine and vine.

Quickly, bring me a beaker of wine, so that I may wet my mind and say something clever.

—Aristophanes

Prologue

STUCK IN THE MIDDLE

Red Mountain, Washington State
March 2011

I died a woman content. And yet here I am stubbornly holding on, hoping to help the man I left behind. That's what love is, isn't it? From this strange vantage point, I can see my husband, but for him, I'm merely a memory now, an unbearable ache in his chest. I can only imagine what it would be like to still be in my human form and wake in our bed to realize that the person I'd spent more than forty years with, my soulmate, my best friend, my everything, was gone.

If I have any ability to reach him now, I will.

Otis and I found each other when we were lost but lost each other once we were found. My sweet but often sour berry of a man spent decades trying to break free from his cocoon. Once he did, the grand puppeteer shook up his universe yet again. The days must be rolling on like decades, and all I can hope is that he has enough remaining resolve to keep fighting.

He's sleeping in the chair in his office, his head cast to the side, a scowl on his face. He's been snoring since I've left him—a result of his overindulgence in drink and his return to smoking a pipe—so he doesn't hear the cries from the wounded coyote pup in the vineyard. If he did, he'd be out there in the vines searching. He'd realize that he's still needed. But how do I wake him?

I try saying his name, and then yelling it, but I can't break into his dimension—if that's what I might call it. No one has given me a guidebook to navigate this realm I now inhabit.

As I watch him sleep, memories pour through me. I can see back to the Summer of Love, back to August 1969, when we first fell for each other, both of us lost souls aboard a purple bus en route to Woodstock. Who would have thought the buds of humans we once were would find our way to flowering? Never mind that it took a lifetime to blossom. Of course it did. That's the point of the chunk of time we're issued on earth. When our time comes—and we don't know when that might be—let's hope we have realized, or at least *tasted*, the sweetness of our own potential.

Otis had tasted his potential more than most, but whoever pulled the strings gave him a heck of a run for his money. I wasn't the biggest fan of my husband's pessimism, but he often made me chuckle when he spoke with such dramatics apropos his misfortunes, how he constantly saw his own shadow like a defeated groundhog, how he lived half his life under a ladder like a man doomed, or how black cats always crossed in front of him. In a way, he was right. He'd been tested more than most. That's what made him and his wines great. Because he had more heart than any man I've ever met, and despite the countless battles, he pressed on.

If only I could remind him of his own resilience.

Who could have known that the out-of-place kid I sat next to on the bus back in 1969 would become my husband of four decades?

Otis Pennington Till was certainly my kind of handsome. His thick and wavy hazelnut hair was all over the place, the perfect indicator of his inner turmoil. Like a mood ring, his eyes turned from blue to emerald and back again depending on his emotional state, and let me tell you, they changed often. His nose was a notch too broad to categorize him as gorgeous, but I wasn't into gorgeous.

Of all things, his most attractive quality was his forehead, right where his third eye—the gateway to his higher consciousness—fought to shine through his doubt and skepticism. Though he'd deny he even had a third eye, his emotions lingered there, sometimes dancing together, often warring like feuding siblings. Along with his fears, he radiated a determination and curiosity that only the best of artists showed. Throughout our years together, no matter what we were going through, I was always proud to slip my arm into his and call him mine.

Even on deck to fifty-nine and broken in grief, and despite his thinning hair the color of ice that's been in the freezer too long, he remains as attractive to me as ever.

What a life we lived. It is said that the grapes that make the best wine are produced by vines that must fight to survive. If the same were true for humans, then Otis and I would have made a magnificent wine. Aside from some financial help along the way, nothing had been spoon-fed to either one of us. We had carved our existence out of stone. Unfortunately, Otis still has a hard row to hoe, as he remains the last of us, the only surviving member of our family of four.

We lost our oldest son first. Camden died in Otis's arms, and it took everything we had for the three of us to recover. As if that weren't enough, Michael and I sipped our last breaths less than a month ago, leaving Otis to fend for himself.

Two rivers and three deaths. That'll make more sense later.

As one can imagine, after so much loss, Otis barely shows any signs of life. Not that I can blame him. The only thing that keeps me connected to the fragile line of humanity is that I don't want to let go till I know he's wrapped his fingers back around the dream we shared. We fought too hard to find our place in the world. If only he could remember that—all the work we put in, the sacrifice. All the hard-earned growth we experienced. If only he realized that he's so much of why our two boys grew into the great men they were. Despite endless challenges, he never gave up, and that can't change now. The memories of our past could be the fuel he needs to keep fighting.

How can I make him remember, though? Unless . . . *if* I could pull it off. One thing at a time, Rebecca. One thing at a time . . .

I understand his pain, why he isn't eating, why his body looks like a bag of bones. Why he cries at night. Why he lies to my family and friends and tells them that he spread my ashes in the vineyard. The truth is that what's left of my earthly remains rests in a piece of pottery on the mantel in his office, the office where he sleeps now. Otis can barely bring himself to go into our bedroom, let alone sleep in our bed. It's all he can do to take care of the animals. If it weren't for Brooks, Otis's right-hand man, the vines would shrivel, and the wines would be poured down the drain—something that *has* happened before, believe it or not.

Never have I met a man so plagued by life, yet so invested in it, so high on it, so committed. Otis is an artist who wears his heart on his forehead and is always one dial on the knob away from the right frequency—so close, yet so far. He is a long way from perfect. For that matter, *I* was a long way from perfect too. *We* were a long way from perfect. But he was my Otis, and I was his girl, and we were as meant to be as the trees and rain.

I sense that I'm soon off to join our boys, who wait for us. A piece of me died when we lost Camden, but now I'm working my way toward finding him, and I've never felt more alive. I suppose death is the final step toward life.

I believe Cam is already with Mike, two brothers reunited in a place that I won't dare attempt to imagine. There's love there, I know that. More love than any human could know. I'll get there soon enough, but I'm not ready yet.

I attempt to brush Otis's cheek, but my fingers pass through his skin like sunlight through air. "My dear, dear Otis," I whisper to him, "you've weathered a million storms; this one is no different. When the time comes, I'll be waiting. Mike and Cam too. When the time comes, we'll *all* be together again. Because I'm your forever girl, and we're your forever family." I nudge closer to him, detecting the faintest woody scents of the man I loved till my last breath. A man I still love.

"But right now," I say, "it's time for you to keep living and chasing that perfect bottle of wine. It's time you rise up and answer the coyote's call."

He can't hear a word. Even a scream won't find its way to him. I could slap him silly, and he wouldn't feel a thing, but if I move just right, with the intent coming from what might still be my heart, I may be able to penetrate the wall between life and death.

Drawing from the depths of me, I reach for him and will my finger to break through the dimensions. And it does. It does! I tickle the stubble under his nose. "Wakey, wakey, Otis. You're needed."

The sweetest whisper woke Otis. It was as if a dimmer switch had been turned up ever so softly and gently, bringing him to consciousness. For a long moment he felt at peace, as if all the bad things hadn't happened. A calm flowed in his core, and a forgotten smile teased the corners of his mouth.

Reality came rushing in as he set his eyes on the urn holding Bec's ashes, and he batted back the joy. "Oh, right," he said out loud. "For a moment there, I thought life was peachy." He still hadn't shaken his English accent from the first eleven years of his life spent in London. His voice still caught him off guard at times, as he felt very much a part of this land, and, perhaps, even properly American now. Or Americanized, as he said on occasion. No, he still didn't watch the Super Bowl, but he'd show up at the Red Mountain party for the nachos and cold beer. Well, not this year, but he had in the past. He'd even attended a Super Bowl years ago in Miami, but that was a memory he'd prefer to keep buried.

Stirring in his beyond-worn leather recliner, he kept his eyes on the urn. "When, in fact, life is not peachy at—"

A sound caused him to cock his head sideways; his ears perked up like a dog's. Before he realized it, he was sniffing, as if to detect a fire.

What bones didn't pop, what muscles didn't strain, as he peeled himself off the recliner? He damn near fell to the floor, trying to get his body to work. Almost fifty-nine and he felt ninety-five. That was what three months of barely moving had done to him. Forty years of hard farming, chasing animals, shoveling pomace, and shuffling barrels around, all coming to a halt, allowing his body to finally figure out the truth of his age.

Not that fifty-nine was that old, was it? But Otis was pretty sure that one's body gleefully presented new ailments at the start of each decade. New places hurt; entire organs decided not to function as well as they had. Hell, he could write a bloody book on the trials of living and dying now, all the way from his back square into the depths of his heart.

Rebecca. Cam. Mike.

All gone.

That was where it hurt the most. Forget his back. Forget his knees and the sore muscles. The real pain lay somewhere so deep there was no way to pinpoint it, a hollowness and sharpness at the same time.

The sound came again, a sort of cry. Otis had fallen asleep dressed, which was nothing new. He pulled on his work boots and stumbled into the kitchen. A half pot of yesterday's coffee sat cold and stale on the counter. He poured a mug and didn't even bother heating it up. He slung back enough to get some caffeine in him and then went out through the front door to find the disturbance.

The sun was high enough to offer light, but it still hadn't poked its head up over the top of Red Mountain. Not that it would do much good anyway, as the entire mountain was a dust cloud.

He'd nearly forgotten that it was March, the month of mistrals, the heavy winds that stirred up dust devils that looked like tornadoes, but he was reminded very quickly as a cloud poured in through the door, coating him as if he were Santa Claus coming down the chimney and collecting soot.

Otis coughed and squinted his eyes and cursed, thinking of all the equipment and floors and other surfaces that would need scrubbing. For a flash of a second, he missed Sonoma, where the climate wasn't so harsh. He knew he was where he was supposed to be, but it was nice to remember a time when the Red Mountain dust wasn't coming after him.

Wait, there it was again, that cry. Damned if it didn't sound like an animal of some sort.

Otis pulled a blue bandanna from his back pocket and tied it around his mouth to filter his breathing. He followed the gravel road that ran up through the vineyard, squinting to keep the dust from getting in. His team had pruned all the vines last month, the beginning of a new harvest, and the lines of them looked like young military men fresh out of boot camp. They'd already come to life, and in not too long, they'd produce buds.

The sound again, much clearer now.

Fifty feet from the house, Otis stepped down one of the rows of the syrah block that he and Rebecca had planted. A flash of those exciting and eager days after they'd escaped Sonoma and all that had happened came to him. He could feel the posthole digger in his blistered hands as he jabbed the metal into the earth, making enough of a hole in which Rebecca could drop a baby vine. Those days were a new birth.

Right at his feet he heard the noise, a whimper laced in fear. Bending down, he found, curled up in a ball, a tiny trembling coyote pup, about the size of two hands. White streaks decorated his otherwise indigo-brown fur.

When he saw Otis, his oversize ears perked up, and he flashed his teeth.

"Oh, c'mon, mate," Otis said. "You're the one trespassing."

The coyote pup attempted to stand, but he didn't get very far. A bad leg kept him down.

"Where's your family?" Even as he asked, Otis realized that he could relate better than anyone on earth. One lone dog to another. "What's going on with your leg?" He stretched out a gentle hand.

The pup growled again.

Otis retracted at the sight of the teeth. "We're not going to get very far with you trying to bite me. Trust me, I'm friendly." He thought he might dash back to the house—if dashing was something his old body could do (come to think of it, it wasn't)—and grab a piece of bacon to attempt to lure the poor animal. But he worried the pup would sneak off, possibly hurt himself even more. From what little he could see of the leg, the animal was hurt badly.

Otis tried to get closer, talking as kindly as he could. At one point the coyote stood on his three good legs and started moving away, but then he stumbled back to the ground.

The dust wasn't letting up, but Otis took off his bandanna, hoping he might look a little friendlier. "All right, mate, we need to make some decisions. You need me more than I need you."

More forceful this time, Otis reached over and finally got a hand on him. The pup went after him with a bite that proved somewhat harmless.

Otis grinned. "Okay, you're younger than I thought." His teeth had barely come in. Otis had seen rabid; this one was not. "Don't worry, I'm the last person on this mountain you should be afraid of."

Otis knelt and did his best to gently scoop up the animal. The pup cried as the damage to its leg revealed itself. The bone was broken below the knee.

Handling the coyote delicately and speaking in gentle whispers, Otis returned to the house, finally escaping the dust. Unsure what to do, Otis set him down on the rug in the living room. Standing on three legs, the pup looked around nervously but stopped growling.

Fetching a bowl of water from the kitchen, Otis dipped in his finger, splashing it. "It's safe to drink. Some of the best water you'll ever have. Well water from three hundred feet down."

The pup sniffed it and turned away.

"Are you being finicky? Some sort of water sommelier? You won't find better in the world." Otis could still recall the moment he'd first tasted the water from the well they'd dug in '94. He'd never tasted anything cleaner in his life.

Eventually the pup inched his way toward the bowl. Now that they were in the light, Otis could see the maimed leg better. He'd have to take him to the vet when they opened. What in the world was he going to do with this guy?

⌇

Later that morning, Otis returned from the vet holding a much cleaner and happier coyote. The vet had issued feeding instructions and given the little guy a painkiller and bath and wrapped his foot in a cast. With a cone around his neck, the pup lay glazy eyed and groggy in Otis's arms.

"What do we do now, little one?" Otis carried him into his office. "Shall we watch a show?" Otis had never kept a television in his office until recently. He'd moved it in from the bedroom.

As he thumbed through stations, he asked, "What am I going to call you, amigo?"

The pup barely opened his eyes, even when Otis nudged him.

"No opinion whatsoever? Somehow I doubt that. A name means a great deal. It must speak of one's strength and character, no? How about Amigo? That seems to fit well."

A silence ripe for an ambush of the heart filled the room.

"You know, Amigo, you really came to the wrong bloke if you're looking for pampering. I'm all out of everything. Cupboards are as bare as my soul." A memory seized him, of seeing tire tracks in the snow, realizing Bec and Mike had gone out into the blizzard, the agony of trying to get a hold of them.

The lifeless faces of his wife and second-born son at the morgue had burned into Otis's brain, and he would never stop seeing them. He never *wanted* to stop seeing them.

Otis sighed as he stroked the coyote's back. The poor dog had found the worst man ever to rescue him. He couldn't even rescue himself.

—

That night, the coyotes howled with a longing that reverberated within.

Otis was no stranger to the desert dogs that he'd first met in Montana as a boy. He'd felt a connection with them since his family relocated to the US, and when he'd first howled as a teenager—at Bec's encouragement—he'd released emotions that had been trapped in his chest all his life. As their calls came piercing through the night, both Otis's and Amigo's ears perked up. Amigo maneuvered well enough with his leg in a cast and jumped up on the back of the couch, which pressed against the window. He didn't howl back, but he longingly stared into the darkness.

"The vet says you need a month. They'll still be waiting on you." Otis hoped so, at least. Letting him out now would be a death sentence.

Amigo pawed at the window and opened his mouth, as if he might howl back, his way of saying, *Mama, I'm in here!*, but only a whisper of air came from his lungs, barely enough to cause a whistle.

Heartbroken, Otis scooped him up and tried to comfort him, but Otis knew better than anyone that only your loved ones, only your family, could offer the comfort they both sought. Only your loved ones could teach you how to howl.

—

In the morning Otis drank his coffee with Amigo on his lap. Though the news disgusted him, he watched anyway and cursed under his breath at life and all the kooks lucky enough to still be alive but not acting that way. He didn't count, of course, as he'd already been sentenced to death. No man should ever outlive his children.

On the way to retrieve a second cup, he was passing by a shelf of books when one came tumbling down at his feet, nearly striking his toe. "What in the . . . ?" As he bent down to pick it up, he realized that he'd been attacked by the fancy leather journal that Bec had given him after Camden died.

He picked it up and stood in slow motion, remembering exactly the conversation he'd had with Bec. Joan Didion's book on grief had inspired her to attempt to write her own way through the loss of their son. She'd toiled away for months before burning what she'd written. Of course, Bec had done better than Otis in the aftermath of Cam's death, and in true Bec form, she had tried to lift Otis along with her.

He'd been annoyed when she suggested he start writing his memoir. "A memoir?" he said with a contorted mouth like he was eating a fried cricket. "Who would want to read my memoir? What would I have to say anyway?"

"Um, you were a writer when I first met you. Just like your father. It could be good for you." She had a seemingly endless well of patience for him and ignored his negativity as she placed a kiss on his lips. "It's not about the product; it's about the process."

"I assure you I will never write a memoir."

She pulled away but still kept a hand on his chest. "Then call it something else. A diary."

"A diary? What am I, a twelve-year-old girl?" In a mocking and exaggerated British tone, he said, "Dear diary, the wines don't taste the same anymore. Quite frankly, I want to tie my ankle to a cement block and jump into the irrigation pond. It's a terrible vintage anyway."

Bec let out her own dramatic sigh. "You're beyond impossible. Also, I'm far older than twelve, and I still write in my diary."

"But you're . . ."

"What?"

"I don't know. Elevated. Introspective. Hopeful."

She finally turned, saying over her shoulder, "For God's sake, Otis. Just call it a journal. Or a notebook. Quit making such a fuss. Pick up a pen and see what happens."

He realized the kindness of her gesture and how much of an arse he was being. He chased after her and kissed her forehead. "Thank you, my dear. I'll see what I can do." To himself, he thought, *And why not, with all the time I have on my hands? The vines these days, they grow on their own. The wines make themselves.*

Back in the present, Otis breathed into the empty feeling he had inside and peeled open the journal. The spine cracked. Of course, he'd never written a word. With the bitter taste of having failed at her assignment, he returned the book to the shelf and continued into the kitchen to get his coffee. Back in the office, Amigo was happily waiting and leaped toward Otis at exactly the wrong time, knocking the coffee all over the chair.

"Aye, aye, aye, dog," Otis said, watching the coffee drip down the leather. "You must be more careful." He was proud of himself for not losing his temper, though perhaps he'd lost the last of his tempers somewhere in the haystack of grief.

On to the third cup of coffee, he returned to watching the news with Amigo cuddled up on him like a bloody Havanese. While the talking head spoke about a crime spree in Seattle, Otis found himself looking back at the darned journal, sitting up there taunting him and testing him and eyeing him as if he had some sort of responsibility to it.

He turned up the volume on the television and tried harder to focus, but his eyes kept going to the shelf.

Bec's voice echoed in his ears. He repeated her words in a mock tone fit for a four-year-old. "It's not about the product; it's about the process."

Otis fought off the idea for another few hours, but he eventually pulled the journal off the shelf and sat at his oak desk and tracked down a pen. As Amigo curled up at his feet, he said into the air, "You see, Bec. I'm full of surprises."

He wondered where to begin.

"Just write, you buffoon."

Something clicked inside, and he felt his hand and the pen moving, almost without his instruction, *almost* like the way his hand had moved the first time he and Bec had toyed with a Ouija board.

The letters collected on the page, forming words and then sentences, slowly dragging Otis back through time.

Everyone has a moment in their lives that changes everything. For me, it was when a hitchhiking hippie princess squeezed in beside me on a crowded purple bus traveling east from San Francisco. From the moment I set eyes on her, I was thunderstruck . . .

Part I

THE CALIFORNIA YEARS, 1969–1993

Chapter 1

Our Own Orbit

August 1969

A purple bus with white daisies, decorated by amateurs with paint not meant for an automobile, waited for stragglers on the corner of Haight and Ashbury in San Francisco. Deep inside sat Otis Till, packed in with a host of barely dressed hippies getting high and singing Woody Guthrie songs along with a long-haired shirtless man strumming a guitar with a rainbow strap. A hand-rolled cigarette hung from the mouth of Sally, the bus driver, and he stood counting heads, his lips moving behind a thick golden beard.

Bumping into Sally as the man passed out flyers days earlier, Otis had been intrigued. Besides the drive from Montana to California, he hadn't seen much of the US. This was a chance for a quick adventure before his freshman year at Berkeley, one last romp before four years of a serious commitment in the pursuit of a career in journalism. He'd been in the city only a month, having come early to get a taste of his new home. Even in Montana he'd heard that San Francisco was the center of the universe for budding freaks and renegades and lovers and seekers and lost souls who were tired of stumbling around like zombies following the footsteps of their parents, tired of letting the government decide who to fight, weary of racing from school to a job that was nothing more than a hamster-wheel-waiting-room for death.

Though Otis was indeed a lost soul, he was a long way from a hippie, but they intrigued him, this life they lived . . . or, at least, tried to live. How nice it would be to drop out of the rat race and go in search of what mattered, whatever and wherever that might be. Not that being a journalist was exactly racing with rats. More like observing and documenting them. He admired the profession and looked up mightily to his father, who'd been a news correspondent for *The Daily Telegraph* in London before assuming his current role writing for the *Bozeman Daily Chronicle*. He'd garnered shelves full of awards and even written a couple of books along the way. Though Otis wasn't the writer his father was, he believed he'd get there in time. He was not quite seventeen and about to start Berkeley as one of the youngest freshmen on campus, an honor he'd earned with a work ethic instilled in him by generations of workaholics.

If anything, he felt torn between the man he expected to become and the parts of him that hung around in the fringes of his soul, the person who wouldn't mind taking a few years off to chase music festivals and expand his mind with psychedelics. He might even find a worthy reason to keep working like a dog.

For the last month Otis had been working at a car wash and crashing in an accordion closet of a two-bedroom flat with two Texans who were trying to open a barbecue joint. They listened to loud hillbilly music, and their place constantly smelled like ketchup and molasses, but the cheap rent and endless supply of pork were hard to beat.

Though he certainly hadn't planned on leaving San Francisco so quickly, the intrigue of this journey to Woodstock had been too tempting. Otis was trying hard not to take another peek at the tennis-ball breasts of the topless woman with hairy underarms who stood in the aisle catching up with a friend, laughing with abandon, as if flaunting her goods were a normal activity among strangers. Had she tried that on a bus in Bozeman, both men and women would've raced to throw a horse blanket over her as if she were on fire.

Along with the luck of a naked woman in his view, he also had an empty seat beside him. With this crew of yahoos, who knew how long that might last, but for now, he had a place to keep his satchel and room to breathe. It was almost like they all knew that he was an outsider. Americans could be so invasive sometimes, as if they had a completely different sense of personal space. Of course, his father had taught Otis that he had to learn to fit in to get a good story. Otis was trying, but this was a tough crowd.

Considering the way he was dressed, his button-down shirt and Sherlock Holmes hat, he supposed there was no hiding who he was. He couldn't quite bring himself to grow his hair out and stick a flower behind his ear and wrap bracelets around his wrist and dance in circles to the rhythm of twenty-five unlearned bongo drummers.

When someone had asked if he'd checked out Zeppelin, Otis had looked up to the sky, wondering whether he'd missed a big balloon.

The guy had laughed. "The band, man. Led Zeppelin."

Otis looked at him like he spoke Mandarin. "The band man?"

The guy put his hands on Otis's shoulders and peered deeply into his eyes. "It's gonna be all right, brother. It's *all* gonna be all right."

"That's quite good to know."

"Ah, listen to that accent. Sweet music to my ears. You're part of the British Invasion. The Stones, the Beatles. You are welcome here, man."

That particular guy now wielded an acoustic guitar and played another song that Otis didn't know. He knew Guthrie and Bob Dylan because his American mother and aunt loved them. Mostly, though, Otis's taste had been formed by his British father, who had raised him on classical music and jazz, the likes of Bach and Bix Beiderbecke. The Beatles and Stones were okay too. That other side of him, the part he'd hidden, could dig what they were about. *Dig.* Wasn't that a funny word?

"All aboard!" Sally yelled as he shut the door. Otis felt a sigh of relief. He'd at least enjoy this first leg sitting by himself. Sally turned back to the passengers and pulled the fag from his mouth. "Okay, brothers and sisters, you gotta sit down. At least while I get out of the city."

No one listened to him.

Sally raised his voice. "Who's ready to go to New York?"

A tepid cheer rose from the passengers.

"I *said*, who is ready to go to New *fucking* York?"

All but Otis yelled and clapped their hands and beat the backs of the seats. "Woodstock, Woodstock!" they chanted, firing up joints and ceramic pipes and grinning like there was no war going on, like all was right in the world.

Without moving his head, Otis peered left and right and up and down through the cloud of marijuana and cigarette smoke. What in God's name had he gotten himself into? He wanted to be this free, but something deep within held him back. He might explore some drugs and crack a smile or two, but he would not be taking his shirt off during this trip. He would not be dancing with abandon. He would not become one with everyone. He'd linger on the outside, watching like a journalist would, studying these people to find what made them tick. Then he'd put his findings into an article that he could turn into his first published piece. His dad would flip, and likely even forgive him for sneaking off to the festival.

Once the commotion died down, Sally gave them the rules of the road, and then everybody returned to their conversations. The guitarist started playing again. Otis pulled out his notebook and scribbled a few observations. He'd *almost* told his parents about this trip. Phrased correctly, his father *might* support the idea of Otis writing a piece about the biggest music festival this country had ever known. More likely, his father would tell him that if he climbed on this bus, he'd be in the biggest heap of shite of his life. The only way Otis would tell his parents about the trip was *if* he could get the piece published.

The bus pulled away, and Otis slipped into his own world, wondering what angle might interest readers. Would they care to read about a young British man's journey east? Or would they prefer a drier form of reporting, ticking off the facts?

The bus stopped abruptly, and Otis's head snapped forward. Looking back, that moment changed everything, the shift in the universe, the sudden stop with the squeaky brakes, the door swinging open. Otis tensed, knowing what it meant: Whoever had paid for the seat next to him was about to get on the bus.

Not that he didn't like people. He enjoyed a good conversation, but these strange beings were from another planet. Otis peered through the smoke and past the braided hair and handmade jewelry and bare breasts and big smiles and eyed the door, waiting to see who would climb the steps. *Whoever it is,* he thought, *may they have showered recently.*

The sight of the boarding passenger made his head fall back. A petite and curvaceous blonde in cutoff jeans and a white crop top apologized to Sally for her tardiness.

"Nah, man, don't worry about it. You made it just in time."

Travel bag in hand, the woman, if she could be called a woman, a girl maybe, looked down the aisle. Her sandy-blond hair fell into a mess of curls. Her necklace was even longer, a collection of feathers and copper beads dangling from a leather strand. A variety of bracelets wrapped around her wrist. Her eyes were the color of the sagebrush back in Bozeman. She stood a foot shorter than Otis, but she didn't carry herself small. She looked like the kind of person who could hustle people with her size, fooling them into thinking she couldn't fend for herself. Those eyes, however, told a different story. *I might appear innocent,* they said, *but I know how to defend myself.* There was a lot to like about her, but he was instantly drawn to her wild hair and those don't-mess-with-me eyes.

She got about halfway down the aisle before she noticed him. With her ballerina legs imprinted on his mind, Otis turned away faster than if he'd come across a bear back home. Shoving his book into his satchel, he peered through the window, looking out over the city, his heart thumping so hard it could break his ribs if he didn't figure out a way to settle down.

"Anyone sitting here?" she asked.

Her voice wasn't petite either. It was an exotic silk that hit his bare skin and raised goose pimples.

Otis looked down, acting as if he hadn't noticed the empty seat. "Oh, yes, I do believe it's available, to my knowledge."

She smiled and shoved her bag onto the rack above them, then eased into her seat, giving off scents of sandalwood and herbs.

Otis escaped with another look out the window. He wasn't trying to be rude, but his body betrayed him. His legs tensed up, and he tapped a foot, pretending to be purely focused on a terribly important affair right outside.

He was relieved when the bus kicked into gear, and he was still holding his breath when she asked, "Do I scare you?"

As if he were prying open a door with a crowbar, Otis forced himself to turn to her. She was simply a young woman. A skeleton covered in flesh. A human with the same flaws and issues as all the rest. And exquisite braless breasts with nipples poking through the thin cotton of a top better suited as a napkin. "Of course you don't scare me."

She pulled her hair from her eyes. "You look afraid." She had soft-looking skin sprinkled with a few freckles. Her mouth, shaped like a flower, puckered into a blooming smile.

By God, had she seen herself? Of course he was afraid. She was enough to rupture time, to alter the course of history! So much for playing it cool. Considering the spell she'd put on him, there was no fooling her, no way of pulling a fast one.

Instead, he let out the air in his tires and said with the most authenticity he could muster, "Okay. I'm petrified."

That got a smile out of her. It did something to Otis too. He puffed out his chest. *So she likes honesty and perhaps a pinch of self-deprecation. It might not be such a long drive to New York after all.*

"Why would you be *petrified* of me?" she asked, mimicking his accent.

Otis looked at her like, *Why wouldn't I be petrified of you?* He examined her up and down, and she let him, smiling the whole time and then breaking into a laugh.

"If you weren't so harmless looking," she said, "I might be offended."

Otis froze, then stumbled for words as his cheeks warmed. "I didn't mean to—"

She poked him in the side; her bracelets jingled. "Chill, man. I'm not offended. Tell me . . . where you from?"

He almost claimed to be an Aussie as some sort of joke but resisted at the last moment. He was never funny when he tried. "A faraway place."

"Okay, man from far away, why are you afraid of me?"

He found her eyes this time, willing himself not to break away. "I won't insult you by complimenting your looks. Perhaps it's not even your appearance." He considered the question. "Honestly, I don't quite know. You have this way about you that's terribly . . . I don't know . . . not *un*settling. It's quite soothing, actually."

"You're really good at playing the innocent cute one from a faraway land, aren't you?"

"I'm not playing at anything. Simply trying to come up with the right words. They've escaped me."

"It's probably just love at first sight." Not even da Vinci could have painted her sly look after that one.

Otis chuckled to himself. The only thing he had on her was a few inches. He was a farm truck on the racetrack in Monaco. She was the lead car, but he had to keep his head.

"Love at first sight," he mused out loud, grasping for that one elusive atom of confidence that he had in there somewhere. "I don't know that I'd go quite that far, but I can only speak for me." To the dear Lord he prayed she couldn't hear the timidity clinging to each syllable that left his mouth. "Have I taken your breath away?" He smiled at his own audacity. The atom swelled into a molecule.

She apparently found him entertaining, as she looked at him like she was engaging in a comedy bit with Walter Matthau. "Who is this man that I've sat next to on the bus?" She asked it almost like she was on stage reciting a monologue. *Who is this man and why hath he been brought into my life?*

Otis pictured the runt of a litter stumbling into the prize puppy. All the effort he'd put into creating this confident facade suddenly felt exhausting, and he retreated into his shell.

For a minute there he'd impressed a girl. For a microsecond, he was a normal kid falling in love. Wasn't it nice? No, not nice. And not sweet. It was extraordinary, a ride on a magic carpet, like those Steppenwolf fellows sang about on the radio earlier.

Otis turned away, hating himself for doing so but unable to wield the false bravado for even another breath.

She poked him again, a strong index finger right in the back.

"What'd you poke me in the kidney for? Do you plan on assaulting me the entire ride to New York?"

An angelic giggle poured out of her. "Kidney? What are you, an anatomist?" She didn't wait for his response. "I don't know what I'm planning. I've certainly hit a nerve, though, haven't I? I don't even know your name."

He took a desperate breath, as if he'd sprinted across the Golden Gate Bridge.

"Am I wearing you out?"

Her demeanor changed in a moment, a trait that Otis would come to see as her defining one. She always claimed to have two heads, as any good Gemini should. Otis would soon see a thousand more. The person she changed into at that moment was the sweetest, kindest, most understanding woman in existence. That side of her would always be his favorite.

She set her delicate hand on his, nearly stealing his breath. "Can we slow it down and just talk? I've had a shitty day, and I need someone who won't judge me."

Her words brought him out of his own head. Suddenly she was more than a pretty face and petite and delectable body. She was as human as he was, someone who deserved more than what he was giving her.

His heartbeat slowed to an easy rhythm, and he gave in to a calm surrender. "I'm Otis Till. Of London, by way of Montana. What's your name?"

"I'm Rebecca Bradshaw. A somewhat proud daughter of the Golden State. A searcher of sorts hoping I'm not a lost cause."

If her looks had torn through to his heart, her voice—that silky voice—and what she said, the way she spoke, they penetrated his soul. The boy who had climbed on the bus took a step toward becoming a man, simply by falling into her presence.

Had someone asked Otis if he had imagined they'd spend the rest of their lives together after that brief first encounter, he would have laughed mightily and responded, "Yes and no. I was smitten, and she seemed to be smitten too. We were the same person, and we found ourselves on that bus, two birds who'd fallen from the nest coming together in what I could only call magic. I didn't believe in myself and questioned everything I did or said, but yes, I had a sneaking suspicion something would come of us."

Those first few hours went by in a blur. Otis forgot about the world and the people around them, the place they were going. It was simply Otis and Rebecca rotating on their own orbit around the sun.

Chapter 2

THE POWER OF LOVE

Otis and Rebecca spent the first three hours on the bus dissecting politics and religion and playfully jousting in cultural warfare, but when they diverted toward personal topics, when Otis tried to maneuver past her defenses and learn more about her life, she'd sidestep and deflect.

He explained what had brought him to the States, how his American uncle, Jim, had been diagnosed with cancer, leaving his aunt Morgan to take care of a cattle ranch. Otis's father had not hesitated when he'd heard of their troubles. In no time, they were on a Pan American flight soaring to a land Otis had never seen. Their belongings—the remnants of their English life—followed behind in a slow boat.

Being the new kid proved to be an ongoing fight throughout his grade school years. Not only was he new, but he was a city boy from London so different from his new classmates. His London education had far exceeded that of the Bozeman public school system, which was why he had skipped a grade and would only be a few weeks into seventeen when he started at Berkeley.

In Montana, he'd found himself surrounded by cowboy types who lived off the land. Dads who rode the rodeo and raised animals, 4-H kids lined up to follow suit. Otis had tried his best to fit in, even tried wearing cowboy boots and a wide-brimmed hat for a while, but in his later teenage years, he'd given up and accepted his role as an outsider.

In the five years since he'd moved to the United States, he hadn't found a shred of clarity—until now, in the earthy tones of this girl's eyes, and in the endless universes behind them. But he couldn't quite muster the courage to tell her that, so he mounted his own defenses, this time insisting that she talk about herself for a while.

They were passing signs for Reno when she finally acquiesced. "Okay, okay, if you really care that much."

"I do!" he insisted, grabbing the attention of everyone sitting near them. In a lower voice, he asked, "How can I know who you are without knowing your origins?"

She frowned. "Let's hope who I am is not a product of where I come from."

Realizing he'd gotten himself into trouble, Otis passed a hand through the air. "Please forgive my intrusion. It's none of my business."

"No, it's fine. Maybe it's good for me to talk about it." She took a moment to sift through her thoughts and then fed Otis a few morsels about her life.

Rebecca Bradshaw had been raised by unambitious and troubled parents in Santa Rosa, north of San Francisco. Her father was a carpenter who could be a good man when his affection for beer and his La-Z-Boy didn't get in the way. Her mother was often plagued by a noisy congregation of regret—her lack of ambition, her poor choice of a husband, and her often misguided relationship with God—but she had bouts of strength, chunks of time, sometimes months, where she found renewed hope in the world. Rebecca said she vacillated between the defeated housewife and the optimist who always found a second chance at life. Either way, her mother always attempted to take care of everyone in the family, even at the expense of taking care of herself.

The Bradshaw household was one of bipolar dysfunction, and it had turned out two seesaws for children, Rebecca and her older brother,

Jed, both of whom could be propelled by the winds of life, but could also be swept up like debris in a tornado by them. Jed, in particular, had been troubled since birth, plagued by dark clouds, and Rebecca said that she'd always had to protect him from her father, whose disappointment knew no end.

Rebecca understood her family dynamics in such an incredibly self-aware way and described them with such eloquence that Otis thought she'd make a great writer herself. He feared his own elocution would stymie his chances of possibly pursuing something with this young woman. Not that he was sure that she was interested in him romantically. He hadn't determined whether she looked at him as a safe co-traveler or as someone with whom she might be interested in a relationship. If it was the latter, then she certainly had a screw loose. Of course, it sounded like her mother had poor taste in men as well, so maybe Otis would get lucky.

Cars zipped by the purple bus as it chugged along through the sweltering desert. The enthusiasm of the hippie passengers had slightly waned, quite possibly because they were all knackered by the copious amounts of weed they'd already smoked.

Things got sticky when Otis asked how often she went to visit her folks. Rebecca closed in on herself.

"We don't speak right now," she finally said. "Long story. Blah, blah, blah." Catching herself, she came back to him with more enthusiasm. "And you, my new friend. What are you going to do with a fancy degree from Berkeley? Write for a newspaper like your old man?"

Otis allowed yet another deflection, not wanting to subject her to any more of the pain that had glimmered in her eyes. "Yeah, write for a paper somewhere, or a magazine. I'd love to write for *The Atlantic* or *Forbes*. Maybe *Life* or *Time*."

"Look at you," she said with wide eyes. "It must be nice to have it all lined up ahead of you. Sixteen years old, and you know exactly what you're meant to do. What a rare specimen you are."

The potential sarcasm in her voice disturbed him. "My father says you must pick something and go with it. That's how you get ahead. The passion will come later."

"Sounds like an ambitious man."

"You have no idea."

"That's a lot to live up to."

Otis let out a chuckle. His uncle had said something eerily similar on his deathbed. Uncle Jim had been days away from succumbing to cancer when he'd grabbed Otis's forearm, squeezed *hard*, and said, "You have big shoes to fill, kid. Don't let your family down."

Rebecca dragged a delicate finger across her chin. "My father always said that ambition breeds disappointment. He taught us to dream small and to accept our place."

"Not much of a world-is-your-oyster kind of fellow. I hope you know he's wrong."

Gloom lifted her eyebrows. "I guess we'll see, won't we? So you inherited your father's gift for words then?"

There she went again, batting away his intrusions. "I know my way around a typewriter, but my dad says the secret to becoming a great writer is leaving a lot of words in your wake."

Rebecca sat back and looked up at the roof of the bus. "You're lucky. I feel like I'm a long way from even figuring out which direction to point myself. Forget about what I'm *meant* to do or what I would *love* to do."

Otis sat up straight, desperate to make a point. "I'm not sure that I *love* writing. I'm good at it. School comes rather easily to me, but it's not something that I wake up eager to do. Perhaps it will grow on me."

She twisted toward him. "It's kind of sad, isn't it, the idea of just going with something? Not that I have a contrarian argument."

Otis crossed his arms and looked down at his lap.

"What?" she asked.

"This is not the pep talk I need a month before I start school."

"Sorry, should I go sit somewhere else?" She started to get up.

He grabbed her arm, almost too desperately. "Are you kidding me? If you get out of this seat, I'll jump out the window."

She smiled and sat back down. A welcome moment of levity descended. "If you jump, then I'm going to feel bad the rest of the trip, and then I won't be able to enjoy the music."

"Oh, dear. I wouldn't want to spoil your trip."

"Not to mention, who's going to shovel you off the pavement? How about the traffic pileup you'd cause? The emotional damage to all involved. And if I miss Crosby, Stills, Nash, and Young, I'll come find you in the afterlife and throw you out another window."

"You're right. It would be terribly selfish of me."

They looked at each other with subtle smiles that threatened to crack the bus wide open.

"It would be nice for the vultures," Rebecca added, not breaking eye contact. "They probably haven't eaten all day."

"Fair point. I do love animals." Otis nearly broke his jaw smiling so hard. "Besides, does the world really need another writer?"

She let her smile fade. "I don't know about another writer, but something tells me we do need you."

Otis retreated into his bashful self and looked away. "You just haven't gotten to know me well enough."

Rebecca slipped her arm around him, like the way a boy might do to his pal. "Sounds to me like you're as lost as I am. Maybe we can be lost together, Otis Till."

That moment may have been the first time in his life that he hadn't felt lost.

"It is nice to think about dreams," she mused, half to herself. "Maybe they do come true from time to time."

"And the light doth shine," Otis said. "What would yours be then? Not to stand in the way of your father's murky take, but let's assume achieving our dreams is possible, a notion to which I do subscribe."

"Listen to you, Dream Seeker." She pulled one leg up and folded her arms around it. Her gaze went toward the windshield. "I have no idea, but I'd like to think that I could make a difference, you know. Do something to make the world a little better."

Her simple words shattered him. Perhaps his writing could do something good for the world, but he'd never once considered how what he did could impact others.

He pulled off his hat and held it on his lap. "It's people like you who should be in control. We'd be far better off."

"Who are people like me?"

He met her eyes and patted his chest. "The ones with big hearts."

"My big heart and your big dreams. We make a pair, don't we?"

~

Utah. Wyoming. Nebraska. Iowa. Otis wished they were going to Mars, because all he wanted to do was keep talking to her, keep exploring her mind, soaking up this feeling bubbling inside.

Rebecca had a side that he had yet to unearth, a room with a locked door. Never had he met a cheerier person, but every once in a while, she would retreat into herself. They sat next to each other every day, chatting some with others, but mostly the two of them, an attraction so intense that Otis would look out the window and realize he'd missed an entire state's worth of the drive. Of course, Otis worried that the attraction was quite possibly and most surely one-sided, but he tried not to dwell on that part.

At night, everyone slept in tents or stretched out on the floor of the bus. Perhaps any other man would have made his move by then, but Otis slept out under the stars by himself, bidding good night to Rebecca after dinner. Each night he would walk away, wondering what she was thinking. Was she sad that he left her or was she grateful that he'd understood his place in her world, namely, as a friend? He hated himself for his lack of courage, but he thought her potential rejection would cut so deep that he would never recover.

It was in a campground somewhere east of Chicago when Rebecca came to him at night. Scents of dwindling fires and charcoal grills lingered in the warm Midwest air. Near the bus, the guitarist strummed folk songs.

She appeared, standing between him and the moon.

A skinny band held her hair back over her ears, showing half-moon earrings. Glitter sparkled under her eyes. A floral kimono hung loosely from her shoulders, revealing a crochet bikini top and ample bare skin. An oversize belt held up a pair of corduroy trousers.

"Can I join you?"

Otis should have been more comfortable with her by then, but her question turned him to stone. Unfazed and not officially invited— considering Otis was unable to utter even the simplest response—she lay down and rested her head next to his on the pillow. Otis caught himself with his mouth open, his mind ablaze with the reality of the moment. If she could smell of desire, she did so then. Perhaps he was about to be used, or maybe it was more, but either way, she had come for him.

Rebecca faced him. "What a night."

"Indeed. Very bright stars." *Very bright stars?* Had he just said that, on the precipice of what was to come? *Very bright stars.* His father would take the word *very* and slap him with it.

She didn't laugh at him. Instead, she looked at him as if he were an adorable puppy who hadn't quite figured out how to walk yet. She placed her hand on his chest.

His heart thumped as if a timpanist stuck in Otis's chest were striking his instrument in the climax of a symphony. Could she tell what she was doing to him?

Enough, he thought. *Get out of your head.* A kiss was coming. His legs shivered; he'd never kissed a girl in his life.

"How long were you going to make me wait for you?" Her whispered question startled him, causing the timpanist to fall out of rhythm. He'd probably fallen out of his seat and knocked over an entire row of oboists.

"What do you mean?"

"You're still afraid of me."

"Intimidated maybe."

"So you need an invitation then?"

He chuckled and slid his eyes to her. "Preferably a written one, yes. Don't forget that you'll have to persuade me with your prose. Beware of lazy adjectives and dangling modifiers. I am not easy, you know." Only she could do that to him, give him courage.

"Oh, I've figured that out," she said.

Why did she look at him so, as if she were truly mesmerized and even impressed by him? She saw something that he didn't see when he forced himself to look in the mirror.

A silence that hadn't likely existed since the aftermath of the Big Bang followed. They'd come to a crossroads, a moment in time where Otis was cornered into making the most important decision of his life. Not that it was much of a decision at all, but the self-doubt running through him was still so heavy that he wasn't sure, even after her comment about the invitation, that he was worthy of her physical affection.

People like him didn't get to kiss people like her. Even if he did, what would happen from there? He would botch every moment. There would be no Big Bang about it.

All the doubt in the world wasn't enough to keep him from giving it his best shot, though. As he moved toward her, it wasn't with the feral voracity of a tiger or even the desperate craving of an animal at all. Every millimeter—yes, millimeter, as he still refused to cede the metric system—that he moved toward her felt like crawling into the cave of a monster.

Nevertheless, he pushed through, because this was a chance that he would not miss, and with his eyes closed, he bumped right into her forehead, missing her mouth altogether.

She laughed while he wished that he could disappear. That was it, he'd blown it, and he was convinced she was a second from leaping up like he was a leper and run, run, running away, seeking a man more fit for her perfection.

His face flushed, and he pressed his eyes closed with such intensity that he became dizzy. *Take me away from here,* he begged.

Her laugh wasn't sinister, though, certainly not mocking. Perhaps more a giggle.

Otis opened his eyes, and she was still there. Her laugh had melted to a slight grin. He felt a million things, but the strongest was an inviting, welcoming, forgiving, loving sensation that made him feel like he was home, like he'd been lost all his life and now he was found.

Rebecca reached over and touched his skin, gliding a finger along his cheek and to his chin.

In a whisper as comforting as a feather bed, she said, "Let's try again."

Oh, dear Lord, when their lips met the next time, Otis felt like they'd rattled the moon. All the philosophy they'd discussed, the solutions to the world's problems, the answers to life's purpose, it all came together then.

"Again," he whispered as she pulled away. This time he took more charge. He certainly didn't turn from Bambi to a gladiator, but he felt a cinder of strength ignite deep within.

She liked him.

For some unexplained reason, more unexplainable than the existence of God, she was attracted to him. Perhaps he was merely a play toy for her, but it didn't feel that way.

He couldn't discount what had led them to this point, days and many miles of travel and conversation. What if this was his break? What if the runt of the litter was finally being chosen?

This time the kiss lasted longer, and he actually enjoyed it as opposed to freezing up. This time he used his hands, too, leaning up and letting her fall back to the earth. He straddled her and came at her with a craving he'd never known.

Between moans, she whispered, "There you go, Otis Till. Show me what you're made of."

In what could only be described as a moment of pure freedom, Otis pulled his lips from hers and arched his upper body into the air and let out a howl that came not from a lost boy trying to find his way, but from a dream seeker who had found his princess and slayed his first dragon and tasted what it would be like to live life on his own terms.

"Ahhhwwwwwoooooo!" he called out into the night, hearing the coyotes back in Montana howling with him, feeling the fire in his chest. *"Ahhwwwwwooooo!"* he called, feeling her beneath him and knowing that anything was possible, knowing that whatever had led him to that bus and to the seat beside her was destiny, and he had hold of it, the whole bloody world, and by God he loved her more than he thought it possible to love someone, and . . .

Otis looked down and found her smiling at him, feeding his fire, surely witnessing the true birth of the man inside him. He smiled back, and then she took hold of his collar and pulled him down on top of her.

Ahhhwwwwwooooooo!

⌇

Since the night of their kiss, they'd barely separated for a moment, and as the purple bus decorated with flowers waited in the longest line of cars Otis had ever seen, he and Rebecca held hands and looked out the window at a spectacle that would make any other circus or carnival on earth appear run-of-the-mill.

Otis had never seen more naked people in his life—all totally uncaring of the curious eyes on them or even the forecast of terrible rain. Theirs wasn't the only painted bus by a long shot. They were simply another float in a parade, a continuous river of soul searchers hoping to finally find what they were looking for.

People marched alongside cars and buses and trucks that all blasted different kinds of folk and rock 'n' roll that morphed into one singular song: an anthem for those on a search for the profound. If they were wearing anything at all, they wore bell-bottoms and headbands and bead necklaces and a thousand different bright colors. They carried backpacks or duffel bags and danced their way toward the promise of a stage somewhere up ahead. Their smiles were almost enough to defeat the long lines and coming rain.

Otis heard a match strike, and he turned to find Rebecca lighting up a joint. She took a long, slow toke and handed it over. He couldn't find one reason not to, and off he went into wonderland.

—

A wet weekend it was, but the rain didn't stop the bands from giving their all. Otis was particularly impressed with Carlos Santana, who played like a man possessed. Or was it the LSD creating illusions? Otis wasn't exactly sure, but between the drugs and the music and this princess who'd latched on to him, he was having the time of his life, while also questioning everything that had led him to this moment. The part of him that had been hiding, that piece that questioned the purpose of life, now screamed at him, telling him he didn't have to follow a path paved by his father or anyone else in his family.

He and Rebecca shared a tent, and they grew closer every night, exploring each other's bodies slowly, one hour, one night, one millimeter at a time. The days and nights blended together as they stayed up late, listening to the likes of Canned Heat, Creedence, Mountain, the Who, Jefferson Airplane, and Joe Cocker. They'd return to the purple bus in the mornings to rejoin their traveling circus and talk about how everything they'd been told growing up wasn't the way it had to be. Otis could only imagine how displeased his father would be with him, but for the first time it didn't matter.

This . . . *this* . . . being here with these people and cracking the code to the universe was what mattered. *How can we keep living like sheep?* Expanding your mind and stepping deeper into the present moment mattered. *The here and the now, man!* Letting the music take you to undiscovered worlds mattered. *You hear that? Forget everything you've been told. That's religion, brother! No, that's God!* Above all, being with this girl sitting next to him mattered. *Take it all away, and as long as she's in this space, all is right.*

The last night of performances crept into Monday morning. At around 3:30 a.m. Crosby, Stills, Nash, and Young took the stage. Rebecca pulled Otis through the hundreds of thousands to work their way close to the front. The young barefooted couple were stoned and happy and energized, having escaped the rain earlier and taken a long afternoon nap in the tent. Though the ground was soggy, the rain had slowed. Not that it mattered. Every part of them was soaked.

As the band sat on stools that formed a tight circle at the front of the stage, Rebecca gestured to a man in jeans and a brown corduroy blazer holding a big guitar on his lap. "That's Stephen Stills there."

Right then, Stephen addressed the crowd, not quite shy but certainly taken aback by the sea of people staring at him. "This is the second time we've ever performed in front of people, man." His voice echoed out over the masses.

Bec, as he now thought of her, enthusiastically pointed out the rest of them: David Crosby, Graham Nash, and Neil Young. She absolutely glowed, and Otis fell in love with her for the thousandth time since they'd met. The only life worth living now would be one with her in it.

The band opened with a song called "Suite: Judy Blue Eyes." Rebecca knew it well and danced with Otis to the tune, their muddy feet splashing through puddles. He had never heard prettier singing in his life and knew he'd become a lifetime lover of this band, of these men.

Not only were they perfect and perfect for this moment, but they would always and forever play the soundtrack to the biggest moment in Otis's life. He felt the ring he'd made that morning with a birch branch swelling in his pocket. She was the only question in his life that came with an answer, and he'd decided the day before that he would propose. There was no time to wait, no time to go to school and establish themselves before settling into marriage like most people. Their love was different. The two of them were different. He would not get back on that bus without going down on one knee.

The band played "Blackbird" next. Stephen Stills sang in a voice as bone-chilling as it was beautiful. What brought Otis the most joy was the happiness beaming from Rebecca's face. Though she had her demons, they were a long way away. She was as free as a human could be, taken away and healed by the music.

When they sang of Guinevere, Otis reached into his pocket. Rebecca was nearly off her feet in a glow of joy, swaying and singing along, while staring up at the stage.

"Hey, Bec," he said, tugging at her hand.

She turned with a look of intoxicating beauty and aliveness. "What do you think?"

"I think . . ." His heart kicked hard . . . and he wasn't sure . . . and wondered whether he was being crazy . . . and then he leaped right off the cliff, letting it all go. He lowered to one knee and sank into the soft mud.

Her eyebrows curled in curiosity, but only for a measure or two of the tune. Because his intent soon registered. Her smile took the rain away, took the pain away.

It was all he needed. He held out the ring he'd made, so insignificant but so much more at the same time. He asked, loudly enough to cut through the cacophony of sound, "Will you marry me?"

Their neighbors caught on and created a circle around them. A more magical setting could not have existed. Forget the rain. There they were under the beauty of the night, a small circle opened amid a sea of people, a band singing their hearts out, and a man so desperately in love that nothing else mattered.

And a woman.

A woman so extraordinary that he saw his destiny in her eyes.

"Yes, Otis! I'll marry you!"

Otis lost his breath; tears filled his eyes. The damned happiest moment that would ever be.

Everyone around them clapped, and Otis's Guinevere pulled him up from his knee and let him slip the ring on her finger.

"It's the most gorgeous ring I've ever seen." She kissed him ten times and then held him tightly, and they danced as lovers and best friends.

Later, in the tent, as the sun rose over the festival, they made love for the first time, and Otis said goodbye to his virginity and to his youth. He had no idea what was to come, but he felt a newfound optimism that he'd never known, and he became desperately thirsty to see what happened next.

When his own demons came, when he wondered what his parents would say, how this turn of events might affect his plans for college and life, he simply pushed them away and buried himself deeper into this woman who gave him the courage to break free.

Chapter 3

Skeletons in the Closet

It was a chilly and gray Tuesday afternoon in mid-September when Otis and Rebecca finally pulled back into San Francisco. They'd returned with five less people, some lost to the madness of Woodstock, some deciding to stay on the East Coast. Like the bus that had lost half its paint, those who had returned seemed worn down—a long way from the jolly bunch who'd first set sail. It was time to detox and take long hot showers and sleep for a few days.

For Otis and Rebecca, it was time to face the reality of the exciting life they'd mapped out on the drive home. Rebecca took Otis to her place on Ashbury Street. On the way, she pointed out 710 Ashbury, the former Grateful Dead residence, and then she dragged him through the door of a row house where she lived with five other girls. Though he was no longer a virgin, Otis was still a shy bloke who found the opposite sex both a mystery and an intimidating force, so as this harem swarmed him upon entry, it was all he could do not to crawl under the couch. They couldn't believe that Rebecca—the girl in the house *least* likely to ever get married—had fallen in love and gotten engaged in a matter of weeks.

"He must be a miracle worker in bed," one joked in front of the entire hive of roommates.

"You mean in a sleeping bag?" Rebecca responded before laying a wet kiss on him. "He is indeed." Otis turned as red as Carlos Santana's guitar but stood tall for a week afterward. No one could give him backbone the way she did.

He finally found the courage to call his parents—not that he was ready for an unveiling of truths.

"Otis, where in the world have you been?" his father asked. Five years in Montana had done little to chip away at Addison Till's distinguished British accent. "We've left messages with the Texans."

"I'm so sorry, Dad. What a month."

"With the car wash?"

"Car wash and . . ." He paused, unaccustomed to lying to his parents. "And I took a second job running Thai food for a spot down the street."

"Ah, good for you, son."

Otis wanted to tell his dad about Rebecca. He would proudly shout from the highest mountain that he'd gotten engaged to an angel, but telling Addison Till right now would shatter the world's peace and send Otis tumbling into what might turn into a battle for his future. Sprouting from a family tree of successful men, his father had set a high bar and held even higher expectations of his only son.

～

Two in the afternoon in October, and Otis and Rebecca sat in a crowded Chinese restaurant on Grant Avenue in Chinatown, sharing egg rolls and fried rice. The San Francisco fog hung heavy outside and moved into the restaurant like smoke every time someone opened the door.

A group of war protesters had just marched by. Thousands of miles away, American soldiers fought an escalating war in a country most Americans couldn't point out on a map. Between the seemingly countless soldiers returning in body bags, the talk of possible conscription, and a new president many doubted would make any changes, the dissent back home grew stronger by the day.

All the men dying, fighting a war many didn't even understand, only exacerbated Otis's swelling need to carve his own path. He was more than a month into his education at Berkeley, wondering why in the queen's name he was chasing someone else's dream.

Not that Otis had an alternate idea for a vocation. It had all seemed perfectly brilliant to talk of dreams and to propose to this young lady sitting across from him, dipping her egg roll into an inordinate amount of duck sauce, but the follow-through was more daunting. Especially now that they were back in reality. It wasn't like he *had* to become a journalist. Even if he graduated with a journalism degree, he didn't have to commit to write for a living. So he didn't need to tell his father yet.

But he did need to share that he'd found the love of his life and that they planned to marry the following spring. For that matter, Bec had kept it quiet too. The inevitability of sharing the news with both sets of parents hung in the air like a trapeze artist who'd lost his pants.

Otis still hadn't even told his father that he'd paid the small fine to bail out of his dormitory commitment, opting to continue his inexpensive lodging with the Texans, only a short walk away from Bec's place.

He pointed to her puddle of duck sauce. "Americans eat more condiments than they do actual food. What would happen if there was a ketchup shortage? The country would go to war. Well, another war."

"At least the cause would be clear." She wore a sunflower-yellow dress cut low enough to show the jewel necklace she'd made and a peek of her voluptuous and braless bosoms.

Apparently noticing his wandering eyes, she leaned forward to tease him with an even more tantalizing peek. "I come for the egg roll, but I stay for this sweet, delicious sauce." Her lips split into a smile.

"Well," Otis said, "I come for the fried rice and stay for the fortune cookie."

Holding her egg roll like a microphone, she spoke into it. "What would you want your fortune to be?" She moved the mike toward his own lips and waited for an answer.

Otis grinned and pretended to tap on it, as if testing whether it were on. He cleared his throat and gave a terrible Nixon impression. "I would like my fortune to read . . ." He paused. "Shite, I don't know . . . may gold rain down from the heavens and splash onto the marble floors of our palace overlooking the Pacific Ocean, and may we have ten babies who each grow up to dominate their fields and subsequently change the world."

Bec returned the egg roll back to her own lips. "That would be unlike any fortune I've ever read, but I can dig it. This is Rebecca Bradshaw, live in San Francisco, reporting for CBS News." With that, she took a big bite of her egg roll and sat back with a smile.

Otis wished he could laugh at her exquisite absurdity. He tried his best to hide the wheelbarrow full of strife that came rushing through him as he pondered the fact that he had no idea what fortune or future he desired. Sure, he wanted to be with Bec, but there had to be more. Journalist or not, he needed to do *something* great, to be *someone* great. The hell if he was going to live anything less than an extraordinary life.

"Okay," she said, "out with it. Why the sudden dark cloud over your head?"

"No, no, no, I'm not dragging you down with me."

"Please, drag away. That's what I'm here for."

"That's not true. Please let me deal with whatever this is on my own, and you be here waiting on the other side if I make it back."

"Fine, then, I'll move on to the fried rice and wait for you to poke your head back out, Turtle Boy. Don't mind me." She picked up her chopsticks and went about eating while looking out the window at a few straggling protesters.

"It really must be nice," Otis said, "to not have a worry in the world. Let's float through life and make jewelry and ceramic weed pipes for a living. We can raise our kids on a commune and teach them how to grow organic zucchini and bathe themselves in a lake."

She dropped her chopsticks back into the bowl. "Does this mean I'm no longer waiting on you? Are you back already?"

Yes, dammit, he wanted to chat. She was the only one who could make him feel better when he felt like this, but he was also self-aware enough to know that he'd drive her mad if he couldn't take a break from his worries from time to time.

Turned out she already knew what was on his mind—maybe because he'd nearly drowned her in his worries earlier that morning. "Otis, you're seventeen. You have all the time in the world. We're supposed to be having fun right now."

He crossed his arms, wondering how she could be so easygoing about it. "I just . . . I want to do something that matters. I know you're tired of hearing about it—I'm certainly tired of talking about it—but I can't let it go."

"I adore your hopeful vision, handsome. You're a windup doll with all this incredible energy, waiting to be pointed in the right direction, waiting to pick up the scent. Maybe it's like love, Otis. Soon as you stop looking so hard, it might find you. In the meantime, let's be teenagers. I don't want to be an adult yet."

He sighed out the whole world of his plagued confusion. "We're not exactly kids. We'll be married soon and have kids of our own."

Her cheeks swelled. "All ten of them, right? In our palace on a cliff overlooking the ocean."

"I was exaggerating. I'm okay with the two like we talked about. Still, we must figure out how to feed them, to clothe them. To send them to university. There's no time for fun right now," he insisted. "We must start making plans."

Rebecca reached across the table to take his hand. "One day you'll look back to this moment—you'll taste the soy sauce and egg and green onion on your tongue—and you'll see me over here wearing this dress that I made—and you'll wish that you had fully immersed yourself into this moment and all the other moments that led to you finding what you're—"

Otis hit the table, causing the glasses and bowls to rattle. He wasn't exactly angry, simply bewildered. "I find it extraordinary that you can have such faith."

Her lips straightened. "What gave you that impression? I barely have any faith at all. I don't have big dreams; I don't expect anything. I'm happy where we are, just the two of us, that's all."

"Would you be happy with me scrubbing sweet-and-sour chicken off the plates back there for the rest of my life?"

"Would that mean we get free duck sauce?"

Otis didn't flinch. "You're not nice. That's all there is to it. I will dump duck sauce on your—"

"Otis, any faith that I have . . . is in you. You make me a believer."

He couldn't have loved her any more in that moment. "I don't know what I did to—"

"No way," said a voice from behind Otis.

Rebecca let out a big grin. "Hunter!"

"The one and only." A surfer type approached them and pulled Rebecca into a bear hug. He had a head full of curly hair and caterpillar eyebrows.

"What are you doing here?" Hunter asked, his chest nearly bursting out of his tight white shirt. He looked like he regularly paddled to Hawaii on his longboard.

"Finding my way, you know. Meet Otis, my fiancé."

Otis rose. "How do you do?"

"You're getting married, Bec?" Hunter pumped Otis's hand with unrivaled enthusiasm. "What a lucky guy."

Rebecca slipped her arm through Otis's. "Hunter and I went to high school together in Santa Rosa."

A note of curiosity entered his voice. "Yeah, everyone wondered what happened to you. You didn't even make it to the graduation party."

Rebecca shook her head, instantly drawing a dark cloud over her. "I couldn't take it anymore. Skipped town that day."

"Yeah, I get that. By the way, I'm sorry about your brother. It's heartbreaking."

Rebecca dropped the smile and let go of Otis. "What . . . what happened to my brother?"

"You know, coming home like that."

"Like what?"

Hunter froze. "Wait, when's the last time you were home?"

The temperature of the restaurant plummeted as she struggled to speak. "I haven't talked to my family since I left in May. What happened?"

Otis had detected that she didn't have the best relationship with her family, but she hadn't shared many details.

Hunter swallowed and scratched his temple. "You know he went to Nam, right?"

"Vietnam?"

The guy clearly wished he hadn't opened his mouth. "Yeah. He was hurt, Bec. Bad. He lost his legs."

Rebecca's eyes fell closed.

Hunter's stout posture sank. "I'm sorry to be the one to tell you."

The three of them stood there quietly, both the men looking at Rebecca, waiting for her to return to them. Otis attempted to take her hand, but she pulled away.

"Look, I know that's big news. I'm going to go. You know I'm here for you." Hunter offered her a hug.

Rebecca allowed a quick one and then whispered inaudible words as he departed.

Otis wrapped an arm around her and guided her out of the restaurant and into the fog. For the first time since he'd met her, Bec broke into an awful cry that Otis could feel at his core. She wept for a long time, and when she was done, she said, "I have to go home."

Otis had already put that together. "We do, you mean. I'm coming with you."

She pulled him closer, tighter. "Yes. *We* have to go see him. It's my fault, Otis. I ran off. I can't imagine what he felt like, abandoned by his sister." Her words broke apart.

"You ran away?"

She nodded into his shoulder.

Ah, this was that part of her that she kept hidden, protecting it like a diary. How deep did the mysteries of this woman go? What else didn't he know? Taking her home would certainly peel back some of the layers. As strong as she was, he wondered what was to come. A brother injured in the war. Parents who hadn't seen their daughter since the spring. And here comes Otis, the man she would soon marry. He could hear the rumble of emotional thunder, and he hoped with all his heart that he would be strong enough to endure. That he could be the man she would surely need when the time came.

Chapter 4

A MANNEQUIN IN THE WINDOW

As they drove across the Golden Gate Bridge in a friend's borrowed clunker, Otis took her hand. "It's going to be all right." Wise words from the bozo behind the wheel who couldn't find any meaningful way to ease the pain.

Rebecca hadn't said much since they'd learned of her brother's misfortune the day before, but she let Otis hold her hand, and maybe that was what was important. He couldn't imagine what she was going through. She didn't even look like the Rebecca he'd come to know. She'd opted for jeans and a T-shirt and scraped her curly hair back in a ponytail. No jewelry, no glitter, not a sparkle anywhere.

She'd told him more about running away, how she'd left a note on the counter, then slipped out the door and jogged south with her thumb in the air, eventually hitchhiking to San Francisco. She had written letters to assure her family that she was alive and well, but didn't mention her location or offer a way to make contact.

Though she'd planned on reconnecting with her brother, who was older by two years and had still lived at home when she'd left, it hadn't happened. Her old life stood behind a door that she hadn't been ready to open again, until now.

It was only an hour's drive up Highway 101 to Santa Rosa. On a street littered with garbage, she pointed to a lime-green house with a rusted gutter and a worn-out truck in the driveway. The landscaping left much to be desired.

After a knock, an unkempt man in tattered khakis and a flannel shirt swung open the door. Marshall Bradshaw bore only the faintest resemblance to Rebecca, the shorter stature and the shallow cut of their cheeks. His gray hair was short and sparse and matched the color of the stubble of his beard. Worry lines creased his forehead, and crow's-feet spread from his eyes.

When it registered that his daughter had come home, Marshall simply stared. Rebecca stared right back. He eventually moved his head, a short, all-knowing nod. The fact that he hadn't pulled his daughter into a hug yet was heartbreaking.

"I see," he finally said.

"I'm sorry."

His face exhibited a sudden overwhelm of sadness, his cheeks and chin quivering. "Goddammit, Rebecca." He pressed his lids together, and a pair of tears rolled down his cheeks.

She went to him, giving him a hug that he accepted readily.

"I thought I'd never see you again," he said, wiping his wet face. "Where have you been?"

"Just . . . just gone." She eventually let go of him. "Where's Jed?"

"He's not good," her dad said, looking as if he'd traveled a long road while embracing his daughter.

"I know."

"You heard?"

"I was in San Francisco. Saw Hunter Sampson yesterday. He told me."

Stepping back, her dad looked at her for a while. He was about forty, but looked like he barely had anything left, midlife with a foot in the grave. "He's at physical therapy with your mom right now. He's lost, Becca."

"I'm here now. I'll help."

"There's nothing you can do. There's nothing any of us can do."

As Otis put his hand on her back to comfort her, she said, "Dad, meet Otis." Otis was okay with leaving out specifics. The moment wasn't right for fiancé introductions or wedding discussions.

Otis shook Marshall's calloused hand.

Inside, the walls were bare and in need of a paint job. The tile floors had lost their shine. In the kitchen, a tower of dirty dishes rose from a stained sink. A line of empty beer bottles ran along the top of the chipped counter.

They spoke about more trivial things while her dad grabbed a ring of Budweiser with one of six missing. He took Rebecca and Otis out to the compact back patio bordered by a tall white privacy fence. It was over seventy out, a good warm day. Several crushed beer cans made up a small stack in the corner near a pile of wood. Up high, a few clouds slid by in an otherwise blue sky.

As they sat in wobbly white plastic chairs, Rebecca asked, "What happened?"

Marshall cracked his beer open and took a sip. "You mean since you ran off on us? We looked everywhere. We had the police out."

"I left a note."

"Not telling us where you were going. Then you wait a month to send a letter. Do you know what that was like? No, you don't." He offered them beers, but Otis and Rebecca declined.

"You pushed me, Dad. You don't push me. You don't ever push me." This was the first Otis had heard of it.

"We were going through a lot. Your brother—"

"There's no excuse."

His head bent down. "I know."

"Is that your way of saying you're sorry?"

His eyes snapped to her. "Jesus, Rebecca. Yes, fine. I'm sorry. You try living my life for a while. You had no right to run off."

Rebecca bit her lip. Otis was in way over his head and kept his gaze toward the fence, listening closely. He wondered what her brother had to do with it.

"What have you been doing?" Marshall asked, clearly working hard to be kind.

"It doesn't matter. Just beatin' around in San Francisco. What happened to Jed? Why'd you let him go? What was it, the army?"

An affirmative nod. "You think I had any say in it? As if my kids listen to me at all. Hell, I told him not to join, he did it to spite me. He got tricked by the promises of benefits . . . and fooled into thinking he was going to save this country. United States pride." He saluted. "Ten hut."

A sadder picture Otis couldn't remember seeing. It was no wonder she ran away.

Marshall shook his head in disgust. "He thought he'd go be a hero, save the world from communism. He was there three fucking days, Rebecca. Barely two months of boot camp, then three days in the jungle, and he steps on an M14, what they call a 'toe-popper.' Both legs gone at the knees. Then two months in the VA hospital, and now he's back home and wishes that toe-popper had taken the rest of him. There's your hero."

Bec fought off tears. "Don't talk about him like that."

"I told him not to go. He wouldn't listen. Just like you." Marshall went for his beer like it was a pacifier.

"I shouldn't have left," she said.

He squeezed the can in his hand till it crackled. "You're damn right you shouldn't have left. He might have listened to you. They said they'd pay for college and help him buy a house. Didn't mention that his chances in coming back whole were slim. I told him . . . twenty times I told him."

Car doors shut out front.

"That's probably them." Marshall stood. "I need to help."

In the driveway, Rebecca's mom had pulled open the back door of their car. Marshall raced over, and together they carried Jed out while Otis and Rebecca watched from the sidelines.

Jed had a long and untrimmed brown beard. He was certainly the tallest in the family. His eyes, the color of almonds, reflected pain and rage, and perhaps even confusion. Maybe he'd once been handsome, but he wasn't today. His thick curly hair could use a wash. Hell, all of him could. Swollen muscles and tattoos poked out of the rolled-up sleeves of his army jacket.

"Holy shit," Jed said, noticing his sister for the first time.

"Rebecca?" her mom asked, unbelieving. Olivia Bradshaw was the only one who seemed to care at all about her own appearance. About the same height and build as Rebecca, she wore a long, casual dress with a thick white belt around her slim waist. Straight hair that was more cream colored than blond fell past her shoulders. Whereas Marshall showed his weariness from the nose up, most of Olivia's wrinkles had developed around her mouth, as if she'd spent her life biting her tongue and clenching her jaw.

The sadness that she wore like a blanket fell away as she approached Rebecca and made sure she wasn't dreaming up this reunion.

"I'm sorry," was all Rebecca could manage to say.

Olivia made a series of grateful sighs as she wrapped her daughter in a hug. "Is this really you, Becca? My God, we didn't know what happened to you. I . . ."

Bec offered a few more apologies and squeezed her mom back.

～

Everyone gathered in the living room. Otis couldn't place the musty odor, maybe a spill in the shag carpet that had never been cleaned up. The walls were painted a scarlet red that someone surely regretted. *Let's really brighten up the living room!* they might have thought. Then the day after painting: *What in the hell were we thinking?*

Marshall cracked another beer and handed one to Jed, then one to Otis, who accepted this time. He needed something to calm his nerves, and he silently hoped Bec wouldn't spring the news of their engagement.

"Who are you, kid?" Marshall asked from the La-Z-Boy throne that Rebecca had mentioned more than a time or two. "What kind of accent is that?"

"London, sir." Otis sat in a tattered cloth chair with a coffee stain prominent on the arm.

"How do you two know each other?"

Otis held his breath, thinking Bec had to make the play here.

Sitting next to her mother on the couch, she took the cue. "We met on the way to Woodstock."

"Woodstock. The festival?" Jed asked, rolling forward to join the conversation. "Hot damn, sis. I heard all about that."

"Yeah, it was pretty wild."

"Good, good," Marshall said, denting the can in his hand with not-so-subtle fury. "So you were out getting high with a bunch of hippies while the rest of us were trying to figure out life, trying to help *your* brother find his way after becoming a war hero."

In that moment, in the following silence, a church bell rang, but it sounded like warning bells.

Otis wasn't sure what Rebecca heard in those bells, but the weight of her father's words had visibly come down on her shoulders. She slightly crumpled in stature, her spine bent forward, and her chin dropped enough to say, *I give up.*

Everyone took a long sip of air, together like a choir, a sound perhaps indicating that none of them wanted to step deeper into the darkness.

Finally, Jed spoke. "Don't beat yourself up, sis. You couldn't have stopped me."

"That's bullshit," Marshall said. "You've been listening to her your whole life."

Otis felt like he was growing up in fast-forward motion, seeing a side of life he'd not imagined.

"What now, Rebecca?" Marshall asked. "Are you home? Are you not home? Just here to give a sweet hug and then be on your way with this new *friend* of yours?"

"He's more than a friend."

Otis seized up, a mannequin in a window. He managed to maneuver his eyeballs to find Rebecca, and he sent an onslaught of telepathy her way, saying, *Please bail me out! I can't move my arms or legs or mouth! Even if I could speak right now, I'd bugger it up. You started this, Bec. Please finish it.*

"This is the man I am going to marry."

Bloody hell.

The previous silence had nothing on this new one. There were no church bells this time, no intervention from God.

Still trapped in his malfunctioning body, Otis thought he might let loose his bladder. He could feel everyone in the room staring—no, *boring* holes into him.

No surprise, Marshall was the first to speak. "Lord, have mercy." Otis wondered whether a prayer would follow, but a string of curse words—all together unrepeatable—sprang from this man like bullets. Marshall eventually gathered himself and found a direction. Apparently he'd forgotten Otis was in the room.

"This is a joke, Rebecca," he said. "You're not seriously telling us right now that you went and met some Brit who looks like a dimwit and acts like one, too, and now you're going to marry him."

"Where's the ring?" Olivia asked, suddenly coming to life like someone had pulled a string behind her.

"It fell off," Rebecca admitted. "But you should have seen it, Mom. He made it from a strip of birch tree bark. It fell off on the way back from New York. He was such a romantic, the way he asked—"

"This is rich," Marshall interrupted. "He proposed to you in a sea of hippies with a stick. I can't wait to see how long this marriage will last."

Something flew through the air. A pillow. It struck Marshall in the head. "What the . . . ?"

Jed had slung it at him, and his grin stretched even wider. He either had a big bag of marijuana or a bag of painkillers tucked somewhere in that chair.

"Lighten up, man," Jed told his father.

Marshall wasn't in a playful mood. "Don't you call me *man*."

"Your daughter just told you she's getting married, and you're crapping all over her."

"She's not getting married."

"Ever?" Jed asked. "What is she, your prisoner? Give me a break. Sis, I don't blame you for leaving, not one flipping iota."

Jed was making light of the situation, but it would take more than his jokes to ease the tension. Rebecca's eyes glowed with anger and embarrassment. Her mother had fully checked out, her eyes hazy. And Marshall looked like he might explode, as if there were a lit fuse attached to his rear end.

"Jed, shut your mouth. Rebecca, you're not getting married. Not anytime soon, at least."

Otis was starting to get angry himself. "Sir, I'm sitting right here. Why don't you speak to me directly?"

Marshall finally acknowledged his existence. "What's your name again? How old are you? Fourteen?"

Thank God he wasn't still sixteen. That fact would have made it worse. "I'm seventeen. My name's Otis Pennington Till."

"That's a mouthful of bullshit. Tell me, Otis Pennington Till," Marshall said, making a brutally awful attempt at a British accent, "how do you plan on taking care of my daughter? You still in high school? Not that I'm taking you or this bit of news seriously, but why not tell me anyway? Who is this man that *wants* to marry my daughter?"

"Leave him alone," Rebecca insisted.

"Let him answer," Jed said, stirring the pot.

Otis might have been timid at times, and he was no stranger to turning to stone, but when the roadkill was poked the right way, he proved to be more than alive.

"I'm working hard to find out what it is that I'm going to do with the rest of my life. I'm a freshman at Berkeley, a journalism major, and—"

"Well, at least you're not an idiot."

Otis didn't flinch. "You don't need to question whether I'll take care of your daughter."

"You're being serious right now? Both of you?" He whipped his head to Rebecca. "You're not marrying him."

"We're not here asking for permission," Rebecca said. "We're informing you that we're getting married. This isn't a childish decision. We met for a reason, and we're meant to be together. Once you get to know him, if you can open your ashtray of a heart to let him in, you'll see that I'm the luckiest girl in the world."

As angry as Otis was, he felt a big wave of warmth come over him.

Marshall directed his fury at his wife. "Olivia, you have nothing to say? You're not actually okay with this, are you?"

"What are you going to do, Marshall? Forbid it? Let her go again? She's eighteen. She can do whatever she likes. For the record, you asked me to marry you when we were eighteen."

That shut Marshall up for a second.

"And look at you now!" Jed said, swiping the air with his fist.

Marshall gathered his troops and finally came up with a retort. "We didn't get married for ten more years. Why not go ahead and get a divorce, because we know it won't last? All you youngsters think love is this giddy wave of fun. It's not."

"We didn't notice," Jed said.

Marshall looked like he was about to stand up and wring Jed's neck like a rooster that wouldn't shut up. "Jed, I will roll you out the front door if you continue your antics."

"Come on and do it, Marshall. Wouldn't be the first time you've kicked me out of the house."

"Do *not* call me Marshall."

"But *Dad* seems so sweet and innocent. It doesn't quite capture your Hitler-esque leadership."

Marshall's jaw tightened. "Otis, why don't you hit the road? We need some alone time."

Otis looked at Bec, who nodded her assent, then said, "Why don't you take the car and go find a bite to eat?"

"You sure?"

"Yeah."

Otis stood and touched her shoulder for all to see, then kissed her on the forehead. "I'll be back in two hours, okay?"

She patted his hand. "It'll be fine here."

No one said another word as he left. A part of him—the brave shred that dwelled within him—didn't want to leave her. He'd just found out that her father had pushed her. He should have left with a threat. *You touch her again and I'll rip your bloody head off.* Alas, Otis didn't have it in him, and instead, he let shame chase him out the door.

Chapter 5

WINE COUNTRY

Otis wasn't particularly hungry, so he decided to simply drive. He'd never owned a car, and it was nice to listen to the radio and cruise along SR 12 south of Santa Rosa. Though he wasn't a wine aficionado, he was well aware of Sonoma County's rich wine history, and he was curious to see the landscape.

Rebecca's awful troubles aside, Otis had his own. They paled in comparison to Bec's, or those of the men being drafted or the people warring over civil rights, but his troubles existed, nonetheless. Hell with it, they didn't only exist, they *plagued* him. Was he really meant to be a writer, even if he didn't feel passionate about it the way his father did? Seemed like a recipe for being a piss-poor writer, if you asked him.

Even now, he could hear his father's clackety typing in the other room, as if his old man were still fifteen feet away. Otis could hear Addison talking to himself, too, occasionally cracking up with joy, a man who knew exactly what he should do with his life.

The DJ said it was Aretha Franklin who'd been singing, then talked about the weather—the fog was coming—and signed off for the day. The next DJ kicked things off with Creedence Clearwater's "Down on the Corner."

Otis couldn't help but turn up the volume and pat his hands against the steering wheel. Bec was right—she and Otis were young. He had to let go and enjoy the ride.

Then it happened . . .

Otis came around a bend and set eyes on a vineyard for the first time in his life, cascading rows of grapevines stretching over the land, the leaves a dazzling green. Otis felt as if he'd driven right onto the canvas of a painting. The scent of ripe grapes rushed in through the open windows.

He'd thoroughly enjoyed watching America pass by from the purple bus—when he wasn't too distracted by the boisterous yet petite sensation next to him—and there was no denying the beauty of Montana he had come to know as a teenager, but he couldn't recall ever laying his eyes on such a miraculous view.

The murky stew in his mind faded away, taken over by the sweet fruity smell, the vision of the vines, the taste of the wines to come, the touch of his fingers on the wheel, the sound of Creedence, the sense that he should quit with all the worrying. What a foreign feeling, one he wished he could pull over and quickly bottle, because rarely had he felt so utterly complete.

Otis slowed the car, noticing heads poking out from the rows. They must have been harvesting. Getting a better look, he saw people with baskets full of purple clusters hanging from their necks. Was California wine even any good? He'd had his fair share of wine in San Francisco, the jugs someone would bring home from the store, but he'd not paid much attention to them.

When he saw a sign for a wine tasting, he hit the brakes. He had a few bucks in his pocket. Perhaps he could bring a bottle back to Bec's parents, a sort of peace offering. *Here you go, a bottle of wine for your daughter's hand.* Did they even drink wine?

Otis parked between a tractor and a Ford truck loaded with plastic bins. He headed toward a red barn with a sign that read MURPHY VINEYARDS. Inside, a long plank of wood rested on two sawhorses.

On one end stood a group of four thirtysomethings equipped with wineglasses, laughing together.

The freckled redhead behind the bar waved him forward. She looked to be in her late twenties and wore a blouse with an exposed midriff. Her long thick hair, the color of orange leaves, hung in loose braids. She had piercing cobalt eyes that evoked a sense of knowingness, like a woman who'd been a mystic in a past life.

"Looking to taste some wines?"

Otis's heart rate lowered in her presence, and he sidled up to the bar. "I suppose so." Apparently no one was checking IDs around here.

She set down two bottles that featured a sketch of the red barn on their labels. "We have a chardonnay and a cabernet sauvignon, blended with some cinsault and merlot." She poured the white first.

Otis gave it a sniff and then put it to his mouth like he'd seen his parents do. It took him a moment to put things together, but something about the smell and how he'd just seen the vines that bore this fruit gave the sip extra power.

"They're harvesting reds today. Feel free to walk through those doors and see the action for yourself. Ask for my husband, Paul. He's easy enough to find. Long hair and handsome."

Otis set the glass down. "This is your place?"

"Ours, yes. I'm Sparrow."

"Otis Till, quite the pleasure." He eyed the open doors in the back of the barn. "Should I go now?"

"Sure. Take your glass. Here, let me top you off."

With a replenished glass of chardonnay, he strolled through the back, coming out into the light again. Rock 'n' roll played from a radio perched on the low branch of a tree. About fifteen people were back there, two of whom stood in large bins, stomping on grapes, big grins stretched across their faces. In a patch of grass, next to a stack of crates brimming with freshly picked grapes, several people played a game of bocce ball.

Otis timidly stepped forward, curious as a dog who had caught a scent.

"How's it going?" said a voice.

Otis looked over to see a well-cut shirtless guy with his trousers rolled up. His dusty-brown hair was long enough to get into a ponytail. And perhaps he carried some of that same knowingness in his eyes that Sparrow had exhibited, though it seemed more like contentedness. "I'm Paul Murphy."

"Ah, I met your wife. I'm Otis Till."

Paul apparently did not practice spatial etiquette and wrapped an arm around Otis's neck. "Welcome, Otis. You ever seen this go down before?"

Otis cleared his throat and tried hard to accept such an invasion of his space. "I can't say that I have."

"Want to stomp?" Any closer and Paul would be kissing him.

"Oh, no, thank you."

"You sure, man?"

Otis did want to stomp, though. He looked again at the two people in the bins, dancing over grapes. Then he turned only slightly to Paul, their faces far too close. "Well, are you . . . ? I don't mean to . . ."

Paul *finally* pulled his arm away, and Otis felt like he could breathe again. Otis would find the American sense of privacy funny if it weren't so unsettling. Also, why was Paul so bloody happy? Perhaps he was high, but nevertheless, he looked as if he hadn't a trouble in the world!

"Take your shoes off, brother. You're up next. You'll never forget it. In the meantime, help yourself to more wine." He pointed to a barrel, on top of which a jug rested.

Otis looked down at his shoes, wondering whether he was really about to do this, worried about the sight of his toenails and the cleanliness of his feet.

"I'm just a visitor, you know," he called out to Paul, who had started walking away.

Paul whipped around and stood before Otis, placing a hand on each shoulder and forcing Otis to make eye contact. "We're all just visitors, aren't we?"

"I . . . I suppose so."

Paul leaned in and kissed him on the cheek, returning Otis to the mannequin form that he'd taken at Rebecca's only an hour earlier.

"Everyone," Paul called, "meet Otis. He wants to stomp."

"Hi, Otis," everyone said at the same time.

Otis raised a stiff hand to these strangers. Though he felt violated and exposed, he also, oddly, felt right at home. Perhaps a dose of vulnerability wouldn't kill him.

He removed his shoes, rolled up his pants, and polished off the white in his glass. An easy buzz settled over him. He poured himself the red wine from the jug. Before he took his first sip, he raised his gaze to the slope of vines, where he could still see the harvesters' bobbing heads. The sight seemed to grow more exquisite by the second, as if he were dialing in the focus with each breath of this Sonoma air.

The red wine clung to his mouth before slipping down his throat. He had no idea how to properly taste wine, but the sensations that came over him were almost more than he could handle. He could taste the wine down to his very toes—the unmanicured ones. The soundtrack of everyone's laughter, mixed with the devotion they gave to this task, only exacerbated how he felt.

There were no words, though. Human explanation would have insulted the experience.

With that reverence in mind, Otis took another sip. Fireworks shot off in his mouth and caused a tingle down deep.

"You all right?"

Otis came to, noticing his new friend staring at him. "All right? I'm bloody fucking fantastic."

A smile stretched on Paul's face. "I see a man who's been bitten."

"Bitten?"

Paul clapped him on the shoulder. "The wine bug. It's sunk its teeth into you."

"Is that what you call it?" Otis grinned. "It tastes like God is in this wine."

"Of course he is. What better way of expressing nature than capturing it in a bottle? You're drinking the lyrics to a song that's just been written. You're drinking a year, captured in a glass. Last year's weather, the choices made in the cellar, everything that happened here on Murphy Vineyards. Nineteen sixty-eight in your mouth, man. Never can it be repeated. It's as unique as butterfly wings, a fingerprint of the earth. If last year had a hand, then we took it and pressed an inked finger down. Now you have it in your mouth and stomach and heart. By taking that in, you're one of us."

For God's sake, this man was the greatest proselytizer to have ever walked the earth. Another word and Otis would fall to his knees and weep.

Collecting himself, he managed to ask, "Is this your family's place?"

He shook his head. "My parents are Mormons from Oregon, so they're not big into what I'm doing, but this is my dream."

"How'd you get started?"

Paul pointed at a man dressed like he'd disembarked from his yacht in Catalina. Khakis, boat shoes, a polo shirt. An expensive haircut with a perfect curl on top and a tight shave. He was as handsome as any man Otis had ever seen.

"That guy there. Lloyd Bramhall. He's my ticket. His family owned half of San Francisco at one point, textiles, real estate. Now he's just having fun. I somehow talked him into investing and helping Sparrow and me buy land. Now we owe him a tremendous amount of money, and he owns my soul, but I wouldn't have it any other way. Look at them. Those are my vines now . . . my winery. An impossible dream coming to life."

Otis looked at Paul with admiration. "You lucky bastard."

"I know. Are you ready? Let's put you to work."

With rock 'n' roll blasting, someone sprayed off Otis's feet with a hose—as if that were enough to sanitize them—and then he climbed into a tank loaded with fresh grapes. His feet sank in, and he felt the berries and their stems press into his flesh. The luscious scent he'd first encountered on the highway was even stronger now, a drug in and of itself.

A smile rose out of him that could have blasted the clouds out of the sky, and he began to stomp those grapes, first little by little, and in minutes he was dancing, this non-hippie all of a sudden a free spirit with wings. He was not only smiling but laughing, a maniacal burst because he'd found something meaningful that he could pursue. Was that even possible in the matter of a few minutes, a life changed, a world turned over?

Damn right it was. Otis felt at one with these people and this place. If only Rebecca were here.

By God, in one year, 1969, he'd had the two most impactful moments in his life. The time Rebecca sat next to him on the bus, and this day, October 15, 1969, when the wine bug sank its teeth into him, and its blood stained his feet.

"Nineteen sixty-nine," he said, looking out over the Sonoma hills. "The year of Otis."

He said it again, uncaring who heard. "The year of Otis!"

Then, for the second time that year, he opened his mouth and howled like a wild dog.

Awhooooo! Awhooooooo!!!!

꒱꒰

That evening, Otis and Rebecca drove back to the city. He hadn't said a word about his experience. Today was about her; his revelation could wait. He'd returned to her family's house with a gift bottle of wine and had been as kind and civil as he could.

Empath that she was, Rebecca certainly noticed that something had shifted in Otis, though. She'd smiled when he returned to her parents' house. "What's gotten into you?"

Otis suspected the rest of the family was wondering, too, probably assuming that he'd slipped off to find a joint. It was far more than that.

As soon as they got on the highway, Otis said, "You didn't tell me that your dad pushed you."

"I know, I know. It's the only time it ever happened."

"Still, a father can't push his daughter. What happened?"

"It was a pretty bad fight. He'd just kicked my brother out of the house—for like the tenth time. 'You're not my son anymore,'" she said, mimicking a drunk Marshall. "'Go get a life!' The same stuff he's been saying for years. He was always disappointed in Jed, but especially because he was still living at home."

Rebecca took a long breath. "I got in my dad's face, told him he was a useless drunk. Maybe a few things even worse. My mom was begging us to stop. He pushed me. Slammed me against the wall."

"*What?* Why didn't your brother do something?"

"He'd already left."

Otis looked at his reddening hands gripping the steering wheel. After a string of curses, he said, "I don't blame you for running away. You don't need to be around that."

"Yeah, well . . . I pushed him back, for the record."

"Good."

She faked a smile. "Trust me, he'll never do it again." Otis decided to let it go, for now.

"Anyway, I have to tell you something, and I'm afraid."

"You should never be afraid to tell me anything."

A tear escaped her eye, and she looked away. "I need to move back home. They're broke. My mom can't work as many hours now that she's helping Jed. And they need me. She says I was always the strongest of them, and I guess she's right."

"I see." In the silence Otis tried to paint the rest of the picture. He didn't want to ask whether he was still a part of her future.

Bec turned back to him and put a hand on his thigh. "I don't want to lose you. Could we make it work while you're still in Berkeley? We'd have to."

Her words came as sweet relief. "Yes, of course. For a moment there, I thought you were—"

"Don't even say it out loud. I have never been surer of us. We won't be that far from each other. Under an hour with the Richmond Bridge."

"I don't care if we're separated by a hundred hours and fifty bridges."

She laughed despite her tears. "Me either."

He couldn't let it go, though. "But they're not healthy, Bec. You don't owe them anything."

"This isn't up for discussion. Maybe I don't owe them anything, but they're family. As screwed up as they are, they're still my family."

Otis bit his tongue. How could he argue? He had to support her. "Okay, then. Well, I might have some business up there before too long anyway."

Her brow furrowed. "Business?"

"What if I told you I think I've found what I want to do." He couldn't stop his lips from curling into a smile.

"What?"

"Take a guess. Nothing to do with writing."

She scrunched her forehead. "A car mechanic then?"

"Um, no."

Her eyes darted around, seeking another guess. "A chef?"

"Wine," he said, feeling it in his bones, hearing the call of the grapes.

"What do you know about wine?"

"Exactly nothing, but . . . I had some sort of awakening earlier. I think I know what I want to do with the rest of my life." He gleefully shared the details, about meeting Sparrow and Paul, and stomping grapes.

"You're full of surprises, aren't you?" It was the first time she'd really smiled in two days.

"I can't even describe, Bec, what happened to me up there. The only thing missing was you."

"What about your journalism degree?"

"I don't know! Why would I need it? I might have to transfer to UC Davis. Or drop out."

Her mouth straightened. "You're not dropping out."

"It's your fault." Otis changed to the slow lane. "A purple bus, a pretty girl, and the whole world shifts from black and white to Technicolor."

He leaned over her and kissed her, tasting their lives together, tasting exactly what courage and faith and partnership could do to a man.

⌒

He helped Rebecca move to Santa Rosa three days later, and as he left, something told him he better not make saying goodbye a habit. She could disappear as easily as she'd come into his life.

Thankfully, he'd always been good with money and had saved every dime his aunt had paid him for working on the farm. First thing he did was buy a black-and-bronze Honda motorcycle that had some good life left in it. The bike allowed him to see her every chance he got, but it didn't take care of the bigger problem: He no longer wanted to write for a living.

The first draft lottery took place on December 1, and though Otis wasn't eligible due to his age, watching it with the barbecue guys wrenched a deep pit in his stomach. If he dropped out of Berkeley, he'd soon become eligible, but Berkeley had become a slog. He made it through the first semester with mostly A's, though he'd barely squeaked out a B in physics. Decent grades or not, Otis could not have cared less about getting a degree. He would close his eyes in class and see grape clusters dangling from vines.

At home for Christmas, his father had given him an earful for the lone B and his lack of extracurriculars. What about the debate team, the school newspaper? Good grades aren't enough these days. *Yeah*, Otis thought, *wait till I tell you what's really going on, Dad.*

Otis didn't mention Rebecca or his newfound love of wine, but back in the city in the first couple of months of 1970, he couldn't stop imagining a different scenario.

Still, his father's voice rang in his ear, warning him off chasing daydreams. Voices echoed from his family tree, telling him the same.

Was there any substance behind this wine thing anyway? Between classes, while seated along the shore of Strawberry Creek, the waterway that ran through Berkeley, he pondered his awakening while also looking for any indications that he'd misread this abrupt about-face in his life.

Otis had fond memories of his mother's garden back in London. They'd had a first-floor flat with a small courtyard that she'd packed with flowers and vegetables. He would lean against the brick wall and watch her work and ask endless questions, desperate to understand how a seed could sprout into a plant, or how humans had discovered which fruits and vegetables were edible, or how a flower could detect the sun and grow toward it.

Seeing the vines at Murphy Vineyards had reignited his enthusiasm. To think a vine could bear fruit that would lead to wine was almost more than he could process, especially once he considered Paul Murphy's words about how each year and each piece of land created different qualities in the grapes. The idea took farming to a new place. Wine production was the ultimate confluence of art and science, an intersection that called to Otis like a gesturing hand appearing out of the fog.

He'd adored so much about the farm in Montana: his mother's much-larger garden, the steady howl of the coyotes at night, the fresh cream and milk, the early mornings where the rest of the world slept as he completed his chores, the constant challenges: a broken fence or tractor, an animal that needed special care, even a door that wouldn't open. The list never ended, and he enjoyed doing his part and learning how to tackle anything that came his way. His aunt and her team of workers had been good about teaching him, showing tremendous patience to a young teen who had far more questions than answers.

But Otis wasn't a Montana boy. He didn't love raising cows, only to send them to slaughter. He wasn't a cowboy. Forgive him for saying so, but he wasn't a big Johnny Cash fan. He didn't favor going to the rodeo, or playing pool and sipping on suds. He'd been an outsider, and that was why he'd moved so far away. Perhaps he was a California man. He could have his nature there but produce something with more appeal—a product with sophistication.

One thing was for sure. He found the idea of farming vines and making wines far more exciting than sitting hunched over a desk like his father stabbing at a typewriter. He had too much energy for a sedentary life. That all seemed clear now.

Was his dream worth giving up on college and facing the wrath of Addison Till, though? Did he need to be in that much of a rush? If he abandoned his current trajectory, he'd risk becoming the first Till in recorded history to not have done something important. Even if he did become someone in the wine world, that likely wouldn't mean much to his family anyway.

"I believe in you, Otis," Bec said one day in February. They were strolling to the café in Santa Rosa where she'd taken a waitress job. "But I'm not going to be the one to tell you to drop out of school. That's your decision."

"You have a sense of these things, though. Am I crazy?"

"I don't know. To take a risk and chase something more appealing? I've never known anyone with ambition like you. Maybe that's all it takes. Before I met you, I didn't even know I should have something to aspire to."

He wished someone knew the answer.

As Bec strapped on an apron and took her first order of the day, Otis mounted his motorcycle and headed to Murphy Vineyards to ask for a job.

"I'll do anything, Paul."

"Mr. Otis Till, bitten so badly by the bug that he's willing to risk it all. You sound more like me every day, brother." He fired up a joint and took a hit. "If you want to join the fellas and prune, that's fine, but that's all the work I have for you right now, and it doesn't pay well. I guess that's where it all begins. That's how I started."

"Pay me what you can. I just want to learn." Otis took a long pull off the joint, then looked out over Paul's vineyard of naked vines that would soon produce leaves and grape clusters, an army of soldiers readying for the next vintage. "I can't exactly explain it, but this is where I belong."

Paul let out a grin. "I know the feeling. Something tells me you're up for the task."

Chapter 6

A Crossroads

On February 27, 1970, Otis said sayonara to Berkeley. He wished he could have kicked it to the curb and not looked back, but the potential for cascading aftershocks of regret was high. Unfortunately, he'd already passed the point of getting any money back, a fact that would infuriate his father to no end. That was why he chose to withhold all information from his family until further notice.

He did not have such a luxury with regard to Bec's parents. Though Otis had never been invited to crash on their couch and stayed in a cheap motel that rented by the hour on the edge of Santa Rosa, the Bradshaws always invited him for a meal. For better or worse, he was getting to know them intimately.

"Let me get this straight," Marshall said to Otis at the dinner table that night. He'd been knocking back Miller High Lifes like his life depended on it. "You've dropped out of one of the best schools in the country and now plan on working in the fields?"

"Correct," Otis said, wiping ketchup off the corner of his mouth, proving his citizenship one condiment at a time. Marshall had a million faults, but the man could grill a mean hamburger. "I have to start somewhere. One day I'll have my own—" He stopped and took

Bec's hand under the table. "We . . . *we* will have our own vines, our own winery."

Marshall ran a hand through his thin gray hair as a yucky grin materialized. The bags under his eyes puddled under fault lines of wear and tear. "I have one daughter, and for some ungodly reason, she's enthralled by you. Should this truly last, I expect you to treat her like the princess she thinks she is. Pipe dreams don't pay the bills, boy. You understand what I'm telling you?"

Otis resisted smacking the man's head. No, who was he kidding? He wasn't a smacker of heads. Instead, he met Marshall with fierce eyes and reminded himself that he could not fail. He'd prove to the whole fucking congregation of doubters out there that he was someone special, someone who could do great things on his own terms.

Aware of the venom in his sharp tone, he said, "You don't have to worry about your daughter. I'll give her and our life everything I have."

"Let's hope that's enough," Marshall said, unwavering. He picked a green speck of lettuce from his teeth. "I guess if you need a job, I can find you something."

Otis nearly threw the rest of his burger at him. Did the man not hear what he was saying?

"When's the last time you built anything, Dad?" Jed asked, saving Otis, who was seeing double with a silent rage. "What favors could you call in?"

Marshall's eyes narrowed. "You have no idea what I do or who I know, son."

Boy. Son. Marshall's words dripped with condescension.

Rebecca gave Otis a peck on the cheek. She was fighting her own demons but somehow kept finding a way to prop Otis up when he needed it. "Dad, there's a whole lot to worry about out there, but you don't need to worry about us. Those who underestimate this man will end up eating their words. I promise you that."

Otis took her words two ways. One, her cheering him on and standing up for him was love like he'd never known. Two, failure was not an option.

＿

In the morning, Otis and Rebecca drove in her mother's car to check out a place that Paul had told him was for rent in the hills around Kenwood. The property manager met them at the door and showed them around, telling them a businessman bought it as an escape from the city but that he'd been too busy to use it lately.

The sparsely furnished one-room cabin stood on an acre of land tucked down a gravel drive off Bennett Valley Road. A walk in almost any direction led to vines. Otis sat in one of the two chairs on the tiny front porch and soaked it all in, the gnarly old trees rising from the grassy hills, the trickle of a nearby creek, the happy song of birds who didn't have to go far in the winter.

"What do you think?" Bec asked, lying on the wooden planks of the porch, stretching her arms out. The property manager had crossed the street and was speaking with the only neighbor in the near vicinity.

"I think you should move in with me."

"You know I'd love to."

"Then why not?"

"Because my family is a disaster. You saw them. I do everything now."

"That's because they push it on you. They're taking advantage of you, Bec. You're cooking all the meals, now bringing home most of the money. Dragging Jed around."

"We only have one car."

"Yeah, but . . ."

"Otis, I've always looked out for Jed. He's different, you know. It's not what happened that made him this way. He's always been . . . I don't know . . . troubled. Sad."

Otis gave a nod that extinguished the tension. How could she not see the truth, that she was trying to make up for running away by becoming the caretaker of the entire family?

"Can I say one thing, though, and you won't get mad at me?"

Rebecca sat up. "I guess."

"If your dad touches you again, even if he raises his voice at you, then you're moving out, okay?"

"He's not going to do anything again. He learned his lesson, trust me. He wasn't always like this, not until he lost his job a couple of years ago."

"But he's like that now."

"Trust me, I won't tolerate it. He gets one pass, that's it."

They held eye contact for a while. He hoped she was right.

Otis coughed up three months' rent, a deep dent in his savings that reminded him that this was the beginning of a race against countless odds.

⌒

While Rebecca worked at the café and attempted to reassemble her family, Otis spent his days on Murphy Vineyards, pruning vines with two Mexican men who called him *gringo*. When Otis finished each afternoon, he hung around the winery to soak up as much information as he could. In the lab, he'd peek over Paul's shoulder as he tested sugar, acid, and pH levels of the new lots, and he'd pepper him with countless chemistry questions, half of which Paul couldn't even answer. He appreciated Paul's artistry, how he didn't get bogged down by the science. In the cellar, Otis would watch the workers, known as cellar rats, as they followed Paul's various work orders: racking wines that needed air, pumping finished lots from tank to barrel, thumbing out samples with a barrel thief, and cleaning incessantly.

A good ten years older than Otis, Paul had come upon the vines for the first time when he was hitchhiking from his home state of Oregon to San Francisco. He recounted the tale as he cut strips of tape and labeled various containers of wine. "I made it as far as Santa Rosa when I overheard a man talking about being short on workers for harvest. I was in the fields a day later plucking cab off old vines with a grin I'd never known. I eventually worked my way to cellar rat for the Charles Krug Winery. Peter Mondavi was the one who taught me the good stuff: micro-filtering, cold fermentation, inoculated secondary. The guy's a legend."

Otis craved such knowledge. "How'd you come upon Lloyd?"

"His dad was a longtime friend of the Mondavis'. Lloyd was up visiting one time, and we shared a glass of wine after work. He was building a portfolio of small wineries that he could finance. His trust fund had kicked in. Mr. Mondavi had said good things about me, and Lloyd asked if I'd be interested in starting something up with him. Sparrow and I scraped some money together, secured some ownership interest, and signed on the dotted line."

Paul was a long-haired hippie who was barefooted more often than not and would never turn down a couple of tokes from an afternoon joint, but he took his wine seriously, and Otis grew to respect the man greatly as he studied under him.

At night, after visiting Rebecca, Otis would pore over the many books he'd borrowed from Paul, topics covering wine chemistry, viticulture, geography, and philosophy.

Glimpses of the wine life began to reveal themselves, and Otis found them even more intoxicating than he'd imagined. Once the vines were retrained and pruned, they focused on irrigation. Otis's Spanish-speaking skills grew by the day. When the leaves appeared in April, they thinned the canopy to open a window to the sunlight. Witnessing the birth of the vintage was nothing short of a marvel, and everyone at the winery would close out the days in camaraderie, sharing a glass and a few stories.

On the weekends, Paul and the employees and other friends and family would sit at long tables, enjoying delicious spreads of family-style food and bottles of wine, and ramble on well into the night about wine and music, religion and politics. That was where Otis and Rebecca began to learn how to taste, and it was where the wine bug had finally gotten to Rebecca too. It wasn't only about what was in the bottle; it was the way of life that pulled her in.

Rebecca looked up to Sparrow, loving the life she lived: entertaining guests, tending to her garden, selling her fruits and vegetables in the tasting room. The two of them would disappear for an hour or two, and Rebecca would always come back glowing, as if she'd put another piece of life's puzzle into place.

On those long, wonderful nights, the group would often do blind tastings and discuss geography and taste profiles. Coupled with his reading at home, Otis was becoming more proficient. He could name the crus in Beaujolais and the classified growths in Bordeaux. With a quick whiff of the bouquet, he could often tell if a wine came from the Côte d'Or or the Côte Chalonnaise. When they were lucky, Lloyd Bramhall would drive up from San Francisco with a bag full of wines that the rest of them couldn't afford with a month's salary. He was a generous guy like that, always willing to share his wealth. He was also the kind of guy who pronounced chardonnay *sha-do-nay*, as if he were requesting a glass from his butler, and his privilege irked Otis, especially when he'd find Lloyd staring at Rebecca.

~

One particularly warm Saturday afternoon in June, Lloyd brought a case of Bordeaux wines that he happily uncorked and put in brown bags. "By this time tomorrow, we'll all be experts on Right versus Left Bank Bordeaux. Remember, the Right Bank is predominantly merlot." He spoke with an exquisite accent of colorful origins. Though he was born in San Francisco, he'd spent part of his childhood in London and Paris as his father expanded the family's textile fortune.

Otis pondered how this cherub of a man had become so lucky. Paul had told him about his jet-setting life, how he dabbled in the wine business for fun as he bounced around the world with various gorgeous women, staying in the most exquisite of hotels and mingling with the most elite of high society. When he wasn't traveling, he returned to his monster of a home in Pacific Heights with a garage full of fast cars and a cellar overstuffed with the world's finest wines. All that and he was only twenty-five years old. What in the world did he lack? Turned out Otis would find out soon enough.

They discussed the merits of each Bordeaux, calling out the acidity, the balance, the structure, swirling and studying their color, sniffing the nose, gurgling the liquid on their tongues.

"That has to be merlot, no?" Rebecca said with a smile that glowed in her eyes. "It's so much softer."

"Right you are, my dear," Lloyd proclaimed, pulling down the brown bag to expose the label.

She glowed with delight, and Otis was thrilled that her love of wine was growing parallel to his own. He was not, however, as thrilled by the length of eye contact Rebecca and Lloyd shared.

"I've got one more to taste," Lloyd said, setting a brown bag in front of him. He had his own glow about him. He loved being the center of attention, the benefactor of them all. Despite his eye for Rebecca and his confident-bordering-on-cocky demeanor, though, he was a hard man to dislike.

"Another Bordeaux?" Sparrow asked.

Lloyd ran two fingers across his mouth. "Mum's the word." Carefully concealing the top of the bottle as to not give away any hints, he poured a healthy taste into each person's glass.

Like the rest of them, Otis let go of his surroundings and put his focus on the ruby-red wine. Everything else around him, the people, the vineyard beyond, even the table, fell away. He wrapped his fingers around the crystal stem and turned it a few times, looking for browning on the edges, an indicator of age. There was none to speak of, so it was likely made in the last few years. He brought it to his nose, expecting either the voluptuous blueberry silkiness he'd come to know as merlot or the classic vegetal notes that crept into every cab he'd tried.

He smelled nothing of the sort. The wine in his glass wafted off scents that his virgin nasal passage had never known. Sure, he detected fruit: berries and even stone fruit. Then a pleasant brininess. Was that possible? Sure it was, if the vines had grown close enough to the ocean. It was the balance, though. It had enough tannins to create girth but not so much as to zap his mouth of its saliva. The fruit sprang from the glass like a silk scarf rising up and wrapping gently around him.

With this particular wine, the alcohol wasn't evident, simply an element of the structure, a vertebra in the backbone of an extraordinary effort.

He hadn't even tasted it yet. He let the wine splash into his mouth and rest on his tongue, then held it there to see what it had to say. It wasn't Bordeaux, it couldn't be. It was altogether a different region.

Pleasure painted Bec's face as she spun her own glass and made her own discoveries. Though he wasn't necessarily the competitive type, he did want to get this right. He wanted to show everyone at the table that he had promise. Oh, the hell with it. He wanted everyone at this table to know that he had the nose of a basset hound and the potential to be an extraordinary winemaker. The desire resonated in his chest. To make a wine, to have his own label, to be called a winemaker, it was a dream in a bottle.

Otis let the wine fall down his throat, and he enjoyed the slight burn, but even more, the cool silkiness, that scarf now touching his insides. As it settled in his belly, he could taste it in his toes.

There was something else, though. Something far beyond the fruit and savory characteristics, or even the structure. There was a tang of authenticity. There was . . . his vocabulary lacked the words. It was like shaking a man's hand and looking into his eyes and seeing his soul. This wine . . . it came from the very essence of the earth.

Otis grinned into his glass and then leaned over to kiss Bec, tasting the wine on her lips too. This was a hell of a thing to do, sitting around with loved ones and friends, dissecting the terroir of the world.

Terroir was a funny word that Otis had never spent much time thinking about until lately. Ultimately, a wine's job was to taste like the place it came from, its *terroir*. The beauty of that was every piece of land on earth could create a unique wine.

"Who's ready to make a guess?" Lloyd asked, pacing alongside the table.

"I think I got it," Rebecca replied.

"Vintage first."

"I'm going late sixties."

"Okay. Country."

She looked around. "Has to be France. Not Bordeaux, though. There's something old world about it. This is Gandalf the Grey in a glass. Tons of wisdom."

Otis chuckled at that. She was his girl.

"I'm going Loire Valley cab franc. Nineteen sixty-eight."

Everyone at the table let out a collective *ah*. Lloyd went round the table, finally landing on Otis. "Okay, Brit Boy. What say you?"

Otis tried not to let the nickname bother him, but it did. It certainly did. "It's a tad bit older than '68. I'm going '61 or '62. There's a sophistication that can only come from bottle time. And I'm going out on a limb here. This is not a European wine. There's something about home in it, the marine influence. You can taste the whisper of the fog, the way it carries the ocean. It's kind of . . . dirty. Not dirty, but earthy. A scoop of our clay. I don't know who could have made it, but I get the feeling its origins are dangerously close."

Lloyd's eyes brightened. "Oh, my, Mr. Till, well done!" No one else had guessed that it could have come from California.

There had been the moment Otis first set eyes on Bec and the time he'd first come upon this ranch, finding his purpose. But this . . . this moment of being right was the boon Otis needed. He damn well felt wings sprout from his spine. He even felt more partial to Lloyd in this moment.

"It's a Carmine Coraggio. Glen Ellen. Nineteen sixty-one," Lloyd said.

"Sixty-one?" Paul said. "No way his wine aged that well."

Lloyd grinned like a teacher might standing over his students. "His wines always age that well."

"Who's Carmine Coraggio?" Rebecca asked, beating Otis to it.

Lloyd drew the dusty green bottle from the paper bag and held it up as if it were a newly forged sword. The black-and-white sketch of vines looked like they'd been drawn in haste. *Coraggio* was stamped across the top.

"Carmine is a winemaker's winemaker. He doesn't produce much, and he has his bad years, but when they're good, I don't know what's better."

Otis took the last sip and decided that he would have to find Carmine Coraggio. This was the kind of wine he wanted to make.

As the buttons of the night came undone, everyone grew bolder. Otis had been blocking Lloyd's advances toward Rebecca all night and was getting closer to making a firmer stand when Sparrow took over the conversation. She wore a wreath of orange flowers. Beaded necklaces of all lengths hung from her neck. She was such a gentle soul, but when she spoke, her voice commanded attention.

"Otis, I know your story, and I think what you've done is incredibly brave, but I'm curious. Are you happy?"

Everyone else overheard and tuned in.

"Am I happy?" he asked. "That's a loaded question, isn't it?"

She brushed her red hair from her face, revealing eyes that could see through a man—not unlike Rebecca's. No wonder they got along so well.

"I don't mean to put you on the spot, but I do. You've done this incredibly brave thing, resetting your compass, and you've found this amazing woman that I adore, but I sense that you're still craving something."

Otis pondered his answer as he fiddled with his hands under the table. "I'm happy, yes. I suppose a bit scared. I'll be happi-*er* once we find our footing. Certainly happier once my parents know that I've dropped out of Berkeley."

He thought he'd answered well enough, but Sparrow hit him even harder with her cobalt eyes, staring into him, almost dredging more from him.

"You're enough, though," Sparrow finally said. "You know that, right? I think you're such an extraordinary human, and I hope you know that."

Otis turned to Rebecca. "What have you been telling her?" he asked in the most playful way the moment would allow.

Bec started to answer, but Sparrow kept going. "It's more what I'm seeing inside of you."

Otis wanted to dive under the table.

"Don't be shy, Otis. We're family here. We all want you to know that you're enough, that you're incredibly special, and we want you to be at peace in your heart."

"Now everyone is talking about me?"

Had he a set of ninja stars, he'd start throwing them at all fifteen people at the table.

"Only because we see what you don't, Otis."

Rounding the table, Sparrow squeezed in between Otis and Bec. She smelled of fresh fir and spice. She took their hands and rested them on her lap, uniting them. Her head swiveled back and forth, meeting Otis's eyes, then Rebecca's. An easy smile lingered on her lips.

"Otis, all this will take the time it takes. Don't be in a rush, okay?"

"You might as well strip me naked and make me dance," he said, blushing like never before.

"What would be wrong with that?"

Otis heard the throb of his heart in his eardrums. He started to speak, but his tongue wouldn't move.

"Maybe that's all it is," Sparrow said. "Let go and live a little. Your dream is coming, and we'll all be by your side."

He realized he'd lost his breath and drew in a heap of oxygen. "Okay, enough of that. I don't like being exposed."

"So no dancing naked on the table?" Paul asked.

"You first."

"Fine then." They all watched with wide eyes as Paul popped to a stand, shucked his clothes, and then leaped onto the table as if he were light as a feather. With his private bits hanging free for all the world to see, he held out his hands and looked up toward the sky. "This is me," he called out. "Paul Murphy, in all my glory."

Sparrow stood on the bench right between Otis and Rebecca, and Paul pulled her up to the table. She tore off her dress, revealing every bare inch of herself, and then she wrapped her arms around Paul, and they danced naked in the moonlight.

Otis returned to the safety of the mannequin body that he knew all too well, too stunned to move, too stunned to look away. The next thing he knew, Rebecca stood on the bench and offered her hand to Otis, pleading with him to climb aboard this madhouse ship of naked loony tunes. He shook his head in a way that made his case clear: There was no way in the flipping halls of Satan's dark den that he was about to drop his drawers and dance on a table. She didn't push and instead took her place on the table and lifted her dress up over her head.

Did no one wear underwear in this country? For a slick moment, he enjoyed the absolute wonder of Bec's body, the delicate feline curves moving in waves a body could only move in if she didn't have a care in the world.

Only for a moment did he worry that everyone—including Lloyd—could see every kibble and bit of his lover, but he let it go and found a sense of joy in watching his partner in life express the absolute essence of herself, letting go like only so few could do. God bless her for starting to shake off what happened to Jed and break free from her difficult childhood, and God bless her for not worrying about dreams at all, but simply finding joy in the here and now.

Dammit if Otis didn't end up being the only one of those fifteen who didn't shed his clothes. When the table started to shake under their weight, they all hopped off and spun and danced naked together in the grass. Otis had never been more mortified. No amount of drugs and alcohol on earth would allow him to feel so free. Perhaps he could undo a button or two, perhaps kick off his shoes, but his trousers would stay on, and he wasn't about to join them, clothed or not, in this wonderful yet terrifying baring of their souls.

～

Late in the evening, after some of the clothes had made it back onto their bodies, everyone lay on the ground in a circle formation, making wishes upon the stars. Lloyd said, "Give me a case of '45 Romanée-Conti, the last vintage before phylloxera set in. To me, that is the holy water of the church that is Burgundy. I'd open a bottle right now and pour you all a fat glass."

Paul wished for a good harvest; Sparrow hoped for world peace. No, really, she did. After a few others, it was Otis's turn. "Oh, c'mon, fuck world peace. Want me to be honest? I want a place like this of my own, vineyards that weep into the bottle. Before I die, I want to one day make a great bottle of wine."

Rebecca, lying next to him, took his hand. "It will come."

The desperate hope for such a wine rattled him inside. "How about you, my love?"

She winked at him. "I want to marry you and start a family and give our children what I didn't have growing up."

Otis almost made a joke but bit his tongue. Her sincerity filled his heart.

No, the hell with it. He had to make a joke. "So Rod over there wants a Corvette. Lloyd wants a case of one of the most coveted wines on earth. Sparrow wants world peace. And all you want to do is marry me? God bless you, deary. I must teach you to set the bar higher."

Laughter ran around the circle of bodies.

Rebecca sat up and then pressed her lips to his. "You're like a Rolex priced at ten dollars at an estate sale, but I know what you're worth. You know what? I'm living my wish right now. You're my destiny, Otis Till."

"Wow!" Paul said, sitting up. "That's a whole lotta love right there." He began to clap, and then everyone joined in.

Otis became serious. "Okay, okay. Well . . ." Otis searched his fiancée's eyes. "My biggest wish is that I one day be worthy of being your husband, because I . . ." Fear ran up through his spine and teased his tear ducts. "I don't know that I feel worthy right now."

They looked at each other as if they were the only two people on earth. "You might not feel it, but you are," she whispered. "And I will be by your side till the day I die."

He pressed his eyes closed and felt the tears squeeze out and drip past his temples to the ground.

"I guess now's a good time to tell them," Paul said, bringing Otis back to earth.

"I agree," Sparrow said. She waited until she had everyone's attention. "Paul and I would like you to get married here. Otis, you're eighteen in August, right? You should get married on the eve of harvest. What could be more magical?"

"You'd do that for us?" Bec asked, nudging her way deeper into Otis's legs.

Paul pulled a joint from his mouth. "We'd be honored, but that means Otis has to spill the beans to his folks."

"I know, I know. Believe me, I know." His father was weeks, if not days, away from Berkeley alerting him to what his prodigal son had done. One way or another, Otis was running out of time.

Chapter 7

ESCALATING DISCOURAGEMENT

As July drew near, Bec told Otis that she wanted to attend Sonoma State University and study business. She'd spent the night at the cabin, and they were both getting dressed for work. "I could get a better job," she said, "make more money."

Otis, who currently made less than her, tugged on his jeans, knowing *exactly* what this was about. "You can't keep carrying your family, Bec. You're not even twenty years old and paying their bills, giving them cash like . . . like they're children getting an allowance." When she didn't reply, he kept going. "Doing the laundry, the shopping. Ushering Jed around."

Rebecca pulled a dress over her head. "You'd do the same thing for your family—if you had to."

Otis glanced at her before reaching for a flannel shirt in his closet. "Do you have to, though? Or are they taking advantage of you? I don't see why they can't pull their own weight. They're all capable of working, including your dad."

Annoyance clung to her words. "What do you want me to say, Otis? My dad prefers the welfare checks and pretending like he's retired. Jed's collecting VA money, but it's not enough. He risks his life for this country, gives his legs, and they barely give him enough to get by. The least I can do is chip in."

Otis shoved an arm into his shirt. "And your mom?"

Rebecca lifted her hands, palms up. "She's looking for a job, but if I go back to school, then I won't be able to help as much, which means she won't have time to work. Jed's not capable of taking care of himself right now. On top of the issues he already had, he's having to figure out living without legs. Can you imagine? I'm not going to abandon him right now."

Otis could hear the annoyance in his own voice escalate as he said, "It might be the best thing for him. All he's doing is drinking and drugging away the money the VA's giving him. Maybe your dad should kick him out again."

Rebecca turned red. "Stop. Please quit pestering me about it and understand that I have to do what I have to do. With a college degree, I can help them *and* make more money for us. When we start our own winery, I'll have money saved and the skills we need to run the numbers. Lloyd said if I got my degree, he could help me find a good job with another winery—something I could do in the meantime to gain experience."

Otis stopped buttoning his shirt. "Lloyd? How . . . when did you talk to *Lloyd*?"

"He had lunch at the café."

Of course he did, Otis thought, bile creeping up his esophagus. "I'd be careful with him, Rebecca."

"Oh, c'mon. He's harmless."

"Yeah, well . . . he has his eye on you."

She approached the mirror in the bathroom and began to apply what little makeup she wore. "What does that matter?"

He followed her, buttoning his shirt with angry intensity. "So you're admitting to it."

She pointed at him in the mirror with her blush brush. "Otis, what I'm saying is that it doesn't matter how he feels about me. Don't insult my integrity because of your insecurities. Matter of fact, why don't you get off my back? I was telling you that I wanted to go to college. I'm excited about it . . . and you stomp on it."

"I'm excited for you. What do you want me to say? Your family wears me out sometimes." Properly put in his place, Otis leaned against the wall and watched her for a while. "I'm stressed out, Bec. I don't mean to take it out on you. I'm calling my parents later, finally tell them what's going on, and it's . . . really wearing on me. I'm sorry."

Rebecca took a long time to respond. Finally, she turned to him. "I accept your apology. As far as your parents, think how nice it will feel when you finally get it over with."

"I hope you're right."

—

"Dad?" Otis wouldn't have been surprised if he'd felt a warm trickle run down his leg. He'd dialed the number while sitting, but he sprang up from the couch once Addison answered.

"Hello, Otis, caught me at a good time. How's summer school?"

Slow breaths, ol' boy, he told himself. The lies had perpetuated, spiraling off one another, first the discussions about how spring classes had gone, then how he'd met a girl but nothing much had come of it, and then how he was going to stay in California for the summer to sneak in a few courses and get a jump on his sophomore year.

The mess that he'd made had reached its tipping point, and any peace that he'd found was moments away from tumbling down into the abyss.

"It's . . ."

The lies had to stop.

"You might want to sit down, Dad."

"What is it?"

Otis wished he wasn't tied to the phone cord, as he needed room to move. Relenting, he sat back down, depositing his derriere just so on the edge of the raggedy couch. *Out with it, you twit,* he said to himself. *Not one more minute of this charade.*

The words wouldn't come, though.

A seething fury transported itself from Addison to Otis through the line. The man knew something bad was coming.

Poke a balloon and it pops. That was what it felt like when Otis finally opened his mouth. "I've been lying to you. I don't know why. Well, I do. I was afraid to fess up, afraid to disappoint you. I dropped out of school in February and moved up to Sonoma."

A silence born of the Ice Age chilled the air.

"What is this, a joke?" His father's taut British tone carried a terrifying bite.

Otis could only grin, knowing he was in the doghouse now. "No joke. I met a girl too. We're going to get married later this year, once I turn eighteen."

"I'm in no mood for this," Addison said.

"I can't imagine you are, but it's all the truth now. I apologize for not telling you sooner."

"Where are you exactly?"

"What do you mean?"

"What is your address? I'm coming down."

Otis stiffened. What had he expected? That Addison would hop up and do the Watusi and say, *Oh, you do say, sonny boy. How wonderful. Your mum and I will be delighted to pop down for the wedding.*

No, there would be none of that.

His father pulled up to Otis's cottage in a car he'd rented at the SFO airport. Though it might have been wise to have recruited a witness for this potential murder, Otis was glad Rebecca was dealing with her own family troubles tonight and wouldn't be stopping by.

As usual, Addison Till was fashionably dressed in slacks and a button-down nearly as stiff as his upper lip. His Rolex peeked out from his cuff enough to offer a sparkle. While he worked at his desk, Addison obsessively raked his dark hair with a nervous hand, and after years of that, his hair seemed frozen in place. His pale skin indicated that he was still working like a dog behind his desk, likely more so now that he was free of raising a child. Rarely did the look of discontent leave his face, but today the cold eyes hiding behind his thick-framed glasses knocked Otis to his knees. What Otis noticed most, even beyond the disappointment, was that for once Addison didn't look like the hero Otis had always considered him to be.

Addison locked his fists on his waist and shook his head. "The whole time I was driving up here, I kept hoping this was all a dream . . . or a nightmare."

Filling the doorframe, Otis folded his arms. "I guess we're skipping the hug today." Coming face-to-face with his father only encouraged the defiance that had taken seed on the purple bus.

"Don't be cheeky. This is serious business."

Addison followed Otis into his small place and expressed his disgust with a groan. Otis pointed to a table in the corner, and they both took a seat, the chairs grinding against the old wood.

With one lone green apple, sour as a lemon, resting in the bowl between them and serving as the only mediary, Otis told his father exactly what had happened. To his credit, Addison listened intently without interruption, though his clasped fingers indicated he was working hard to quell his volatile emotions.

As Otis wrapped up, he said, "I'm sure you're frustrated with me, but I bet there was a day when you realized that you loved writing, that it was your calling. In like manner, I've found my purpose, in both Rebecca and in this wine world, and I hope you'll return with Mum in September for the wedding."

Addison let out a slow breath so long that Otis wondered if he had a third lung. Clearing his throat, he pushed up from the table, chair legs again sliding or wood. He approached the window and looked out toward the road. Otis could only imagine the war in the man's head, and he appreciated that Addison hadn't flown off the handle. That wasn't his style anyway. He was a calculated man, equanimous even. It was also clear, though, that this was one of the biggest battles he'd ever fought.

"I'll reimburse you for school," Otis said to his father's back. "Every dime." Addison's cropped hair had a clean taper where it met the neck; no man visited the barber more.

Addison finally turned and shoved his hands into his pockets. "I'm afraid for you, Otis. I know what it's like to be young, to have dreams. Even more so these days, all the kids thinking they need to rebel, to fight the system. To break away from the routine. It's a fine thought, but put into practice, I fear you'll discover reality wins in the end."

Otis waited for more.

"What am I supposed to say? You'll turn eighteen soon, so I can't make you go back to Berkeley, but I think it's the biggest mistake of your life. Get in the car with me. Let's drive down and go to the admissions office, tell them you had a change of heart. Fine if you love this girl, but why the rush? Finish school, for God's sake. You might change your mind about wanting to be a winemaker. No one knows what they want to do when they're seventeen. It'll change twenty more times. Why not at least have a degree? Otherwise, you very well might find yourself with no means to ever upgrade from this"—he scoped the innards of Otis's humble domain—"this cramped and meager existence. Don't live a life of regret, dear boy."

"That's exactly why I'm here," Otis said with shaky defiance.

They went back and forth for a while, finding no more common ground than Nixon could with the Soviets.

Addison finally sat back down. The apple in the bowl jiggled. "You're a teenager making adult decisions that will impact the rest of your life. I can't condone . . ." He bit back what he was going to say.

He's a good father, Otis thought. *Trying his best.* This was a lot for him. "I know I lied to you," Otis said, "and that's really where I messed up. I've been terrified my whole life of disappointing you, of not becoming the man you want me to be. Of not being as great as you. It got the best of me. I need you to know that I'm not some lazy wanker who's going to sit around all his life and . . . I don't know . . . rot away. I'm going to make something of myself, but on my terms."

Addison didn't flinch. Otis could have balanced the bloody apple on the top of his father's head.

"I want you to meet Bec. She's a lot like Mom. Caring, wise, funny. So, so much better than me. She'll be a great mother one day. I hope you'll be a part of our lives."

Addison raked back his hair. "I've tried to teach you the ways of the world, what it takes to survive. I'm trying to appreciate your youth and these feelings that you have, but you will one day tell me you messed up, and I wish with all my heart that I could prevent it now. How do I do that? Do I grab you by the ear and drag you back to Berkeley? No, I can't do that. But I can't support these decisions. I love you, son, and I . . ." He choked up. "I'm going to walk out this door and let you mull over what I've said. Right now, I'm lost. I'm lost for words, lost for advice, lost for how I can save you from a devastating blunder."

Addison turned and walked to his car, his disappointment and anger silently emanating from his body. As the rental car kicked dust, Otis collapsed onto the stoop and cried.

Up to the last moment, Otis wasn't sure if his parents would attend the wedding. He had many phone conversations with his mother, and he could feel his father stalking in the background, his patience worn so thin, this test surely crushing him. Addison Till had been raised to conquer the world, and he'd set out to teach those same lessons to his son, ushering Otis all the way to a wonderful university, only to fail in the last lap.

Otis sensed the turmoil in Montana as he talked to his mother, a proper American ranch woman who took no shit from anyone, a woman so different from Bec's mom. She was smart and soft, but like Bec, you couldn't let that fool you. Eloise Till ran the show in her house, and Otis knew that she was coaching Addison on how to handle losing control of his son.

They flew in a day before the wedding, and Otis was wound so tight he felt like something might pop inside. He wanted his mum and dad to fall in love with Bec and to see this life at the winery and finally understand that he'd indeed found his own calling. He also needed them to get along with Bec's parents, who were not exactly their type.

They met for the first time in downtown Sonoma, because Rebecca's mom didn't want Otis's parents to see their house. So there they stood, outside of a casual spot called Baby's Kitchen, where Otis had secured a table for seven. September had brought with it a helping of cool air, and the clouds threatened rain.

"Mum, Dad, meet Rebecca Bradshaw."

"What a pleasure," Eloise Till said with a smile, exhibiting an eagerness to snuff out any negativity. Leaving Bec out of it, Eloise was the most charming woman within a mile. She moved back and forth easily between a rancher in jeans and boots who wasn't afraid to pull a stuck calf from a springing heifer to a classy, stunning, and witty woman in an elegant white dress who could keep up with any Ivy League, big-city intellectual. As she usually did when not mucking about in work boots on the ranch, she proudly showed off her exquisite legs in a dress with stilettos that could double as ice picks. No doubt, she'd threatened Addison with them a time or two, as he seemed to be on his best behavior, smiling and nodding like this was the proudest moment of his life.

Rebecca hugged both of them, showing extraordinary poise, confidence, and beauty, proving she was as much of an anchor as Eloise. Otis prayed his parents could see that he was marrying someone who only comes around once in a lifetime. You don't pass that up for a degree.

Addison tried his best but could have been warmer. Bec didn't let it bother her, though she surely sensed it with her magical powers that Otis was seeing more of every day. She might not be able to see the future, but she could see people's souls.

The dinner went well enough. The electricity of the wedding seemed to put a sparkle in both Eloise's and Olivia's eyes. Marshall Bradshaw was on his best behavior, too, sipping slowly on only two beers and proving that he was also under spousal command—or arrest, rather. He could be charming when he wanted to be, and he and Addison started off about the weather, then wound their way toward politics before finding common ground in sports, which dominated their conversation for the rest of the night.

Bec put most of her attention on Jed, trying to include him as best as she could. She had a bleeding heart and worked hard not to get dragged down by her brother's decay, but she was still doing double duty trying to make up for her guilt for abandoning her family.

The following morning, Otis was relieved to wake up to clear skies. He couldn't have it raining on their wedding day. The stakes were too high, the opposition and doubters too strong. While the moms took Rebecca out for a spa day, Otis took his father around vineyard country and ended the tour at Murphy Vineyards, guiding him through the vines, showing him what he'd learned. Then he took him into the cellar and tasted him through juice at differing steps of fermentation. In his own voice, Otis could hear all the knowledge he'd gained in the six months he'd been chasing his wine demons. Could his father tell that he was working as hard as he ever had in pursuing this dream?

～

Otis stood next to a preacher, because all the parents had insisted a preacher marry them, and he watched as Marshall awaited his daughter, whom he would walk down the aisle. Vines bursting with grapes on the edge of ripeness dotted the hills. The sun lay suspended on the horizon, splashing vibrant colors over the sky.

Then she appeared, as radiant as an angel floating toward him.

Otis had no business marrying such a woman, and when she finally stood before him, he said, "You're so far out of my league we're not even playing the same sport." His eyes watered, taking her in, the strength of his girl shining like a comet.

"Will you hush?" she whispered. "Stop trying to be funny."

Otis had worked on his vows for weeks, tearing up paper, marking through lines, nearly giving up a time or two. Even as he read them before his bride and family and friends, he knew that he could have done better. No words could capture his feelings for her.

Rebecca followed with loving vows she'd scrawled on a napkin but read like she'd been working on them all her life. She ended with, "I can't believe I'm saying it, but you've made me a believer, Otis. I don't know what's ahead, but something tells me you're going to take me places I could have never dreamed."

As she finished, he made a silent vow to do just that.

When the time came, Bec said, "I do."

"You sure?" Otis asked, invoking a chuckle from the preacher and a few in the front rows. "No turning back."

Bec glared at him, but she couldn't smother the smile that rushed to her face. For some ungodly reason, this woman truly loved him.

They were both grinning as their lips met, and for those seconds, his feet left the ground as his heart thumped joyfully.

He *would* have driven away with Rebecca in a state of utter bliss, if he could only shake one image away from the night: the way Lloyd and Rebecca had danced together as the night ended. He saw Lloyd whispering into her ear, and she'd laughed like he was the funniest man on earth.

As Otis drove them away, and as the cans tied to the back bumper rattled on the road, that haunting image wedged its way into his psyche.

Chapter 8 (Interlude)

PESKY SPIDERS

Red Mountain, Washington State
March 2011

Lloyd Bramhall. He always came back into our lives like one of those pesky spiders that never failed to appear on our windowsills in Red Mountain with the warmth of spring. Lloyd was kind, handsome, funny, charming, well traveled, and *rich*—not that his wealth drew me in. I could look past his ego, because how could he not have one? Otis didn't like him one bit, and I could understand why. Though I often denied it or attempted to dull the potency, Otis was right, Lloyd had a desperate crush on me. More than once, Otis had compared Lloyd's cravings for me to how Eric Clapton had felt for George Harrison's wife, Pattie Boyd. Indeed, I was Lloyd's Layla, and if only we could have known what sort of trouble he would cause.

As I look at Otis now, his glasses resting on the tip of his nose, his pen resting on the page, this adorable coyote pup curled up against his feet, his head resting on Otis's ankle, I hope he won't linger on too much of the bad. Lloyd brought out the worst in him, a jealous and often angry teenager, but when all was right in the world, Otis was soft and cuddly. When it came to wine, though, he had an obsessive focus.

He became relentless in his pursuit to capture terroir, relentless in his vision and in making sure no one stood in his way.

I delight in what this journaling is doing to him, the way a spark of joy rises amid the ashes of his grief. We really do have a story.

Perhaps a stir will force him to pick up his pen again. I certainly don't want him stopping with Lloyd on his mind. Yes, Lloyd nearly destroyed our lives in so many ways, but we forged through. Enough about him, though. For now, anyway. I'm sure Otis will reveal all eventually.

Otis felt for Amigo, giving him a rub on his head. "I think we've done enough for a while." Amigo stirred but continued sleeping. Since Otis found him a week earlier, the pup hadn't left his side, following him everywhere, even into the bathroom. Little did he know, he was about the only reason Otis hadn't put a gun to his head.

Perhaps the journaling hadn't hurt, either, though Otis hated to admit it. Bec was always right, and it often drove him mad. There was a magic in getting it all out, in revisiting all the wonderful things that had carried them through, even amid the turmoil of damaged families and assholes like Lloyd Bramhall.

Otis was about to stand when his pen moved, rolling over as if it were a dog itself. He rubbed his eyes, thinking he'd been staring at these pages far too long, a week of reliving memories. He pushed back, pulling his leg away from Amigo. "Sorry, little guy, it's time I step away from this thing. The memories are sweet, but they cut too."

The pen moved again, this time toward him, taking several rotations as if rolling on a sudden incline. He lowered down to see if he'd just changed the angle of his desk while pressing against it. Nope. The pen had moved on its own.

"What'd you put in my coffee, Amigo?"

His eyes went back to the last page he'd written, and he recalled the Chinese lanterns hanging over the tables at their wedding, the sparkle of the evening, despite Lloyd attempting to steal his girl. She'd moved into the cottage with him that night, but they had to forgo a honeymoon, even though Addison offered to pay for one (a kind gesture likely instigated by Eloise), as harvest was all-consuming, and there was no way in the shiny spit of Adam that Otis was going to miss his first harvest. The Murphy team worked countless hours, barely sleeping, and who cared because there was nothing like harvest, nothing like bringing in the fruits they'd labored over all year.

Bec and Otis were mostly happy in the following year. Poor, but happy. Turned out they were lucky too. On August 5, Rebecca and Otis held each other on the couch with barely a breath between them as they watched men in black suits draw numbers to determine the fate of American men born in 1952. Only did they breathe a sigh of relief after two hundred blue plastic balls had been pulled. His number ended up being closer to three hundred. Unless the war took a massively awful turn, he'd never be called up.

Rebecca was going into debt attending school, but Otis tried not to harp on it. They'd simply pay it off making wines harvested from the vineyard they *didn't* have. Perhaps even more worrisome was how much energy she was devoting to her family: cooking meals, food shopping, cleaning the house, attempting to help Jed find sobriety and a path forward. Despite the school debt, she was still giving her parents money on a weekly basis.

Though it was a full-time job not to lose his mind over how depleted Bec was, Otis took side jobs when he could, helping acquaintances with various construction projects, running errands for the owner of the café where Bec still worked when she wasn't studying, reluctantly doing jobs for Lloyd, who paid well despite his ass-holiness. Mostly, though, Otis set his sights on making good wine. When he wasn't at Murphy Vineyards, he hunted down other winemakers, offering to buy them a drink if he could ask them questions. With all the money he didn't have, he bought and tasted countless wines from around the world.

Thinking about that unwavering spirit that possessed the younger him, Otis chuckled to himself and picked up the pen.

As long as she didn't get pregnant, everything would be fine.

Chapter 9

A NOBODY WANTS TO BE SOMEBODY

Nineteen seventy-two came down with a shower of heartache. The Bloody Sunday Massacre reminded them that it wasn't only Southeast Asia and the United States that were in trouble. Humankind had reached a tipping point.

Much closer to home, Jed was struggling and becoming more like his father with each depressing day. Still living at home and propped up by his VA disability compensation, he showed no interest in finding his way toward a career. Instead, he spent time with a crew of Vietnam veterans who drank and drugged their troubles away.

When Rebecca and Otis saw him, he'd knock back straight whiskey and rant about the war and Nixon and how he'd been spat on by a protester, how "the whole damn world" was on fire and burning its way to the ground. With each visit, Bec would die a little inside, and Otis wished Jed would stay away from home until he cleaned up his act—if he ever cleaned up his act.

In early February, as Otis was sharpening his clippers and about to join the crew to start pruning and prepping for a new vintage, Paul clapped him on the back. "You know that block of zinfandel on the north side, up past the tractor shed?"

"The one you keep neglecting?"

"That's the one. I was thinking you could take care of it this year. If you can get some fruit out of it, it's all yours. I'll give you a corner in the winery to make some juice. You gotta buy your own barrels, though."

A smile leaped to Otis's face. He'd hoped to buy some fruit during harvest, but this opportunity would allow him to make a wine from scratch. "I don't need barrels. Just lend me a stainless tank."

"Suit yourself."

When he first walked up the hill to assess his block, he hadn't quite realized what he was getting into. It was a half acre of mostly zinfandel, perched on a steep slant that made it hard to farm—he certainly couldn't use a tractor—which was one of the reasons Paul hadn't bothered with it. Having never been trellised, the vines lay curled on the ground like snakes. Paul didn't have irrigation up there, so they'd eked out their existence on what little rain had come the last few years.

Otis didn't see a hopeless cause. What he saw was an opportunity to bring these orphaned vines back to life.

～

A life is built with moments. Ever since the day he met Rebecca, Otis had been collecting moments that were becoming a foundation for a life worth living. Moments that were building his confidence and turning him into the man he sought to be. Twenty years old, and he'd found what he wanted to do for the rest of his life.

Twenty years old, and he'd made his first wine.

His first wine.

Almost ten months after Paul had given him a block to farm, Otis stared at the tank. He'd been tasting it every day, and it wasn't exactly horrible. It was maybe even palatable. Maybe even delightful.

The multivarietal fruit had looked good when he harvested it two months ago in October. Paul had eyed the bounty with wide-eyed surprise. "How you managed this, I do not know, brother." Under judicious temperature control, the juice had fermented easily after pitching the rehydrated yeast. He hadn't let anyone taste it, as this was his baby, and he wanted to guard it till it was perfect.

On Sunday afternoon, Rebecca was holed up at the cottage, studying to ace another economics exam. Earlier in the week, the government had hosted another draft lottery, promising to tear more men away from their families. That same day, *Apollo 17*, packed with three astronauts and five mice, had launched from Cape Canaveral and was due to land on the moon tomorrow.

Otis cared deeply about what was happening in the world. He was tired of hearing about more men like Jed coming home without limbs, tired of seeing clashes between protesters and cops, tired of all the bloodshed. There wasn't much he could do, though, so he put his head down and kept working.

To many, including his father, making wine seemed like such a small thing. Sure, he wasn't performing surgery. He wasn't sending people to the moon. But it wasn't a small thing at all. Not to him.

Making wine was his way of shining some good light out there in the world. Wine brought people together. How many bottles had graced the tables of family reunions, of celebrations of new births, of lovers tying the knot? How many bottles had graced simple moments, new friends gathering to share like-minded conversation, reminding themselves that they weren't alone. How many bottles had transported people, tasting a wine from very far away and being taken to a different place and pulled back in time, being touched by the souls of farmers dedicated to bottling the heart of their vineyard.

Just as Otis had done with his first wine.

This particular tank didn't have a sampling spout, so he cracked the racking valve to let the wine spill out into his glass. December was quiet at the winery. Otis had been in every day, learning from Paul and anyone else willing to teach him.

He lifted the wine to his nose, expecting a bouquet of berry and stone fruits. A fresh and fruity wine. Perhaps not ageable but certainly sessionable. Something of which he could be proud.

Long before the vines had even flowered, Otis had dreamed of what his label might look like and imagined how it would feel to one day pull the cork on his creation.

As the scent traveled through his nasal passage, his mouth curled in shock. It smelled like rotten eggs. With a curse, Otis cast the wine down to the cellar floor, letting it seep into the drain. He cracked the racking valve again and poured another sample, hoping for a different result. With his nose deep down into the glass, he confirmed the existence of hydrogen sulfide, a volatile sulfur compound that he'd learned to detect in his work with Paul.

Bile rose up Otis's esophagus; a whole year turned bad.

He'd bragged to Bec, telling her the whole process had been easy. He'd told her—he'd told his dad too—that he'd shown a natural talent for fermentation. For the whole bit.

His shoulders slumped, and his heart ached as he chucked the rest of the reductive wine from his glass into the drain, his liquid dreams rushing away from him. This was supposed to be his break. It wasn't simply a tank of wine; it was the beginning of his winery, the beginning of . . . no, he couldn't say it. Couldn't even think it. He'd already come up with the name of his winery, even designed the label in his head, and this wine was supposed to be its first vintage. He'd planned on holding back cases of it, sharing it with his children and grandchildren.

In the following days, Otis went to work on the wine, racking it with desperation, hoping a ton of oxygen might save the day. He was too ashamed to ask for help. Trying another technique he'd learned, he added copper sulfate and crossed his fingers. Days later, it had only gotten worse.

No amount of air, copper, or any other winemaking trickery could save this batch. He'd blundered his chance.

He pulled at his hair and yelled into the cavernous tomb of the cellar: "You fucking buffoon!" His words bounced off the concrete floor and the stacks of barrels, shouting back at him, assuring him that he was indeed correct in his assertion.

"What's going on, man?" Paul's voice cut through the void.

Otis came to, realizing his eyes had leaked tears. He wiped them quickly and nodded toward the tank. "I've made the most reductive wine in history."

Paul was good under pressure, hard to rattle. He kept his cool as he grabbed a glass and cracked the valve for a taste. Otis looked at the wine like it was poison, proof that he did not have the natural talent it would take to own a winery. He wanted to be some kind of savant, someone with inborn talent, but his nose wasn't extraordinary, and now he was proving his instincts were no better.

Paul took a whiff. "Oh."

"It's wretched, isn't it?"

"It's a . . ." He sucked in his lips. "Let's rack it."

"I've racked the bloody hell out of it."

"Copper?"

"Yep."

Paul looked over at him. "It's your first wine. It's not supposed to be perfect."

"I don't want perfect, Paul, but I want drinkable."

"I'd drink this . . . you know, after a few tequilas." He grinned.

Otis couldn't even kick-start his facial muscles. All of him drooped.

"You're not the first guy to screw up his virgin batch."

"It was going fine. We went to Montana for a few days. I should have been here."

Paul shook his head. "If it were easy, everybody would—"

"Don't patronize me. What do you think went wrong?"

"Probably not enough air, man. You have to find that perfect balance of protecting it without suffocating it." Paul stepped forward and put a hand on Otis's shoulder. "We'll get 'em next year."

Otis didn't have years. They were broke. This would have earned them some money, something off which to build. He wasn't dumb enough to think he could have made a wine worthy of Carmine Coraggio, but he at least wanted to pull off a wine that he could share with his family and friends, something to show them that he could make his dream reality.

What it felt like, what this wine *tasted* like, was an omen, his last chance to get out while he still could.

Fear rushed in his father's voice the bugle call for an army of doubt, but he pressed his eyes closed and shut it down. He wasn't going back to Berkeley. He wasn't giving up.

~

Rotten eggs still on his tongue, he drove through the valley to the only man who he thought might save him.

Shortly after first tasting the wines of Carmine Coraggio, Otis had learned that Carmine's farm wasn't too far away. Only a few miles south.

Several times in the last two years he'd wanted to go by and talk to the man, to ask if he might study under him. Paul Murphy was a great winemaker, but Otis wanted to expand his knowledge. Every time he thought he'd found the courage to go introduce himself, though, that courage would die a fast death. Once he'd even gotten close to the legend's house before turning around. He couldn't follow through, terrified of the rumors he'd heard, terrified that he wasn't worthy of even breathing the same air as such a great man.

From what he'd heard from Lloyd and Paul and other natives of the area, Carmine Coraggio didn't like people—especially after losing his wife—and wasn't fond of visitors. He had no phone. No tasting room. Signs warning off visitors supposedly hung on the gates.

Desperation could either kill you or break down barriers. Today, it broke down barriers. Otis didn't turn back and wound his way through the hills of Glen Ellen with unwavering determination. The drive was stunning, despite the season. Though many of the trees were bare and the flora had paused its growth till the spring, this land projected poetic majesty. The sun shot through the canopy of the forest, splashing light through the lingering mist. A deer raised his head from the grass and then shot off into the distance. On occasion, a farmer's tiny vineyard revealed itself. Otis could already see why Carmine's wines were special.

If it weren't for the lack of signs, the severely eroded gravel roads, and its overall remote nature, this part of Sonoma would have been inundated with wineries, but the business-minded winery owners knew that tourists spent their time and money on the Sonoma Highway, so that was where they planted their grapes.

Rounding one last bend, Otis knew he'd arrived. Over a wooden fence coiled with barbwire stood a farm beyond description, a winter oasis bursting with vibrant energy. Twisty ancient vines wrapped gnarly canes around their trellises. Random oak trees poked out of the earth. Black sheep like Otis had never seen wandered the rows with their heads in the grass. Birds cut through the sky in search of prey. A small wooden house hid at the end of a long drive. A plume of smoke rose from the brick chimney. Another building, presumably a winery, stood next to it and called to Otis as if with open arms.

After he'd parked, a steady whisper filled the air, a constant note as if God were holding down a low key on an organ with his left hand. This buzz crept into Otis and caused a stillness within him. He'd been chasing around the idea of how wine was art, that it was the ultimate expression of man working with nature, but only now did he truly grasp the spiritual element of wine, how a true farmer didn't only work with nature; he broke bread with it, sharing communion, cracking into the utter core of what mattered.

"Hello," he called out.

The black sheep lifted their heads to view the intruder. A dog barked. Off in the distance, compost piles gave off steam.

Otis found the latch on the gate, deciding that this would be an okay way to die if Carmine came rushing out with a gun. He locked the gate behind him and started down the gravel drive with his eyes on the vines, soaking up more in this moment than he had in all the years leading up to it.

A gruff voice shot across the farm. "Can I help you?" A man marched his way.

Otis put up his hands in surrender. "Mr. Coraggio?"

Carmine looked like the pictures in the articles Otis had read, a former navy man who'd seen his share of battle . . . or a Hells Angel who had grown weary of the road. His scars reinforced that idea. He was scrawny in places but muscular in others. Big biceps, a disheveled beard. His long gray hair hung in two braids. It looked like he'd lived in the woods for years, uncontacted by the outside world.

"Who's asking?" he asked with an Italian accent, plucking a cigarette from his mouth. Parts of his beard stained yellow from tobacco.

A nobody, Otis thought. *No one that deserves to speak to you.*

"Don't worry, I'm not selling anything. I just came to . . ." This could be the most important moment of his life. Here he stood in the presence of greatness, a man who'd flipped San Francisco upside down with his wines. A man who made wine like Picasso painted.

"Sir, I'm a fan. Not that I've had tons of your wine—I can't afford them—but I've been blessed with a few sips."

Carmine looked at Otis like he was about to shoot him.

Otis had nothing left to lose. "I've been working with wine for almost three years and have been reading and studying, doing everything I can, but I need guidance." Otis raised his head and met the man's gaze. There were songs in Carmine's eyes, ballads of angst and sadness, a life imprisoned behind the twelve bars of the blues.

"I came by to see if I could study under you. If you might have some work for me."

The old man's head kicked back. "Ah."

"I'll work for whatever you pay. I just need to know what you know. I've never wanted anything more in my life than to make great wine. To make something that people won't forget."

Carmine laughed at that. "That's not the goal in what we're doing here."

"What is it then?" A note of pleading lingered in the air.

"It's not something I could even teach, *ragazzo*. All I can say is keep trying, keep doing what you're doing. I'm not much of a teacher. There are better ones all over the valley." The evidence of Carmine's Italian heritage became more obvious with each word he spoke. In the last few decades, many Italians had immigrated to California and planted grapes.

"I don't want other teachers. It's *your* wines that speak to me."

"I appreciate that, but it's not something I do."

"Surely you have a cellar rat or two."

Carmine pinched his cigarette between thumb and forefinger and drew in a puff. "I'm done teaching people. I'm wrapping up. My career is over. My vineyards are folding in on themselves. Go study at Davis. Learn the chemistry. Go get a job at Gallo. Learn how to sell. 'Cause it don't matter how good your wine is, selling's the hard part. Good luck."

Otis took a questionable step forward. "With all due respect, this is all I want. To be a winemaker and to put my name on something to be proud of."

Carmine held his ground, and for a moment Otis thought he might come around. But then: "Good luck, *ragazzo*."

~

"I'm dumping it."

"Don't be a . . ." Not one to name call, Bec held back. "It might improve."

"I've tried all the tricks. There's no hope for it."

They were at a Sonoma taco joint they frequented. The floors were greasy, the windows hazy, but the tacos were good enough to serve to the Queen Mum.

Otis felt a rumble in his belly as he fidgeted with the bottle of habanero hot sauce. "I don't want anyone to ever know how much I messed up. I don't want to ever be reminded."

"Maybe that's the point. Maybe this wine is the most important you'll ever make because it marks your Neil Armstrong moment, your first big step."

"You mean big stumble?"

"Oh, here we go again. You know I love a good 'woe is me' with my tacos."

He pinged the hot sauce bottle down onto the table. "Is that being funny? Is this my wife cracking jokes? In my desperate hour of need."

Were it anyone else, he'd be mad, but her face glowed with love and joy. How could she find life so agreeable? How was she not terrified? "This is your life, too, you know. You've put all your chips on me. On Otis Till. We very well could be picking up the pieces of a broken dream before too long."

"You're a fox when you're passionate. A big sexy fox."

He glared at her.

"I'm sorry," she said, allowing some of her annoyance to shine through. "Did you think you'd make a perfect wine right from the get-go? Who gave you that impression? Making wine, growing it first, it's not an easy thing. You've been doing this, what? Three years? How long has Carmine been at it? How many vintages has he screwed up? No, you don't pour that wine out. You catalog it and taste it every year to remind yourself of your hard work. When you finally make a wine you're proud of, you taste them next to each other and remind yourself for one damn minute that you're capable of extraordinary things. You hear me?"

Her speech was *almost* enough to lift his spirits. "I still want to pour it out."

Bec laughed at him.

"You're kicking me while I'm down. And I'm down, Bec. I'm not some child who broke his toy in the tub."

"No, Otis. I'm not laughing at you for that. I'm laughing because I've never seen someone with such a desperate want to create something wonderful. You're a miracle."

He was the one to laugh this time. "You really must stop doing all those drugs. I'm afraid you see something in me that's not there."

Bec reached across the table and took his hand. "One day, when you're the most famous winemaker in this state, when people cry as they taste your wines, will you please tell me that I was right all along?"

"Ha. Sure. Someday, as I hoist myself onto my unicorn and hold up my bottle like Excalibur, I will tell you that I was always great and that you were always right."

She sat back with satisfaction. "Good. Now that we have that settled, I have some news I want to share."

Otis suddenly remembered how much of a selfish arse he could be, always vomiting his issues onto her. It was time he listened, for once. "Forgive me," he said. "Tell me what's going on with you."

"What's going on with me?" Bec looked around, as though she were about to confess to robbing the bank next door. "You know. School. Learning numbers. Being Jed's chauffeur. Waiting on you to make enough wine to hire me. Oh, and did I mention that I'm pregnant?"

The air was sucked out of the room.

In an instant, Otis forgot all about the terrible wine he'd made and the epic rejection he'd received from his hero. It felt like his insides had been removed, leaving him hollow, especially in his gut, where a hole had been blown into him.

"What kind of face is that?" she asked, her words echoing through the numbness.

He fruitlessly commanded his body to take a breath. He told himself he better get it together, that Bec needed him to smile. This was a big moment—the biggest. Using the same weak commands that he'd attempted to force himself to breathe, he told his mouth to bend. His lips moved into a curve that carried with it no sign of elation.

"You're turning blue," she said. He heard: "You're turning *blue blue blue blue blue blue* . . ."

Finally, he was able to suck in air and gather himself. "I'm so happy," he said lifelessly. At least he got it out. "Really, I'm thrilled. Just . . . surprised."

"Are you . . . surprised?" She leaned forward and said in a whisper, "That's typically what happens when you can't stop chasing your wife around the house."

He was relieved to see her smiling, despite his botched processing of the news. "I don't think it was the chasing that did it."

They both laughed, and he reached for her hands. Their gazes fell into place like a key twisting in a lock. "The whole biology thing really does work, doesn't it? What a miracle."

She smiled, the kind that could take away someone's pain. "Only you, Otis."

Here she was, the woman he'd spend the rest of his life with, the woman he'd raise children with. "It really is a marvel of science. I wonder if it's a boy or a girl."

"What do you want it to be?"

"A girl," he said so quickly and forcefully that the light above them rattled. "Unquestionably, a girl. I can't imagine bringing up a boy, dealing with all the things boys deal with."

She let go of his hands, but in a teasing way. "So girls are easy and don't deal with things?"

"Yeah, but their things are far more . . . graceful."

"Ah, I see."

After sharing a smile with her, he asked, "And you? Boy or girl?" They'd had the conversation a few times, but now the question had the potential to drum up different answers.

Rebecca stared off into the middle distance for a while, then said, "I want whatever's supposed to come. I'm just . . ." She suddenly teared up.

"What?" Otis was coming back to life more by the second. It hurt to see his lover upset. He leaned in. "Tell me."

A veil of earnestness fell over her face. "I want to do it right. I want our little person to grow up happy and safe, always knowing that we'll love him no matter what. I don't want our baby to grow up like I did."

"She won't." Otis shook his head, reality settling in. "I swear we'll give her our all." He saw a little girl running into his arms and became determined to bring the joy back to this moment. "I'll give her my all, and we're going to live one big and bold and beautiful life."

—

Long before anyone else had made it to the winery the next morning, Otis stood in the cellar, staring down at the tank that held the first wine he'd ever made. He considered what Bec had said about bottling it as a reminder of how far he'd come. A sparkly thought of one day sharing this wine with his child—daughter (please, God, let it be a daughter!)—gave him a lift. Perhaps a day would come when they could all laugh about his failed inaugural effort.

It was a nice thought, but a far stronger force was at play. If he bottled this wine, then he'd be gathering evidence against himself. He would be bottling proof that he wasn't capable of greatness. He would be verifying that yes, in fact, his father was correct in warning him off dropping out of college. Otis could imagine Addison's horrid reaction if he ever tried this wine.

No, Otis had to get rid of it and move on as if it had never happened. Before Bec's words again played in his head, he knelt down and opened the bottom valve. His reductive wine flowed out of the spout, splashing onto the concrete and then running like a river toward the drain. He didn't turn away until the tank was as empty as his heart.

Chapter 10

A Harvest to Remember

Rebecca bailed on the fall semester of Sonoma State, as Camden arrived in September 1973, a plump baby born three days after his due date. Otis was right in the middle of harvest but had rushed to Santa Rosa Memorial Hospital when the call came. Though they'd been plagued by more money troubles—his bike breaking down, Bec siphoning too much of what little money she made to her family, Otis barely making enough of a salary to call it a job—Camden was a welcome bundle of joy.

Otis's parents flew down, mixing with the in-laws as best as they could.

"He's a harvest baby," Otis proclaimed, assuring his family he would be one of the best winemakers in the world, that he was already aligned with the grapes.

Addison Till nodded his head with a morsel of encouragement, but Otis suspected that everyone, maybe Bec included, prayed that the wine bug wouldn't get close to biting this young boy. Otis could see how all eyes glazed over when he spoke of *terroir*, or about the latest trends in farming, or about the writer and farmer Jack London and what he'd done to bring ancient Chinese techniques to California. No one needed to say that Otis and Bec weren't in the financial position to have brought a child into their lives. In addition, Otis's decision to dump his first batch of wine had drawn unsolicited reminders from both Marshall and Addison that the admissions office at Berkeley might give him another chance.

This year Otis was trying again, working that same block of orphaned vines. He'd spent countless hours loving on them, dropping fruit, pruning—perhaps too heavy-handedly—talking to them, begging those vines to give him the chance he needed. Fear had a grip on him, and with every bite of ramen noodles and hot dogs they ate, he reminded himself of the stakes.

As soon as the 1973 harvest ended, and while his latest wine fermented, Otis worked with Marshall on a new project renovating an office building. He figured learning the construction trade would be invaluable when—not *if*—he found a way to buy his own piece of paradise. It was a bloody miracle that Marshall had gone back to work, and Otis made a stab at building a relationship with the man out of love for Bec.

Throughout the winter and into the spring of 1974, even as the vines came alive, Otis worked both jobs while somehow attempting to help Bec at home. He found that he could survive on four hours of interrupted sleep as he balanced his heavy load. He would have complained to Rebecca, but she'd been the one peeling herself off the pillow for Cam every night. Of course, she handled her lack of sleep so much more gracefully. Otis was the Scrooge of Sonoma, while she still managed to smile.

They were getting very little help from her parents. Marshall and Olivia would pop by on occasion, but there was no babysitting, no casserole delivery. Barely a diaper change. Uncle Jed was no uncle at all. He'd shown no interest whatsoever in Cam's existence. All that Bec had done for those three, and they couldn't return the love. It was heartbreaking.

At Murphy Vineyards a year after Camden's birth, Otis filled a bottle without a label—what they called a shiner—from the tank he'd used for his first vintage and carried it out to the tables where everyone had gathered for a preharvest dinner.

The scene reminded him of their wedding. Stretches of Chinese lanterns hung overhead. Everyone had brought a dish. Sparrow was the salad person, sharing the rich bounty of her garden. Paul always prepared an enchilada casserole that his mother used to make back in Oregon, and it was barely edible, but no one had the guts to tell him. He was a terrible cook but too kind and happy for anyone to want to burst his bubble. Bec had made mac and cheese, and it disappeared before Otis had even gotten a bite. Lloyd had arrived in a shiny new convertible Jaguar and brought with him a selection of French wines and several tins of Caspian Sea beluga caviar. Otis would have thought him to be a show-off had he not been so eager to enjoy his first caviar experience.

Perhaps what made the night different from their wedding was Cam, the young hellion always by their side. Their son sat in the grass, playing with building blocks. He'd finally discovered his tongue and rambled on about God knows what as he built his toy empire. Otis felt proud to raise his boy amid the vines and couldn't wait for the day that Cam took a seat at the table.

After chatting briefly about the economy and stagflation, they played the usual game, guessing country, region, producer, and vintage of each mystery wine. For this particular tasting, everyone had brought one bottle to contribute.

They finally got to Otis's offering—the wine he'd made. He'd tasted it every week since he'd picked the fruit eleven months prior, and he'd come to know it as if it were his second child—one who did not require diaper changes.

Like a Parisian chef eyeing his patrons, Otis studied his friends' faces as they tasted, searching for clues in their expressions.

"Oh, my," said Paul. "That's got to be a . . . is that? I don't know. I'm thinking Bordeaux."

"Whatever it is, it's groovy," said one of the cellar rats.

"I think it's California," Bec said. "Tchelistcheff?" She was referring to André Tchelistcheff, the legendary Russian winemaker whom Georges de Latour had recruited to transform Beaulieu Vineyard in the Napa Valley.

If only she knew what her guess meant to him.

"Yeah, maybe," Paul agreed, elevating an eyebrow with his nose still stuffed into the glass.

Lloyd harrumphed. "You know half of Bordeaux sneaks syrah into their wines to give some extra panache. I wonder if that's the case here. Who brought this?"

Otis ignored the question and splashed the wine around in the glass before jabbing his nose in for another sniff. He took a sip and let it dance on his tongue. It really was delightful, utterly alive in the mouth. The savory taste lingered like an outgoing tide, and Otis thought that maybe, just maybe, he had what it took.

"Moment of truth," Paul said, drawing the bottle out of the bag. "Hold on, is this one of our bottles?"

Otis smirked, but in his depths he glowed like a star coming to life for the first time. "It's my wine," he said, unable to stop himself from swelling with pride.

"Get out," Paul said.

Others chimed in, telling him he'd done it, made something spectacular. A fellow vineyard worker clapped him on the back. Bec slipped her arms around him.

"A wine this good needs a good name," Paul said. "Are you ready to share yet?"

Otis hadn't even told Rebecca the name he'd chosen, as he was worried he'd jinx it and end up pouring another vintage down the drain.

The time to fess up was now. "Just like Bec and me when we first met, that block Paul gave me is a lost soul. There you go, the first vintage of Lost Souls."

"I'll be damned," Lloyd said. "You show talent, Otis. There's something special about this juice. It's a good name too." His head bobbed up and down with approval, marking the first time Otis sort of liked the man. He still wanted to punch him in the mouth for eyeing Bec, but maybe Lloyd Bramhall wasn't a total piece of shit. Perhaps a bit of scat, though.

A round of applause rose into the air. Otis couldn't remember feeling prouder, and he stood and kissed his wife, then scooped Cam up from the grass and met his eyes, whispering, "I'm paving the way for you, my son."

"People are going to fight for this wine," Paul said. "Have you thought about a label?"

With Cam in his arms, Otis turned to the man who'd given him his first chance. "Every day since you and I met."

⌁

Carmine Coraggio's farm burst with a haphazard and overgrown explosion of life, so very different from the manicured country-club wineries lining the highway. The cover crop—the plant life around the vines—rose nearly as high as the vines' trunks, camouflaging them. A red-tailed hawk kept watch atop a foothill pine. The meandering sheep had cut zigzag paths down the rows, no doubt leaving nutrient-rich manure in their wake. Carmine must not even mow the rows. Just over the heads of the animals, two warblers chased after one another. Loose grape clusters peeked out from behind uneven canopies of bright-green leaves that had become a playground for bees and butterflies. This land was alive, every atom of it.

Otis heard that whisper that he'd noted last time, perhaps more a feeling than a sound, reverberating out over the land and easing its way up Otis's legs and causing a stillness in his chest.

At the end of the long gravel drive, a dog alerted Carmine to Otis's presence. It was a mutt of some kind, scraggly as the old man, who stood near the shed spraying down bins. He wore cutoff jeans and nothing else. A thin gold necklace with a locket hung from his neck. A pink scar ran across his chest. Tattoos marked his shoulders and biceps. His withered skin hung loose over fading muscles.

Otis knelt to pet the dog, then raised the bottle in his hand. "I brought some wine. My second vintage, bottled last October. Would you please try it with me?"

Carmine turned off the hose. "You're a persistent one, aren't you, Otis Till?"

"I don't know anyone else making wines like you."

"Oh, c'mon. The whole of Europe is forging wines like me." He fired up a smoke.

"Ten minutes of your time, that's all."

Carmine relented and led him to a picnic table surrounded by old barrels. Down the hill, a creek trickled through a thick tuft of trees. Carmine produced two foggy glasses marred with fingerprint smudges. Otis had to suppress his urge to ask if there might be more polished stemware somewhere.

With his heart rattling his ribs, Otis pulled the cork and poured the wine he'd forged from the depths of himself. Carmine stared with squinted eyes at the color as he sloshed it around in his glass. The anticipation nearly killed Otis, and he shared the details of the wine with a shaky voice.

Finally, the old Italian man took a sip. Otis waited with a breath caught in his lungs. He wondered how Carmine had any palate left with all the cigarettes he'd likely burned, but who was he to question the man's ability? Carmine had a funny way of tasting, moving his whole head to shake the wine in his mouth, then he looked up to the sky and let gravity drop the juice down his throat. He smacked his lips and then closed his eyes.

"This is your second vintage?"

Otis nodded proudly.

Carmine set the glass down and pulled on his beard. "You've been working hard, haven't you? How are you learning?"

"From Paul down at the Murphy Vineyards. Reading everything I can get my hands on. Tasting as much as I can afford."

Carmine was quiet for a long time. "You have a good name. Till. That's what I would have called it, but all you young kids don't like using your last names. I'm okay with Lost Souls, though. That speaks to me. Here's the thing. You need to forget what everyone's been telling you . . . what you've read. What I taste here is damn near perfect, scientifically speaking. No strange flavors. No VA. You kept it away from oxygen. It's clean. You filtered, I'm assuming?"

"I did."

"And you picked at a good time. I like the balance."

Otis sat up straighter.

"It's not my kind of wine, though," Carmine said. "To me, it's boring. Tastes like every bulk wine from every country in the world. There's no heart in there, Till. Can you tell that?"

Otis had gone from having the best day of his life to falling on his ass. "I thought it was pretty good. Everyone seems to like it."

"Who is that, your mom and sister?" He chuckled to himself. "It's fine. Delicious even. In the same way that orange juice is fine. You've made something that is entirely palatable, but you're here telling me you want to make something great."

"That's right." Otis wanted to fling himself in front of a tractor. *Entirely palatable*. Wasn't that a phrase for the ages.

"Filtering is your first problem. If you use anything tighter than a window screen, you're stripping the marrow from your wine. If a drinker complains about sediment, they can go fuck off. More importantly . . ." He recalibrated. "Stop trying to please others and stop trying to make something great. I keep hearing you talk about yourself. You, you, *you* want to do something great. That's not how you make a wine that's true. You need to get out of the way and let the land speak."

"How do I do that?"

"It's taken me a lifetime to figure that out." Carmine laughed, then tapped Otis's head. "Stop creating with this." Then he jabbed Otis in the chest. "You make it here. With your heart. Your essence."

Chills traveled up Otis's spine. Carmine didn't make clear how to do such a thing, but the sentiment was powerful.

Carmine stomped on the ground, shaking Otis. Scaring him. "When I see you again and ask you what you want, you know what you should tell me?"

Otis didn't dare speak.

Carmine leaned in, his pungent sweaty-and-smoky smell invading Otis's nostrils. "That you want to turn your land to liquid, that it's not about you and your silly dreams. It's about tapping the vein of your farm and running a line of it right into the bottle." A gold tooth in the back of his mouth sparkled.

He bent down and gathered a handful of dirt, then held it over the glass and let it fall through his fingers. The soil splashed into Otis's wine. Carmine spun the glass in a sharp, angry motion, then tossed the wine into the back of his throat.

Otis about shit himself.

"Become one with your land. Speak her language. Know when she's sick, know when she's mad. Tend to her with the respect she deserves. Get down on the ground and make love to her. Eat her dirt and let it spread under your flesh. You understand?"

"I . . . sort of?"

"You're not even a shepherd. You're a pair of hands, the only opposable thumbs on the farm, the only being who can do the math. So pick the grapes, move them from tank to barrel, do your measurements, and get out of the way. Don't worry about making a wine that tastes good. Taste has *nothing* to do with it. Make a wine that sings the sermon of the earth!"

Otis exhaled, as if he'd narrowly missed a bullet. He had no idea what Carmine was talking about, and yet he'd learned more in the last twenty minutes than he would the rest of his life.

Carmine kept going, sharing wisdom that Otis would try to wrangle into reason for years to come.

"What is it?" Carmine said after a while. "I can see you have a question."

Otis rubbed his eyes, wading through a minefield of question marks. "I don't mean offense, but—"

"Out with it, Till."

"You say I have to take myself out of it, but then you tell me I should have put my name on the bottle. That's what you do."

Carmine stuffed a cigarette into his smiling lips and drew in a long puff. The red cherry glowed. Out with the smoke came more wisdom. "Just when I worried that you were another pawn falling in line. Now you're thinking, *ragazzo*. It's a hell of a question, a complex one. To make a great wine, you must take ego out of it. You have to let your farm lead the way and take all the glory, but the reality is that to sell a wine, we need to sell ourselves too.

"In a perfect world, my labels would be blank. Or better yet, I'd just press some of this dirt into them, but we must consider marketing. If we are to be the stewards that usher juice into people's mouths, we must give them a brand. But what we put *in* the bottle is not the brand. It is life, nature . . . God. Brands are a short-term tool forged on the impatience of the human capitalist perspective."

Otis laughed at that. This fellow had a way with words.

Carmine helped himself to another glass and knocked it back. "I have work to do. Aren't you sorry you came to see me?"

"I'm begging you . . . let me help around here. I'll work for free."

"I don't need help, and you're not ready."

"Why not?"

Carmine stood and looked down at Otis. "For one thing, you need to go to the Old World. Go to the church of wine. Go to Burgundy and Bordeaux. Go walk the magical hills of Tuscany. You know what? Go baptize yourself in the Mosel. They started making wine there in the fifteenth century. Soak that up. Then go buy a farm and learn how to tend to land. You're up there working a block at Murphy Vineyards. It's not about working a block, *ragazzo*. It's about working a farm. You see all these trees around here, you see those animals, the biodiversity? You hear those bees? Fermenting wine is the easy part. All right, class dismissed."

He found a pen and wrote his number down. "So that next time I don't shoot you for trespassing, at least call first."

As Otis took the paper into his hands, tears welled under his eyes.

⁓

Otis would never forget his first trip to the Mosel Valley, courtesy of his father, who'd paid for it as their honeymoon trip. Carmine was right—the hills were damn near cliffs. The naked riesling vines descended steeply down from the mountain mist and stopped just shy of the ancient fairy-tale town of Bernkastel-Kues, which straddled the Mosel River. A grand church tower stood over the half-timbered *fachwerk* buildings that made up most of the architecture.

Before they even unpacked, Otis was dragging Rebecca and Camden out the door. They'd barely slept, but he was wide awake. They enjoyed sausage and sauerkraut and beer and then wandered along the old stone wall that created a border between the town and the vines.

Whispers trickled down like fog descending a mountain.

"Do you hear them?" Otis asked.

"What's that?" Rebecca asked.

"The vines. They're talking."

Rebecca smiled. "I've never seen you like this."

"And I haven't even tasted wines like this. My God, Bec. We're on holy ground."

Thanks to Lloyd, they had an afternoon appointment with a five-hundred-year-old winery. In the depths of a musty cellar underneath the town, as Camden lay on the floor drawing in a coloring book, a German man with shaggy hair and a plaid scarf guided them through a lineup of rieslings. The first few vintages were crisp and delightful *quaffers*, but nothing that sent Otis reeling.

Then the man pulled corks on older wines from the early sixties that blew Otis's and Rebecca's minds. It was as if riesling slept for the first decade before coming alive and running in a million different directions. Wines from grapes grown only meters apart tasted like they'd come from different parts of the world.

"This is how the riesling works," their host explained in stilted English. "The wine needs many years for it to find its way."

"Just like us," Rebecca murmured.

Otis stared into the golden hues of a '61. "I have never understood wine till this day."

Rebecca wiped Otis's eyes. "What am I going to do with you?"

"My whole world has changed. It's flipping fruit juice, Bec, but it means so much to me. Being here. These wines. This town. The history. They were making—no, *growing* wines here *five hundred* years ago on those unbelievably steep slopes." Otis stuffed his nose back into the glass and spoke in reverent whispers. "I'm eager to get back to California and tap in, but another part of me wonders why I would even try. How can we ever find a piece of land back home that would be worth devoting our lives to?" He looked at the dusty racks of wines dating back hundreds of years and sighed.

"The how doesn't matter. All we have to do is will it."

"Will it? Are we back to this Seth thing again? You and Sparrow really need to settle yourselves."

Sparrow and Rebecca had become best friends, despite the decade that stood between them, and Sparrow had pulled Rebecca down into a wormhole of New Age thought. They'd both recently read a book called *Seth Speaks*, which supposedly captured the wisdom of a spirit named Seth who had written a book through a channeler named Jane Roberts.

Otis thought that the two women might have eaten too many magic mushrooms, but a small part of him—an infinitesimal part—wondered whether perhaps he was missing out on something. The way Bec spoke lately, she'd changed. It was like she'd stepped into herself, tapping into a power of which she hadn't been aware.

Lately, she and Sparrow had been talking about manifestation. Apparently Seth talked about how mind created matter, that humans, either intentionally or unintentionally, drew their own reality as if they were sketch artists.

"Okay, magic genie woman," Otis said, his sarcasm thicker than the Beerenauslese they were about to try, "I want fifty acres on a hillside in Sonoma County. A place near a river with centennial vines parked on a south-facing slope."

Rebecca gestured to his wine, the '61. "Smell that again."

He did so.

"Wake up and smell the riesling, my love. There's no room for doubt right now."

"Wake up and smell the riesling," Otis muttered. "That's a bumper sticker waiting to happen."

～

Back at the hotel, Bec jammed a metal rod into the spokes of Otis's peaceful evening. Camden slept in a crib inside the cramped room, and the adults sat out on the balcony in the chilly night air, looking out over the lights of Bernkastel-Kues, a place barely touched by modernity. The stars burst overhead.

"I want another baby."

Otis had taken a sip of Spätburgunder and coughed it out onto his shirt. "Another baby?" He wiped the pinot noir from his chin. "So now we're buying land and wanting another baby? When are we winning the lottery?"

"I've always known we're having two." Her playful side took over. "What's the problem? Have you lost your attraction to me?"

Otis pulled her onto his lap. "Moi? Lost my attraction to you? I'd put a poster of you on my wall."

She turned and whispered over her shoulder, "Then take me, Otis Till."

"Right now?"

"Why not?"

"Camden, for one."

"He's asleep."

"Yeah, but . . . we're kind of on display up here." He gestured toward the people wandering the street four stories down.

"Fine, you know what? I'll go down to the bar and see if there are any handsome German men who might be more interested." She popped open a button on her blouse, then another. "Catch you later."

"You wouldn't dare." He slid to his knees and rested his hands on her thighs. "You're mine and no one else's."

"Ah, there's the Otis I like. Tell me again, what is it that you want?"

He attempted to slow the sexual craving rising up from within. "Fifty acres on a hillside. Centennial grapes. A farm that we tend. Animals. Two rug rats. How about you?"

She took a moment to solemnly consider the question. "For a while I thought that I was stealing your dream. That I needed my own. But I realize now that we're the same. I want to help you tend to our farm, to do my part to make the wines sing. I want to live off the land, to build a sanctuary where we have a giant garden and fruit trees of every kind, maybe even a U-pick farm. I want to make my own honey and jam and bread and sell it at the market. You do your vines and wines, and I'll do the books and manage the rest of the farm. I don't want to worry about money anymore."

He glided his fingers on the back of her neck. "Me either, lovey."

Bec cast her gaze up toward the North Star. "I can see it now. For the first time in my life, because of you, Otis Till, I think—no—I *know* we can make it happen."

For the first time in his life, Otis did too. Even if that sense of knowingness existed only up there on a balcony overlooking the Mosel River on this one night, the feeling was real, and he would revisit that memory and this place as often as he could, for the rest of his life.

Bec slid her fingers down his chest and abdomen and farther, igniting a carnal awakening from deep within. "Now take me, Otis, you lost soul you. Put a baby in me . . . and don't wake up the whole town with your howling. Then, when we get back home, let's go make this thing happen."

The howling came soon enough. With his clothes piled on the floor, Otis stood at the railing and beat his bare chest and howled into the night like he never had before, calling up to the moon, demanding that the universe make way for their dreams.

Chapter 11

LOST SOULS

In late January, Otis burst through the door with a case of wine in his hands. "Ladies and gentlemen, today is a good day."

Bec and Camden huddled over the table, drawing with crayons. "Hi, Daddy," they both replied.

Otis set down the wine and kissed the tops of their heads. He pinched Cam's cheek and said in a baby's voice, "Guess what Daddy has in this box? Your birth vintage. Can you believe that? When you're old enough, once you've cut your teeth in the cellar, we'll pull a cork together. What a day that will be."

Otis looked to Rebecca. Bags collected under her eyes. "You okay?"

She looked away. "Yeah, just tired."

Otis knew it was more than that. Maybe seeing the wine would turn her around. "Can we take a look?"

He pulled back the shipping tape and drew a bottle from the box. "Here we have it, the first vintage of Lost Souls."

Bec had been instrumental in the design. They'd studied countless labels, noting how Carmine Coraggio and Inglenook and Martini and dozens of others used a painting or drawing of their château or their vineyards. Others, like Mayacamas or Foppiano, focused on a logo. Otis and Rebecca opted for simplicity with a white label and black text.

LOST SOULS
1973
Murphy Vineyards
Sonoma

"You did it, baby."

"Are you kidding me? *We* did it. This bottle wouldn't exist had you not been pushing me all along."

She worked hard to hold her smile. He was losing her. He could feel it, the way she was pulling back. It might not necessarily be about him, but she'd lost herself, or, at least, the part of her that Otis had come to know best.

He slipped his hand into hers. "I know, I know. I'm too focused, but we have to do what it takes right now. Losing your paycheck hurts. I have to work overtime. I'm trying to get to a place—"

"I get it," she said in a tone that suggested that no excuse would justify how little time he was spending with his family.

He held eye contact with her for a while. What she didn't get was that she'd been taking out her frustrations on Otis. Her parents had proved to be terrible grandparents. Still, she continued to try with them, always inviting them over for dinner or taking Cam for a visit. Jed's drinking and drug use had gotten worse, and Bec had become highly invested in convincing him to go to rehab. He was a complete jerk half the time, but Bec kept trying to love him and reason with him. It didn't help that she and Otis still hadn't conceived another baby. Sometimes she acted as if another baby would fix everything.

Though she was an expert at hiding her troubles from Cam, Otis saw all of it: the way she got up in the middle of the night, sometimes for hours, the creases on her forehead, her lack of patience with him.

Could she not see the truth? That she was still trying to make up for running away.

Otis did his best to support her, but he was no good at it. When she simply needed him to listen, he'd always jump in with solutions, and that never went well. Maybe the best role he could play was as the target, someone to bear the brunt of her inner turmoil.

Not that Otis was trying to eschew all the blame. He *was* working too much. How nice it would be to ease his workload and make more time for Bec and Cam, but he simply had to keep his eyes on their dream. She understood more than anyone what it was like to be broke. The only way they could ever pay back their school debt and eventually build up some kind of financial cushion was if he relentlessly pursued the growth of Lost Souls and eventually found a way to purchase their own land.

Even as he thought it, he could hear his father cheering on his demise, ready to say "I told you so" at the finish line of his failure.

After dinner, Otis took a bottle to Carmine, and they cracked it open. Puccini played loudly on the record player. "It's coming around," Carmine said. "And the label's nice. I'd consider washing my feet with such a wine. Maybe even give it to the dogs."

Otis melted into the earth.

Carmine smacked his back. "Oh, lighten up. It's far better than what I made with my second vintage. You and your wines are growing on me." A long beat of contemplation ensued. "Come back Monday and I'll put you to work."

Otis looked at him dumbly.

"You asked for a job, didn't you?"

The next morning Otis shipped a case of his wine to his parents and then went to visit Paul to tell him that Carmine had offered him a job. "I get it, Otis. Work here when you can, but go learn from that guy. Maybe share some of his secrets with me. In the meantime, that block is still yours. I can't get enough of Lost Souls."

Otis wasn't a hugger, but he stepped forward and pulled Paul in. "I'll pay you for the fruit."

"Nah, just give me a few bottles every now and then. A man like you needs to have his own vines to farm."

~

Carmine threw Otis right into the mix, first pruning with two other guys who'd worked there for twenty years. Every day was a master class on organic vine, pest, and weed management, using only holistic treatments. So much of the talk centered on energizing the soil and the ecosystem.

He learned that cover crops attracted beneficial insects—pollinators, ladybugs, wasps, and spiders—as well as prevented erosion. Cover crops also made the vines compete for water and nutrients, forcing them to struggle, which made them focus on reproduction, which meant activating their own antioxidant-rich, stress-resilient pathways that would energize the fruit.

No matter what, Carmine did not allow synthetic chemicals on the property. "Chemicals permeate the vine, poison the berries, and kill their potential. Then the toxins end up in your wine! Do people think that the process of fermenting can kill chemicals? No, it can't."

More than once, Carmine would dig into the earth with a shovel and show Otis the health of his soil. "You see the earthworms, the life. My soil is a living thing with bacteria and fungi, an environment ready to thrust its sexual energy into the vines." He winked to inject some humor, but he was deadly serious.

"A balanced vine means a balanced wine," Carmine would often say.

Every week they would move the black Hebridean sheep from block to block so that the animals would mow the tall grass, softly agitate the topsoil with their hooves, and leave their manure as fertilizer.

Carmine had a way with those sheep. They'd come running to him like a dog might. He could clap his hands, and they'd follow him into the next fenced-in area, where the tall grass waited. They'd even eat out of his hands. Carmine was the one who ignited Otis's own love of animals.

When they weren't tending to the awakening vines and the animals, they scrubbed clean the cellar, sterilized pumps, topped off and cleaned barrels, racked the wines, and monitored them through tasting and testing. It was a never-ending cycle of work that repeated itself year after year.

Carmine also taught him the art of taking notes. For a guy whose outward appearance exhibited disarray, he wrote down *everything*. A notebook for each vintage offered meticulous information on each cellar task and monthly tasting notes of each lot and their chemistries. Even at his age and his level of mastery, he always strived to make the next vintage better.

Experiencing the truth of what made a good wine, Otis fell in love all over again.

~

In early April, Otis's father sent a letter that included a newspaper article from *The New York Times*. Addison wrote:

> Thanks again for your bottle of wine. I'm including a clipping of a writer I've come to admire, a Sam Ledbetter. Not sure if you've heard his name, but he has a column in the *Times* called Vine Matters. Might be interesting to send him a bottle, see what he thinks. I expect he could give you some tips.

In the article, under a black-and-white drawing of the man's face, Ledbetter reviewed several wines of the last year, featuring particular favorites from André Tchelistcheff's latest efforts at Beaulieu.

Otis knew his father meant to help, but he felt a dent in his pride. Even when his parents had called to thank him for the wine he'd sent, Addison hadn't exactly praised him. He certainly hadn't acknowledged what a feat it had been to farm a block of vines and create a passable wine.

In the morning, as they compared wines from Hungarian and French barrels, Otis asked Carmine, "Do you know of Sam Ledbetter?"

"Oh, sure, that old curmudgeon. He makes me look like a happy guy."

"He's tasted your wines?"

"Sure, he's tasted everyone's wines. He comes out every year to meet with folks."

"What's his opinion on yours?"

"I hear he likes them, but I don't seek out the articles. All I can do is my best. How they're received is not my problem."

~

Ovulation meant the Olympics of sex every month, as Otis and Rebecca had yet to make another baby. Nineteen seventy-five was a feeding frenzy for Bec's libido. She'd even track him down between the vine rows and tear the shears from his hand and rip down his pants to seize the opportune moment.

Though it had started out fun, a desperation began to fill her eyes . . . and Otis started hiding from her.

One day in mid-July, when he came in for lunch, she fired a finger at him. "Take your pants off. Let's go."

"Bec, I'm . . . let's give it a break till tomorrow."

"This is my window. Now. Pants off, c'mon. Cam's going to wake up any minute."

Otis felt no stir at all down below. In fact, he said, "Bec, my lobster tail is rubbed raw, and you have to get me excited in some way. I'm not a fornicating machine."

Bec crossed her arms; her eyebrows curled. "Is it really so much to ask for you to make love to your wife?"

He waved a hand through the air. "This isn't lovemaking, what we're doing. Maybe that's the problem. Let's go out on a date, perhaps even seduce each other. I can't keep doing it this way. You're going to create an aversion." As soon as he said it, he knew he'd made a mistake.

"An aversion?" She nodded in that way that showed him he was going to the doghouse no matter what he said.

"You know what I mean," he said sweetly.

"I do. This is about you getting tired of me. Six years together, and now I don't even excite you anymore."

"Excite me? You got me excited twice yesterday and once already this morning! That's about all I'm good for. I need to recharge."

Her eyes could have put holes through glass. Otis took a timid step toward her and offered a hand. She swatted it away.

"C'mon, Bec. The baby will come when it's supposed to come."

"Unlike my husband," she said without any hint of humor.

Otis sighed but stepped closer to her and opened up his arms. "Come here."

She reluctantly let him hug her, and he pressed his cheek to her head. Her hair smelled like dried rose petals. "I want to say something, but I don't want you to get mad at me. We're in this together. You have to always know that."

No response. *Oh, the hell with it,* he thought. "I think you're struggling right now. Yes, part of it is me and how I'm distracted by work. Of course it's how you're giving everything you have to Cam. But there's something bigger at the core." He let his words settle.

"Is my husband trying to be my psychotherapist right now? I can't wait to see how this goes."

He held her tighter. "I'm guessing not well, but I'm going to say it anyway. I think you're still blaming yourself for not being home to stop Jed from enlisting. So you're constantly trying to make it up to your family. You give and give and give, all the time, despite them not giving back. And you're so hung up on things needing to happen. Jed going to rehab. Your mom eating healthier. Your dad drinking less and working more. Us having a baby. It feels like it's all related."

The only sound for a good minute was the hum of the window unit.

When she didn't respond, he said, "It wasn't your fault. You don't owe them anything. You don't owe *Jed* anything. You were seventeen, growing up in an awful home. You did the best you could. Jed, and Jed alone, is responsible for his own actions. I know they're your family, and you have to do what you have to do, but stop doing it for the wrong reasons."

He pulled back and waited till she was looking at him. "You have to live *your* life. God, I hate seeing you hurting so."

A tear escaped her eye.

He wiped it and then kissed her cheek. "It's time to put yourself first for a while. Can you do that?"

She shrugged her shoulders. "Maybe. I still want a baby, though."

"I do, too, my love, but let's not rush it, okay? Trying is supposed to be the fun part." He kissed both cheeks and then the tip of her nose. "You're my everything, Rebecca Till, and I love you and am attracted to you more today than I was to that sexy girl on the purple bus six years ago."

"You sure?"

"You're the only thing I'm ever sure of."

They kissed, and Otis could feel some of her pain fall away.

"Did you really call your penis a lobster tail?" she asked, as they pulled apart.

A smile split his lips. "I was trying to be . . . polite."

Laughter spilled out of both of them, and Otis fell in love all over again. She had her own demons, but they'd be no match for her in the end. Otis believed that with all of him.

—

Often the years were determined by the vintage, whether it was wet or cold, hot or dry. Carmine was a dry farmer, meaning he didn't use any irrigation, and as the warm months came, he cursed when it didn't rain, saying he used to get all the rain he wanted, but now God had it out for him.

The '75 harvest, the first since the end of the war, settled into a steady climate that brought the grapes to a nice balance. Carmine liked to pick after midnight while the fruit was cold. As they dumped grapes into the crusher/destemmer, he would blast Italian opera music, insisting that his wines demanded to be celebrated as they made their journey toward the bottle.

Otis soaked up as much as he could from his teacher—how carbonic maceration staved off oxidation, how sulfur could paralyze a wine if it was overused, how a bladder press was far gentler on the grapes and easier to clean than a basket press. Like Paul, Carmine had recently sworn off redwood fermenters and used only double-lined stainless-steel tanks, but that was one of the few modern techniques that he embraced.

"You need to unlearn some of these things," Carmine said. "They're good tools for larger wineries. Gallo has to use machines to pick, has to filter, to load up the sulfur. What we're doing here allows for less intervention. This is liquid poetry. You don't filter poetry, do you?"

At home, Bec always played the latest records. When Otis complained about how much she spent on them, she'd remind him how much that last bottle of Barolo or Barbaresco had cost them.

Pink Floyd's *Wish You Were Here* spun constantly on the turntable. Otis was still more of a classical or jazz guy, or hell, even some bloody silence, but rock 'n' roll had its place, and he especially appreciated his fellow Brits, who rocked in a way the Americans couldn't figure out.

He'd come home from a long day's work, shut his truck door, and hear the familiar sound of Roger Waters's voice coming from the open windows. He'd find Bec inside chasing Cam around, or maybe dancing with him, and he'd smile at her strength and promise himself that he wouldn't work as hard next year.

⁓

In late October, after everyone else had gone home, Otis plopped into a chair across from Carmine and let out a long sigh. These long harvest days were not for the weak. They cracked a couple of beers, because it takes a lot of good beer to make great wine, and spoke about the future for a while.

"Stop doubting yourself," Carmine eventually said. "You don't need half the fight you have to make good wine. I'm scared for the wine world, scared of what you're going to do to it. I hope I make it long enough to watch it happen."

Otis sneaked into bed that night, thinking that Carmine had given him the finest compliment of his life, but when he woke and found the other side of the bed empty, something in his gut told him he'd royally fucked up. Couldn't Bec see that sacrifice bred greatness? Couldn't she hold on a little longer?

He found Bec curled up on the comfy chair, cradling a steaming cup of coffee. Her cheeks glistened from fresh tears.

He sat down in the chair beside her. "Am I in trouble?"

She barely acknowledged him.

"Harvest is over. We made it."

She smiled despite the tears. "You've been working seven days a week since you moved here—harvest or not. You haven't once looked up."

Here we go, he thought. "I'm trying to carve out our life, Bec. This isn't the time to act like we're retired. We must fight so one day we can sit back and enjoy it."

"That's not the way it's supposed to work. Life isn't a fight. The only opposition is what you've created in your head." Tension coated her tone. "You're fighting because you think you have something to prove. Just stop for a minute. You have a son that needs you. *I* need you. Nothing in this world matters more than what we have within these walls. Don't you dare try to blame my frustration on my parents . . . or my brother. I get the part they play. This isn't about me or them. It's about your absence."

In her eyes he saw a future without her, and it seized him with fear. "Oh, Bec. Please. I'm making our dream happen. I just need a little more time."

"You *need* to find balance."

"I agree, it's just—"

"I know, and I support you. I love your desperate want to make something great, but we have a lifetime to get there—"

"But we don't. Though I do need to spend more time with you and Cam, I also need to pay the bills. I need to make more than six bucks an hour. I need to get us into a bigger house, to own a house. I need to . . ."

She touched his face and looked into his soul. "You need to let go of your fears. We're eating. We're healthy. You're doing exactly what you want to be doing. You told me to stop trying to rush having another baby. Take your own advice. Stop trying to rush your dreams. All the good things are coming. What we need is to be here now, for each other and for Cam. Don't wake up one day when he's twenty years old and realize you missed it. There's not a wine in the world you'll make that will ever matter as much as our son."

If only her desperate words were enough.

Then the land came.

~

"It's not fifty acres—it's forty-nine—but it's close. And it's on a hillside."

Otis scratched his head. Never mind that it was exactly what they'd dreamed of. "We're buying this with what?"

"I don't know that part yet." Bec had returned to her other self and showed a kind of enthusism that Otis couldn't quite muster.

"I'm not sure that's a currency."

"Let's go see it."

"Why, Bec? So we can be reminded of what we don't have?"

"No, so we can realize what we want."

"You don't even want this dream anymore. You think I'm working hard now. Wait till we have our own place." He resisted the urge to say that she'd been discouraging lately, to say the least.

"Otis. We want the same thing, but you don't have to work so hard to get it. Don't you see we made this happen in Germany? We created this."

Oh, he saw it. Talk about adding fuel to her fire. She'd never stop her mysticism now.

"Well, we might have talked about it, but we're a long way from owning it."

"I already see it, Otis. We live on this farm. You're making the wines of your dreams."

Otis rolled his eyes. "Oh, here we go again. I'm going to make you stop hanging out with Sparrow."

She didn't like that comment. "So I should just roll up my sleeves and work myself to the bone too? Your way is so much better, isn't it?"

He sighed. Why was she always right? "How much is it?"

"Two hundred thousand."

"Two hundred thousand dollars?"

"No, two hundred thousand guineas. Yes, dollars. It's chump change. Let's call the Realtor."

As if he'd ever win this one. "Fine, let's go see what we can't have."

~

"This was the worst idea in history," Otis said, standing in the middle of what might have been the prettiest piece of land he'd ever seen. "Now I really want it."

The real estate agent currently wandering around inside the house had no idea that his clients were late on two bills and had dined on hot dogs topped with canned chili for the third night this week.

Bec looked at him like he was an idiot. "Of course you want it. It's going to be ours. It's already ours. That's how it works."

She'd said the same thing about having another boy, and that still hadn't happened. He knew when to keep his mouth shut, though.

"I know, I know. Mind creates matter. Seth said so, so it's true."

"It's science, Otis. Don't belittle my beliefs."

"You can't know that this is ours," Otis said, looking out over a piece of land that he'd give both kidneys for. Other than the birdsong and the swoosh of the breeze pushing the trees, there was absolute peaceful stillness.

The farm was called a ghost winery, as it had been left abandoned during Prohibition. The land lay at the end of a winding gravel artery that threaded back into the rolling knolls of Glen Ellen, near to both Jack London's Beauty Ranch and Carmine's vine oasis. Weeds and wild bushes had taken over. The vineyards hadn't been pruned in ages, the canes swirling like barbwire. Birds had made this land their paradise. Frogs croaked from lily pads in the overgrown pond.

The charming stone house had been built by an Italian family in the 1870s. A line of Douglas firs protected it from the setting sun. This was not a place for potato chips and chili dogs. This was a domain where chefs prepare their meals for the gods, a place for someone with actual money to create a paradise ripe for hosting friends and family, where kids ran with reckless abandon, where a poet of a winemaker could carve his place into history.

Almost all the property, including the stone wall that wrapped around it, was crumbling, but it had potential, like a dust-covered masterpiece found in the vaults of the Louvre. The vineyard was enough on its own, scraggly vines of mysterious varieties that begged for a caretaker to bring them back to life. Beyond the vines, a forested hill hosted countless species of trees. Below the house lay a meadow of wildflowers.

Otis scratched his head and said to Bec, "The things you do to me. For the rest of my life, this place will be the one that got away. I can only imagine this is how Jack London felt when he set eyes on his property. Yet he had the money to pay for it."

Bec slipped her arm into his. She smelled like fresh flowers and looked prettier than he'd ever seen her. "Let's make it happen."

"How? Some rich sap is going to swipe this up in the next day or two. We don't have two hundred dollars to spare, let alone two hundred thousand."

"Then we need investors."

He found her eyes, and he saw that she was blinded to any of the obstacles in life right now. "Who could we talk into investing with us?"

The answer appeared like Norman Bates pulling back the shower curtain of Otis's mind. "Don't say it, Bec. Don't say his name."

She shrugged. "We'll need a few investors."

"Including you-know-who." Had he a wine bottle, he would have smacked himself in the teeth.

Rebecca picked up a stone and placed it back on the wall. "He likes you, Otis. He believes in you."

"First off, what are you doing repairing the wall? This isn't ours."

"It will be."

"So matter-of-factly. You're impossible sometimes. One day you want me to quit chasing this wine thing, and today you want us to jump into the deep end. I don't even know why we're here." He threw out his hands. "And Lloyd. When's the last time you saw him?"

Another shrug. "I bumped into him a few weeks ago. He said he believed in your vision."

"You told him my vision? You always tell me not to worry about the how, that all we have to do is envision what we want. That's because *you* were worrying about the how, greasing Lloyd up."

Her eyebrows crinkled. "He's a good man, Otis. He believes in you, and he told me that if we found a place, he might be able to help."

"Of course he told you that. He'll do anything to get in your pants."

She picked up another stone and wedged it into a crack. "Don't insult me. Everyone knows that you have a future in this business."

"Don't try to butter me up. My dream does *not* include Lloyd Bramhall, and I don't appreciate you working behind the scenes."

Something he'd said caused her to back away. "You know what? If you don't need me, go do this on your own. Buy it or don't." She turned and began to walk back down the path that led to the truck.

"Oh, c'mon. Where are you going?" He raced after her. "You know how I feel about Lloyd. It's impossible to not feel defensive when you bring up his name."

Bec snapped back toward him. "It's about trust, Otis. If we don't have that, then what are we doing here? How many times do I have to tell you I'm not interested in him?"

"Every . . . day? Multiple times a day. Jesus, Bec, look at him."

She drew in a long breath. "You exhaust me."

"I exhaust myself. Remember, *you* said yes when I proposed to you, and you said, 'I do.' No one was holding a gun to your head."

She shot arrows out of her eyes. "Is that how you want to end this conversation?"

"I'm sorry, okay?"

She shook her head.

"Lo siento."

"Ah, we resort to Spanish when we have trouble expressing ourselves?"

"Si, señorita. Te quiero." He opened his arms, seeing a path toward forgiveness. *"Lo siento, mi amor."*

Finally letting him hug her, she said, "I'll let you off the hook this time, but I'm tired, Otis. Take some deep breaths. Quit trying to take over the world by tomorrow. For God's sake, have a little faith in me . . . and in yourself."

~

In the morning Otis drove into the city and marched into the tall building where Lloyd Bramhall kept an office. Otis still didn't know what the man did, other than manage his trust fund. On the fifth floor of what was called Bramhall Enterprises, Otis entered an office with high ceilings and several giant windows that looked out over the Golden Gate Bridge. A photograph of Lloyd behind the helm of a sailboat hung next to his degree from Stanford. Large-format bottles of wine rested in fancy wooden boxes.

"There he is." Lloyd pumped Otis's arm like he was trying to get oil out of him. Up close, the man was even more arresting. He should be in a watch ad. Probably was. And the darn smile. Once again, Otis found it very difficult to dislike this chap. Ten minutes ago, he was ready to warn him off his not-so-subtle pursuit of Rebecca, but now he was ready to hug the guy. Or ask him to stand there for a minute so Otis could study his godly beauty.

Sharp cheeks, a jawline that would make Rembrandt weep, eyes that could pierce through armor. Forget about his body. Apparently, before he walked through the doors of Bramhall Enterprises to do whatever it was he did every morning, he spent an hour or two toning his physique. Who was Otis kidding? He stood no chance. If this guy wanted to take Bec from him, all he had to do was snap his fingers.

"I appreciate you making the time."

"For you, anything."

Otis sat on the edge of one of the leather chairs facing the desk and rested his hands on his thighs. "Bec mentioned to you that we've been looking for a place?"

Lloyd's eyes lit up. "You found it, didn't you, Brit Boy?"

Otis swallowed back his urge to smack him for the terrible nickname. "There's a spot that's come up for sale in Glen Ellen, an old ghost winery from back in the old days. Forty-nine acres, thirty of which are planted with a hodgepodge of whites and reds. Wine hasn't been made from the fruit in many years, as far as I can tell. The vineyards have been neglected but have enormous potential."

"You think you can make some good wine?" Excitement flashed in his eyes.

"We're in the business of capturing terroir, and I can't imagine wanting to capture anything more exciting, an entire host of microclimates. But I need investors, people who would put some faith in me to build up a brand."

Lloyd turned to take a look out the window, and Otis wondered what the man was thinking. Otis had only made wine for five years. He didn't deserve a chance like this, but he needed it. He wanted it.

"Lost Souls, huh?"

"That's the idea."

Lloyd twisted back and leaned over his desk. "What kind of terms are we talking here? How much are you ponying up?"

Otis held one nonnegotiable in his mind. "I can get half. Just need the other half. Well, I want fifty-one percent, because this is my baby. Then I'll need some additional cash for the winery. That part, I'll pay back first."

Lloyd steepled his fingers. "What's in it for me?"

"You'll get your money back with interest, a share of the proceeds, and you get to hitch yourself to my wagon." Otis raised a finger in the air, confident as he'd ever been. "I will make some of the most exciting wines in California. I have no doubt."

Lloyd's beautiful golden eyebrows rose. "Tell me the details."

Otis expanded on his thoughts, touching on his vision for the land and for Lost Souls. "Just give me a chance to buy it back from you; I'd need that in the contract." It felt like a deal with the devil, but Otis would do anything.

Sitting up with an erect spine, Lloyd flashed another grin. "Let's go see it."

~

Lloyd bit. He loved the place and said to count him in, that he didn't want to miss out. Lawyers went to work drawing up paperwork, and Otis put on his sales hat and attempted to lure more money from other people in his life.

145

His first call was to his father. Addison had some money tucked away in a savings account that might be enough.

"Otis, you can't ask that of me."

"I know but . . . I am anyway. Dad, do you remember when you realized writing was what you were supposed to do? You've told the story a million times, how you were lost as a teenager and had no compass and then your English teacher said you had a gift and how her words set you free?"

An epic clearing of the throat traveled through the phone line. "I know the story."

Otis pushed harder than he ever had. "Winemaking does for me what writing does for you, and I need help right now. Sure, I can do it another way. I can skip this land and buy some bulk juice, but I'm a farmer. It's in my bones. I swear I'll pay you back."

"What if you don't, Otis? Or what if it's too late? Your mum and I will need that money for retirement."

Otis sat back in the chair and considered his words. "There is no way I will fail."

For the next ten seconds, as he listened to his father breathe, Otis hoped he might enjoy the sweet sound of a yes. It scared the hell out of him, but he still hoped.

"I'm sorry, Otis," Addison finally said. "You'll have to look elsewhere."

Dreams rise and dreams fall. Hopes crumble like old walls. And the heart turns to ash. He didn't hear anything else his father said afterward.

⌒

Thank God Bec and her ocean of positivity made up for Otis's weaknesses. It had always been that way and would be till they met their end. Using what she'd learned in school, she helped Otis draw up a business plan that included specific growth expectations, a marketing guide, an analysis of competitors, and a hopeful outlook on the state of both Sonoma Valley and California wine. Potential investors bent to her will with the promise of a more favorable interest rate than any bank in the country, lucrative dividends, put options in the contract that would give them a way out, and the pride of knowing that they could own part of a winery. Her only requirement was that the investors could be bought out at any time.

Otis and Rebecca stayed in constant contact with the Realtor, hoping no one else would swoop in to buy the property during their fundraising campaign. There had been interest but no offers yet.

Lloyd sent the paperwork over to Otis, and he and Rebecca combed through it carefully. They couldn't afford a lawyer but asked every question they could think of before signing. They just needed a little more time and a few more big checks.

While they were still well short, the property went under contract to Gallo, and Otis died a small death. Of course they had no business even entertaining the idea of owning a piece of property so exceptional, but a tiny part of him thought Bec might be right, that somehow and someway it would be theirs.

And yet he won a victory too. Never had an *I-told-you-so* tasted so sweet. "You see, Bec? Mind doesn't always create matter. Blood, sweat, and tears do. So next time you tell me I'm working too hard, let's remember this moment."

"Don't be a jerk."

"Oh, is this the time for another *ye-of-little-faith* speech?" He was really in trouble now. "Sorry, I don't mean to be—"

"An asshole."

"Yes, that."

That afternoon, his father called. "Otis, I'll lend you the money." If only it weren't too late.

After a day that started at 4:00 a.m. with Carmine, Otis raced to Murphy Vineyards to deal with his vines before tomorrow's rain caused problems. He was down by the barn, dropping clusters into the hopper, when Bec and Cam came to visit. He'd mostly gotten over losing the land to Gallo, though it clung to him like a cold that wouldn't go away. There was all kinds of action at the winery, Paul tossing out commands to his cellar rats, harvesters bumping their way through the rows, tourists tasting inside.

"Look at this," Otis said, taking in the beauty of his bride and son. Little Cam was adorable in his overalls. Rebecca wore a curious look on her face, like she was hiding something.

"What is it?"

Bec plucked a few grapes and tasted them. "Today's the day, huh? This is our fruit?"

"Yeah, it's a little early but rain tomorrow. I don't want to risk it."

"I like the acid."

"Why are you stalling? I love having you here, but . . . what's going on?"

"Oh, did I not mention? I heard back from Eric." Eric was their Realtor. "Gallo bailed on the property."

Otis didn't hear her correctly. He shook his head and then stuck his fingers into his ears to clean them out. The world began to spin.

"He wanted to know if we're still interested." Bec put on that smile that said she knew she was right and that she'd been right all along and why wouldn't he just trust her.

Otis jabbed his hands into his pockets and looked around. Despite all the doubt that ran amok in his head and heart, this little taste of magic was enough to last awhile.

This would be his last harvest at Murphy Vineyards.

Chapter 12
(Interlude)

CHASING RABBITS

Red Mountain, Washington State
March 2011

I so desperately wanted to break through the invisible wall that separated us and wring Otis's neck for smoking that darn pipe. Earlier I'd watched him drag it out from a box in his office, then shove it full of fresh tobacco. Now he was out in the backyard overlooking the sheep while Amigo stumbled around on his three good legs in the grass. At least Otis was outside in the sun and laughing at his new furry friend, who could draw a laugh out of anyone.

Of course, I wasn't the one who had injured Amigo and set him in the vineyard at just the right time. To that end, I'd love to know whether there was some design to it. Was there a man upstairs? Or a woman? I'd never been a believer in something so specific, but I'd long been in touch with what I call Spirit.

Anyway, this smoking of the pipe is not allowed.

I attempt to blow it out, but my breath won't break through the dimensional wall with enough force. Only a soft wind passes by, flaming the tobacco to a brighter red and blowing up the gray hairs on Otis's arms. He doesn't notice, as he's talking to himself between puffs.

"It wouldn't be the first harvest I've skipped, Amigo." He grins. He *actually* grins.

Through an exhalation of smoke, Otis says, "You're a young pup, but I'm at the end of my rope and looking back and wondering where it all went wrong. Don't make the same mistakes as me."

Amigo stumbled toward him and sat down.

Otis reached down and petted his face. "We had some grand times, and it often blazed right by me. Even when we finally got our land, that perfect spot on the globe, even when we started to make some decent money, fear got the best of me. Fear that it would be taken away. Should you find your family again, and I think you will, then don't take them for granted. Don't go chasing rabbits and forget what matters."

I may no longer be on the same plane as Otis, but my heart could still break. The good memories were worth their weight in Red Mountain fruit. Why won't he latch on to those?

Once we bought our land, we hit cruise control, living a glorious existence where the world peeled open like an orange for us. I couldn't believe it, but my father jumped in to help with our new farm, likely because what little competitive streak he had kicked in once he'd figured out that Otis's dad had loaned us his retirement. My dad did some of the best work of his life rebuilding our house. I was reminded of the man who raised me, before things started falling apart. With his help and the help of a few others, we brought the forgotten winery back to life.

Otis spent most of his time on the farm. First thing we did was erect a series of fences for deer protection and to prepare the farm for animals. We'd inherited several blocks of zinfandel-heavy field blends, a medium Otis knew well. To plant additional vines, we hired a team of Vietnam vets with explosive expertise to blast through the giant boulders that poked out of the hillsides like the tips of icebergs. Utilizing a terracing technique, we planted more zinfandel and a few other test varieties, including syrah, which Otis had taken a recent liking to. As Carmine said when he came to visit us, "You don't choose the grapes, the land does." So we made our best guesses and then would see what thrived.

Otis followed Carmine's methods, avoiding chemicals, composting, and employing various treatments to fight leafhoppers and blue-green sharpshooters. He refused to drive tractors down, or even till, the rows. Those vines were his babies.

Jed's condition wore on me. As far back as I can remember, he showed signs of depression, but such things weren't talked about back then. We didn't have a name for it. Even in the nineties, when Michael began to face similar issues, depression wasn't something we considered a mental health issue. Mental health was only talked about when someone was on their way to a psychiatric hospital.

Jed would often lock himself in his room. He cried a lot. Other boys in the neighborhood would ask him to play, but he'd rarely accept. Chunks of time would pass when he barely smiled, let alone laughed. That being said, he did have a wicked sense of humor—not unlike Otis's—that he seemed to reserve only for me, and I cherished those times in our youth when he'd let loose. He was my big brother, after all. He'd sometimes sneak into my room late at night, and we'd lie next to each other in bed talking and giggling for hours. Though it was difficult for him to step outside of his own problems, he always found ways to show that he loved me, from covering for me or even taking the blame for something I did to listening, *truly* listening, when I needed comforting.

As he grew older, he'd do anything he could to avoid school, often getting in trouble for skipping. His grades were terrible, and he fell into a rough crowd that led him to partying hard and causing all sorts of trouble.

My father had zero patience for Jed's behavior. How many times did he tell Jed to "toughen up" or "get your shit together." They quarreled constantly, and it only drove Jed further into his shell. My mom would sometimes try to stand up for him, but that duty mostly fell on me, the younger sister, the only one who knew how amazing he could be.

I was still doing it, still trying to come to his aid.

I'd often go by my parents' house and find him in various states of intoxication. One time Otis, Cam, and I pulled up for a visit and found him passed out in the front yard, drool falling from his mouth, his chair folded over on top of him. An epic fight that included my parents, Jed, Otis, and me ensued, and as we left, Otis told me that he was done, that neither he nor Cam would come back to visit anytime soon.

Jed wore thin my patience a thousand times, but I kept trying to sympathize, because he was a good person who hadn't had a fair shake. No one but me had *ever* stuck up for him; no one but me could see past his dark veil. And yes, Otis was right. I did blame myself for Jed running off to Vietnam and losing his legs, so I was incredibly invested in helping him find his way.

Sometimes I'd go over early in the morning and catch him sober, and I'd push him through the streets of our neighborhood, and we'd catch up and rediscover our connection, and I'd be reminded of who he really was and leave desperate for him to find his way to happiness.

I suggested on more than one of those sibling strolls that he should learn about computers. I even bought him a copy of a magazine called *Computerworld*, saying, "Jed, there are ways to change the world without your legs."

He stuffed the magazine into the saddlebag of his wheelchair. "You've been watching too much *Star Trek*, sis."

"I don't know, I think computers could be the future." I actually said that, all the way back in 1975. I should have gone in that direction myself. Can you imagine? We could have bought half of Napa.

⌐

Despite my familial troubles, we found a lot of joy in the coming years. Stevie Wonder's *Songs in the Key of Life* came out during harvest in

1976, and it captured our lives perfectly. We were running around like crazy, but the smiles were abundant. I'd dedicate all my energy to Cam, then put him down for a nap and race into my office to work out finances. Having known far too intimately what it was like to go hungry, I became hell-bent on our success.

Aside from our arguments about me giving too much to my family—or, as Otis would put it, me letting my family push me around—most of the disagreements Otis and I had back then had to do with him wanting to spend more money than we had. I'd have to shut him down when he wanted to buy new equipment, hire a label designer, upgrade to nicer bottles, or make another run to Beltramo's in the city to stock our cellar. I'd always tell him we had to hold off. Had he been in charge, he would have run us into the ground.

That being said, whatever magic he was making had struck a chord. We had zero trouble selling our production. We'd get calls out of the blue from restaurants in the area—and even in the city—asking for another case or two. Soon distributors in the big cities were begging for cases. Otis was a grump and the worst salesman in the world, but people loved that about him, and people whispered about his wines. A lightness came over us, as the breeze of good fortune carried us away.

Of course this success stoked my continued belief in manifestation, and I constantly managed my thoughts and words and worked hard to see our dream in my mind. Before Cam woke, I'd go for long walks and find a place to sit and meditate. As the sun warmed the morning dew, and the birdsong played counterpoint to the baas of the sheep, I'd shed my worries about my loved ones and connect with the place where worry didn't exist. Where faith was enough.

We even got a dog! She was a runt named Bubbles who loved to lick Cam's face and lived for scraps from our meals.

I'd honed my skills in the kitchen, often with Camden right beside me, and I discovered tremendous joy in hosting family and friends. I learned to bake and could make baguettes that would draw tears. On top of long tables covered with plaid tablecloths, I'd place baskets of bread, cutting boards of cheese purchased from neighboring farms, charcuterie from our favorite store, and dishes made with the various fruits and vegetables I'd grown. Each meal got better and better.

Otis was also coming into his own, finally showing some confidence as he found his stride out in the fields and in the new cellar. I always knew he was in a good place when he'd get frisky with me. Sometimes he was a terrible lover, but when his vines and wines were doing what he wanted them to do, and when he felt like he'd connected with his land, he could make me shiver into countless orgasms.

I suppose that's how it happened.

Michael was born in the fall of 1977, a colicky baby who cried and cried and cried late into the night. I spent so many nights holding him in the crook of my arm, both of us sobbing. It was almost enough to dent our happy lives, but we kept our love strong and embraced Mike with all the patience in the world.

~

Only as the end of the decade drew near did things start to fall apart. I simply couldn't take Otis's ego anymore. Fueled by the growth of Lost Souls and the adulation he was receiving from the wine world, his newly found confidence had risen to the pitch of cockiness. He'd begun traveling and was wined and dined around the country by distributors begging for his business. On a trip to New York, he sold wine to Kevin Zraly at Windows on the World, the new restaurant on top of the World Trade Center. Kevin told him that he was making the best wines in California. Just like that, Otis felt he had made it. If only he would have taken the time to enjoy his success, but he wasn't satisfied.

"They could be better," he always said of his wines.

He was an addict chasing the next high, and he became swept away by the notoriety, spending entirely too much time on the road. I kept telling him that his family needed him, that his farm needed him, that it would soon detect his absence, but he didn't listen. Carmine reminded

Otis that the best fertilizer is a farmer's footsteps, but Otis had decided he knew everything and didn't need anyone's help. Between his growing fame, our growing financial security, and the wear and tear he was putting on his body, he'd lost his way.

Otis still cared for the farm, but he'd spread himself so thin that he couldn't give it the love it needed. He'd work his tail off during harvest, barely sleeping, then take any consulting job he could, as people now offered him ridiculous money for his opinions, and then he'd race off to the airport to further the reach of our empire. He was the Napoleon or Alexander the Great of wine, unwilling to be satisfied until his wine ran from the taps of every household in the world.

Though we paid off a few investors, there was still Lloyd.

Lloyd, Lloyd, Lloyd.

I never told Otis about all the blatant passes he made over the years. Lloyd would corner me and say, "What do you see in Otis? What about giving us a chance?" I'd ignore him. What else could I do? He owned nearly half our company, and he was not someone with whom we needed to go to war. Otis would have lost his mind if he knew the specifics of Lloyd's pursuit, so I hid it and kept deflecting.

I must say, however, there were times when I wanted to rub Lloyd's interest in Otis's face, tell my distracted husband that if he wouldn't pay attention to me, then I knew someone else who would.

Finding my anger, I swung my arm through the air and made contact with my grieving husband's pipe, knocking it to the ground by Amigo's feet. The lit tobacco spilled out. Otis and Amigo both looked with golf ball eyes at it resting in the grass.

When he picked it back up, I smacked it out of his hand again. I was getting the hang of things.

Scrub, scrub, scrub. Amigo hated the bathtub, but he'd gotten into some sheep poop and needed a bath. Otis massaged the soap into him and dirt caked the porcelain.

The phone rang again, and Otis knew it was his assistant winemaker, Brooks. What was Otis to say? That he didn't give a bloody shit if the vines were wilting, or if all the wineries were up in arms once again. Whatever the fate of Red Mountain, he had nothing left to give.

Once he had the coyote pup dried off, Otis poured himself a scotch and sat on the back deck, journal in hand. As if he'd fallen into a time portal, the falling sun took him right back to Sonoma and where he'd left off with his pen. He knew exactly what he'd write next.

There was one man who drove me even crazier than Lloyd, and that was Ledbetter the Bedwetter.

Chapter 13

JEWELED BOOTS AND BEDWETTERS

As the eighties broke, Rebecca fell in love with music that Otis did not understand. Joan Jett, the Clash, Hall and Oates, Rick Springfield, the Go-Go's, Journey, Air Supply. He felt like an old man listening to his kids' music—a sixty-year-old trapped in a thirty-year-old's body. Before too long, he'd feel the same thing when his kids were headbanging to "Smells Like Teen Spirit" by Nirvana; and forget about it when Michael got into his rap phase. That was when Otis knew he'd been left behind entirely.

Besides, who had the luxury of listening to music anymore? Growing wine was a matter of life or death, especially now that zinfandel had lost favor with both the critics and drinkers. Cabernet sauvignon was all the rage, and Lloyd suggested they graft every last zin vine to cabernet.

Needless to say, that hadn't sat well with Otis, and he'd drawn the line. "Till the day comes when Burgundy starts grafting syrah onto their pinot noir rootstocks, I will not pander to wine trends, Lloyd. Our farm is meant for zinfandel. You can't just plug any variety into the ground and expect great things."

"Fair enough," Lloyd had said, proving to Otis that he was in control now. As he should be. After all, he was the flipping winegrower.

Camden and Michael, both spawns of Satan, spent most of their time swatting and screaming at each other, and in turn Rebecca spent most of her time screaming at Otis, telling him, "It wouldn't hurt if you played the bad guy every once in a while. You show up after a long trip and act like Uncle Otis, the fun guy who always wants to play, never scolds."

"Are you kidding me, Bec? Don't you see how they look at you? You're their hero."

She didn't understand how much it took to keep the winery growing. She had a brilliant business understanding but remained stuck in the seventies mindset of "it's all good, man." *All good* didn't sell shite for wine. Forget mind over matter. Otis had proved that it was his determination that had created their reality, not her woo-woo Ouija board sessions with Sparrow.

Besides, she'd taken on more than she could handle—especially considering her bozo parents and brother were barely contributing at all. To their credit, they'd go through phases where they showed that they did actually have beating hearts. Marshall had his good spells where he slowed his drinking, took a job, and behaved like a grandfather, telling a story or perhaps tossing a ball to the boys. *Occasionally*, Olivia would swing by with candy or even offer to watch the boys while Bec took a rest. On rare visits, a not necessarily sober Jed would chase the kids around the living room in the wheelchair, and he'd smile as if he was actually happy for a change.

Bec had stopped complaining to Otis, as it only reinforced his argument that she needed to quit giving so much of herself to her family to make up for her perceived abandonment, but she couldn't seem to stop herself from playing intermediary and therapist, and giving them money, the latter of which was an epic sore spot between Otis and her.

In addition to carrying her family and running the business, she'd also decided to homeschool the children, as she felt sure she could give them a better education, at least in their earlier years. She'd always loved the idea of homesteading, where the children contributed to create a self-sufficient lifestyle. They had their morning chores, cleaning their rooms, feeding the sheep, collecting chicken eggs, cleaning out the coop, and then they sat with their mother at the dining room table for lunch, working through their various studies. She was a good teacher, and both kids learned to read by age five.

Meanwhile, in the vineyards, Otis had upped their wine production, and all the new vineyards had finally come to maturity. Bec had told Otis that he'd planted too much, joking in a not-funny way that if he didn't slow down, he'd be dropping new vines into their bathtub. He admitted he'd planted every possible patch he could, but the demand was high. He had to seize their good fortune!

Lost Souls had become a viable product, and Otis happily bought out smaller investors and paid dividends to the rest. Though they'd had a few arguments when Lloyd had tried to micromanage decisions in the fields and in the cellar, the two men were getting along. Lloyd was proud of Lost Souls and had done his share to spread the word, putting bottles in the hands of important sommeliers, tastemakers, and journalists around the world.

Lost Souls Ranch reached its peak after seven years of incredibly hard work. The stone house stood two stories high. They'd re-created so much of what he loved about Carmine's farm. Now sheep and chickens grazed in the rows. Never once had Otis sprayed a single chemical. Though he'd had his learning curves, the vines thrived, pushing out stunning fruit.

Otis and Bec's room looked east over the oldest vineyard, and there were few days when Otis didn't lift himself out of bed, smile at his bride curled up naked under the sheets, then peek out the window at the tangerine sun rising over their centennial vines and think that he'd finally done it. He'd cracked the code.

～

It was a Tuesday in the middle of August when a new disturbance ruptured the peace. *Veraison*, the stage when the ripening berries changed color, was spreading across the vineyards. Otis had been working since well before dawn, checking off a list that filled two legal pads, and now he'd collapsed onto a chair on the terrace to read the paper.

"The *audaaaaaciteeeeeeeeey!*" he yelled out as he read Sam Ledbetter's latest article in *The New York Times*. Otis sprang to his feet, his mouth agape. "How could Lloyd claim responsibility for any of this? And who does Ledbetter think he is?"

Bec rushed out, barefooted in a sundress. "You're going to wake the boys. What are you going on about?"

Otis held the paper toward her and jabbed a finger at the drawing of Ledbetter's smug face. "Bedwetter's at it again, as is your boyfriend. Apparently I'm a soldier and nothing more. And the wine's shit."

"I'll choose to ignore the boyfriend comment." She took the paper with a gentle hand. As she read, Otis paced the tiles, huffing and puffing like the Big Bad Wolf.

"Lloyd Bramhall has added another micro winery to his quiver. He says he's excited about what he and the team are doing up there. Apparently he's enlisted a fellow from the Carmine Coraggio school, though I don't see the comparison. I suppose the fruit is farmed well enough, but the wines fall flat for me. Nevertheless, Lloyd has a good eye, and I look forward to tasting future vintages and seeing if they find their stride."

She pulled her eyes away from the rubbish on the page. "Oh."

Otis squared up to her. "Not even a mention, Bec. We finally get into *The New York Times*, finally get written up by Bedwetter, and my name doesn't even come up. I'm merely *fellow*. Fellow. Fellow—*fucking* fellow. And Lloyd. The nerve. What *he* and his *team* are doing up here? What in God's name has he done to contribute to this wine? When's the last time he picked up so much as a shovel."

The oh-so-familiar calming hand of Rebecca rested on his shoulder. "Take some breaths, dear."

"I beg of you not to patronize me." He shook his head in a jittery furious motion, a soldier of misfortune—left, right, left, right. He could whip an egg with such force. "I won't take a breath. What I will do is have words with Lloyd. He can't go around telling people he's making the wine."

A note of incredulity rang in her otherwise calm tone. "I don't think he said he's making the wine."

"He might as well have." Otis tore the paper from her hands and dropped it to the floor and stomped on it. "We have to buy him out."

"Then we need to slow our spending."

"Don't get started on this again. We have to keep upgrading equipment."

"How about your travel? Do you have to stay at Ritz-Carltons? Do you need to be drinking Burgundy on Tuesday nights?"

"Burgundy doesn't care what day it is. How can I attempt to make a wine of such caliber without knowledge of the great wines of the world?" He couldn't stand it when she harped on spending. It certainly didn't help that she was the one who ran the finances, so she knew every blasted move he made.

Back to the matter at hand, he said, "He always has an agenda. Now he's taking all the glory."

"What would Carmine say about glory?" There she went with her calm wisdom. Couldn't she see what was happening all around them?

"Carmine isn't the final say on all things."

"He used to be."

"Yeah, well, we've outgrown his production. I've got a few opinions of my own now." Otis gathered the paper, crumpled it in his hands, then tossed it over the railing, where it landed on the wheelchair ramp and rolled into Bec's tulips.

"What did Carmine tell you? Don't listen to the critics."

"Carmine, Carmine, Carmine. Easy for him to say when Bedwetter thinks he's the greatest winemaker in California."

"There will always be obstacles," Rebecca said. "It's how you handle them. Look at you, you're falling apart."

Otis flapped his hands in the air as he spoke. "Please don't Obi-Wan Kenobi me. When we're all paid up and when Lloyd is out of the picture, we'll hire a salesman. For now, I have to do it all, and I'm going to sometimes get a little road weary."

Bec approached him and slipped her arms around his waist. He was ready for her to attack him for saying that he had to do it all, but as usual she took the high road. "What's the point of all this if you're not enjoying it?"

"I *am* enjoying it. Look at me. Look at this smile, this bright-eyed bushy-tailed smile."

She let out a quintessential "Ugh." He'd heard a chorus of those in their marriage. *Ugh, ugh, ugh.* Sure, he might have deserved them, but still . . .

"What? Out with it, Bec. Get it over with."

She paused, doing one of her little meditative recenterings. "You need to slow down. I don't know everything you're doing on the road, but I know you're not taking care of yourself. I see the receipts, the itemized ones. You're eating countless burgers and bacon. You're drinking like you're W. C. Fields."

"You're the one who makes me bring the itemized receipts."

She let her chin fall. "Is that the point?"

He didn't tell her that he'd also taken his first sniffs of cocaine with a distributor in Florida who'd overpaid to get only fifteen cases of Lost Souls. What else does one do on a fast boat in Miami while the speakers are blaring Hall and Oates?

He took her hand. "My dad barely says anything when I send him wine these days. He wouldn't know a good wine if it hit him in the head anyway, but he *loves* to read Bedwetter, and I'm sure this article solidifies his argument. His soldier son, a.k.a. *fellow*, should have done something of which I was capable. I should have finished Berkeley and should be writing for the *Times* right now. Lord knows, the bar is not high, if they're letting Bedwetter in. Instead, I'm the failed and forgotten disciple of Carmine, and a lackey of Lloyd's who doesn't even get a mention."

"A lost soul," Bec said.

"That's right. My dad raised a lost soul."

"Please don't let Ledbetter get the best of you."

"His name is Bedwetter."

"Yeah, well, he makes you act like a child."

Otis breathed into lungs that felt like rocks and looked into the eyes of this nearly perfect being he'd married. She was cheerleading for the wrong man.

Though he wouldn't have blamed her if she'd left him alone with his misery, Bec grabbed him and held him tight, not a word said, conveying her reassuring and unwavering love, holding him till their hearts began to beat at the same rhythm again.

⌐

Later in August, Lloyd came to town, rolling in with an arm crooked out the window of his new Ferrari. He slid out wearing jeweled boots. His jeans were tighter than green tape around a vine. His shirt was pressed with so much starch you could have driven his fancy car over it without making a crease.

Meanwhile, Otis had been repairing irrigation all morning. He stepped out of the south vineyard block and wiped the sweat and dirt from his face. Bubbles had been hovering around him all day and followed him toward the Ferrari. Otis wished he'd taught his dog to attack, but it was too late now.

Lloyd knelt to pet Bubbles and said to Otis, "There's my Brit Boy. How's harvest looking?"

Otis's fists tightened. "What was that Ledbetter article all about?"

Lloyd recalibrated. He apparently hadn't expected a standoff. "He didn't get it quite right, did he?"

"No, he did not." Otis stood three feet from him, looking up at this exquisite specimen of a man.

Lloyd waved it off as no big deal. "Don't pay those things any attention. Hey, at least we got more press. People are starting to get what we're doing."

"What is it exactly that *you're* doing?" Otis asked, standing his ground.

As if he kept reserves, Lloyd unpeeled another layer of handsome. "I'm doing my part. You're making good wine, but I'm pulling strings in the background."

"Pulling strings?" Otis raised a finger. "Don't take credit for my wine, Lloyd. I'm grateful that you helped bankroll this thing, but it's mine and Rebecca's blood and sweat out there in the fields. Don't ever forget that."

A flash of anger threatened like thunder, but Lloyd wrangled it in quickly. "No one is forgetting what you do."

"Bedwetter is. Maybe remind him next time."

"I'll do that. More importantly, I have big news. Bec around? I think she'll want to hear."

Otis didn't like how Lloyd brushed the Bedwetter issue aside, but he was too damned taxed to do anything about it. He'd just returned from two weeks on the East Coast, securing new distribution. He never imagined what slinging juice on the road could be like, the toll it took.

Otis gathered Bec and watched her kiss Lloyd on the cheek. He seemed all too delighted by her touch, and Otis wondered whether anyone would notice if he chopped Lloyd up and buried him in the vines.

They sat on the terrace under the shade of a pergola. A noisy bird called out from the patch of trees nearby. The subtle scent of ripening grapes had started to fill the air.

Lloyd crossed one leg over another. His pant legs rode up, revealing more of his fancy boots. "Gallo wants to buy us."

Heads spun; eyes popped out.

Lloyd directed his attention at Bec. "The brand and the land. They regret not buying the property in the first place. They love the label and wines and see big potential. They'd want you to stick around as winemaker, and you could keep living on the property."

"How much?" Bec asked.

"No," Otis said, his body tightening. "Don't say it. I don't want to know."

"Oh, c'mon," Lloyd said with greed dripping from his words. "You want to know."

"You say a number, and I'll punch you in the mouth." Otis gripped the water glass in his hand so hard he felt the glass bend.

"Otis . . ." Bec said, as if he were a dog who'd stolen her sandwich.

"Don't *Otis* me. I don't want to hear it. This place is not for sale, and I'm not going on Gallo's payroll."

"Everything is for sale," Lloyd said.

"No, it's not. We're getting closer and closer to buying you out, and I'm going to farm this land till the day I die. I belong here, every bit as much as I belong with Bec."

Lloyd uncrossed his legs and leaned forward. His teeth were as white as the pope's robe. "Gallo doesn't go around throwing money at people every day. We can find another piece of land and do it all over again. Well, after a few years. They want you to sign a noncompete."

"This is laughable."

Lloyd looked at Bec as if she were the sane one of the two. He stated Gallo's bid.

"What did I say?" Otis's teeth clenched, the tendons in his neck twisting.

Lloyd kept his eyes on her. "Think about it. I'll stop back by tomorrow around the same time." He glanced at Otis. "I knew you wouldn't jump on it, but let's see if it makes more sense after sleeping on it."

That night, after they'd tucked in their boys, Otis made Bec a vermouth over ice and gave himself a hefty pour of Glenmorangie, because anything other than scotch wasn't strong enough for the forthcoming conversation. He sneaked a large sip and then topped his glass off before finding her in the living room listening to Fleetwood Mac.

Lowering the volume on the record player, he said, "Can we please finish this conversation?" They'd revisited the topic of selling maybe ten times since Lloyd had left, never once finding common ground.

A sigh escaped her lips.

"I know, I know, but we have to. I need us to be on the same page."

"You mean, you *need* me to see it your way."

Otis handed her the vermouth, then set his drink down on the coffee table before sitting next to her on the couch. "Well, yes. Yes, I do. I let you win all the time. This one, I need." He pressed his hands together in prayer position. "I'm begging, Bec. Let this go. I don't want to sell. We haven't done what we're supposed to do here."

She stared into the purple hues of the vermouth. "You don't know what it's like to be poor. Not really."

"We were dirt poor for years after we first met."

"We were kids. We have a family now. This is a chance for us to never worry about money again."

"I'm not worried about money now. You don't need to be either. We're just getting started. We don't need Gallo's money to be rich." Something occurred to him. "Is this about helping your mom and dad out too? Your brother?"

"Not only that, but yes. I would like to take care of them."

Otis shook his head, frustration seizing him.

"I also think it might be a good time for you to take a break. Before you kill yourself."

Otis rubbed his eyes and then massaged his temples. This was the *one* battle she couldn't win. "Look, I'm working on slowing down. We can keep helping your family out. I'll watch my expenses. We'll focus more on saving, but we can't sell this land. You might as well rip my heart out and stomp on it." He found her eyes. "Please, Bec. My soul is here. My destiny."

She set her glass down next to his and sat back. It took her a moment, but then she finally looked at him. "More than anything, I'm worried about you."

"You don't need to be. I am already feeling more relaxed. Let's not give up on what we've built. I'm a new man, Bec. Let me prove it to you, okay?"

She gave the smallest nod possible.

"Is that an okay-we-don't-have-to-sell nod?"

"I'll let it go. For now. But I'm watching you, Otis. I'm far more concerned about the health and security of my family than I am about taking over the wine world."

Oh, he was well aware. "Fair enough. I'm going to prove to you that we can cover all bases. No need to choose." Smiling at this momentous victory, he inched toward her and kissed her cheek. "I won't let you down, my love."

The summer of 1983 was off to a good start. The vines spoke to Otis more than most years. Sales were superb. By June, he'd sold the entire '81 vintage, which had only gone to market late last fall. He was tempted to pull more out of his cellar to sell, as he'd been holding back fifty cases from each of the past few years, but Bec told him he'd kick himself later. She was probably right.

Lloyd didn't stop trying. Every few months he'd return with new opportunities, assuring them that the time to sell was now. Otis stood firm, not even considering the higher offers that started to come in. To Bec's credit, she stopped pushing after that night on the couch, though he knew she'd sell in a heartbeat if he got on board.

The boys were five and nine. Camden was going into fifth grade. All he wanted to do was escape into nature. It had always been that way with him, and Otis guessed that he'd work the vines as he got older. In fact, his boy could already prune with the best of them. Cam loved being out there, playing cowboys and Indians, digging deep holes, building tree forts, chasing Bubbles up and down every hillside.

Michael was more complex. He was all heart and cared so damn much for everyone around him, even at his young age. When Otis or Bec had a bad day, Michael would climb onto their laps and ask what was wrong. He fared much better than Cam at school, eliciting grand reviews from his teachers. Otis's only worry was that he had his mother's tendency to disappear into himself on occasion, that hidden part fighting battles only he could see.

Leaving the boys was getting harder and harder, and Otis was glad he wouldn't have to spend the summer traveling. He needed a break. The road was draining him. Not that he wasn't having fun, but it was *too* much fun. Bec would have killed him if she knew the full extent of what he was up to. Though his father wouldn't have believed it—despite the $10,000 check he'd written the man to settle their debt—Otis had become a celebrity in the last few years. People clamored for his wines and fought for his time. Otis and Bec even had stalkers, wine enthusiasts who would creep by on the road and, in some brave cases, pull over and ask for a tasting. He was on the brink of installing a gate, but for now they'd posted a big sign with painted black letters that read: *We're all out.*

Of course Otis didn't mind the attention. He thoroughly enjoyed his jaunts into San Francisco, where the wine buyers did a double take when they saw him, comping his meals, sometimes even inviting him into the kitchen for a line of blow. The same happened all over the country during his travels—the wine reps and managers from the distributor, the wine buyers and chefs from the restaurants, they all wanted a piece of Otis Till and would wine and dine him and drag him out until the wee hours of the morning.

Didn't mind it? Hell, he loved the attention. Craved it even.

Thank God he had the farm as an escape. Reentry was tough, though, returning from those fast-lane trips to find Bec exhausted from running the entire ship.

"It's your turn," she'd say, the words that became her anthem upon his returns.

"I know, I know, but . . . let me catch a breath." Couldn't she see that he'd worked himself to the bone out there? Yes, she'd been pushing herself, too, but he wasn't giving *her* a hard time.

He'd just returned from Chicago, where he'd landed a glass pour at Gene & Georgetti, a quintessential Chicago steakhouse, and he'd dined later with a host of journalists and wealthy collectors who'd spoken about him in ways that both stroked his ego but also made him feel uncomfortable, as if he were a commodity. They called him the new wave of wine, a god of the grape, a vine whisperer, names that went to his head.

Thank God he was home for a while.

This June day was sensational, blues in the sky that made it look like the ocean had floated up there, greens so vivid it was like living in a crayon box. Otis held Bec's hand, and Michael rode on his shoulders. Camden raced ahead of them, waving them along.

"You wait, Dad." Otis had no idea what Cam had up his sleeve, but he could barely stand the joy of the moment, knowing he was home, and his family was healthy, and they'd finally made it.

Michael drummed a beat on Otis's head, singing, "Can you tell me how to get . . . how to get to Sesame Street?" Otis jumped in with him, singing along.

While they sang, Camden led them deep into the woods, where he'd built a fort like Otis had never seen. Three rooms, all constructed with fallen limbs and a few tarps he must have borrowed from the tractor shed.

"It's my secret winery. I'm going to make the best wine in the world."

Otis grinned and knelt beside him. It was all he could do not to break down and cry. "What an accomplishment, my boy."

Cam shrugged. "You know how Mr. Paul gave you some grapes? I was thinking you might let me have a row. Just to make a little."

Shivers cascaded up Otis's back. "You know I will. Of course. We'll have to set your lab up, too, bring in some barrels."

On the way back, they took a shortcut through the vines. Camden and Michael were chasing each other, and Otis had his arm around Bec. She seemed distant, but it was often that way when he first returned from a trip.

"I'm home, baby. I know it's been a lot, but we're almost there."

"Are we?" she asked.

"You were right all along. We did it."

She looked away, a signature move lately.

"Hey, I'm serious."

"You don't look good, Otis. You're killing yourself."

"Oh, don't do that. No more travel for a long time."

"I've heard that before." It was bound to happen. Her exasperation with the man she'd married teetered on the edge of climax. "You promised me that if we didn't sell, you'd start taking better care of yourself."

"And I *am*. It's us and the farm now, the rest of the year. I have our distribution in place. Now it's up to you to set pricing. I'll tell our network I don't want to travel as much next year. Not even for a sales meeting. We're right where we need to be."

She nodded half-heartedly.

He lifted her chin. "Things are going to change."

"How many times do I have to—"

Over her shoulder, something caught his eye. He brushed past her before she could finish her question. "What is this?" he asked, reaching for one of the many millions of leaves on the property. Holding the stunted green leaf in his hand, he saw what looked like warts covering it. "Bec, is this . . . ? No."

Down the entire row, nearly every leaf looked the same, and it had happened so fast. All the elation he felt, all the hope, it fell to the earth like a hot air balloon that had lost its air.

—

Otis climbed up onto his John Deere and drove toward the vines that he and Bec had planted. She and the boys were in the house, and he'd asked her to keep them there, because he didn't want them to see him this way, didn't want them to see their father's descent.

Never had he failed so utterly and completely. He'd heard whispers of phylloxera sneaking into California, but Otis was confident that their vines would be okay. His older vines had survived for a century, and he'd chosen the perfect rootstock for all the new plantings. At the recommendation of the local nursery, they'd gone with the AXR1 variety, which UC Davis touted as a dream rootstock that was easy to cultivate, issued high fruit quality, and resisted phylloxera. Then he'd forgotten about it.

Of course, he knew about phylloxera from his studies, how the pests had decimated France in the eighteen hundreds and how France had saved itself only by acquiring rootstocks from California, but they'd had to replant and start over. It was like a pandemic, this phylloxera. Since first discovering it on that day walking with his family, Otis had consulted Carmine, who'd confirmed his fears. He'd also found others who were suffering the same fate. It wasn't the leaf damage that was the main issue. Those same insects, the tiny yellow lice, had burrowed into the ground and fed on the roots, making them vulnerable to fungi that crept in and finished them off.

Sadly, there was only one solution. Dig up the vines, burn them, and rip the soil with ripper shanks. Then inject methyl bromide to kill everything, *including* the trillions of healthy microorganisms in the soil. Afterward, they would cover the land with plastic tarps and start over with properly resistant vines. From what he'd learned so far, he'd go back to the tried-and-true St. George rootstock.

All that hard work lost; he could barely stand it. Two-thirds of his vineyards were dead vines walking. All that he and Bec had planted, all those vines coming into their own. Even the legacy centennial vines that had once attracted him to the property had also been hit.

And the soil . . . how many years would it take to bring it back to life?

Carmine had told him to get the vines out of the ground as quickly as possible, then to burn them, but Otis held on until he saw the spread, how the infestation was hopping blocks. Now he sat behind the wheel of the tractor, bandanna on his head to keep the sweat from burning his eyes, wishing that they'd sold to Gallo when they had the chance.

Tears fell as he jabbed the front loader into the earth, and the vines began to fold over. These vines had made him who he was. These vines had bought back investors, paid for their lives.

He'd attempted to keep the news quiet, begging everyone with whom he'd consulted not to mention it, but there was no smaller world than Sonoma Valley, and by now everyone knew that Lost Souls had been hit hard. Likely, his competitors were shaking their heads and saying he'd done something wrong while also scrambling to spray and do whatever it took to keep the lice from getting their crops too.

Row by row he went. It felt like having each nail plucked from his fingers, ripping up as many vines as the front loader would carry and then driving them to the far end of the property, where his vineyard guys had cleared an area ready to burn. It would take two years to get any fruit from newly planted vines, which meant he'd lost at least two years of income from his estate plantings. It would take another seven to ten to grow fruit worth talking about.

In two days, he had wrung from the earth a lifetime of dreams. He slept on a stack of hay bales that abutted the outside wall of the tractor shed, desperate to avoid Bec. Shame caked his insides. Had he let her win, none of this would have happened.

The second morning she came out with a peanut butter and jelly sandwich and begged him to eat.

"It took so many years to get here, Bec."

"We did it once, we can do it again." She was always optimistic, but he could hear the note of doubt in her voice.

He ran a hand through his hair, looking out over the empty rows, knowing that he had to treat the soil and get to planting if he wanted the roots to take before winter. "We won't have anything to sell for two years, Bec. Even then, it'll be too young to offer any complexity. People will say that what we do have in barrel is tainted. We're already the laughingstock of California."

"People will stand behind you, Otis. Lloyd will be here tomorrow, and we'll work it all out."

"Lloyd? How can he help? I don't want more of his money. I don't need his advice. I want him out of my life. Out of yours."

Later that morning, with his men standing beside him, Otis struck a match and lit a section that he'd doused with gasoline. His assistant vineyard manager, Scooter, a calloused-handed man from Santa Fe who'd been with Otis three years now, stood by with a hose for safety.

The flames rose as high as the trees and kicked off a heat that burned Otis's skin. Sweat dripped down his face and neck. He turned back and saw his boys watching through the window.

A sharp pain took him by surprise and caused him to reach for his chest. His legs gave way, and then all went black.

~~

Otis woke in a hospital bed. Monitors chirped. An IV drained into his arm. He felt a warm, familiar hand slip into his.

"What happened, Bec?"

"You had a mini heart attack."

"A heart attack?"

In her eyes he saw so much loss and pain. He'd done this to himself, and the reality of it came at him like a train. He'd been pushing for so damn long and hard, and this was what he got.

"Where are the boys?"

"With my parents."

Bec slid onto the bed and cuddled up with him and began to weep. He squeezed her. "No, don't do that. I'm fine."

"It's gotta stop, Otis. You're not fine. You're thirty and had a heart attack. You won't make it to forty unless you stop."

"I'm going to slow down."

"How? We have to start all over. Do you know how many acres of vines we need to get into the ground?"

Reality gut punched him. She was right. He hadn't earned anything, certainly not tenure with his farm. The following years would be the toughest of his life.

He didn't know where to go from here. "I'm going to change, Bec. You've been right all along. I can't keep going this hard. We'll have to get more help. I'll settle down. If you want to sell the farm, we'll sell the farm. Maybe it's time I go back to sch—"

"Oh, right, so you can be miserable about it the rest of your life. We have to replant, Otis. We're not stopping now, but you have to change. Your behavior on the road has to change. How many times do I have to tell you that what you put in your bottles doesn't define who you are? You take it too seriously."

Otis stared up to the white ceiling. "I don't know how else to say it, but that farm and those wines, Lost Souls, it's my oxygen."

Bec petted his face, there for him even when he didn't deserve it. "We're your oxygen, Otis. Me and Cam and Michael. You're missing out. You're missing the boys grow up. All Cam wants to do is go fishing with you, and you haven't taken him once. They just watched you collapse and be carried unconscious into an ambulance."

She climbed off the bed and stood over him. "I didn't marry your wines, Otis. You're a great man, even without them. The problem is that you're the only one who doesn't see it, the only one who doesn't realize that you let the quality of each vintage determine your greatness. That's not healthy."

"But it's true. What's wrong with that? The quality of Rembrandt's work had to do with his paintings, not how he brushed his teeth. Keith Richards isn't known for the way he dresses. It's his guitar playing. I'm an artist, and I am absolutely defined by my output. I only get so many vintages in a lifetime, and it already feels like I'm running out."

She slapped the air. "You don't get it. You will make better wine when you stop trying so hard. You'll make better wine when you can find balance in your life. What does any of it matter if you have another heart attack and don't wake up? You talk like you're in your eighties. You're thirty. Doctors are getting out of their residencies in their thirties. Most people at our age still have no idea what they want to do. You know exactly. You're way ahead, but you have to sit back and smell the riesling—"

"It's not that easy, Bec."

"It is. Yes, you only have a finite number of vintages, but what about the finite amount of time you have with your boys? With me? I could be gone tomorrow."

Otis saw a flash of a life without her, and it caved in on him. "I hear you, Bec."

—

Bec didn't leave the changing up to him. Having read it in one of her cuckoo books that she kept on her cuckoo bookshelf, she decided the first order of business was to institute daily recess for Otis.

Recess.

She laid out the whole plan with a straight face too.

He was back home from the hospital and feeling okay. Along with the doctor's instructions to eat healthier, start jogging, and stop drinking so much, he had a long list from Bec, including her instructions to "take an hour every day to play."

"Play?"

"Yes, play."

"For God's sake, who has time to play?"

She didn't respond, didn't have to. He'd already promised. He could hear himself back in the hospital. *I'll change, Bec. I swear to God.*

Worst promise he'd ever made.

"Guess what," Bec said, determined to fix him, "you have two expert boys outside who can teach you how to play. *When will the replanting happen?* you might ask. On either side of recess."

"Do you hear what you're telling me to do? I'm not seven years old."

"You're going to start acting like it."

Chapter 14

PAC-MAN AND WHITE ZIN

Sitting on a beanbag in Cam's room, Otis mashed down the controller and steered Pac-Man toward the enemy. "You can't take me alive!"

"Not that way, you git. They'll eat your face off!" Cam screamed from his tiptoed stance; he hadn't sat down for thirty minutes.

"Let's not call names," Otis said. He had to be careful what he said lately, because Cam had turned into a parrot.

Otis had no idea what monsters he would create when he surprised Camden with a new Atari game console a week ago. So much for them ever doing their farm chores again. Michael sat cross-legged only a couple of feet from the television. At five, he hadn't quite figured out how to play yet, but he was mesmerized by the game's visuals.

Otis's recess had just started. He'd been dropping new plantings into the ground when Rebecca rang the bell. To call Otis in from the vineyard, she'd purchased an old church bell from an antique store and hung it from the pergola that rose over the terrace. When that bell rang, Otis had minutes to race to the house to join the boys in recess.

Or else.

Or else was her new *ugh*. It was extraordinary how sassy his hippie princess could get. Perhaps he was the one who'd turned her that way. There was no more Mrs. Nice Girl when it came to his well-being.

She'd taken the same route with Jed and her parents, no longer letting them take advantage of her. Tough love was her new attitude, often even resorting to blackmail. Though Lost Souls didn't have the income it had, Bec was still giving her family money, and she'd threatened to cut them off if Marshall and Jed didn't attend AA meetings. She'd even sit through the meetings with them, making sure they participated. Indeed, although they were attending the meetings, Otis doubted the two men were actually sober. Apropos Olivia, Bec was constantly bickering with her, telling her that she had to learn to stand up for herself.

Most of these details Otis learned from afar, as he avoided the Marshall family as much as he could. He had his own command from Bec anyway: Learn how to play.

It wasn't always video games. They'd already set up Cam's pretend winery, attempted and failed to solve a Rubik's Cube, played tag and hide-and-go-seek ad nauseum, and thrown the football and Frisbee till Otis had torn a muscle in his shoulder.

When Otis was finally eaten in the game, he widened his eyes and said, "Now who else can I chomp?"

"Not me!" Cam yelled, running toward his dad, tackling him.

Mike followed suit, leaping into the air and landing right on Otis's stomach. "Oh, God, boy, you weigh too much these days."

Neither of them let up, attacking Otis from all angles, poking him in the side, trying to tickle him under the armpits.

"Is this fair? Teaming up on me? Don't make me unleash Pac-Man."

Cam and Mike laughed but continued their onslaught.

"Okay, that's it. Turbo mode coming right up. Chomp, chomp, chomp." The boys clung to him as he stood and shook them off and chased them out of the room.

Rebecca stood in the hallway, a smile dancing on her lips. Otis realized the width of his own smile, patted her on the bottom, then yelled after Mike: "Make way for Daddy Pac-Man!"

During this short hour every day he let go of his worries about their lack of money or the work ahead. For the first time in his life, he was truly connecting with his boys. Maybe Rebecca was right again. Of course she was. She was always flipping right, and he felt grateful to her, but he had a hard time saying it.

The bell rang again in the afternoon on Saturday. Bec had said she didn't want him to work on the weekends. He found that as funny as a skit he'd seen on *SNL* a week earlier. Till that impossible day came, they'd settled on him taking off Saturday afternoons to visit L&N Donut Shop, the place where Otis had first met the wine legend August Sebastiani, who had always kindly shared his wisdom over the years.

It was a scorcher outside, almost ninety degrees. Otis could only imagine how early he'd have to pick this year, if things didn't settle down.

As they pulled up to L&N, Cam said, "Oh, crap. That's Melanie."

Three young girls with bows in their hair stood in the long line, giggling.

"Shall we buy their doughnuts?" Otis asked.

"I'm not getting out of the car."

Otis turned to the back seat of their station wagon, a purchase made right before the fall of the Till empire. That's what he called it. They had some cash on hand, but the bleak future promised headwinds. No sprinkles or any other extra toppings today, that was for sure. The only exception would be a small scoop for Cam's potential love interest.

"So you like her?" Otis asked. "It's the first I've heard her—"

"He mentioned her the other day," Bec said, reminding him of his absentmindedness. "He met her at Isaac's birthday party. She's the one in red."

"Ah, yes." Was it him or was everything she said coated in a thin film of condescension? Either way, she did a great job of socializing the kids to counteract the homeschooling.

Little troublemaker that he was, Mike rolled down the window and called, "Oh, Melanie, Cam's in love with—"

Otis turned in time to see Cam punch his younger brother in the gut. Mike started crying, as Cam yelled, "The bloody wanker asked for it!"

"Cam!" Bec said, whipping her head around. "Watch your mouth!" Then she set angry eyes on Otis.

"What? I didn't teach him that."

"Who else would teach him to say *bloody wanker*?" She cracked a smile. Otis smiled back, then did something that he thought might surprise her.

He got out of the car and climbed into the back. Both boys looked at him with wide eyes, the toes of their bare feet clenched. He'd never sat in the back seat before. Though he wasn't one for spanking his children like his own father, Cam and Mike looked at him like he might strike.

"What this is, gentlemen," Otis said, "is the start of your experience with women. It's a long, hard road of joy and pain, but this is why I'm here, your dutiful parental coach."

Bec let out a laugh. "Oh, you're going to teach them about women?"

"Naturally."

"Hopefully not about the birds and the bees."

"What about the birds and the bees?" Mike asked, his newly missing front tooth causing him to slur his words.

"Nope, we're not going there," Bec said.

He put an arm around Cam. "I wasn't going there. What I thought I might bestow on them was a bit of my hard-earned wisdom from my years chasing women."

Rebecca pressed a palm to her forehead. "Boys, don't listen to a thing he says. He's never chased a woman in his life."

Otis eyed her in the rearview mirror. "Let's pause for a moment and consider the fact that I did land the finest catch in the ocean. I might have been rough around the edges, but there is no denying my skills." Otis winked at the boys.

Mike let out a giggle.

"Here's the thing. That Melanie over there, she might not act like it, but she wants you to say hi to her. To make conversation."

Cam shook his head sternly.

Otis pulled his arm away and smoothed his hands together. "Hear me out. You, too, Mike. Your time will come soon enough. If you master this now, you won't have trouble the rest of your life."

"This is rich," Bec said, shining the way she did whenever Otis gave the boys his all.

"Never mind her. Cam, I want you to go out there and strut your stuff and say, 'How's it going, Melanie?' Or can we call her Mel?"

"No," Cam said. "I'm not getting out of this car till they're gone."

"I'll go with you." Otis put a hand on the door handle.

Cam knocked it away.

"Fine, she's all yours. Tell her you like her shoes. Then maybe ask about the weather."

"The *weather*?" Bec said. "You're so lucky that I found you charming."

"In addition to handsome, sharp, quick-witted. Talk about a catch, boys." Otis jabbed his own thumb at his chest. "Back in the day, every chick on the block would turn my way."

Rebecca let her head fall.

Otis whipped out his wallet. "Ten bucks in your pocket if you go out there and say hello to her. Yeah, you heard me?"

Otis got out first. As Cam stood, he looked over to the three girls, who were now ordering. The push and pull of tween emotions showed in Cam's eyes. He took a step forward, then stopped. "I can't."

"Bwaak, bwaak," called Mike, giving a solid chicken impersonation.

Otis held up a hand. "Michael, give the young man time." To Cam, he said, "You *can* do it. Believe in yourself."

After a few more long seconds, Cam's bravado won out, and he started their way.

Otis stood proudly, his arms crossed. Mike climbed into the front seat to get a better look through the windshield. Otis heard a Brahms piano concerto in his head. This was the moment of truth, a man facing his greatest fear.

Cam walked with guarded hesitation, but as he drew near, he raised his hand into a subtle wave, said hello, and then started a conversation.

Otis quietly clapped his hands. He bent down to look at Mike. "You see that! That's courage, Mikey."

Cam gave a slight glance back to his family.

Otis couldn't help it and raised his arms in the air. "My boy," he said. Then he leaned down again and peered at Bec. "They have their father's charm, don't they?"

~

If only Bedwetter hadn't gone after Otis, he might have been fine for the rest of '83. He might have been okay returning to ramen noodles and hot dogs for a while, though he did miss the mushy peas of his childhood. He might have even started using ketchup. But something about Bedwetter and his writing jammed a screwdriver in Otis's eye.

Of course it had to be over the phylloxera debacle. Bedwetter had done an entire article discussing how phylloxera had taken over California, and he'd zeroed in on Otis, mentioning his name for the first time.

Under the drawing of his face—the fellow was as ugly as a groundhog—his words read:

I've been watching the youngster known as Otis Till, a new face in the Sonoma wine scene. I've written about him before. He's a part of Lloyd Bramhall's growing portfolio and a disciple of Carmine Coraggio. Let me say: I don't get it, and I might be the only one. I don't remember a newcomer splashing onto the scene in such grand fashion, and yet . . .

The harder they come, the harder they fall. I don't know if it was Otis's poor choice of plantings or his negligence in the field, perhaps even his bad luck, but the word is that he lost nearly everything. Once again, a climb to

the top knocked down by this wine world that eats
its young.

Bedwetter went on like that for a while, and Otis read with fury
rising. He folded the paper and slapped it down onto the breakfast
table, jostling his mug of coffee and the glass of grapefruit juice.

"Bec, I have to go to New York and get this man off my back.
As if I don't already have enough to worry about. He's confirmed
that we're the laughingstocks of this state. Of the whole flipping
industry."

Rebecca stood barefooted in cutoff jeans at the counter, making
breakfast. Otis had hoped to smell bacon, but he had a sneaking
suspicion she was making avocado toast again. She'd been threatening
vegetarianism, which was worse than becoming a communist.

"Honey, half the state is dealing with phylloxera. Quit acting like
you did something wrong. Also, I don't think people spend as much
time judging you as you might think."

"Oh, deary, you have such an optimistic outlook on mankind."

"If you think they're out to get you," she called over her shoulder,
"then they will be. I choose to see the good in people."

Otis rested his elbows on the table. "I choose, I choose, I *choose*. You
and your careful wording." She was still convinced that whatever one
said or thought became reality. "Well," he started, "I choose to take the
next flight out of SFO, track down Bedwetter, and throw him off the
top of the Empire State Building. That's *after* I ram a phylloxera-ridden
vine trunk up his arse."

Bec turned from the counter, butcher knife in hand. "It's
extraordinary how you let some guy you've never met affect you so."
She pointed at him with the knife. "Put your focus on our young vines.
Do what Carmine says, give everything you can to the wine, and then
move on. Don't worry about the reception."

"That's so easy for you to say."

Bec stepped forward, gripping the knife like she was going to use it on him, his beautiful sandy-blond butcher wife. "We have enjoyed the great opportunity of replanting exactly how we want. A fresh start."

"Are you going to kill me with that thing?"

She looked down at the knife. Her exhaustion with him dissipated, and a smile flashed on her face. "If you're not careful."

It was nice to share a laugh.

"I can't wait to hear what my dad has to say."

Rebecca sighed, realizing he hadn't heard a word she'd said. "Will you stop worrying what everyone thinks? My tolerance for your self-absorption is high, but you're pushing it. You're walking a pity path that's starting to become a paved road. So what if we have to tighten up for a few years. You can buy grapes and still make wine. And you have your consulting."

"Tighten up for a few years?" Otis asked with exasperation. "Have you stopped running the numbers? Do you know how many payments we have due? For glass, the new John Deere, the new press."

Rebecca returned to the counter with her blade. "Then you might have to stop drinking first growths for a while."

"I rarely drink first growths."

"Bullshit." To her credit, she'd never once blamed him for not selling to Gallo or taking any of the offers that had come their way before their vineyards were infected. Still, cutting off his access to first growths was playing dirty.

"I'm going to have to sell my soul," he said to her back. "No, wait, I already sold that to Bramhall. Do you mind if I sell your soul? No, yours is too pure. Maybe the kids'?"

She turned back around. "I'm just going to say it. Maybe this phylloxera mess is the best thing that ever happened to you. The way you've been with the boys lately, the way you've been with me. You've been so free. Don't let Ledbetter—"

"Bedwetter."

"I'm not calling him names."

"I have to go see him."

"You're not going to see him. You're not going to do anything but put your head down and keep making good wine."

This was one of those times where he probably should have listened.

⌇

Addison couldn't even wait a day to call and rub Bedwetter's words in his son's face. "Finally made the *Times*, did you. You didn't mention the phylloxera."

"Because I knew what you'd say." He hated that he'd had too much scotch and his words were slurring. "Bedwetter's a clown."

"He was writing about California long before Spurrier came in with his 'Judgment of Paris,'" Addison said snidely.

Otis poured himself another.

His father loved to talk about the "Judgment of Paris" and how Otis should have chosen to throw anchor in Napa. "Dad, the whole 'Judgment of Paris' thing . . . Sonoma made the chard. Not Napa, and yet they claim it." How many times had he told his father this fact?

"It was Chateau Montelena, son. One of my favorite properties. Trust me, they're in Napa."

Deep breaths, Otis told himself. "Yes, Mike Grgich made the wine at Montelena, but the chardonnay was grown in Sonoma by Charles Bacigalupi. I'm exactly where I want to be."

"For God's sake, Otis. Quit being sensitive. Get him out there to taste the wines. Perhaps he could give you some tips."

Otis paused and swallowed back a geyser of f-words that wanted to leap from his tongue.

There was not enough whiskey in his house, nor in Sonoma, nor in all of California to drown his troubles. He had damn well tried to prove it this evening. Rebecca wasn't speaking to him, likely because he was belligerently drunk. She'd tucked the boys in and retired herself, probably up there meditating or reading *Way of the Peaceful Warrior* or talking to herself, going on about "I choose, I choose, I choose."

After the call Otis marched out to the terrace with the rest of the bottle and collapsed into a chair. He took another gulp. Goddamn that burn was nice, but it still wasn't enough.

Could he survive two years of no income? He hadn't saved like he should. Once the money had started coming in, he assumed it wouldn't stop. So despite Bec's warnings that they remain thrifty, he'd loaded the cellar with wines and upgraded the tractor and the irrigation system. He'd opted for the most expensive label designers and glass. He'd also insisted on traveling in style, always renting the nicest cars, staying in the nicest hotels, indulging in often-excessive meals.

Scotch in hand, he pressed his eyes closed and sought solutions. He'd replanted the vines. Nothing he could do now but hope they would take. Had he lost his momentum? That would be Bedwetter's next article. *Otis Till has lost his mojo!*

No matter what Bec said—or Carmine, for that matter—Otis needed to resolve this Bedwetter issue. What if Otis invited him out there? Perhaps it was all a misunderstanding. The writer of abysmal wine prose came out once or twice a year to taste, and not once had he reached out to Otis. Perhaps there was a reason of which Otis wasn't aware.

In the morning, while Bec and the boys were feeding the sheep, collecting eggs, and cleaning out the chicken coop, he called *The New York Times* and asked for "Sam Bed—I mean—Ledbetter. It's Otis Till, a winemaker out of Sonoma."

"He's in France right now," a jolly young lady said, "but I'm happy to leave a message. He returns tomorrow."

In a friendly tone that wasn't exactly genuine, Otis said, "Please tell him to give me a call. I'd love to visit with him when he next comes out to Sonoma."

"I'll do that."

Tomorrow came and went. And the next week. No callback. Each time Bec left the house, he'd reach for the phone and dial the number with the New York area code, but then he'd hang up before the call connected. He couldn't beg.

Until he did a week later. "Yes, it's Otis Till, from Sonoma again. I've been trying to get in touch with Sam Ledbetter."

"One moment, please."

A distinguished American voice came on the line moments later. "Ledbetter here."

"Hi there, Sam. It's Otis Till, Sonoma winemaker of Lost Souls."

Agonizing silence.

Otis cleared his throat. "I wanted to see if you might be interested in including me on your next visit to Sonoma. I feel like . . . I don't know . . . that providing some context might help you understand my wines a little more."

"Uh-huh. It does work that way sometimes, doesn't it?" He spoke the way Otis imagined people who summered in the Hamptons spoke, with a fancy lilt, likely inherited from generations of martini drinkers holding their noses high at anyone less well to do.

The door swung shut, and the boys came running in. He held a finger to his lips.

"Let me consider, Otis. I'll have my secretary reach out in the coming months."

"That would be—"

Bec came into the kitchen with curious eyes. "Everything okay?"

Otis pressed the phone to his chest. "I'll be right off."

She began to put away groceries behind him.

"Yes, that would be great," Otis said into the phone.

"No promises, though."

Otis wanted to reach through the phone and strangle the man with his own ascot, tell him that he wasn't worthy of stepping onto the great land of the Lost Souls Ranch, but he couldn't say a damn thing now, as Rebecca wouldn't speak to him for a week if she discovered who was on the other end.

All Otis said was, "I understand. Look forward to hearing from you." After he'd hung up, Bec kissed his cheek. "Who was that?"

"Jack over at the farm shop. The brake disc for the Mahindra isn't in yet."

⌐

October used to be the month when Otis shone, when he felt the wolf howl within him. During October 1984, he had moments, especially with his boys, when he did feel okay, like life was almost normal, but right now, he was walking his vines, talking to them, and pleading that they take root and yield grapes that could make a worthy wine sooner rather than later.

Lost Souls Ranch was a sad affair during the harvest. With two-thirds of the vines standing only a few inches tall, there were barely any berries to take in. Otis had been forced to let half his staff go, as money was tight and there wasn't as much work to do. He'd committed to some purchased fruit grown north a few miles, but even the *idea* of making terroir-less juice hurt him. Otis Till was not a bulk winemaker, the kind of businessman who sells juice to churches for communion, or that off-loaded jugs to grocery stores. He'd built a name on his farm, and he didn't want to lose that reputation.

The worry ate at him. He was thirty-two and could very well be steering his family into a place from where they couldn't recover. Sure, they could sell their land, pay back Lloyd, and live off the rest while he found another means of income, but they'd put so much into it.

The sound of the bell rang out over the fields.

Otis looked back toward the house. Was it already ten? Rebecca had given him a hard time—in a soft Rebecca sort of way—for taking so long to report yesterday, so today he hustled and tried to shuck all the worry clinging to him.

One year of recess, and he and his boys had done about everything imaginable. As he came up the hill, he saw Mike and Cam tossing the football. They were that age now where they loved playing ball more than anything. Otis didn't quite understand sports, American or English, but he'd occasionally sip some whiskey and cuddle up with his boys to watch the San Francisco 49ers run up and down the field. He found it curious, these men tossing balls up into the air and being paid so much to do so.

Nonetheless, he'd decided to learn for his boys' sakes. "Recess has commenced!" he called, stretching out his arms as he came up the hill to the lawn.

Cam smiled and slung a spiral in his direction. Otis made a play for it, but it fell through his hands. Needless to say, Addison Till had not thrown him long balls back in London. Or in Montana, for that matter. Otis picked it up and slung it back as best as he could.

"That's not a spiral," Cam said, catching Otis's ugly toss. His son jogged toward him. "I told you, you have to hold it by the threads."

Otis took the ball. "Like this?"

"That's it."

"Go long."

Cam took off down the long gravel drive and then twisted at the last moment. Cam caught it perfectly. Who would have thought he'd raise two sports boys? But wasn't that the way the world worked?

Mike didn't have the athleticism that Cam did, but he had the determination. He joined in, and they stood in a triangle, tossing the ball back and forth. "So what's your mom teaching you today?"

"Math."

"Math? That's great. Every winemaker must be a mathematician. Just this morning, I was using division *and* multiplication. What I want to know is which one of you will work in the lab and which one will work in the vineyards." He already knew the answer, but he let them sort it out.

"I'm doing both," Mike said. "Like you."

"Yeah, your mom says I work too much. The duties would be best split."

"I'm working the vines," Cam said.

Otis agreed. The kid liked the outdoors more than anyone he'd ever met. "Would that be okay with you, Mike? I see you as more of the man in the lab, the one making the calls in the cellar. The fermentation artist. Typically, that means you'd go out and sell too. Go see the world, dine in some of the—what's wrong?"

Mike had caught the ball but hadn't thrown it back.

"I don't like to think about you not being here."

"Oh, I'll be here." Otis approached and lifted up Mike's chin. "I'll be on the terrace with your mother, sipping lemonade. Believe it or not, there will be a day, likely decades from now, when I want to step back, watch you boys do all the hard work. Besides, you'll both have a couple of sprogs running around. I want to focus on being a grandfather. Who else is going to teach them to throw spirals?"

"You can't throw spirals," Cam said, grabbing the ball from Mike.

"Fair point." Mike's shoulders were still slumped. Otis pulled him in. "Don't worry. Your mom and I aren't going anywhere for a long time."

A tear fell down his cheek. "I hate dying."

"Hey, why are you even talking like that?"

He raised his gaze, his eyes dull with heartache. "Mom said that Bubbles won't live as long as us."

Otis felt his son's pain. "Yeah, that's true. Dogs have shorter lives, but death isn't a scary thing. I'd like to think that, in some ways, it's just the beginning."

"What does that mean?"

Otis knelt and wiped Mike's face. "We can't know what's out there, but something tells me this little life we're all living here on earth is only a small part of the plan." He sounded like Rebecca, but he really did believe it. "In the meantime, that's why we must work hard to do something special. Because our time on earth is limited."

Once the boys returned to their schoolwork, Bec and Otis sat on the terrace to catch up. Otis sat in his favorite wrought iron chair, which faced up the hillside. "I'm worried about money, Bec. I see our little guys so happy here. Thriving. I don't want to lose the ranch."

"We're not going to lose the ranch."

"Do you really believe that or are you just saying that to manifest it?"

"It's the same thing, isn't it?"

Sometimes he wanted to explode when she refused to validate his fears. "You know what I mean. There's reality, and then there's you saying what you want to happen. Back here on earth, I'm looking at logistics."

"We did it once, we can do it again."

"I'm worried that those days were short-lived, that . . . I feel like a fraud. For a minute there, we had it figured out. Was it all an illusion? What if our fruit doesn't taste the same? What if people don't believe in me anymore? What if our distributors don't want the new wines when they come online? There are new players in town now. Napa is taking over. Hell, people are even buying Oregon wine these days. Can you believe that?"

The phone rang inside. A minute later, Cam called, "Dad! It's Paul." Otis pushed himself up and went into the kitchen. The boys hovered over their books at the table.

After a hello, Paul said, "You know Ledbetter's in town, right?"

Otis almost dropped the phone. "What?"

"Yeah, he came by to taste my wines. We're all doing dinner at Hamilton's tonight, a bunch of winemakers. Want me to see if I can get you in?"

Otis could have cried. He felt exactly the way he felt during lunches in the cafeteria as the new kid in Bozeman. Three hundred cowboys and cowgirls and one lonely English bloke with a funny accent.

"Nah, thanks, though. Have fun and tell everyone hello."

Otis set down the phone and stared at it for a while. Never had he felt more like a fraud.

⁓

Otis hated lying to Rebecca, but she was keeping far too close an eye on him. The whole recess thing wasn't the end of it. She seemed to always be watching when he refilled his glass of wine or if he got a second helping of food. It was her bloody fault for learning how to cook so well! Either way, it was not like his body showed evidence of overindulging. He was still in fine shape. He had a bit of a belly, but good God, all he'd done on the road for years was eat and eat and eat. Foie gras for breakfast, a big fat burger for lunch. Why wouldn't he order the bone-in rib eye for dinner?

Truth was, he knew to keep certain things from her. Like a man of days of old who left his village to fight enemies or to hunt for meat, it was best he do his work and not speak of it afterward.

Tonight he drove away from Lost Souls Ranch with the excuse that he was going to meet Carmine. She loved the man, loved how the old Italian had the right things to say, so she wouldn't think twice.

In reality, Otis beelined it straight to Sonoma Plaza. He slid his truck into a spot a block down. Stepping out, a small part of him thought, *Nothing good will come of this. Get back in the truck.*

A larger part of him screamed, *Oh, c'mon, don't be a coward!*

The maleficent Otis won, and he marched down the sidewalk till he reached a polished front window with HAMILTON's printed in gold letters. It was the best steak restaurant in the valley, certainly Otis's favorite. They even had his wine on the list.

He pressed his back up against the wall and took a guarded look inside. It didn't take him long to locate a table filled with Otis's competition. Sam Bedwetter sat at the end, in the middle of telling a story. He looked even more smug than he did in the cartoon drawing of him that always accompanied his repulsive writing. There must have been ten men there, and twenty open bottles, everyone's hard work from the previous harvest. Bedwetter spun a red wine in his right hand while telling a story that must have been funny as hell, because every winemaker there laughed like he was Johnny Carson.

Otis pulled back out of sight.

Of course, there was something else at play. Bedwetter held the keys to the kingdom. More and more, people were letting critics tell them which wines were good. People sought out the wines that Bedwetter mentioned in his articles. Same with the new fellow in Maryland, Robert Parker, who scored wines with a number.

Why were Americans so impressionable when it came to wine? With music, people liked what they liked. Same with food and even art. But wine had become intimidating in recent years. Maybe because so many had lost access to it during Prohibition. They didn't grow up with it the way Europeans did.

Otis looked again. Paul, with his hair pulled back into a ponytail, sat next to Bedwetter and kept touching him on the arm. Almost as if they were best friends. Otis loved Paul, but how could Bedwetter find Paul's wines more intriguing than that of Lost Souls? Actually, Otis knew every winemaker at the table. They were all decent men, but their wines weren't any better than Otis's.

Excuse him for saying so. His thinking was presumptuous, but it was true. He knew the methods of these men, and in comparing them with his own, Otis made truer wine. Of course, Bedwetter didn't know that because he didn't know a thing about Otis and his practices.

He wasn't sure what to do. There was one empty chair at the table. Had that been destined for him? Not that Bedwetter had asked him. Paul had asked. *Want me to see if I can get you in?*

No. Otis didn't want to be squeezed in. He wanted Bedwetter to invite him with a handwritten plea delivered with a goddamn coat of arms on the letterhead. Bedwetter should be begging to hear Otis speak of his farm and his wines and his miraculous climb to fame. Who else had their wines in the World Trade Center and Delmonico's? None of those guys.

He pondered what Rebecca might say, knowing she'd tell him to race back to his truck and get out of there. But this was his department. She oversaw the boys and the rest of the farm. The vines and wines were his.

He smoothed down his trousers and readied to enter. He'd pop in and pretend like he was taking a seat at the bar. *And, oh, I didn't realize*

you guys were here. Ah, Ledbetter. Nice to finally meet you. Who knew
what would happen from there? Otis might offer to buy a bottle, or
perhaps present a nice uppercut to the jaw. Or a jab in the abdomen.
Then he'd say, "No, thank you, I don't care to join. Just here for a filet
and a glass of a taut Haut-Brion."

Every step he took threatened to take his breath away. He opened
the door and readied for war.

Then he saw a man coming out of the restroom, and he froze.

The gorgeous Lloyd Bramhall was wiping his soft wet hands on
his pleated khaki pants. That empty seat was his. How had Lloyd not
mentioned that he was in town or that he'd also been invited to join
Bedwetter for dinner? Of all people, Lloyd knew exactly the issues Otis
had with the writer. It did make sense that Lloyd would be invited, what
with Paul there, but still . . .

All these thoughts came in a rush a second before Otis started to
turn away and make a run for it. It was too late, though.

Lloyd caught his eye and said, "Otis!" Loud enough for others to
hear. Loud enough for the whole table of winemakers to hear.

Otis spun around and darted out the door. He didn't look back as he
passed the large glass windows that he knew were filled with the gawking
eyes of the other winemakers. He wanted to turn around and face them,
but it was too late now. All he could do was disappear. He raced back
into his truck, clamoring for the keys. People in the plaza were laughing,
pushing baby strollers, licking ice-cream cones, tossing Frisbees. They
couldn't possibly know the wine wars being fought out here.

As he backed up, he saw Paul standing outside of the restaurant
with his hands held high, looking at him. His friend waved for him to
come back, but Otis did the only thing that occurred to him. He offered
a middle finger of defiance, and then spun away in a trail of dust.

Chapter 15

Zin and the Art of Implosion

Otis had stomped around the vineyard all morning, unable to stop thinking about how he'd embarrassed himself. Even now, he couldn't stop wondering what they'd said about him after his humiliating retreat from Hamilton's.

That was when the bell rang. That god-awful bell.

He could feel Bec rattling it with a big smile on her face, ready to see Otis come scurrying back to the house. She was sure that this recess thing had been his salvation, but you know what? Today he wouldn't come running at the ding. He was fed up. Fed up with all the misfortune. Fed up with Bedwetter and Lloyd and all the plays being made behind his back, and with being called like a fucking dog by a dinner bell!

Otis took one last look at the house and then continued his work digging a hole to put in a new post. Each jab of the dirt was a stab into Bedwetter's chest, not dissimilar to the stabs in his back from both the writer and Lloyd. He couldn't believe—

"Your boys are waiting."

Her voice came at him like his father's.

"Not today. I'm not feeling well." Another jab in the dirt.

Though she still walked around barefooted most of the time and still clung to her sixties and seventies mindset, Rebecca had started to shed some of the hippie attire of her youth. In her mid-thirties she wore skirts or pleated pants with button-down shirts, often accompanied by light wool sweaters—all in either stark white or pastels. Even her jewelry had changed. She didn't have the time to make her own anymore and now wore a series of thin gold chains around her neck and a Cartier watch with a thin leather band around her wrist.

She crossed her arms. "Did you drink too much with Carmine?"

"No, I did not drink too much. We were just tasting *and spitting* some of the new wines."

"Since when do you and Carmine spit?"

He still hadn't made eye contact. "Oh, I spit."

"Uh-huh. Well, it's time to take a break. Your boys want to throw the football."

Otis set the shovel down. "Bec, I can't help but feel a little exhausted by these games. I am not your child. I can't keep running to you when you ring the bell." He finally looked up. "Don't you see how awful it even sounds, you ringing a bell for me to come, like an obedient dog?"

"I'm not belittling you," she said, her face crinkling in insult. "Until you buy us a mobile phone, how do I get in touch with you? We both know you get lost in your work and lose time. I have to stick to a schedule, for the boys' sake. We have math at eleven."

"I'll buy walkie-talkies."

Bec saw right through him. "I hate to psychoanalyze, but the bell is a metaphor for your frustration."

"Here we go. Want to go grab Sparrow so you guys can do a soul reading?"

"Hey, I wish you'd learn your lesson. You had a heart attack at thirty—"

"A mini heart attack."

She ignored him; rightfully so. "You *still* have a hard time slowing down. More than that, your boys are growing up right before your eyes, but you don't see it."

"That's bullshit. I have played with them every day. Most fathers are at offices all day. I'm right here."

"I know, and I appreciate it, but it's because I'm making you. You're not giving me a choice. I love you too much to lose you, and I'm worried."

Otis swallowed.

"I don't know how else to drive it home. You're working too hard, and I wouldn't be surprised if you brought on all this bad luck as of late, including the phylloxera, and the tax hike. Heck, even the press breaking down. I think you might be creating this reality for yourself."

A sigh escaped him. "Here we go again. You're right. I brought a disease down upon us. Because I am God, Bec. I have the ability to spread plagues in the vineyard."

"That's not what I'm saying, and you know it."

He jabbed the shovel into the earth. "Then what are you saying?"

"That you're not living with any joy. You're so *damned* focused, and you're forgetting what you have. You're marching around as if the whole world is coming after you."

He looked around. Couldn't she see it? "Well, it is."

"If you think it, then it will be true."

"Please don't spit this New Age mumbo jumbo at me. The only reason we're here is because I pushed when I had nothing left."

"If I remember correctly, the reason we're here is because I pushed you to come see the place, to believe we could have it."

"Yeah, with the help of your boyfriend. At least I know I'm messed up. Sometimes I think you forget that you're human too. You've never been the same since you found out about Jed, always feeling like you have to make up for leaving. Why not, for a minute, focus on yourself? Why do you have to fix everyone around you? Why can't you stay in your own lane for a . . . ?" He pulled back the reins.

She cut him with angry eyes, and he knew he'd gone too far.

"I'm sorry," he said. "I didn't mean to say that. You're . . . you're the rock in this family. Despite all you've been through."

"No. I'm done here." She turned and marched away, her bare feet padding on sacred soil.

Otis grabbed the shovel and smacked it against the post till the handle splintered in two. He huffed and puffed for about five minutes before he realized that he was in the wrong in all ways. He had no right to speak to her so.

Returning to the house, he saw his boys tossing the ball and picked up the pace. Burying his frustration, he attempted to appear light and airy. "Hit your old man with a long one."

Breaking into a grin, Cam reeled back and tossed a beautiful ball to his father. He now played wide receiver for a flag-football team in Santa Rosa, and he'd asked if he could attend school in town so that he could join the seventh- and eighth-grade football team. It was only a matter of time till Rebecca gave in.

After twenty minutes of football with his boys, Otis had come back down to earth, his anger settled, and he was about to climb the steps to apologize to Bec when the familiar sound of Lloyd's Ferrari came purring through the Glen Ellen hills.

Otis's fists clenched. He had hoped Lloyd would return to San Francisco without a word spoken about last night.

The boys had taken a liking to Lloyd, for multiple reasons, and they raced over to welcome Sir Shitbag. Dressed in shiny leather shoes, gray suit pants, and a tailored blue shirt, Lloyd sprang out of his fancy car with a white bag for each of the boys. It was either doughnuts or candy. Was it any wonder the boys liked him? He bribed them with sugar. Then, of course, Lloyd took the ball and sent it long to Mike. Mike and Camden stared with eyebrows high at Lloyd's extraordinary spiral.

"How do you do that?" Cam asked with enthusiasm that crushed Otis's heart.

"All in the legs and waist, kiddo." Lloyd retrieved the ball from Mike and twisted back and forth, showing the motion.

"You're the best I've ever seen," Mike said with admiration that should be reserved for superheroes, running up to him, staring at him as if he were Joe Montana, the quarterback for the San Francisco 49ers, whose poster occupied a spot on Camden's wall.

The front door swung open, and Rebecca descended the steps and joined Otis. "What's he doing here?"

Otis shrugged his shoulders.

Lloyd broke away from the boys and approached. "Good morning, guys. Thought I'd stop by on my way back to the city." He kissed Bec on the cheek, and Otis was pretty sure he took a big sniff of her, too, taking all of her in. He still barely tried to hide his infatuation with her.

Otis almost didn't shake his hand but accepted after letting Lloyd wait for a few seconds, his arm suspended in the air.

"What happened last night?" Lloyd asked. "I thought you might join us, but you disappeared?"

Otis's shoulders tightened.

Bec swiveled her head to Otis. "You didn't tell me Lloyd was at Carmine's too."

A dog knows when he's destined for the doghouse, but he must try to evade his owner's wrath first. "I don't always report when Lloyd's in town."

Whether Lloyd detected the issue, he didn't attempt to bail Otis out. "We were at Hamilton's with Sam Ledbetter—I was there with Paul—and Otis showed up."

"At Carmine's?"

"No, at—"

Otis jumped in before he got in even more trouble. "I stopped by Hamilton's. Just for a drink."

Rebecca's eyebrows curled. "By yourself?"

Otis squirmed. "Carmine wasn't home and . . ." He let his words trail away. What could he possibly say now?

The following minute carried a serrated edge that could have sawed down a tree.

Finally, Lloyd cleared his throat and changed the subject. "I had an idea I wanted to run by you."

Never was Otis interested in Lloyd's ideas until right now, when it could provide such a welcome distraction. "Oh, yeah, what's that? Why don't we sit down on the terrace?" Otis wiped the sweat off his brow.

Lloyd pulled back his sleeve and glanced at his Patek Philippe watch. "I have to get back for a meeting in the city but wanted to put something out there. It was the heavy topic last night."

Otis could only imagine.

"White zin," Lloyd said.

"What about white zin?" Otis asked with a bitter taste coating his tongue. White zinfandel was made by limiting the amount of time zinfandel grapes spent on the skins and then stopping the fermentation with sulfur to keep some of the sugar content, making for a slightly sweet, pink wine.

"As you know, it's the new rage."

"Because people are idiots."

"Maybe so, but there's money to be made."

Otis pointed to the last of his old vines. "Let me guess. You want me to use our babies to make a wine that has less soul than Sprite?"

"I was thinking bigger than that. I was thinking we buy bulk and make a shit ton of wine. This is an opportunity like none I've ever seen."

"You better go," Otis said, praying to God Bec wouldn't get behind the idea.

"Oh, c'mon. Think about it. You need money. I'm giving you a way to earn some." Lloyd's eyes tracked to Bec, hoping she'd jump in.

"I'm not making white zin," Otis said. "Thanks for the idea. It's good to see you. And goodbye." Otis put his arm around Rebecca and attempted to guide her back to the house.

Bec shook him off. "How much could we sell? What kind of FOBs are we talking about?" *FOB* meant *freight on board*; it was the price at which Otis and Rebecca sold their wine to distributors.

"We could sell more than we could ever make," Lloyd said, greed dancing in his voice. "People are begging for it."

Otis set his fists on his waist. "Don't even tell me you think this is a good idea, Bec."

"I think we need money."

"We also need our souls. I'd rather rob a bank."

The boys walked up. Ball in hand, Cam said, "Dad, did you see Lloyd's arm? I've never seen anyone—"

"Yes, I saw Lloyd's arm," Otis said sharply. "Boys, we're wrapping up an adult conversation. Do you mind waiting inside?"

"But, Dad," Cam said, "we wanted to see if we could get a game going. Me and Lloyd versus you and Mike."

Mikey threw his hands in the air. "What? No, it's Lloyd and me versus you two."

Otis's jaws tightened like a coyote trap. He had to pry them open to say, "I will not ask again."

They took his meaning and retreated inside with slumped shoulders.

Otis reverted his gaze to Lloyd and stepped toward him. "Lloyd, let me make two things clear. We're not ever selling this place, and I am not ever making white zin. I don't care if the world is on fire and white zin is our only hope. I don't care if the White House is begging for it. No. White. Zin."

Lloyd's eyes went to Bec.

Otis snapped his fingers. "No, don't look at her. Look at me."

When Lloyd did, Otis said, "She runs the books and the farm and about everything else, but the vines and wines are mine. I'm not making white zin, and if you ever bring it up again, I will knock you in the mouth."

Handsome smile alert. He didn't even seem fazed by Otis's threat. "It's just a suggestion. I know money's tight."

Otis didn't say a thing. Bec didn't dare.

Lloyd took the hint, said a quick goodbye, then retreated to his race car and sped away.

Otis tried to take Rebecca's hand, but she pulled it back. "You need to grow up."

Christmas of '84 was anything but joyful. Otis and Rebecca had been at each other's throats throughout harvest. After one of her rants, Otis would throw himself on the sword. "You're right," he would say. "I *am* impossible. I don't want to compromise my art and make white zin or fucking blue cabernet. I want to continue making wines that matter."

She'd quieted about the white zin thing, though he suspected she'd been speaking to Lloyd on the side. If he found that out for sure, he would absolutely lose his mind.

What brought it all to a head was Rebecca's statement—not question—on Christmas Eve. Bec's parents had just left, and the boys were asleep, and Otis and Rebecca were playing Santa Claus. Rebecca wheeled in a new bicycle for Mike. Otis had gone to work setting up a train set for Michael that promised to take three hours, what with the awful instructions.

"Jed wants to go back to rehab," Rebecca offered.

"Oh, yeah?" Otis had a proper buzz from having drained almost two bottles of wine. Marshall and Olivia's presence always forced him to overindulge. Marshall had a never-ending evil eye, and Olivia's fragility was too difficult to be around even halfway sober.

"I want to pay for it."

"Pay for what?" He stuck a screwdriver into a hole in the track.

"We're going to pay for Jed to go back to rehab. The VA is being difficult, and they won't pay for a good one anyway."

"What does he need, a Four Seasons?" Otis took a soothing breath, set the screwdriver down, and tried not to show how maniacally angry he'd become in a matter of seconds. "With what money?"

"With our money."

"We don't have money."

"We do. We have savings."

"What happens when we need our savings?" Their words came out faster by the second.

"We'll be back in greener times by then?"

"How could you know that?"

"I know."

Otis wanted to eat his wineglass when Bec started talking like that. He picked up the screwdriver and went back to work with determined fury. "What an epic waste of money. Like last time, he'll go right back to using."

"It doesn't always take."

"Isn't that the truth."

"He's my brother, and he wants to get better. Can you imagine what he's been through?"

"I appreciate that, but we can't put our security at risk for him." Where was the bloody whiskey bottle?

"He's family."

Even as he continued to protest, Otis knew she would win. Was it any wonder why he had to work so hard? Sure, he'd simply spread himself a little thinner, because he had *plenty* of time and energy and money. Who needed sleep? He could whittle his four hours down to two.

~

The real rage rose on the day the San Francisco 49ers made the Super Bowl. Rebecca, who wasn't much of a sports fan at all, had suggested the wonderfully stupendous idea of inviting everyone over to watch the game. Not just everyone, but *everyone*. Otis's parents in Montana. Her parents. Her now-sober brother—coming off a rehab Otis and Bec had paid for. All the employees. Carmine. Paul and Sparrow. *Lloyd.*

The boys had run outside to throw the ball after losing their minds over the win. Otis and Rebecca still sat with Bubbles on the couch, facing the television. A reporter was wrapping up an interview with Joe Montana. A giant bowl with remnants of popcorn rested on the coffee table beside an empty bottle of rosé Champagne.

"You want to invite Lloyd?" Otis asked, wishing he could get away with opening a second bottle without being scolded.

"He's our partner."

"He's evil."

"You're a child."

The conversation felt like a hundred they'd had in the past.

"I know you don't like football," Rebecca said, "but this is about the boys. Look at their joy. Let them see what a real American life is like, getting the family together the way it should be."

This was always her way, giving, giving, giving, and always talking about the perfect American life. How far she'd come from her hippie youth.

"There's one thing, though," Rebecca said, pouring both of them more water from the carafe. "With Jed getting out of rehab, I'd like to make the party alcohol-free."

Otis's head spun all the way around, 360 degrees of mind-bending shock. "You're kidding. Just when I thought you had lost your humor. Not bad, actually. You nearly gave me another heart attack—not even a mini one, a full-blown affair. You're funny."

She wasn't laughing. Hell of a poker face.

"Wait, you're not being serious. Hold on. You are. You want to host a party with our extended family and friends—many of whom are in the wine business—and yet ask them to abstain from alcohol."

Apparently Otis was having a conversation with himself, as she collected the bowl and bottle from the table and headed for the kitchen.

He hated this, how she let him process things verbally on his own. She didn't even have to participate in their arguments sometimes.

"If you are, in fact, being serious," he called out to her, "this is not funny and not even a discussion. You win everything, but not this one. No way."

Not a peep.

"With my father there. Your father. With Jed? Oh, I'll be drinking. Everyone will be drinking, or it will be a nightmare. You're going to punish me for Jed's drug abuse?"

He followed her into the kitchen and waved a hand in front of her face. "Anyone in there? Do you hear me? We're either having a party with alcohol flowing like the Nile River, or we will not be hosting anyone at all."

She finally spoke, her deceptively sweet little mouth peeling open. "I don't think it would hurt you to take some time off from drinking anyway."

"Oh, here we go again. I only drink too much when I'm stressed out. That happens to be a lot lately."

She went quiet again.

He knew he couldn't win, but he tried anyway.

"I beg of you. Let's not have a party. No one says we have to. I'm not inviting people to our house, to our vineyard and winery, and asking them not to drink. What they put in their mouths is their business. What I put in my mouth is *my* business."

Rebecca, ever patient, reached for his hand. "I love you."

Otis's shoulders slumped. He knew she'd won. No other woman on earth could control him like her, by bloody blue gods; that was why he loved her more than any other man could love a woman.

Her idea was still a bad one, though.

⁓

On game day, January 20, 1985, Lost Souls Ranch resembled a rehab facility. Everyone dead sober. The conversation stale and awkward. Not a smile within ten miles. It fit that it was cold outside. The long tables in the living room where they'd hosted countless wonderful meals inspired by European cooking now hosted buffalo wings, cheese curds, jalapeño poppers, hamburgers, and nachos. What a travesty.

Otis couldn't get past being grumpy. This was not a time to expect everyone to be sober.

Except for Jed.

Otis wasn't a monster. He was happy for Jed. He wasn't happy that he'd had to pay for the rehab and now had to endure a sober family get-together. What was it that Sinatra had said? That he felt bad for a man who didn't drink, as he woke up feeling the best he would all day. Sinatra's heart would break for Otis right now. Actually, Sinatra would have had his people take care of Jed—and Lloyd—a long time ago.

This would be the last time Otis paid for rehab, though. If Jed slipped up, then Otis would enjoy one of the finest "I told you sos" in history, then make Rebecca sign a document agreeing that Jed was on his own next time.

The other thing. His father didn't like football any more than he did. Addison Till sat next to Otis in a vacuum of awkward silence. Why? Because there was no wine to numb Addison's ever-present grudge toward Otis for having dropped out of school, a grudge that would last until his dying breath. Talk about "I told you sos." Addison could slam you with one without ever saying the words. His eyes shot "I told you sos."

"How's the new book coming?" Marshall asked Addison, surprising everyone with his attempt at making conversation. "What's the topic?"

Addison dabbed his mouth with a napkin like he was inside Buckingham Palace dining with the Prince of Wales, then said, "I'm tackling the influence of modern culture on the time-tested traditions of the past." He kept going for about five minutes, but Otis tuned him out. Had his father not done the same to him all his life?

The man should write a book on how to set a bar so high for your son that he'll spend the rest of his life parked in the shadow of a paternal dark cloud. Addison hadn't said a word about the quality of the wine from the last vintage. Barely a thank-you for the case of wine Otis had shipped to Bozeman. Shipping wasn't getting any cheaper, by the way. Next year it might be a bottle, if Addison was lucky.

If that weren't enough, Lloyd's presence swelled like a malignant tumor at the table. Carmine was the only one who had turned down the invitation. Not because of the booze but because Carmine didn't do parties. What a freaking hero. Here Otis was hosting one that he didn't even want to attend. Why couldn't he be like Carmine and simply say no? No, no, *no*. What a lovely motto.

Otis came back to reality only when he heard Ledbetter's name. Making it even more excruciating was that it came from the mouth of Addison Till.

Addison had said to Lloyd and Paul, "Superb mention in Sam Ledbetter's article."

"Aw, thanks, man," Paul said, holding his hands in prayer position. Despite how wonderful Paul was, Otis had an urge to throw a corn dog at him.

"I'd love to taste your wines sometime."

"Sure, come over before you go back. I'd be happy to walk you through them."

"Thank you," Addison said. "I just may. He's a great writer, isn't he? Quite humorous, in a dry way, of course. Lloyd, have you tried to get him to taste the wines here?"

Otis wondered whether his father realized the evil of his ways.

Lloyd set down the can in his hand. That was the other thing. Beer. Sure, beer was fine, but a long lunch like this required a Vouvray, not a lager. Why was it that football brought out the heathen in everyone? Hold on, that wasn't a beer because *no one was even drinking beer*. It was a bloody soda!

"He'll get to us eventually."

Us? What in hell did Lloyd have to do with Lost Souls?

Addison finally turned to his son. "It could be the name. You see him mostly writing about more traditional-type wineries. Lost Souls has a sort of childish quality that could be turning him off."

Otis's blood simmered in his veins, nearly scorching his insides. "Right, Dad. Maybe I should change the name of the winery so that Samuel Bedwetter can piss all over—" Otis stopped and turned to make sure the boys were out of earshot. "So that I could get some miserable old man in Manhattan to mention me in his *shit* column."

Addison groaned disappointment. "I don't think it's shit. In fact, I find it very useful to have a guide of what I might find at the local stores. The retailers don't have a clue what they're doing."

Otis was ready for battle. "That statement couldn't be further from the truth. The people in retail stores are the ones who can get to know your palate and steer you in the right direction. What do you think they do all day? They study wine, talk about it, meet with reps, taste wines. They know more than you'll . . ."

Hearing his tone, Otis stopped just as he was getting going and looked over at Rebecca. She was staring at her plate. Dammit, the doghouse was calling again.

Lloyd stood. "I'm going to toss the ol' pigskin for the boys."

Otis cut him a look. "Yeah, you do that."

Silence fell over the entire table. Addison didn't even clear his throat. Otis wished to be anywhere. The jungles of Vietnam, front row at a heavy metal concert, supine position at the dentist office staring up at a power tool, prison. Yes, prison. Hell, he'd rather be neck deep in a tank of white zin.

Jed broke the silence with a laugh that crescendoed like a Mahler symphony. When he garnered the attention of every single human present, he said, "For God's sake, will everyone please get a drink? This is awful."

Another beat of silence, this one more anticipatory.

Otis didn't move a muscle, simply waited to hear Bec's voice. She was the mayor of this town. He could almost feel her weighing the decision.

One.

Two.

Three seconds.

He counted to ten before an answer came.

"Fine. Otis, would you like to grab some—"

Before she'd finished the sentence, Otis was already in the cellar, gathering his largest formats, a three-liter of an '81 Morgon Beaujolais and a five-liter of a '79 Lost Souls. He'd never been so eager to have a drink in his life. No one has ever seen a man open two large formats faster.

Within five minutes of Rebecca's surrendering her hope of a sober party, Otis had filled glasses for everyone in attendance sans Jed. Apparently it wasn't only he who'd been desperate for a sip, as by the time he'd sat down, half the glasses were empty.

⌒

After the game, which was apparently a stunner—Otis hadn't watched—he went back into the kitchen to do dishes and found Lloyd and Rebecca speaking in low whispers in the corner under a rack of copper pots.

Lloyd backed away quickly, almost too quickly, as if Otis had stumbled upon them on the edge of a kiss.

Rebecca's eyes glowed with guilt. "We're just catching up."

Otis looked from one to the other. "Right."

She likely understood what he might have assumed and cut it off at the pass. "I was asking Lloyd about potential numbers if we did the white zin."

Otis smiled an unhappy smile. "I see. I thought we'd already discussed and closed this topic."

"We're just talking."

"Just, just, just," he muttered, then more loudly: "You mean going behind my back. I am the winemaker here. I'm telling you that we will become the laughingstock of California. *Again*. First we succumb to an infestation, and now we're discussing making a wine without even an ounce of terroir, a wine that isn't art at all. A wine that is no different from the damn sodas we tried to serve out there."

"People like it," Bec said. "They're demanding it. Not every bottle has to bleed terroir."

Otis clutched his heart. "You sound like him now." He refused to make eye contact with Lloyd and pointed at him instead. "We're not in this business to follow trends. You always bring up Carmine. He's not making white zin. He wouldn't make it if the lives of his children hung in the balance. This has to be a joke."

Bec moved toward Otis, breaking away from her boyfriend. "We need the money. You can still make your terroir wine. Why not make a guzzler too?"

"Because we will never outlive it."

Lloyd leaned against the wall. "Otis, I get you. You know I'm a terroir guy. I live for a wine that speaks of its place, but we're just saying that—"

"We? So you *are* colluding? How many times have you two spoken without me there?"

"There's no collusion, my man."

"My man? I am not your *man*."

Rebecca put a hand on Otis's back, as if that might extinguish his rage.

Lloyd smiled a smile that could break clouds apart. "We're simply talking about taking advantage of a trend that's not stopping anytime soon. I worry that we'll be scratching our heads in five years, wondering why we didn't take the money. Think about it. That kind of green can set you up to do whatever you like. You'll be able to make deals. 'Take thirty cases of my terroir wine and you can have a pallet of my white zin.'"

Otis peered into the eyes of his lover. This must have been how Napoleon felt when he learned of Joséphine's infidelities. "My heart is broken right now. Truly shattered."

"Take a deep breath," Rebecca said.

"I'm not taking a deep breath." His voice escalated. Others had come into the kitchen. He could feel them watching like gawkers witnessing a bar fight.

"We're not pushing it on you," Lloyd said. "We want to reason with you."

Otis pointed his finger at Lloyd and then at Rebecca. "I dare you to say *we* one more time. I know you have eyes on her. Or for her, whatever the hell. I know that you would love nothing more than for her to divorce me so you could have a chance with her."

"That's not tr—"

"I'm speaking."

"Otis, stop."

He lifted a hand. "Bec, I've had enough. Lloyd, I want you out. Of my house. My life. You are a silent investor that gets a check. Very soon, I will buy you out. Exactly what it says in the contract."

Lloyd grew prickly. "I don't want to be bought out."

"Tough shit."

Lloyd opened his hands. "Otis, you don't want to go down this path. Be a good partner."

That felt like a threat; Otis stepped forward. "You want me to be a good partner?"

"Otis, stop it," Rebecca said.

"How about *this* for a good partner?" Otis timed the punch perfectly, and Lloyd was too clueless to know Otis had nothing left to lose.

The man's head smacked against the back wall and blood dripped from his mouth.

Rebecca screamed, as did someone else from behind.

Otis reared up to hit him again, despite Lloyd not retaliating.

Then Rebecca's pleas to stop filled the air, and he caught himself. He lowered his fist and dropped his head. His chest heaved.

"There is no *we*," Otis whispered.

He turned and started out of the kitchen, passing by Marshall and Olivia, and his own mother and father. His boys looked at him like he'd lost his mind. He touched their heads and whispered that he was sorry.

As he reached the front door, he turned back and screamed one last time, "There is no *fucking we*!"

Chapter 16

Ring the Bell

Ten o'clock the next day came and went, but neither Rebecca nor the boys hammered the bell. Absolute silence penetrated the farm. Otis and Scooter and two other men had been pruning canes all morning. The guys had figured out pretty quickly that Otis wasn't in the talking mood, so there'd barely been any chatter, only the snap of snipping shears.

Otis kept reliving the look on his father's and the boys' faces. He understood the way Bec felt now, all those years of standing by him, allowing him space to grow, hoping he'd come around, only to realize that Otis was Otis, and perhaps she'd made a mistake in marrying him. His fear and disgrace weighed him down like armor. He'd finally screwed up beyond repair.

At eleven o'clock, Otis couldn't take it any longer.

He marched back to the house. Bec's car was gone. He wound through the rooms, calling, "Hello?" She'd taken Cam and Mike. He looked into the primary bedroom, wondering whether she'd packed a bag. Who could blame her? Her bag was still under the bed, though.

Back downstairs, he went to the terrace and looked up at the bell, that shiny stupid fucking bell that had rung every day since he'd returned from his stint at the hospital. The bell that had called him back to his family reminded him what mattered. The bell that had connected him with his boys.

The bell that hadn't rung today.

A hollowness spread through his core. Tears falling down his cheeks, he reached up for the chain and began to ring it himself. *Clang, clang, clang.* Each chime shot out over the ranch and up and around the hills, filling the air with his failures, all the shit he hadn't said, all the shit he hadn't done. It sang of how his father would never be happy with him, and how Otis had failed his children, and how he'd failed himself, and Rebecca. The runt that he was had been given a chance. No, endless chances. This perfect being had come into his life, and he hadn't been and still wasn't the man she deserved.

Ringing the bell harder and harder, he shook the pergola, his head shaking with it, tears spraying and splattering to the floor. His own curses shot out into the daylight along with the clang, a madman who'd finally cracked.

Otis swung that chain till the hook that held the bell ripped out of the ceiling and crashed to the floor. He was full-on crying as he picked it up and flung it down, then again, screaming obscenities and wishing he weren't here, wishing the heart attack had taken him away.

When he finally collapsed, he looked up and saw them—his family. He hadn't heard them pull up. Now all six of their eyes watched him from inside the car.

Right then he knew exactly what it felt like to be a failure.

⁓

Strolling next to his mentor through the vines, Otis glanced over. "I don't know where to go from here, how to get back."

Carmine didn't respond. He'd been silent for a while, listening to Otis speak about how they'd lost so much with the phylloxera infestation and how Bec and Lloyd were willing to compromise everything by making white zinfandel to climb back on top.

A wet chill bit the clean air. Carmine and his crew hadn't even started pruning yet. The sheep, ripe with wool, stood quiet in a fenced area ahead.

Carmine wore a weary sweater that had been torn apart by moths. It looked like he hadn't shaved in weeks. "Take it easy, *ragazzo*." He grabbed Otis's neck and pinched his trapezius muscles, strong hard hands digging into the tissue. "You take yourself too seriously. You take it all too seriously."

"Why wouldn't I?" Otis tried to pull away, but Carmine pinched him harder, not letting him go. Otis stopped fighting and let the man's fingers dig in deep. Soreness rose through his arms.

"You know what I see?" Carmine asked. "A man who feels like he's in control. A man under the illusion that he's steering. Where's your faith?"

"Faith? Far as I know, faith never fermented grape juice. It never built an empire."

"Without faith, what's the point in building anything?"

Otis couldn't answer the question. Now into his sixties, Carmine had perhaps strayed too deeply into the ethereal.

The old man let go of him, and they started strolling again. "You see all this? I didn't do it. I'm just along for the ride. The best thing is, it all exists without me. I'm simply a passenger. Soon as you realize and accept that, the ride gets so much smoother."

"I have no idea what you're saying."

"The best wines are made when you know enough to control everything but are wise enough to control nothing. Balance comes from guidance of a natural process, not forcing an outcome. Come here." Carmine lowered to his knees at the base of a vine and wrapped his hands around the trunk. "Down here, Otis. Now."

Otis reluctantly obeyed.

"Closer, closer, what are you afraid of? Hold the trunk like it's a . . . no, not what you're thinking. Hold the trunk like it's the metal rod on a carousel. There you go."

They sat on their knees, facing each other, the vine between them, their hands wrapped around the trunk.

"You feel that?"

Otis focused on his fingers and felt the tingle, a surge of electricity—a life force—traveling from the vine to him. It had been a long time since he'd connected in such a way.

"This vine and every other vine in this vineyard will go on with or without you. All you can do is arm yourself with faith and hold tight. Let them carry you; let *life* carry you."

Otis offered a slight nod.

Carmine wrapped his hands around Otis's. "This spaceship we're on . . . there's something else steering. It doesn't need you. You don't matter." He laughed to himself. "In not mattering, you will find your reason."

Carmine retracted his hands, and Otis let go of the trunk.

"The world is sprouting before our eyes, vines growing from the ground, trees, humans, bugs." He tickled the air with his fingers. "If you fight it, if you for a moment think you have any control over it, you'll be swallowed whole. Find the balance, Otis. Find that space where you're a passenger who trusts in where he's going. We're so unimportant to this wondrous world . . . and yet, vital, but you have to quit white knuckling the wheel. Do you hear what I'm saying?"

"I suppose so."

Carmine waited till Otis looked at him. "What I'm really saying is . . . loosen up. Take it easy on yourself." He jammed his fingers into the soil and brought up a handful of clay. "No matter what, we all fold back into the earth."

"Are you saying that you'd compromise everything you've worked for to make white zin? That you'd sell yourself to rebuild?"

Carmine's cheeks swelled with a kind and gentle smile. "I'm glad I'm not faced with the decision, as I'm not sure. But I do know, *mio amico*, that if you shake off the fear, that if you quit trying to prove yourself and simply climb aboard this ride, the answer will land on you like a butterfly on your shoulder."

Otis understood what his mentor was saying, but it was too much. He felt far away from faith and connection, so very far from finding his way back.

~

Though the butterfly did not land, and the bell no longer sounded, Otis returned to the house at 10:00 a.m. every day to play with his boys. In early April, he hiked up the hill eager to join Cam and Mike for an hour of play, only to find several cars in the drive. Paul and Sparrow and Carmine stood from a circle of chairs to say hello. Above their heads hung the bell.

"What's this?"

Rebecca stood and took his hand. She wore a silk blouse half tucked into jeans. Worry showed in her eyes. "Will you sit down, honey?"

He looked at his friends, then back to Bec. "Where are the boys?"

"With my parents."

"What is this?"

"We want to talk to you."

"About?"

"Sit down."

Otis reluctantly sat and rested his hands on his knees. How dare they ambush him.

"Honey," Bec started, "we're worried about you."

"Right." He felt a smirk rise on his face; he was the only one who knew the truth: His hard work was the reason they'd made it this far.

"We're here because we love you, and we're here to tell you that you need to slow down." He could see that she'd been pondering what to say for a long time.

"This again? Shall we double recess time?"

"This isn't about recess, and I'm sorry if my idea belittled you. Can't you see that hour of recess is the best thing that's ever happened to you?"

He didn't answer, because he would have had to agree, and he didn't want her to be right.

"We can't tie you down. All we can do, as the people who love you most in this world, is tell you that we think you've lost your way, and we want to help you rediscover it."

"What the hell does that mean?"

Paul spoke up. "We love you so much, Otis, and that's the only reason we're here. We're worried. You're a tractor running without oil, grinding your gears into oblivion. You freaking punched Lloyd in front of everyone."

"Because he's a thief, stealing everything from me. My wife, my vineyard, my kids."

"We're still here, Otis," Bec said calmly. "No one is stealing anything from you. It's time you take a big step back. No more travel for a while. Period. Our distributors will be fine. The new vines are in the ground and doing well. Reconnect with what got you here. Reconnect with what Carmine and Paul taught you. Find that joy again. Because I don't see you having fun right now."

"Oh, I'm having the time of my life."

Otis looked at Carmine, who rocked silently in his chair. They held eye contact for a while; then he finally spoke. "It's like we talked about, Otis. The only thing getting in the way of your dreams is you. You're a passenger trying to take the pilot's seat."

"What pilot, Carmine?" Otis asked, unable to stay calm.

Carmine barely moved and kept his voice low. "Maybe we don't need to know who or what it is, but to make a great wine, to be a great man, requires a certain amount of . . ."

"Faith?"

"Or trust. You've just lost your way for a while. We've all been there."

Everyone nodded.

"That's why we're here," Sparrow said, "to help you find it again."

Bec took over. "I think you need to take a step back, Otis. Recharge. Rediscover the young man who I met on the bus, the young man who set his eyes on vines for the first time."

"I've heard all this before," Otis said, seeing too much red to hear exactly what they were saying.

The conversation kept going, all of them taking their turns, Otis folding in on himself with each word.

After they'd left, Otis said to Bec, "I've gotta go for a little while. I'll be back. I need some time."

Tears puddled in her eyes.

"I'll be back, I just . . . I need some . . . time." He wanted to thank her, but he couldn't. What she couldn't see was that nothing anyone said could help him now.

～

After four days of hiding out at a hotel overlooking the Pacific while pondering the death of terroir and his own ego, Otis came home and found Rebecca and the boys at the table, eating dinner. Simon and Garfunkel played on the record player. The word *Daddy* sprang from his sons' mouths. Rebecca stood and went to him as if he were actually a good man. She wrapped her arms around him.

"I hear you," he said. "You're right. About all of it. I'm going to try. Harder than ever before."

Her deep breath sounded of relief.

"We can make white zin this year."

She pulled away and touched his cheek. "It's not about that."

"I know, I know, but this is the symbol. This is me letting go. Let's make white zin and let's have some fun doing it. You want me to quit taking myself so seriously. There is no better way." He laughed in a sad way. "No better way at all."

～

As the spring of 1986 gently wrapped her fingers around the hills of Sonoma, Otis stood at the bottling line of a custom crush facility in Santa Rosa and watched twenty thousand cases of bottled white zin get plastered with labels. More than a year had passed since Otis had punched Lloyd.

Giving the effort all he had, Otis had made a wine that he knew was good—in its own way, of course. There was no terroir to speak of. This juice had been made from multiple batches of conventionally farmed overcropped zin that he'd bought from various large vineyards across Sonoma, but he knew it was good and that Americans would absolutely adore it.

Turned out he was right. They sold every case for a ridiculous amount of money, and it required absolutely no travel on his part. He'd called his most loyal distributors, and the conversations had all gone in a similar direction.

"What? Otis Till makes a white zin? Never would I have imagined."

"Me, either, trust me, but we must give the people what they want, right? Are you interested?"

"What's it called?"

"Heartbreak. It's my heart on the label with a crack of lightning across it." He'd almost called it Goldrush, which was the other truth behind the wine.

"I'll take as much as you'll give me."

Times got better from there. Otis started jogging a few times a week and eventually got up to seven or eight miles. He didn't require the bell to remind himself to take breaks, and he took them often. He didn't take one airplane, didn't even drive down into the city. He hid on the ranch and let himself heal. He could feel his body tightening and detoxing. He even joined Rebecca and the boys in meditating, although those occasions were as rare as a full moon—or perhaps a supermoon.

The money poured in. It was enough to take a leap of faith and triple the production of white zin for the '86 harvest, bringing in purchased fruit from other farmers. Was it a gamble? Bec felt sure of the potential, so Otis went along.

The only deep sadness came when Bubbles succumbed to kidney disease. They buried her in the forest and marked the grave with a cross that Cam made with two-by-fours. It was the boys' first introduction to death.

~

Nineteen eighty-seven was a banner year for sales. They sold every damn case of Heartbreak without even shipping samples. Not only was Otis featured in *Wines and Vines* and the *San Francisco Chronicle* and other magazines and papers across the country, but he got his first *Wine Advocate* rating *and* a mention from Sam Bedwetter.

Firstly, the *Advocate* score. Robert Parker had come to town a few months before, and Otis had sent his single vineyard syrah and zins to the wine commission for the tasting. Carmine had warned him not to, as he despised scores, but Otis had shrugged and said, "It couldn't hurt."

Robert Parker gave him two 93s, which were solid numbers and above the pack of other Sonoma and Napa wines he'd rated. Otis thought he'd deserved better, but he'd take it. Wine drinkers now loved scores, and retailers had started posting those scores on shelf-talkers, the small cards with text promoting each wine that hung under bottles on shelves.

Bedwetter's gentle mention wasn't enough to make Otis refer to him by the man's real name, but Otis did feel his pride swell when he read the article. Otis Till of Lost Souls is laughing all the way to the bank with his Heartbreak White Zin. His new SKU is one of the bestselling wines in the country. Sutter Home better pay attention, or he'll steal their shelf placements in grocery stores.

There was no mention of his estate wines, which hurt him some, but Otis did enjoy the idea that the many readers of *The New York Times*, including his father, would see that he'd climbed out of the hole and was getting back on top. He would rather be called a terroir god, but he'd take *laughing all the way to the bank* in the meantime.

Enjoying a taste of not having to worry about money, he decided that he could certainly sacrifice a bit of his soul to feed his children, buy out Lloyd, build a new facility to accommodate the growing production, *and* purchase a few things they needed.

Like a bladder press from Italy. The finest of crusher/destemmers from Germany. A fancy fountain for the courtyard. A vertical of Château Margaux, cases of Dujac and Leroy. Several cases of cru Beaujolais. It felt good to spend money and know that they still had plenty of it.

⁓

A few days before harvest began, Otis was standing in Rebecca's office, chatting with her about the construction plans for the new facility, including their own bottling line, when the phone on her desk rang. Bec picked it up and chatted with the man on the other end for a moment. She covered the mouthpiece as she handed him the phone. "It's Howard from Beltramo's."

Otis took the phone and tried to match Rebecca's charm as he greeted the buyer from one of the best bottle shops in the Bay Area. "Howard, how are you?" He was a heavyset fellow who refused to spit wine, and he was infamous for drinking all day with his distributor reps and finding himself fully drunk by noon. At that point, he would expect someone to take him to lunch. Otis had volunteered more than a few times, and those lunches had often led to dinner and beyond. More to the point, he was a knowledgeable and kind man who never dodged his salespeople and had a long list of wealthy clients. It paid to stay on Howard's good side.

"I know you're not traveling right now, but I have someone who wants to meet you. An important client. You a football fan?"

"Not really. My boys are."

"They might know Joe Montana, the quarterback?"

"Oh, yeah."

"He loves Lost Souls and wants to meet you. Could you come down this weekend?"

Though Otis was no football fan, he perked up at the idea of Joe Montana even knowing his name. Joe had played his way into California stardom.

After the call, he said to Bec, "I'll get some autographs for Mike and Cam, maybe even some tickets. Good seats this time. What do you say?" He'd taken the boys to a few games over the years, and it was no exaggeration to say that the games were the highlight of their lives.

Bec had no qualms, and that Saturday, he drove down to Menlo Park and stepped into Beltramo's. If there was any place he'd want to hunker down after a nuclear attack, it would be here. Otis walked the shelves lined with the finest wines from around the world as if he were strolling through the pearly gates to shake hands with God. With the amount of money Otis had spent here over the years, he should have owned part of it, but the place had been in the Beltramo family since 1882.

In the center stood the discount racks and the more popular SKUs. Otis was glad to see Heartbreak White Zin held a premium endcap position. He didn't like the price, but he'd bring that up with his California distributor later.

Howard stuck out a fat hand. A thick gold bracelet wrapped around his wrist. "So glad you made it down. Joe will be here shortly."

"Thanks for the invite. How are sales?"

Otis hated small talk and hated selling, but he'd learned a thing or two over the years. The two men discussed sales and the latest trends until the door swung open, and then there he stood: Camden and Mike's true hero.

Joe Montana, otherwise known as Joe Cool, wore jeans with brand-new tennis shoes that were as white as Lloyd Bramhall's teeth. Joe was a few years younger than Otis and wasn't much taller. Otis had expected a giant to walk through the doors. He was certainly in better shape, though. The man played humble well and made Otis feel like he was the celebrity. Hell, maybe he was.

"I'm surprised you were able to get away," Otis said. "Busy time of year."

"For you and me both," Joe said. "How's the vintage looking?"

"Could be a great one, depending on what we see in the coming weeks. It's been a hot summer. How's your back?"

"Good as new, thanks." Joe held eye contact for almost too long. "I can't believe we're finally in the same room. Lost Souls speaks to me. I'm a huge fan of Carmine's, and when I read that he'd taught you, I jumped all over it. I have several vintages in my cellar, and I want more."

Trying to not be starstruck, Otis said, "I'm sure we can work that out. How much are you looking for?"

Joe stated a number, and Otis tried hard to stay cool. "I expect we could do that."

After some terroir discussion, with Joe holding his own nicely, Otis said, "You know, you should come up to the winery sometime. Bec and I would love to host you for a long lunch, taste through the older vintages. My boys would love to show you their skills with the pigskin." *Had he just said* pigskin? *Dear Lord.*

Joe gave him a firm handshake with an arm that was ruling the world. "It would be an honor. I'm actually considering how I could get into the biz, so I'd love your advice. In the meantime, how about some tickets to a game?"

"Oh, Cam and Mike would love it."

"Consider it done."

<hr>

Otis sat between his two boys on the fifty-yard line of a 49ers-Oilers game in early November at Candlestick Park. "Your mom would tell me that working hard is not the answer, but let the proof be here. A little hard work never killed anyone. So tell me who's on the field? Which one is San Francisco?"

"You're joking, right?" a fourteen-year-old Cam said. Each year brought more attitude.

"The purple team?"

"Red and gold. Oh, my God."

Michael, now a tween, slapped his forehead.

Otis put his arms around them. "I'm kidding. I know that. And I know that guy behind the helmet—like, actually know him." In truth, Otis was more intrigued with football now that he and Joe had become buds. The quarterback had come up for a lunch during the offseason, and they'd talked business and tasted nearly every wine Otis had ever made. They meandered the grounds, and Joe talked about his aspirations for one day owning his own, and then he'd tossed the football for two young boys who would tell that tale the rest of their life.

As the game progressed, Otis looked around and thought that he might have finally made it. All the hard work had meant something. Maybe, for the first time, he felt worthy. This was the culmination of everything he'd ever done. Sure, the money had come from committing the ultimate sin against his art with Heartbreak, but at least it funded his noble pursuit of bottling the terroir of his Glen Ellen estate.

He'd come such a long way from that puny bloke on the purple bus.

The boys were sugared up and out of control on the way home. Otis had bought nearly every bit of 49ers paraphernalia, and Camden was now hitting Mike with a big red foam hand. The old Otis might have lost his temper, but this Otis was different. He didn't feel anxious today. He felt like, maybe, just maybe, he'd finally learned his lessons and had come into his own.

They pulled into the driveway, and all three of them had big smiles on their faces. "Race you to the—"

Rebecca stepped onto the terrace and descended the steps with drooped shoulders. When she looked up, her eyes told a devastating tale.

Chapter 17

BUILT ON THE BACK OF WHITE ZIN

They held the funeral at Saint Philips in Bozeman. No one mentioned the sparse attendance, though Otis knew it weighed as heavily on his mother as it did him.

Afterward at the ranch, people gathered in the kitchen of Otis's parents' house—one of the two houses on Aunt Morgan's ranch—to celebrate Addison's life. Wide-brimmed hats hung on the outside railing and coatrack; cowboy boots clicked on the hardwoods.

Aunt Morgan held court in the living room, making people laugh amid the sadness. "Did I ever tell you about the time my husband drank a case of Budweiser and decided he was a matador? I didn't find Jim till I came out the next morning to feed the cows. He was laid flat in the bullpen with a welt the size of a cantaloupe on his head." She'd lost Jim—Otis's uncle—years earlier and had found her way through it with remarkable grace.

Cam and Mike played football with several other kids. Rebecca had gotten pulled into a conversation with Otis's one and only girlfriend from all those years ago. *Mortifying* wasn't a strong enough word to capture Otis's cringey feeling. He made chitchat with many of the people he'd come to know in his five or six years living here. When

Otis told them of his wine adventures, most of them had looked at him like he spoke an alien language.

A few literary types showed up, fellow journalists who had worked with Addison. They shared their sweet stories of Addison, and the theme Otis picked up was that his father had always been the first in and the last out. Never had they seen a man with a stronger work ethic.

Otis wasn't sure what to make of it, but his mouth was dry, and he was worn out on conversation when he saw his mother disappearing up the stairs. He followed and found her pushing open the door to her bedroom.

"Mom?"

"I need a break, that's all." Her voice was brittle.

"Yeah, you and me both."

"Come in."

Stepping inside, he breathed in the familiar scent of his parents. Eloise sat on the end of the unmade bed and kicked off her heels, digging her toes into the rug. She'd aged so much, and Otis wondered where the time had gone. It seemed only yesterday that she'd squeezed him goodbye as he departed for California years ago.

Addison's bedside table hosted a stack of books, all nonfiction, including his own. His Rolex rested on a small porcelain plate along with his gold wedding band. On his mother's side, a Bible rested under the soft glow of a petite lamp.

Eloise patted the bed. "Sit with me."

Otis sank into the soft mattress only inches from his mother. She attempted to say something, then let out a long sigh. "I hope you know how much he loved you."

Of all the things she could have said, that was what she chose. "I suppose so. He had to, really."

"He wasn't good at showing it, dear."

Otis chuckled at that, feeling his belly kick with the absolute truth of the statement.

She shook her head for a while, her mind clearly ablaze with . . . what was it? Grief? Regret? Or perhaps simply the bewilderment of what the hell we were doing on this planet for this finite amount of time. That would be more in line with how Otis felt. What was the purpose of it all? His father had lived such an extraordinary life, had done so much, and had died at his desk doing what he loved.

For what, though? All that was left of him was a long trail of words and a closet full of suits and a Rolex and ring that no longer had a home.

"He wasn't happy, Otis. That's the truth of it. He wasn't able to express how he felt for you, because he didn't love himself."

"I think he gave himself a hard time. Held himself to a high standard."

"More like an impossible standard," she corrected.

A need to defend his father came over him. "Yeah, well, he gave up a lot moving here. He gave up so much of his career to help Aunt Morgan after Jim passed." Otis recalled the day they'd closed the door to their London apartment and climbed into a taxi to the airport. "He was a good man for doing that."

"I made him do it."

Otis's head jolted. "What?"

Eloise paused, clearly wondering whether she wanted to say more. "I was about to leave your father, honey. I don't know if I should tell you this or not, but a lesson could be learned. There's something in the Till blood. He had it; his father had it. His grandfather. And you have it. This desperate love of—or is it a need for?—work. He couldn't shake it, and it was tearing us up. He was barely home, and even when he was, he wasn't. You'd beg him to play, to take you out to Hyde Park to kick the football. I'd suggest that he take me on a date. Maybe do something special for an anniversary. Sometimes he'd find the time, but mostly he worked. Christmas Eve, Christmas Day, New Year's. The news always came first. He was a good man, your father, but he wasn't a good father or husband, and he'd stopped taking care of himself that last year in London. He was down to one hundred and thirty pounds when we left."

Otis swallowed back an eruption of confusion, not recalling such frailty on the trip to Montana. "He was a pretty good dad."

"No, honey, he wasn't. Not then. He tried, but he wasn't. I was leaving him. I drew a line in the sand. Your uncle was sick, and I wanted to go back home. To get you away from what your dad was doing to himself. He relented, because he did love us. He wanted to be a better man than he was, but he held the move over my head till his last breath."

His mother had obviously gotten some of this wrong. "Oh, c'mon, he was . . . he did it for the family."

The pitch of her voice rose. "Because I forced him. Always in the back of his mind, he wondered what could have been, what he might have accomplished back in London. Always in his head, he was living that alternate reality."

"Thinking that maybe he shouldn't have gotten married or had me?"

She stretched her feet out. "Or wondering why I couldn't have just let him do his thing."

Otis let go of his mother's hand and stood. "I think you're grieving, Mom, and seeing things in an uglier way than they were."

Eloise locked eyes with her son. "He let whatever it was that was hanging over his head defeat him. He didn't like himself. He was never happy or satisfied. It was always on to the next thing. It was never ever enough. He died lonely and sad . . . his fingers on his typewriter, halfway through an article about how Interstate 90 needed repairs. I asked him to take me out to lunch; he said he was too under the gun with a deadline. Now I'm left wondering the point of all those words he left. That's all he talked about, his words and his deadlines."

Otis stared into the middle space, lost in thought.

"His only interactions with you were his desperate attempts to steer you toward the success he never realized for himself."

Otis sifted through her meaning, a miner looking for flakes of gold.

"All the while," she continued, "he was getting it wrong."

Otis pulled back the curtains of the window and looked out over the ranch. Cattle grazed in high grass. Snowcapped mountains shot up with jagged edges on the horizon.

"What do I know, Otis? I try not to give you advice. Your father had enough for both of us, but I don't want you thinking of him as your hero any longer. I don't need Rebecca to tell me how hard you've been going."

"He's not my hero. Hasn't been in a long time."

"I don't want you to end up like him. That's all."

_____

On the plane back, Otis sat between the two boys. Bec had the seat across the aisle. Mike wore headphones, and Otis had asked him to turn down the music several times. Whatever it was, it was heavy. Metallica or something like that. Otis and Rebecca had talked endlessly about letting him listen to such intense music, and after multiple conversations with Mike, they'd realized it seemed to pacify his mind. How could they take that away?

In the last year or so, he'd been quite down about himself and his lack of friends. Whenever Otis spoke to Rebecca on the phone from the road, Mike was the first topic she'd bring up. She'd say while sobbing that Mike was exhibiting a lot of the same behavior Jed had as a kid. "I'm worried about him," she'd say. "He's not happy." When Otis was back home, he would try to talk to him, but Mike was too closed off to share his feelings.

Otis sipped on a virgin Bloody Mary and was making conversation with Cam, who was pretty good about connecting with his dad for a teenager. He wouldn't let his parents hug him in public, but he seemed to understand that he needed to try because Otis was trying. In that way, they were able to have some often-lovely chats about life.

"Dad, can I tell you something?"

"Oh, boy. Don't tell me you're getting married."

"Worse." He pushed up the drink tray and locked it in place. Then he peered over at his dad. "I don't want to go into the wine business. I don't want to take over the farm."

Otis nearly spilled his drink, but he collected himself quickly. "That's . . . you don't need to make that decision now."

Camden lowered the tray back down. "I know it's what you want. That it's your dream for Mike and me to take over the farm. It's not my thing, though."

It took everything Otis had to hide his sadness. He recalled Cam's enthusiasm as they worked together to build his own little winery on their property in Sonoma. Where had Otis gone wrong? Had he pushed too hard?

"I understand," Otis finally said, but inside, maybe he didn't understand. He could only hope that Camden would have a change of heart. He still had a long way to go before he had to commit to a profession.

⌒

The winter of 1987 to '88 was a blur. Addison's death and Eloise's words on the day of the funeral hung over Otis. He buried himself in work and was short with Bec and the boys, and even the workers. Any attempted apologies fell flat.

"I know I'm being awful," he told Bec during the first week of the new year. "Please know that I'm trying."

"You know I have all the patience in the world," she said in a weary tone, "but it's wearing thin. You're allowed to grieve, but you still have to love the ones you're with. Though you were physically here, you weren't actually here during the holidays. How many more Christmases do we have with the boys? And I don't know, maybe you should allow yourself to grieve more, as opposed to distracting yourself, running around like everything is on fire."

A burn flared up in his chest. "My father just died, Bec. Cut me some slack." He knew better than anyone that all she'd ever done was cut him slack. That's what she did with everyone. For some ungodly reason, she surrounded herself with broken people and then fed them slack like she was helping a climber rappel down a rock face.

Bec wisely ignored his defensiveness, which only made Otis angrier—at himself, more than at anyone else. "Let's not forget all this money pouring in, the success we're having. Do you know how many wineries out there would kill for it?" He fired his index finger into the air. "That doesn't happen if I'm sitting around stewing in my grief." Every word that escaped his mouth fueled his self-loathing.

It was true, though; they'd become unstoppable.

His growing friendship with Joe Montana didn't hurt their momentum. Photos of Joe drinking Lost Souls were as good as marketing could get. Other celebrities began to contact Otis, and all of a sudden, he was experiencing his own celebrity. Especially around San Francisco. He knew every chef in town. None of them would let him pay for a meal. Instead, they'd come out and shave fresh truffles on his pasta or pour him four fingers of Pappy Van Winkle. Otis got that level of respect everywhere he went.

Rebecca wanted nothing to do with it. She told him that she had to take care of the boys and the farm and that she wasn't interested in going out on the road and schmoozing.

Otis bought a convertible BMW 325i and slapped a ZINMAN license plate on the back. He'd don a silk scarf, crisp white button-down, khakis, and loafers and drive his new car fast up and down the coast. Not even a couple of speeding tickets slowed him down. He'd splash into San Francisco, catch up with some of the big retailers, and take them out on the town, thanking them for all the hard work.

He knew he had to stay away from his family till he got it together. He didn't want to poison them with the pain he felt inside. What his mother had said about his father's failures stuck to him like flypaper. Had she been confused?

Otis made a bold decision. Being a successful winemaker required following trends, and now that he'd sold his soul to the devil with white zinfandel, other lines began to blur.

Robert Parker's *Wine Advocate* continued to grow in popularity, and many new writers had started scoring wines on the one-hundred-point system. Though Otis didn't agree with attempting to objectify wine, he also knew that high scores made life much easier.

Whenever he nabbed high scores, the phones rang. He could hike the price, and no one would balk. Or, if they did, he'd say, "I'm sure I can find another home for it." He became a shrewd businessman—and winemaker—in that way.

Fortunately, the recipe to make a high-scoring wine wasn't too difficult to follow: Pick the grapes late; add enzymes to enhance color, flavors, and texture; age in new oak barrels; add back a touch of sugar and gum arabic; and then sterile filter the holy hell out of it . . . and whatever else it took to make the wines big and bold, giving them the oomph they needed to stand out in a tasting. You wanted someone to pull the cork and be knocked over by the power of the juice. If you could do that, then the critics would eat it up.

Otis had already begun to succumb to the temptation. During the previous harvest, with hurt feelings over the 93-point ratings he'd received, Otis had picked his estate fruit later than usual, at higher Brix. An element of shame pierced his soul as he walked his land, but he kept telling himself that a few years of this would mean even his grandkids would never have to work again.

His sins didn't stop there. Once the wines had fermented, he'd racked them into all brand-new, heavy toast French oak barrels, which would over time soften and smoothen out the tannins and impart notes of graham cracker and toasted marshmallow, along with seductive vanilla and baking spice flavors. This practice was a far cry from his previous regimen of using mostly used barrels, which didn't mask the expressive fruit and allowed the geography to shine. Now that terroir was dead—and it was—what the hell.

In March, he decided to push it even further by transferring the wines into yet *another* set of brand-new barrels, a proverbial touch of additional plastic surgery that would make this particular vintage absolutely irresistible to consumers and critics alike. Otis was no longer capturing a time and place in a bottle; he was the Willy Wonka of wine, the King of Smooth, bottling fluffy clouds of cotton candy that might garner the first 101-point rating in history. *Otis Till has made the first wine that's actually beyond perfect!* There would be no authenticity to speak of, but who cared anyway? It was all one big sham. If he was going to abandon his beliefs, why not drive a Lamborghini while doing so?

Otis didn't tell a soul—not even Bec. It would be too hard to say out loud. Only the vineyard crew and cellar rats could see what he was doing, and he found himself avoiding eye contact with them when he gave them the latest instructions. "Make it smoother than smooth, fellas," he'd say, knowing they'd all be happy when he handed them their fat bonuses.

Distributors started giving Otis a hard time for ignoring them, and that was the excuse he used when he said he had to start traveling again soon. Escaping the man he'd become on his own land was closer to the truth. There were days when he'd walk through the rows and notice that the reverberant whisper of his farm had gone silent.

"Just a few months of working the market," he told Bec. "My face is being forgotten. The white zin market's crowded. I want to stay front of mind. Besides, I don't even know if the trend will continue. We can't start getting lazy." He often found a way to sneak in another barb. "Don't forget, this was your idea, building this empire."

Perhaps in the back of his mind, he did sound like his father, making up excuses to keep working. He tried to remember his childhood. He sought clues to his parents' unhappiness. How in God's name had they fooled him into thinking that it had been Addison's decision to move? Eloise had made it seem like he was a hero. She'd painted this version of Addison for him, that he was the greatest man to walk the earth.

Then, in a few short words, she'd cut it all down.

Starting in April, Otis hit the road. He'd land in a town hungover and drop his bags at a hotel; then one of the reps for the distributor would drive him around all day to meet with the most powerful buyers in each city. Otis had found that he was far more personable after a nip of wine, so he didn't spit when he tasted with them, even if it was ten in the morning. By eleven, he'd have a nice buzz and would wax poetic about his practices in the vines to buyers who gathered around him at long tables in back rooms of restaurants like he was the final word on terroir.

It was in the bathroom of Le Bernardin, an exquisite restaurant in Manhattan led by the genius chef Eric Ripert, when Otis's backslide took an even worse turn. He was on a whirlwind trip on the East Coast and hadn't been home in three weeks. Having decided to embrace his artistic side, he wore a flashy silk shirt with a few buttons undone to expose a gold chain. He was there to meet with all the higher-ups from his new distributor.

One thing he'd started doing in the late eighties was replacing distributors. They'd started getting lazy on him, and he had no room for it. "Don't tell me sales are down. I'm giving you something easy to sell. And look at the scores!"

They were sipping on Manhattans and about to order dinner when one of the reps slid a bag of cocaine into Otis's hand. He hadn't touched it in years, not since a trip to Chicago years before, but nothing kept him from it tonight. The truth was that he was exhausted. He was out of energy and tired of talking to people, tired of being in the spotlight. Three weeks on the road, and he'd barely slept, and he couldn't keep up the facade much longer. No quantity of Manhattans or Negronis would help.

He took the bag into the bathroom, rolled up a bill, and sniffed a line as long as his middle finger. Woo, it woke him up. Suddenly all that weariness disappeared, and he returned to the table more charming than he'd ever been.

Easing back into the seat with confidence, a smile on his face, he said, "I ever tell you about the time Carmine Coraggio dumped dirt into a glass of my first wine and then tossed it back without a care?"

Otis couldn't believe how all eyes went to him as he spoke. Sometimes he forgot what he'd achieved. Not many winemakers would ever reach such a level of success. It felt so good that he sneaked back to the bathroom three more times.

The next morning he peeled himself from the bed of his suite at the St. Regis—still dressed from the night before—and realized he must have forgotten to set his alarm. He was first up presenting at the general sales meeting.

With his hair wet from a shower, he rushed out the door. Bits and pieces of what had happened after dinner slowly came back to him in the taxi. A late-night show at the Village Vanguard. Or was it the Blue Note? Countless more cocktails. Otis recalled slapping down his American Express card multiple times to cover the bill. He dreaded looking through the receipts in his wallet to see the damage done. Bec would certainly have something to say upon his return. He had terribly vague memories of nearly getting into a bar brawl, and there was also a possibility that he'd thrown up into a trash can in Times Square, but maybe that had been a dream.

Twenty minutes later, Otis leaped up the stairs of an office building in SoHo, where everyone waited for him. He stood in front of forty sales reps and several managers and only then realized that his fingers were shaking. On the table beside him waited his wines.

"Well, here we are. I can't lie. I had a late one last night. Le Bernardin and then who knows what." He wiped his brow, capturing a layer of sweat. "Hair of the dog anyone?" He pulled the cork from the first wine and poured himself a glass, then tossed it back.

Once the liquid soothed him, he looked up. "Well, that did it. I'm back, folks. Back for more. Where are we having lunch?"

Everyone laughed, and Otis began to pass around his wine, so that each person could pour their own.

"I suppose there's a reason that I'm best staying back home and working the fields. In all honesty, I've been on the road too long, but it's important. I want to meet you guys, see who's out there pushing my juice so that I can keep doing what I do. I appreciate your help, and all that I can offer is to give my all every year in the vineyards . . . and then climb out from my cave every once in a while for a visit."

He poured himself another glass. "My land, my farm . . . I treat her like a princess. We've had our years, our challenges, but I've learned that the more love I give her, the more she responds. The more these wines speak. We've been to hell and back, but I think she's coming around now, giving us vintages that we'll never forget."

Otis carried on for a long time, and when he finished, everyone gave him a standing ovation. In the back of his mind, he knew it was all bullshit. Just as he knew what people wanted to drink, what critics wanted to praise, he knew exactly how to spin his pitches. In truth, if his land could talk, she'd berate him for what he was doing, what he'd become.

But it was too late now. Just too late.

~

By the time he returned to Glen Ellen, he was a wreck. Rebecca's jaw fell open when he stumbled into the front door with his bags. Even his boys noticed.

He slept for two days, barely coming out of the room. Rebecca finally came in and peeled back the blinds. It was July; the last few months were a blur.

"Okay, that's enough, Otis. Get out of bed and get back to reality."

He wiped the sleep from his eyes. "Come climb in with me."

She shook her head.

He realized then that he was in the guest bedroom. "Bec, we haven't slept together in months." He felt himself swelling under the sheets, his libido in desperate need.

"I wonder why." Of course he knew why.

She opened the rest of the curtains and walked to the door. "Mike has trumpet lessons at eleven. You're taking him. Later, we need to go into town for school supplies and some new clothes. Camden has nothing to wear."

"Can you buy me a couple of more days?"

She didn't even respond and turned to leave the room. Otis rolled over and closed his eyes again. He kept an eye on the clock, and at ten thirty he stepped into the shower, then found himself in the mirror.

It felt like the first time he'd seen himself that year. He hadn't shaved in a few days. Black rings collected under his eyes. New wrinkles ran across his forehead. Damn, forty was coming on him quickly.

"Let's go, Dad!" Otis heard from down the hall.

He slapped himself and then raced to the closet to find something to wear.

Once he and Mike were in the BMW, Otis asked, "Since when did you start playing trumpet?"

Mike was almost eleven now, almost a bloody teenager, and Otis had seen firsthand with Camden what it was like to raise a boy going through puberty. Click the seat belt and close your eyes! Michael's voice hadn't dropped, but pimples had collected on his brow. He was a handsome little devil, thick dark hair and bright-blue eyes. If only a shadow didn't follow him around.

"I got tired of the trombone," he said in a monotone voice.

"You look good, son. Tell me what else is new. I'm so sorry I've been gone, but I'm done for a while now."

"You look strung out."

Otis's eyebrows curled. "Strung out? What do you know about strung out?"

His son shrugged. Kids knew way too much for their own good.

"Have you talked to Joe Montana lately?" he asked.

Otis was glad that Mike was willing to speak with him. It wasn't always that way. "Not in a while."

"I think they're going to win it all this year."

"Yeah, they're looking good, aren't they?" Otis had no idea how they were looking, but he'd pretended that he knew when folks around the country had brought it up. He'd caught himself more than once bragging about his budding friendship with Joe, even mentioning a time or two that they'd considered a project together.

Which was true. Nothing had been set in stone, but Joe kept pushing. Otis kind of liked stringing the quarterback along a little bit, staying on equal footing, as it were.

—

Otis spent the afternoon with his family in Santa Rosa. They ate tacos at their favorite Mexican place, then dropped into the drugstore for school supplies and stepped into a couple of clothing shops for the boys. Then, while the kids went into Sound Control, the CD store, Bec and Otis got a chance to talk.

Otis sat on a bench and motioned for her to join him. She sat a good three feet away. She would turn forty in the next few years, but no one would have known it. While Otis had been digging his grave with red meat and drugs, she'd been living off the land, meditating, and doing everything she could to take care of herself. The only sign of her age and of her weariness with Otis and raising children and taking care of her extended family was in her eyes, in the way the bright light that had always glowed deep in the galaxies of her pupils had slightly dimmed.

Though she dressed with more sophistication, she was still a hippie at heart, still barefooted and braless most of the time, still listening to the latest music and insisting that vinyl was better than CDs, still fine with taking an evening toke—but only once the kids were asleep.

"I know you're not happy with me."

She let out a staccato laugh that she'd been holding back for years. "What makes you think that?"

"Hey, it's not been easy. I'm coming back. I'm here." He reached for her hand. "I'm not going anywhere."

She withdrew her hand and rested it on her lap. "Come November, right?"

"No, that's not what I'm saying."

"I don't know what you're doing on the road, and maybe I don't want to know, but it's gotta stop."

Tired of having to defend himself, he said, "I'm doing what it takes to sell wine."

She cut a quick look at him, then diverted her attention back to the storefront. "Mike said you didn't even realize he played trumpet. Is there any wonder why he's sad? He misses his dad."

"I thought he was still playing the trombone. Come on, same thing. Trumpet, trombone. You can't put what he's been going through on me. That's not fair."

"Otis, he's struggling. He needs his dad, right now. Maybe if my dad had been there for Jed, then . . . then things would be different."

Otis didn't even touch that comment. "He has me. I'm giving him everything I can. I'm giving him security. Remember, that's the thing you told me you wanted them to have above all else. I've made that happen."

Michael and Camden and Rebecca needed more than that now. Otis knew it as well as anyone.

He sat back and crossed his legs, threw an arm up on the back of the bench. His fingers grazed her shoulder. "Believe me, I don't want to travel anymore. I'm home."

"Jed's using again. I can't have you getting lost in the same cave. You owe us more than that."

"I'm not using."

She stood. "You need to get your shit together, or we're going to have a problem."

"Don't do this, Bec. Is that a threat?"

She didn't turn back.

Damned if the 49ers didn't make it to the Super Bowl, and damned if Joe Montana didn't call Otis and offer him a ticket. "I wish I had one for each of the boys and for your wife, but I'm limited."

"No, I understand. And thank you. You know I'll be there."

Otis should have anticipated Bec's reaction. They were in their bathroom getting ready for the day. Otis wore a monogrammed twill robe with matching slippers, a gift he'd recently given himself. A man of his stature should look good in the morning.

He'd decided to hit her with the news while she was fresh. "It'll be the only trip I do this year." It was a hard promise to make, considering it was January 4.

Bec had been wearing a robe lately. The woman who had always slept and got ready in the morning naked now shielded herself from her husband. Yeah, he knew what she was doing, that she was repulsed by him, that she didn't want him looking at her body. Forgive him for still being attracted to his wife, for wanting to look her up and down like the old days.

"I don't like who you're becoming," she said, "and you're fooling yourself. You were barely here for the holidays. The boys don't know who you are. ZINMAN. That's the person you've become. Who has a license plate like that? And the robe and those slippers. We all know what you're doing in the fields and in the cellar, picking later, manipulating the juice, over-oaking it, doing *everything* you never would have done a few years ago. I hate to crush you, but the wines aren't even that interesting this year."

Now that hurt. "You're just mad at me, so you're not tasting them with an open mind." He stuck his toothbrush in his mouth before he reminded her for the one zillionth time that he—and her stupid fucking boyfriend—had forced him to make white zin.

"No," she said, "that's not it."

Once he'd finished brushing, he spat the paste into the basin. "Well, I tried to get the boys tickets. Joe only had one."

"Then stay home and watch it with them. Why do you have to go to Miami?" Bec reached for her brush.

"For one, I was invited by the quarterback of the 49ers to attend the Super Bowl. This isn't just a game. This is the event of the year."

"You hate football."

"It's growing on me. Besides, it's about being seen. Joe said he might even be able to get me an introduction to the marketing guys at TAG Heuer. Can you imagine? Your husband, that punk you met on a purple bus, becoming the face of a watch brand."

"You know what? I far prefer that punk on the bus to who you are now."

Otis stuck his toothbrush under the running water and ran his thumb over the bristles with ferocious intensity. "Do we have a problem here? You seem to be dropping some serious threats."

"What do you think, Otis?"

Otis began to lather his face with shaving cream. "I think you're worn out and need some help. Let's hire an assistant, someone to run the kids around. Cook some meals. You're exhausted and taking it out on me."

Rebecca squared up to him. "Fuck you, Otis."

Then, per the usual lately, she stalked away.

Otis didn't feel regret as he boarded the direct flight from SFO to MIA. He flew first class, and he sipped on Woodford Reserve the entire flight. He didn't feel regret when he stepped out of the airport and slid on his shades, nor when he checked into the Four Seasons, the exact hotel where the 49ers were staying. He thought nothing of it when he pulled open the minibar in his suite.

This was what he deserved. You make sacrifices so that you can one day reap the rewards. No way would he turn down this opportunity. The tropical air was ripe with the Super Bowl madness, and what came with it was this wonderful sense of arrival. Everyone with a ticket to that game had *arrived* in their own way, taking their place on the podium of life.

What an absolute tragedy that his father had died before actually knowing who Otis had become. Sure, Addison might have worked too hard and put a lot of pressure on Otis to achieve what he hadn't, but it had worked. Whatever he'd done, it had worked, and now Otis had finally done it. Achieved his wildest dreams.

By the time he claimed his reserved table at Joe's Stone Crab in South Beach, he was properly sozzled. A quick Negroni warmed him up even more. His words stumbled out of his mouth as he ordered a loaded baked potato, creamed spinach, and a twenty-ounce New York strip done Oscar style.

"Live like you're gonna die, ol' boy," Otis told the young server, who then tried to push a ridiculously priced cult Napa cab on him. "No, no, a bottle of that Château Lynch-Bages would be a far better pairing."

One in the morning, Otis woke in a sweat and kicked off the covers with a curse. After a stumble to the toilet, he turned down the air-conditioning to sixty. Back in the bed, his mind started racing, so he flipped on the television for a while. Tomorrow would be murder if he didn't fall back asleep. Thirty minutes later, he popped a benzo and chased it with a mini bottle of Crown. *Finally*, he faded away.

⁓

Over an indulgent room-service breakfast and a pot of coffee, Otis read the new Sam Ledbetter article in *The New York Times*.

In the article, Bedwetter highlighted several of his favorite producers, then got to Lost Souls. Otis's hangover quickly took second place to rage.

> I tasted through Lost Souls' lineup recently and was
> not surprised to find the wines syrupy and overdone. I

suspect this trend has been happening for a long time. Till's Heartbreak White Zin was proof that he's in it for the money, and now I believe he's pandering to the critics. Perhaps I shall ask: Who could blame him? Otis Till could urinate into a bottle, and his loyal followers would happily lap it up.

When Otis called Rebecca, he was drunk off three Bloody Marys. "Bedwetter strikes again."

"What, Otis? It's early here."

"I know. Sorry. But I had to tell you. Listen to what he said." Otis read the entire mention. "Can you believe that?"

She sighed. "I don't care, Otis. I'm so tired of you going to war with this man. Are you drunk? You're slurring."

"No, I'm not drunk. It's eight in the morning."

"Okay, well, I'm going back to bed. Forget about the article and be safe, okay?"

"I love you," he said.

The phone clicked.

The thing was . . . there were times when being in the doghouse was an acceptable trade-off. Any male in his right mind would agree that attending the Super Bowl made up for the punishment. *Give me a Super Bowl in Miami, and, honey, you can put me in the doghouse for a month!*

⌒

Over seventy-five thousand people were crammed into Joe Robbie Stadium. Otis had club seats with access to the full bar in a fine lobby with a crowd of celebrities. He took a double Crown and Coke and a hot dog and sat down on the fifty-yard line. People wore costumes. They'd painted their faces and bodies. The air was electric.

Otis was properly drunk and had a hard time seeing the jersey numbers, but he made out number sixteen taking the field. "Joe!" he yelled. "Let's go get 'em!" The whole crowd roared with him.

"He's my friend!" Otis yelled. "Let's go, Joe Cool!"

He looked beside him to see his boys' reactions, and then remembered they weren't there. They would have loved this. He wondered who was at the house for the Super Bowl back home. He hadn't even asked. Maybe they'd see him on television.

He took a long sip of his drink, then another.

Sitting back down, he bit into the hot dog. Relish. Mustard. Ketchup. And regret.

That's what he tasted. It was a meager hot dog, but it was so much more, taking him back through the years to all the hot dogs they'd eaten and the hard work they'd put in to get to where they were. Never could he have done any of it without Bec.

He looked at the bozos on either side of him, wishing that she and the boys were there.

Regret.

He shouldn't have come.

It was as if he'd been ice-skating on a frozen lake, happy and carefree; then at once a crack had formed. Then another.

He looked down at the hot dog, the red and yellow and green. The countless hot dogs they'd eaten when they'd first started chasing this wild dream appeared before him. Here they were, they'd finally—

No. Here *he* was.

They'd made it, but he was here by himself.

Another sip of Crown, then another. The thoughts wouldn't go away.

A big play happened on the field, and everyone jumped to their feet.

Otis stayed in his seat, staring at the hot dog. What his mother had said back in Bozeman rang in his ears, about how his father had died at his typewriter, having skipped out on a lunch with her, so that he could finish a piece about road construction.

Was this any different? He could not have cared less about being here, about who might win. But he felt like he *should* attend this game as a successful entrepreneur. How could he say no to Joe?

His chest felt heavy, and his body began to tingle, like when he'd had his heart attack years ago.

Otis set down the drink and hot dog and stood. He pushed through the aisle, people's knees angling sideways, and when he got to the steps, he started running.

"I'm coming," he said. Quiet, at first. "I'm coming, my loves." Tears pricked his eyes, and he ran harder, up and down the steps and out of Joe Robbie Stadium and into a waiting taxi.

"I just want to go home," he said, his face now a mess of tears.

"Where's home?" the cab driver asked.

"Where Bec and my boys are . . ."

Chapter 18 (Interlude)

THE MENTEE

Red Mountain, Washington State
April 2011

I thought I'd lost him. The boys were old enough to think it too. How many more times could I keep answering their questions with "Your father's grieving. He'll be okay"?

Otis came back from Miami a new man, though. As he sits at his desk now, almost three weeks after finding Amigo, a hint of a smile plays on his face. Despite all the regret I know he feels, the same regret that ate at him in the years after coming back from the Super Bowl, I can detect the gratitude he feels for having climbed out from the darkness.

I didn't know about the cocaine. Not till now, as I read the words over his shoulder. Of course I suspected that he'd experimented on the road, but I didn't ask—didn't want to know. What with Jed's substance abuse issues, I might not have been able to handle it.

I suppose I'm reliving with him, and I feel no need to scold him. What I feel is unbridled joy. We went through the wringer, but we came out the other side. Not unscathed, mind you. No, not at all, but we did come out on the other side.

If I might say something about my sweet Otis, it's that he was such a focused man, that balance was hard for him. While he spent those first years in Sonoma breaking his back for his terroir, then the next few focused on growing our finances, he returned to Sonoma with an entirely different attitude.

As much as you don't want your husband to overwork, you certainly don't want him to underwork either. I loved Otis and adored having him around, especially when he was in a good place, but there comes a point. I didn't need him telling me how to better organize our finances, or how to manage the starter for my bread. I certainly didn't need him involved in the laundry, because thanks to his efforts, he, Camden, and Mike were all running around with pink underwear.

Upon his return, I could tell something had broken inside. Teary eyed and vulnerable, he had assured me that he'd finally realized how lost he'd been and that he was dedicated to change. He started to tell me about his life on the road, but I'd shushed him. "I don't want to know, Otis. All that matters is what you do going forward."

I'm not surprised cocaine was part of the equation. Though he's had his bouts of drinking too much, he would always dry out, taking months off at a time after being on the road and spitting when he tasted. Now I know there was something else at play. It makes sense that Otis started being kinder to Jed, taking him out to lunch, inviting him over, teaching him how to drive the tractor. I wonder what conversations they had, as Jed started to show a transformation then too.

It's April. The winds have died down. The Red Mountain sun has begun to warm the dusty soil. Days are longer. Otis still isn't doing much. He takes Amigo out to play in the yard. He checks in on the animals, though the vineyard guys do most of the work. My husband still hasn't gone up to the winery since Mike and I died. If it weren't for Brooks, those wines would be in trouble.

Otis picks up the pen, and I look forward to seeing where he goes from here, jumping into those happier times. Before ink meets the page, the front doorbell rings.

It's Brooks. A lightness comes over me. There aren't many better men in the world than him, and I know that he's doing everything to bring Otis back. As hardheaded as Otis can be, it certainly takes a village.

~

At the sound of the bell, Otis whipped his head around. He was in no shape to see anyone. By God, he hadn't looked in the mirror in days, but he could imagine what he'd encounter. Nevertheless, he scooped up Amigo and put him in his crate, then headed to the door.

Brooks stood there. Tattoos from his years as a runaway troublemaker branded his body. He once had a sadness in his eyes, a lost sense about him, but in the five years since he'd been working with Otis, a glimmer of hope and even excitement had started to sparkle. Otis considered the young man a third son; Brooks looked up to him as a father figure.

"You're not answering my calls," Brooks said.

"Yeah, my phone's probably not charged." His voice came out in an ugly croak.

"How's Amigo?"

Otis turned back to the inside of his house. "He's coming back to life. Gaining weight. Cast comes off in three weeks."

"Then?"

Otis cleared his throat, tasting stale tobacco. "I guess I walk him up the mountain and see what happens. I hear his family out there, calling for him. Hopefully he'll make it." Amigo had been a steady companion, and the idea of not having him in the house was unsettling.

"He's doing better than you, then," Brooks said. It wasn't a question.

Otis gave a weak laugh. "He's far more on the mend."

Brooks looked at him so long that Otis had to turn away. "Don't worry about me."

"Are you kidding? Look at you, Otis. Everyone's worried about you."

"No need to be. A man can grieve, can't he?"

"Of course, but you need more sunlight. A shower. You need to let people visit with you. The whole mountain is worried. You're the leader."

Otis laughed. "If this mountain is counting on me right now, I don't know what to say. You're all in trouble. My time has passed."

Concern rang in Brooks's tone. "Would you let me say something like that? Do I need to remind you how you found me, the shape I was in? Now it's my turn. I understand a man must grieve, but there comes a time when you have to put one foot in front of the other. Let's start with the wines. You haven't even asked about them."

"I haven't agreed to forge ahead."

"I won't allow too many more days to go by. I'll drag you out of here kicking and screaming if I have to."

Otis mustered the courage to find Brooks's eyes for a moment. "I don't want to know about the wines. I . . ." His heart slowed to a drip.

"It was your last vintage with her. You have to care."

Otis tightened. "Do not tell me what I have to do."

"Oh, I know I can't do that, but you'll one day regret it if these wines don't sing. You're going to want to remember what you and Bec did your last year together."

"Why would I want to do that?"

Brooks's silence won the argument.

"What's it been, five years with me? You know as much as I do about wine."

"Hardly." Brooks took in a breath. "I need your help. The syrah, the cab. Even the merlot, they're not coming to life. There's a dullness to them. It's almost like they know what's going on . . . like they're waiting on you too."

Otis chuckled. *It's going to be a long wait,* he thought.

"I know it's only been a couple of months, but you can't keep hiding. We have work to do."

"I have nothing left to give."

Brooks crossed his arms defiantly. "Do you really believe that? You talk like you're in your eighties. You're not even sixty."

Otis raised a hand. "While I appreciate the pep talk, I need the time I need. Right now I don't want to taste the goddamn wines that mark the end of what I had left."

"What would Bec say?"

Fury shot up Otis's back. "Don't bring her into it."

Brooks nodded. "I apologize, but someone has to say it. She wouldn't want this. It's time you finished what you started. Get out there and show these people what you're made of. Red Mountain's not done with you, not by a long shot. This vintage in barrel now needs you. The vines need you."

Otis studied his apprentice. "I don't know what to tell you, Brooks."

"Consider this notice then. Clean yourself up. I'm coming for you. The only way out is through."

Oh, there was more than one way out, but he didn't say that to Brooks. What he saw reflected in Brooks's eyes was a man too ashamed to walk out that door and try to pretend the world would keep spinning.

Because no.

It would not.

Chapter 19

WELCOME TO THE NINETIES

Otis had something to prove in the year after the 49ers won the Super Bowl. He had to show his family that they mattered, and he had to prove to himself that he could take a step back and recalibrate. What was all this for if he lost the ones he loved?

He'd been slipping for a long time, and that had to stop.

Now.

For the first time since he'd jumped on this terroir merry-go-round, he didn't help Scooter and the team prune. Instead, he made the family breakfast, including masterful cappuccinos for the adults, then dressed in casual, unflashy clothes with Birkenstocks and took the boys to school. He ran or lifted weights for an hour afterward. Then he'd devote much of his day to Bec, sometimes sharing a late-morning second-round coffee, or taking her out to lunch, or simply a long wander through the hills. He committed to meditation in the afternoons, but mostly it led to napping.

He also took her into the city to see music: David Crosby, Paul McCartney, REO Speedwagon, the Grateful Dead. Otis thought that the Grateful Dead were a lot like Carmine, making art that took a moment to understand, but if you gave them the time, then you'd find a world of wonder between the notes. As a family of four, they went to see the Red Hot Chili Peppers and Radiohead and Green Day, and Otis hadn't even used earplugs.

While leading this improved life, which included working his way through a few of the spiritual books on Rebecca's shelf, an idea started to form in his mind. He wanted to be as minimalist as possible with the wines. Hands off. If he was meant to work less, then, oh, he'd do that. They had money, so now he could simply play around, see what the vines and wines did when set free. He committed to doing as little as possible, an experiment of postmodern philosophy.

It was his family who needed him now.

Mike had grown into a lanky thirteen-year-old with cropped black hair, rather pronounced ears, and angular features all around. Tall for his age, despite Bec's height, he excelled as a forward in basketball and had a mean three-pointer. He also had an innate gift for engineering and mechanics. What had started as a love of building blocks had turned into him taking apart anything he could get his hands on.

But he still often went to a dark place. He would get lost in his head and spend chunks of time in his room, cranking loud music. He'd often skip dinner, saying he wasn't hungry. Sometimes he'd beg to call in sick to school. Rebecca would worry over him constantly, endlessly comparing him to Uncle Jed, worrying that her son might follow a similar path.

Otis gave Mike as much time as he could, attending Mike's basketball games, grabbing him after school and taking him for a sundae, going for hikes, and even working together on the farm and in the cellar. While Cam had made it clear that he wanted nothing to do with the wine business, Mike seemed to be gearing up for it. He could and often did change the oil and brakes on the tractors and farm trucks, and he was nearly as adept as Otis and Scooter at fixing the bottling line, the press, the irrigation equipment, or anything else on the property.

As far as Cam, he had only one more year of high school before setting off to college. Otis tried to feel grateful that he still had some time to connect with his son before he set off into the world. He looked far more like his mother, with sandy-blond shaggy hair and a rounded handsome face with electric eyes that had turned him into a magnet for the girls. Somewhere during tenth grade, he'd decided he'd rather chase them than running backs, so he no longer played organized sports.

Cam had chosen CU Boulder, the campus tucked up against a vast wilderness. He was still far happier out in the woods, a long way from everyone. He and his friends loved camping and would take off after school on Fridays to go backpacking and fly-fishing. Otis's idea of camping was spending the weekend at an expensive resort along the coast that had a lovely wine list and an adults-only pool, but he sacrificed his comfort to join Camden on a trip up to the South Fork Eel River to fish for steelhead trout, or, as Camden called them, "steelies." Otis slept exactly zero minutes on the first night but bit his lip as he hovered near the fire the next morning and didn't complain at all. Thank goodness Cam had learned how to make a wonderful cup of coffee over the fire.

Otis didn't know the first thing about fly-fishing, but Camden taught him with admirable patience. They stayed for three nights, hunting steelies by day and sitting around the fire by night. Though Otis far preferred roughing it in the L'Auberge de Sedona as opposed to a few meager hours of interrupted sleep followed by ridding his bowels in the woods, he wouldn't have traded anything for that trip. He even caught a fish, which delivered him unexpected delight.

"Dad, do you think Mike's going to be okay?" Cam asked on the way back home. Otis was proud of himself for not even mentioning the fish smell currently permeating his BMW.

It was a damned good question, and Otis wondered whether this was a time to be honest, or to skate the truth. Instead, he spoke from his heart. "He's a fighter, Cam. We all have our struggles. Some more than others."

"What do you think's wrong?"

Otis decided not to tell him that the depression could be genetic, passed down on Bec's side of the family. Michael and Jed were both chased by dark clouds.

He shook his head and slid his eyes to Cam. "You keep doing what you're doing. Show us all how to live. Your brother will get there. We'll do everything we can to help him."

—

If only Lloyd Bramhall would vanish into the ether. The old Otis might have wanted to tie him to the back of a farm truck and drive in fast circles over sharp rocks, but this new Otis wanted the guy out of the picture. The problem was that the cost of buying Lloyd out wasn't a fixed number. It moved with the success of the winery, and in 1990 they were certainly clearing more than they ever had.

The tenor of their meetings since their . . . altercation, if one could call it that, was barely on the side of civil, thanks to Bec steering the way. Where they used to plan their strategies over a bottle of wine and a long lunch, things had changed.

Today, the third of May 1990, Lloyd slid into the driveway in his Ferrari. The car didn't sound like it used to, didn't shine anymore. Nor did Lloyd. He finally showed some chinks in his armor, a few new wrinkles, a tad less confident in posture.

No hands were shaken. He did kiss Bec's cheek, though. Then he sat at one end of the dining room table as Otis took his place at the other. Rebecca took a spot between them, her readers on so that she could see the numbers in front of her. She was the accountant, the business leader, and mediary. And object of desire for both parties, but Otis tried not to dwell on that fact.

Otis had notified her of his recent decisions regarding taking a big step back. She'd agreed with what he had in mind. As much as she liked the financial security, enough was enough.

He actually looked forward to watching Lloyd squirm as he said, "We've decided to push back opening the new facility and the tasting room." Otis added as if he were twisting the knife he'd shoved into Lloyd's gut, "Perhaps permanently."

Instant tightness gripped Lloyd's jaw. "No."

Otis inclined his shoulders.

"Why would you even consider that?" Lloyd asked.

"I'm slowing down."

"Slowing down? We're just getting started." Lloyd apparently had lost all ability to stay composed, and he reddened by the second.

His fury calmed Otis. "I didn't like the man I was becoming, and that's because of this exact mindset. I don't want to make Heartbreak anymore. I don't want our finger on the pulse of the newest trends. All I care about is this family and my time with them, and then this farm and putting it into bottle. Lost Souls is the one and only project now, and I don't want to grow production. It stays where it is."

Lloyd looked to the woman who he surely wished was his wife. "Rebecca, tell me you're not on board with this. We have worked too hard. I've got giant retailers, hell, I've got Annette Alvarez-Peters at Costco begging for our wines. We have a distribution network that any winery would kill for. You can't tell me you're going to kill Heartbreak . . . or drop production."

"I prefer the word *slash*," Otis said.

"So you're no longer interested in making money?"

Otis drew in a breath and sat back against the chair. He took his time crossing one leg over the other. "I'm taking a step back before I kill myself. We'll see what the future holds. I don't want to miss out anymore on my boys' lives, or my life with my wife. Time with them is what I want right now."

Lloyd's grin faded, looking a notch less handsome. "You know what I see? A man who has lost his way. When I met you, I had never seen such ambition. I gave you money. A lot of money. We made a deal. I have helped you with countless connections. You would not be here without me."

Otis kept his relaxed position, but he didn't mince his words. "Slow down, Lloyd. You're going to get yourself popped in the mouth again."

"Don't threaten me."

"I'm the one under the gun here. We've done great things, but I'm taking a step back, and we're not asking permission."

Lloyd raised a finger, his big flashy watch sparkling under the light of the chandelier. "Don't make me talk to the lawyers."

"Put your finger down, Lloyd."

Bec held out her hands to keep them from going at each other. "Lloyd, I don't think threats are going to get us to common ground. Otis is right. This is what we want."

Lloyd lowered his hand. "I'm tired of him, Bec. Your husband is losing his damn mind. Last time I talked to you, you wanted more money. You wanted your boys to have an inheritance. You wanted to know that you guys won't starve. Growing production is a must. We have the network, the name. We're totally set up."

"You just want people to talk about you," Otis said, finally having swallowed one spoonful of bullshit too much. "You want people to know that you're a part of this thing."

"Isn't that what you want?"

"Not anymore." Otis sipped a breath; his heart rate lowered. "I'm done. At least for a while."

Lloyd took a repositioning breath of his own. "What I know is that we have built something that's worth a lot of money, and we have to ride that wave." He paused. "Take some time. You're exhausted. It's been a hard run. We'll hire a sales team. You don't have to go on the road. Just build the goddamn facility, and let's move on."

"I'm not building anything. There's nothing in our contract that says I have to grow at a certain pace every year. You're along for the ride."

"We'll see what my lawyers say. You don't want to make me an enemy, Otis." Lloyd looked to Rebecca.

"Nope, don't look at her," Otis said. "I think we're done here. Pack your briefcase and hit the road."

Lloyd shoved his papers into his case and stomped out the door.

"That went well," Otis said to Bec, as they heard Captain Dirtbag descend the steps.

"I don't think it's a good idea to make him an enemy, Otis."

Standing, Otis drew her in and kissed her mouth. "He's been an enemy for a long time. Don't underestimate me, my dear. He can bring his lawyers if he wants. He will not take advantage of us any longer. I need a break, and I'm drawing that line in the sand right now. Isn't that what you want?"

She gave him a smile and pressed her body into his. "I know that you're a man of extremes. Find the middle ground. Don't upset him. Yes, take care of yourself, but don't start a war."

Just then, the Ferrari puttered to life, and Lloyd tore out of the driveway.

"Wah, wah," Otis said in a baby's voice. "My name's Lloyd, and I'm not getting what I want. Wah, wah, wah."

Bec shook her head sternly.

Otis kept going, determined to get a laugh out of her. "Wah, wah, Bec. Your husband won't listen to me. He doesn't want to work anymore, and now I'm—"

She finally smiled, and Otis said, "Ahhhh. That's all I needed, my love." Then he went in for another kiss.

—

"That's what he told me," Bec said, shining with delight in a way that only she could. "He said he was going to jump out the window if I left the seat."

"So he blackmailed you on that bus," Cam said with a charming grin, drawing smiles from the rest of their little family, all sitting together around the kitchen table. With every passing month, he grew more into his body, filling out and growing stouter.

On a butcher block rested Marcona almonds, cornichon, Castelvetrano olives, cherry tomatoes from the garden, walnuts from their trees, one of Bec's lovely baguettes, and two cheeses: an English cheddar and Humboldt Fog. It would be the perfect meal if it were accompanied by a few fine shavings of an acorn-fed *jámon Ibérico* or even *prosciutto di parma*, but Bec was on another vegetarian kick, God bless her. Though Otis smelled bacon in his dreams, he was determined to ride out this rabbit-food diet, if only to prove his discipline.

"That's why we were eventually conceived?" Cam asked. "The reason we're all here? Because he threatened to jump out the window if you left his seat."

"This is the grossest discussion on earth," Mike said, putting his head in his hands. He'd taken to wearing black jeans and white T-shirts every day, and they hung loosely on his skinny frame.

Otis cleared his throat. "If you say it like that, I guess so." He held a glass of an exquisite Bernkasteler Ring Riesling that he and Bec had picked up at auction in Germany.

"I was going to Berkeley to major in journalism, as you know, to follow in my father's footsteps. She had just pointed out—rightly so—that maybe I should do something I actually *wanted* to do. Kind of like the stand Cam has made. The same one that is welcome by Mikey, if he chooses not to take over the farm. Of course, I'll jump out the window if he bails on me, too, but hopefully I'll survive." He winked to make sure they knew he was being playful.

Their laughs filled Otis's heart.

"For the record," Bec said, "I was mesmerized by his ambition, but he needed to point it in the right direction. Same goes for you two. That's why we want you to chase your own dreams. You're the one who has to live them. Not us. We understand if you don't want to be a part of the farm."

Otis swirled the nectar in his glass. "I can't imagine you'll find anything more noble than making wine, but . . ."

Bec eyed him.

Otis broke off a chunk of bread; crumbs spilled onto the table. "I'm kidding. Your mother's right. You can't live our dream. It has to be yours. That was the first of a million lessons your mother taught me over the years. No matter what you do, find a partner like her, someone who can see past your flaws and find the good in you and lift you up. You understand?"

Both boys nodded.

"Make sure you find someone who knows how to make bread like this too." He moaned with delight as he dipped a piece in a bright-green olive oil made down the road.

"I'm just trying to figure out what Dad brought to the table," Cam said. "I've seen the pictures. He was funny looking."

"Funny looking?" Otis said, scrunching his face and flaring out his nose. "What's funny looking about this?"

More laughter filled the air, and Otis felt at ease.

September was here. Harvest was here, starting tomorrow morning with the chardonnay. It had been a hell of a vintage: easy temperatures, the perfect amount of rain, manageable pest pressure. Otis had been completely hands off. They'd barely pruned, let alone applied treatments for pests or weeds. What he'd been working for since he took over the farm had finally happened. He'd created such a happy environment that it had thrived on its own. Which was all to say that Rebecca—and Carmine, for that matter—were right once again. Otis didn't need to work himself to the bone to make good wine. He needed to stand back and let nature do the hard work.

Why had it taken him this long to understand?

Rebecca reached for his hand. "We pick on our dear Otis, but he had so much going for him back then. I was the lucky one. In this house, we talk about achieving our dreams, creating our own reality. I didn't understand these concepts growing up. My mom and dad had a far bleaker outlook. When I met this handsome devil—"

"Handsome, charming, brilliant," Otis said.

"All of the above, that's right. He blew the doors off my vision of what my life could be. Are you kidding me? I never imagined any of this: the farm, you two, the wines we've made, the experiences. The traveling around the world. That's your dad orchestrating it all. He's the one with the powers, the vision. He might look a little funny, but he's my hero."

Otis's eyes watered with delight. Damn it felt good to be back.

Puberty had hit Mike's body, and his voice cracked when he said, "That's what Dad always says, that he's going to jump out the window. He never will."

"Don't test me," Otis said, wagging a finger. "One day it might happen."

"I doubt it."

"You don't think so. Hey, I'm a man of my word. Don't make me do it right now."

"So stupid," Cam said. "You're all talk."

"Please don't encourage him, boys."

"Nope," Otis said. "It's too late. I see how I'm looked at around here. A funny-looking man who doesn't stick to his word."

He approached the closest window, the one looking over Bec's herb garden, and slid open the latch. "It was nice knowing you. Never forget, I was always a man of my word."

"This is so dumb!" Cam said.

"Do it, do it, do it!" Mike chanted.

Bec looked at him like, *Did I really marry this . . . this being?*

"Yes, honey," Otis said in answer to the question she didn't actually ask. "You did marry this."

With that, he lifted up the window. Peeking back at his family, he said, "I hope they serve riesling in heaven. I'll say hi to Bubbles. Bon voyage."

Then he went headfirst out the window and tumbled smack into the basil. It hurt far more than he'd considered possible, and he felt his shoulder tear. Nevertheless, looking up and seeing the three heads of his favorite humans poked out the window in rib-rattling laughter made it all worth it.

He'd found his family again, and that was what mattered.

In the morning Otis pulled on his Carhartt pants and button-down shirt and sneaked down the stairs. The sun's early-morning rays splintered through the windows. A peace had come over him in the last few days, and today it felt even more pronounced.

He decided to take his cup out into the vines. Mug in hand, barely having wiped the sleep from his eyes, he meandered into the chardonnay block they'd planted. Steam rose from his mug as he enjoyed a long sip. He spun around, looking at all the vines with their ripe grapes dangling in wonderfully imperfect clusters. It was time to pick.

But . . .

It didn't feel right.

He thought of what Carmine had always said, how you can't keep taking and taking and taking from your vines, taking from your land. You have to give back more than you take. Sometimes you must make sacrifices.

With his free hand, Otis walked through one of the rows, tickling the clusters and leaves with his fingers. "Talk to me. Tell me I'm not crazy."

He listened with his entire being, wanting to hear the whispers that often came singing from the vines. A swoosh of energy passed by in the morning breeze. "Would it be so bad if we took a year off? I need it. I've lost my edge. Lost the fun, even. I'm tired. Perhaps we both are. What if we take time to heal together?"

Several rows later, once he'd emptied his mug, Otis knelt in the middle of another row. The sweet smell of chardonnay grapes teased the air. The sun rose over the horizon and splashed the fall leaves with light, causing the dew to sparkle.

He closed his eyes and listened. The vines didn't speak with words. It wasn't like that. They spoke in a way that could only be felt, like an electric current running right through his heart.

What he heard the vines say was that this vintage should be one of rest. A reset for the vines and the wines and for Otis Till, who had spelunked so deeply into the caves of his own demons that he best return to solid ground before it was too late.

Just as Otis left the row and reached the gravel road that led to the cellar, Scooter pulled up in one of the farm trucks. He rolled down the window. Old country music played in the background. "Good morning. You ready to pick some chardonnay?"

Otis shook his head; his empty coffee cup dangled from his finger. "We're going to let the fruit hang this year."

Scooter grabbed one of the suspenders of his overalls. "What?"

Otis put a hand on the window frame. "I've been going at it too long. We've been taking too much from this land. Let's take some time off. We'll still pay everyone, but we're not making wine this year. I want the grapes to shrivel on the vine."

"You sure?"

"I've never been surer of anything in my life."

⌒

It didn't take long for word to spread. One of the vineyard guys must have said something, because in the next few weeks, Otis got calls from distributors all over the country, asking for an update. When he went to town, all the winemakers and other farmers asked too. "I heard you were dialing back Heartbreak, but now you're not even picking fruit?"

Otis smiled every time, knowing he'd made the ultimate sacrifice. It didn't matter if no one else understood.

Though he hadn't intended it, his choice threw gasoline on the fire of his celebrity. Joe Montana and Tchelistcheff heard about it. Hugh Johnson wrote about his "brazen decision" in *Decanter*. Even Bedwetter jumped into the melee, writing: *Otis Till and his renegade ways have only exacerbated the rabid desperation for his wines from drinkers across the globe. He is to wine what Folkwhore is to music.*

Otis knew Folkwhore well, as they were one of Camden's favorite bands, one of the groups that had come up in the Seattle grunge scene with Pearl Jam, Nirvana, and Soundgarden. Otis might have preferred that Bedwetter compare him to Yo-Yo Ma, but he didn't mind being called a renegade.

Considering Otis had deleted a year of profits from the books with his decision to skip a vintage, it was inevitable that Lloyd would strike again. Otis had felt him silently stewing. He and Bec hosted him for another formal meeting at the dining room table of Lost Souls Ranch. The boys were at school. Lloyd pulled in in his weathered Ferrari. He'd aged even more since they'd last seen each other, gray hairs sprouting on his sideburns. Wrinkles had found him too. His shoes weren't even polished.

He came at Otis hard as they met at the door. "You know what you're doing, right? You're sabotaging our brand. Premeditated murder."

"Premeditated murder?" Otis asked. "That's rich."

"Don't tell me you're doing the same with the reds."

"It's true. We're taking a year off."

"We? So you're in collusion with the vines?"

"Of course we are, you bumbling fool." Otis cackled with all the griminess of a seasoned wine rep talking about how "smooth" the wines in his bag were. "You know, I used to look up to you. I used to think we saw eye to eye. So much so that I ignored your obsession with Bec, but you can't see past the dollar signs, and that's a tragedy. It might be wise for you to take a year off as well; you're looking a bit ragged." Otis looked down. "Growing a belly too. Go spend some time in the fields. I'll give you a shovel. You remember how to work one, don't you?"

Bec came from inside, saying, "Otis, please try to be civil. Welcome, Lloyd."

"Yes. *Welcome*, Lloyd," Otis said. "Please come in and poison our house with your toxicity."

"Otis, seriously," Bec said.

"Sorry."

Lloyd stood there like a statue, clearly trying to decide his next move.

Otis pulled open the door and turned back. "Well, are you coming in?"

"Don't start throwing insults," Lloyd said. "I told you. Things will get ugly if you don't get back to the plan. Pick the red grapes and make some wine. We can put off building the new facility for a year, but you can't skip a vintage. I need you to make forty thousand cases of Heartbreak."

Otis let the door swing shut and squared up to Lloyd. "I'm not making an eyedropper full."

Lloyd crumbled before them. His exquisite jawline splintered. Words he shouldn't say likely lined up on his tongue. Once he'd calmed himself, he said, "I have a buyer. More money than we've ever been offered." He started to say the number, but Otis stopped him with a raised hand.

"Don't say it. We've been down this road before."

Lloyd went incandescent, as if he were plugged into a socket. "Otis, don't make me force you to sell. Because I can. I want to do this in a friendly way, but I don't have to. I own almost half of this winery, and I can make you buy me out. At a number you won't like. Or we can sell and walk away from each other."

Bec finally hit her limit and sharply clapped her hands at Lloyd. "Is this really who you are? It was never about the terroir, was it? Don't you see what Otis has done for this place? For our wines? He needs a break and yet you don't care. Maybe he was always right about you."

Otis gleamed with delight. As much as he wanted peace among all men, he couldn't help but relish in the idea of the epic collapse of Lloyd Bramhall.

"Bec, your husband lost control of the ship. I'm trying to right it."

Otis soaked it up, watching Lloyd dry up like a salted slug.

"We have an incredible offer. You sign the papers and walk away with stupid money. Go buy the land of your dreams."

Otis spoke with the confidence of a poker player sitting on a royal flush. "We've been down this road. This is the land of our dreams. I wouldn't sell for all the money in the world."

Sir Shitbag slid his snake eyes from Otis to Bec and back. "Here's the thing, guys. I can force you to sell, and you're not going to like it."

"Thanks for coming by, Lloyd," Otis said as patronizingly and rudely as possible. "You are *not* welcome here again."

"That's how you want to play it?"

Otis held his hands before his chest like a yoga master. "May you find peace and happiness."

"Don't placate me."

"*Arrivederci*, Lloyd Bramhall. *Bon voyage. Sayonara. Ciao!*"

"You've picked the wrong guy."

Otis rang an imaginary bell, going, "Ding, ding! That is the truest statement you've ever made. May the wheels of your Ferrari all find nails and may your swimming pool be filled with white zin, and may your life be spent drinking sulfurous boxed wine made from inorganic grapes grown in a swamp of glyphosate. Cheerio, ol' fellow!"

For a moment Otis thought Lloyd would come after him, but the man seemed to find a last foothold of self-control and backed away like the cockwomble he was.

Once Lloyd was halfway to his car, Otis turned to Bec and found her smiling. He'd finally won.

"You're gonna get it," she said.

"No, you're gonna get it."

"Did you hear yourself?"

"I'm having fun." He took her hand and pulled her toward him, then propped her up into dancing position. "I'm a new man, deary. Better get used to it."

"The many faces of my Otis Till."

Otis spun her round, dancing to the sweet song of Lloyd's departure. "You'll never grow weary of me, that's for sure."

Chapter 20

Land Sharks and the Wrong Bull

Otis and his team didn't pick one grape the previous harvest. All he'd done was tend to the wines already in bottle. He continued to take care of his body and mind while also repairing some of the relationships he'd let fall to the wayside, including that of Paul, Sparrow, and Carmine. He still put most of his effort into his family.

The boys were headbanging to Nirvana and Folkwhore. They even got Otis to thrash his head up and down on occasion. Otis figured Kurt Cobain would make a heck of a winegrower. Meanwhile, Rebecca was going through a tough time and exhibited a tremendous lack of patience, which didn't bode well for anyone in near proximity, especially Otis Till. For once, though, she wasn't worried about him. It was Jed, who was using again. Mike, who still faced his struggles. Cam, who would soon fly the coop for CU Boulder. Her parents, who were . . . well, her parents. With her impatience, her troubles with sleep, and her glum demeanor, Otis had to be the strong one.

It was January 1991, and Americans were dropping bombs over Baghdad when Lloyd sent a letter of intent. He was suing in an attempt to force Otis and Rebecca to make a move, to either buy him out for an absurd amount, sell to him for a lesser amount, or agree to a new offer from a large conglomerate.

Otis and Rebecca engaged a lawyer from San Francisco. It was a long few months of back-and-forth. They kept requesting that it all be delayed, as Otis and Rebecca wanted to focus on family. Inspired by Otis's early departure to San Francisco before college, Cam had asked to go to Colorado early so that he could get to know the surroundings. Everyone knew what that meant: He wanted to rock climb, find all the good fishing spots, and check out the girls before the semester began. At least there was no Woodstock to attend. Otis didn't want to say it out loud, but he suspected Cam would never make it to his second semester. His extracurriculars paired with his good looks might prove to be his undoing.

By spring, Lloyd started pushing harder, and the reality of what might happen began to settle. On the day of their departure to Boulder, all of them crammed into the station wagon with Cam's trunk and outdoor equipment, their lawyer called. "He's got too much money. He'll keep going and going until you relent. As much as I like your money, I don't want to take all of it. It's our advice that you accept the offer and wash your hands of the whole thing."

Otis hung up the phone and let the news settle. He'd decide later. What mattered most was Cam right now. They drove up as a family and spent two weeks in Boulder. Otis and the boys fly-fished. Bec did the spa thing. The four of them hiked and shared meals, and Otis knew that this mattered so much more than what could become of the ranch.

Still, the idea of losing what they'd built hurt, and he didn't want to go out without a fight.

—

"You're doing what?" Scooter asked. "Otis, you're the pro, but it's early. Late July? Earliest I've ever heard of in the valley."

"For sure. I'm talking the reds too."

Scooter removed his hat, showing off his bald head. "You're the boss."

It felt right in Otis's bones. Not only because he wanted to shove a big cedar stake up Lloyd's tight bum, but because it was the right time to pick this year. It had been unbearably hot. The grapes were behaving like stubborn jerks, an insult as Otis took it, as he'd given them a year off. Now they seemed to feel as if they didn't need to work at all.

Why couldn't he pick grapes in July? Because no one else did it? Otis couldn't handle the homogeny taking over the wines in the valley. Everyone was trying to make the same thing, grocery store wine that tasted no different from the one next to it. If Otis were to pinpoint the culprit, it would be the critics who had decided that they had the final say in what was worthy of being consumed in America.

Robert Parker had a lot to do with it. Even Parker would admit that his scoring system had become too powerful. Nearly every critic used the number system to define a wine, and countless winemakers did what they could to cater to the most powerful critics' palates, making the wines bigger, bolder, and darker, with more alcohol and less acidity.

Otis could only judge so much, as he had sent his fair share of wines in to be scored, and he'd even manipulated a few along the way to make sure he'd get high scores for the year. Now, though, as he entered this new phase of life, as he stepped deeper into the relationship with his vines, he saw the truth in new ways. No longer could he sacrifice his art for fame and fortune.

Could art be defined by a number anyway? Could any art be objectified in such a way?

The answer was a giant fucking NO.

Also, who said Robert Parker had the right palate? When he put a high number on a wine—and he had with Otis's on occasion—it just meant that he, one person, liked it. The wines that typically claimed the high scores were the over-extracted beasts that stood out in a lineup. If Parker sat down to taste through one hundred wines, which ones would he remember? Naturally, the ditzy blondes with the giant knockers and hourglass hips. Those kinds of wines that screamed at you. Not the subtle intellectual efforts that made you seek them out, made you cuddle up next to them and get to know them, made you ask questions.

Forget what was supposed to be good. Forget a high score. Otis wanted to make something different. It had been the hottest year in the valley that he'd ever known, and these grapes would make a fine wine. Sure, they might pucker up a mouth or two, but it wouldn't be like drinking lemon juice. It would be like biting into a blackberry that wasn't quite ripe. This would be a year to make sessionable wines, low-alcohol beauties that had an acidic cut to them.

Perhaps more than all this, Otis wanted to show himself and others that wine wasn't life or death. Yes, they were making art, but they had to stop taking it so seriously. Wasn't that exactly what Carmine had said?

For Lloyd and the critics and Otis's sons, who needed to know that you didn't have to follow the rules, and for Otis himself, he said, "Let's pick it all this week. Get ready for an interesting year."

Scooter rested his hat back on top of his head. "You know they'll never let you live this down, right?"

"Scooter, if you ever again find me making wines while worrying about what others think, hit me over the head with a rake."

"Aye, aye, boss." Scooter broke into a smile that showed a flicker of the metal in the back of his mouth.

An hour later, Scooter's team was out there plucking grapes that seemed slightly angry about leaving their mama vines so soon. Otis was right there with the fellas, a basket around his neck, shears in his hand.

As the sun poked through the clouds, Otis tromped to the end of a row and dumped his basket of grapes into a half-full bin. Had the grapes been human, they'd scream, *We're not ready!* However, Otis would offer fatherly assurance with: *Trust your papa, my children. Besides, I'm the one with the opposable thumbs.*

"What's going on?" came Bec's voice as she strode down a row barefooted.

This early pick was an ask-forgiveness-later situation, and he knew he was in trouble. Had he a tail, it would have curled up under him.

"It's picking time," he said matter-of-factly.

"Late July?" Not counting the year prior, they typically picked in early October, so she was rightfully surprised. "They're barely purple; you're too early."

Otis held up a finger. "Early on what scale? You know, Bec, we always follow those that came before us. We make wines that we're familiar with. Not this year. I think the fruit's ready. Brix are a little low, but—"

"What are the Brix, Otis?"

"Around sixteen."

"So you're making *ver jus*?" She was jokingly referring to "green juice," an early-picked, unfermented product that had a milder bite than vinegar and did wonders for salad dressings.

"No, it's far too ripe for *ver jus*, though I admire your humor. Veraison started. Who defines *drinkable* anyway? No one owns that definition. Besides, I want to finish early. Let's wrap this thing up and go on a trip. Nothing like Barolo this time of year."

She sighed. "I know what you're doing, Otis. I know you better than anyone. It's obvious."

"What's obvious?"

"Don't play dumb. This is you hitting Lloyd's bow with a torpedo."

Otis couldn't stop himself from smirking. "I hadn't thought about it."

"Don't mess with him."

He raised his hands defensively. "I'm trying something new. Let's have a year of tart wines. They'll age forever. You wait till you taste the juice . . . loaded with flavor. These guys who stick to the rules, always waiting until the fall, they're going to have a bad year."

Bec peered up the hillside to the other pickers. "I'm not going to fight you over it, but I know that Lloyd won't take this well. This is nothing more than a protest, and you and I both know it."

"Other than making something interesting, I suppose it's also a way to play my hand. I'll admit that. He needs to see he can't push me around. If he'd like, he can sell to us and we go on doing what we do." Otis raised a finger. "*Or*, he can sit back and watch me pick in July—if I pick at all. He can watch our bottom line dwindle."

"That's your play?"

"That's all we got, Bec."

⌐

Far more important than the wines, Mike acquired a girlfriend. Or perhaps she acquired him. Sure, they were young and weren't likely getting married, but the glow in Mike's eyes was so welcome in the Till household. Or Château Till, as Otis had started calling it.

Only a few weeks into this budding romance, four days after the last of the grapes had been harvested, Mike climbed onto the stool at the island in the kitchen. He wore what he always wore, a white T-shirt and black jeans. Whereas Cam was fiendishly handsome and graceful, Michael was battling acne and moved his lanky frame awkwardly.

"Can I take Annette to *Point Break* tomorrow?"

"*Point Break?*" Rebecca said, wearing a *Mama Hen* apron and feeding her sourdough starter, a culture that Sparrow had shared with her years earlier. "No, sir. I'm sure it's rated R."

"Who cares?" Mike said, desperate lust for a girl in his eyes. Otis knew it oh so well.

Bec put another scoop of flour into the jar. "We care. Help me out here, husband."

Thursdays, Otis always cooked, and he currently sipped on a glass of water while putting together a curry tofu dish that would be topped with fresh herbs. No, that was not true. Halfway through a bottle of Franciacorta, with a cabernet franc from Bourgueil on deck, Otis topped off the oil in his deep fryer, preparing to make the best frites his family had ever tasted, which would accompany three wonderfully marbled rib eyes.

"I don't know what *Point Break* is," Otis said. "Seems fine to me."

Rebecca gave him the stink eye.

Otis fell in line, put his "father" cap on, and inclined an eyebrow toward his son. "But you're not going to see an R-rated movie. Nevertheless, all those tricks your old man taught you are paying off."

"What about *Hot Shots!*?"

"What's *Hot Shots!*?" Otis asked, wanting to say yes.

"It's a comedy with Charlie Sheen."

"What's it rated?"

"PG-13."

Otis pointed to Bec, who had her back turned, and silently whispered to his son, "She's in charge. I'm okay with it."

Mike mouthed back, "Help me."

Bec had eyes in the back of her head and said without turning, "Otis, don't make me the bad guy."

"Mom, please."

Rebecca turned, drying her hands on a towel. "Let me see if they talk about it in the paper."

"I'm thirteen," Mike pleaded. "I'm old enough to see PG-13 without even asking."

Rebecca let out a long motherly sigh. "Fine, but I'm the one driving you."

"What?" Otis said. "It will be *I* who chauffeur the young lovers."

"Not a chance," Bec said.

"Then we'll both go."

"No way," Mike said.

⌒

Rebecca and Otis had drawn straws. Otis had won and was driving along Highway 12 in their new sedan while bestowing further nuggets of wisdom to his young whippersnapper.

Mike was already exhausted by Otis's advice. He checked himself in the mirror and straightened his white T-shirt. "Dad, I know how to do it."

"I did the same for Cam. Let me do my dadding."

"Things have changed since the twenties."

"The 1920s?" Otis said. "Is that how old you think I am? I'll have you know I first pursued your mother in 1969, the Summer of Love. It wasn't that long ago."

"Trust me, things have changed. You probably didn't even have movies back then. Or electricity."

Otis slowed down and looked over. "Okay, a few things have changed, though we did have electricity; however, many things have been the same since Adam and Eve. You open the door for a girl. You give her a compliment. Tell her she's pretty. You pay for her ticket, buy her whatever she wants. Skittles, popcorn. Twizzlers. Treat her with respect, you understand? Don't you dare kiss her, as much as you might want to. Maybe hold her hand, but you have to read the situation first."

Mike looked up to the roof of the car. "Why me?"

When they pulled up to her ranch-style house in Santa Rosa, Otis slid to a stop. There wasn't a vine in sight, and he wondered whether he could trust these people. God, what if the parents weren't wine drinkers? "Want me to walk up with you? I should probably meet the parents."

"No, please, I'm begging you." He spoke quietly, despite no one being around to hear. "Mom already knows them."

"You think I'm going to embarrass you?"

"Yes."

"Very well. Remember: eye contact; shake hands; be respectful."

"I know."

Otis set his hand on his son's arm. "Never forget, she's the lucky one."

His second-born son climbed the steps and knocked on the door. Otis loved seeing the warrior in Mike, especially after struggling with bullies and depression and all the other shit that life throws at a kid.

Here he was, though, propped up by a girl. Like father, like son.

Mike looked uncertain as he escorted his girlfriend back to the car. They'd been together almost a month now, sealed by a box checked on a handwritten note, but they barely spoke and stayed a good distance from each other. Otis was beyond sure he didn't have to worry about Mike kissing her.

Yet.

Mike opened the door like a gentleman, and Annette climbed in. She was adorable, brown hair topped with a beret. "Hi, Mr. Till. It's nice to meet you."

"And you, Annette. I've heard so much about you."

~

The way things worked, though, when one member of the family reached the top, another fell. Bec would say it was a self-fulfilling prophecy and warn Otis not to say such things, as if he were the conductor of this dark, dysfunctional orchestra of mad violinists, cellists, and the like.

"So you think that if I say it's going to go well," he suggested en route to her parents' house, "then it will go well?"

"Not in front of Mike."

"He needs to hear, Bec." He turned to the back seat and gestured for Mike to pull off his headphones. Once he had, Otis said, "Please be on your best behavior. It'll be over in a blink of an eye."

"Otis," Bec said, "this is my family you're talking about."

"They *are* kind of difficult," Mike confessed.

"I know," Bec replied, finding her son's eyes in the rearview mirror, "but they're your grandparents. You'll be sad one day when they're gone. And your uncle loves you, despite his troubles."

Otis cracked into a laugh that he tried to keep to himself. Jed was the engineer of a slow train to hell. Otis had tried—God knows, he'd tried—to help. There had been moments, too, when the two had connected. Otis had taught him to drive a tractor and paid him for months at a time to work the land. He'd also encouraged him to stay clean, telling Jed what he hadn't shared with Bec, that he'd made a promise to himself never to touch the hard stuff again.

Jed had made yet another false promise, telling Otis that he was done too. Otis had hoped it would stick.

It didn't.

Bec tensed with each mile. *This is the problem,* Otis thought. *She's being a martyr, forcing herself—and dragging her family along—to show a family love that barely deserves it.* They weren't bad people, but they were damaged . . . perhaps beyond repair. The gloom that hovered over their heads never dissipated, and their complaints and negativity dominated every get-together.

However, Otis reminded himself, *they are family.*

Armed with this acceptance, he took Bec's hand, as he had the first time they'd pulled up to Marshall and Olivia's humble house, and made it clear that he had her back, no matter what. Apparently unfazed, Mike raced out of the car to get his hands on whatever sugary treat Grandma Olivia had rustled up for him.

"Hey," Otis said to Bec, waiting till she turned to him. "You're amazing. You know that, right?"

She gave him a close-lipped smile that was barely a smile at all.

"You've given them everything. Don't let them take any more."

—

They gathered outside around a picnic table dressed in a ratty plaid tablecloth. The usual condiments and a tray of toppings covered in Saran Wrap rested in the center. Marshall presided over the grill, beer in hand. He was happy to not be working. Since Otis and Rebecca had found more success, her checks to her parents had grown in size. Essentially, the Tills were paying for the lives of Rebecca's family, and Otis had long ago stopped fighting Bec about it.

The smell of charring burgers wafted into the air. A few empty soldiers already gathered in the grass by the fence that barely offered any privacy from the neighbors, who had more than once called the cops on Jed.

Mike sat at one of the tables, playing his Game Boy. In normal circumstances, Otis would never allow it, but the conversation had already taken a negative turn, and he preferred that Mike hear as little of it as possible.

Jed, who was high on something far more powerful than the Jack Daniel's that shot from his breath, had become the world's greatest master of political thought, and he chose now to share his opinions. His chair sat pressed up to the picnic table. The red Solo cup holding his strong cocktail rested before him. He wore his army jacket rolled up at the sleeves, revealing needle marks and razor scars from the hell he'd put himself through.

He raked his fingers through his long beard as he spoke. "You know Cheney's pulling the strings, right? Bush doesn't know his head from his ass. The only reason we're in the war is Cheney chose to put us there. Is it any surprise? He's getting kickbacks from every fucking sheik over there, and he's got his hand up Bush's ass like a puppeteer." He lifted a hand and opened and closed his thumb against his other fingers like a sock puppet. "My name's George Herbert Bush, and I will do anything Dick tells me. Because Dick is the only one with balls around here."

Marshall smacked the spatula against the top of the grill, a smack heard round the world. All heads turned. "Jesus, Jed. Will you stop with it? Nobody wants to hear your conspiracy theories."

"Oh, I'm sorry. Let's continue being Dick's sheep. Let's keep fighting more wars. Did we not learn anything in Nam?"

"Please, Jed," Bec said.

"I'm not doing anything wrong, sis."

Otis and Rebecca sat together on one side of the picnic table. She dug her fingers into his thigh. Was she saying that they should go? Or that he should jump in and save her? Or was she simply expressing her frustration?

Olivia had a superpowered ability of pretending that everything was okay. "Burgers almost ready?" she asked her husband in a joyful tune. "I'm starved."

Everyone ignored her.

Another dig in his thigh, this one almost deep enough to tear through his trousers.

He put his hand on Bec's back. "Maybe we should go."

It was a whisper meant only for Bec's ears, but Jed picked it up.

"That's right, Otis. Maybe you *should* leave. That's what you people do."

Otis resisted an urge to snap back.

"Who wants potato chips?" Olivia tore open a bag of Lay's. "I think I'll cheat today and have a few."

"The going gets tough," Jed said, "Bec and Otis get going."

"That's not fair," Rebecca said, digging once again into Otis's thigh. Was this a command for Otis to stand and knock her brother in the face? He was considering it.

"Not fair?" Jed laughed. "What is not fair? That you have to come over and see your broken family every once in a while? That the boys have to see what real life is like outside that piece of white-collar heaven that you call your farm? That the world isn't so—"

Otis stood. "Okay, we're leaving. Bec, let's go, please."

Bec slashed a hand through the air. "No, hold on. What have I done to you, Jed? What have we done that makes you feel like you can speak to us this way? Was it the rehabs we've paid for? The money we share? Or was it all the love and patience I've shown you?"

Jed's jaw fell onto his lap. "Love? Where is the love? You're not here for me now, and you weren't there for me then."

Bec raised her voice, damn the neighbors. "I wasn't there for you? I left the city for you. I came back and got a job so that I could help support you and our parents and help take care of you. What part of me hasn't sacrificed for this family?"

Otis looked over at Mike, who still had his Game Boy in his hand but was fully captured by Jed's outburst. Was that a smirk? "Go inside, Mike."

He didn't move.

"Right now!" Otis surprised himself with the authority in his voice.

Rebecca didn't wait until Michael was inside to continue. Otis had never seen her so angry in his life. "What do you want me to say, Jed? That you lost? That you let your injury beat you? That being around you sucks my soul up? I've tried everything, given you so much of myself, ever since we were kids—even at the risk of not giving as much to Otis and the boys. Need I remind you that I suggested you go into computers fifteen years ago; imagine if you had. I gave you a thousand solutions, but you wouldn't listen. I was here for you from the *beginning*."

He pulled on his beard. "Ha. Ha. Ha. Here for me? You ran out on us. You want the truth? Okay. Let's finally get this out." He took a sip of liquid courage.

Otis tugged on Bec's arm, but she shook him off.

Jed slapped his empty cup on the table, then wound up and threw words at her like they were baseballs. "You're fucking right I wouldn't have gone to Nam had you not run off on us. You were the only hope for this family, and you abandoned us like we were nothing more than shit on your shoes."

A tear dropped from Bec's eye.

"That's enough, Jed," Otis said.

"What are you going to do about it? Knock me down like you did Lloyd? Or are you afraid to hit a man in a wheelchair? I'll wipe the patio with you, you pompous British shit."

Olivia sat motionless, staring at the sliced pickles and iceberg lettuce. Even Marshall had nothing to say and kept needlessly flipping the burgers. Maybe they thought this would be cathartic for Jed, finally

283

saying what he'd been harboring all along. Perhaps what all three of them had been harboring.

Otis touched Bec. "Let's go, please."

She found Otis's eyes and nodded in defeat. He took her hand and helped her up. Not another word was said.

⌒

To no one's surprise, Lloyd didn't take the July picking well. Throughout the fall and winter of 1991, he sent threatening letters through his lawyer claiming sabotage and accusing Otis of being mentally ill. Otis and Rebecca's lawyer pushed back but warned them they were skating on thin ice.

"That's my life, thin ice," Otis said. "We're not selling, and he needs to stop forcing it, or I will sabotage in ways that he can't imagine. I will drag the name Lost Souls through the mud, if that's what it takes. I don't care if we lose every dime. I'm not letting him win."

Strangely enough, the market begged for this wine he'd made, and even the critics took note. Bedwetter wrote a long article called "The Sonoma Feud," and he broke down with impressive investigatory skills the collapse of Lloyd and Otis's relationship. He even mentioned Lloyd's possible infatuation with Rebecca. He talked about the Tills' choice to abandon building the facility and stop making bulk juice. He even wrote something rather kind: Hats off to Otis Till. He's proving to be more of a terroir man than I've ever given him credit for. His gall is noted.

Otis read the last sentence a hundred times. His gall is noted.

Pushing the early-pick wines out in February of '92, they sold out in an instant. Parker slaughtered the wines, giving the Lost Souls Zinfandel a 53. No one in the world had ever received anything lower than a seventy. Still, instead of being laughed at, Otis was called the "Grape Messiah," a true artist, a god of wine, an iconoclast. Maybe Bedwetter was right. Otis could urinate into a bottle, and it would sell out.

The problem was that his defiance had an adverse effect. Whereas he thought he'd run Lost Souls into the ground with his bold decisions, what he did was make the company even more valuable, while also creating a demand that was simply impossible to satiate. Who didn't want to get their hands on what the *San Francisco Chronicle* called a "puckering sessionable slosher that throws a middle finger up at what is generally acceptable"?

Was it pride that Otis felt reading these comments and hearing these calls from distributors? All of a sudden, writers who'd never given him the time of day wanted a word with him. When Otis spoke with them, he spoke his mind. No matter what he said, folks enjoyed it. He was now the terroir soldier of California.

—

Nineteen ninety-two brought with it a sense of unknowing. Lloyd remained somewhat quiet, though the lawyers were certainly talking. Otis paid the lawyer fees with the same ask: "Buy me some time. Let's see if he wears down."

He and Bec knew they were delaying the inevitable. Lloyd was not the type of man to wear down, especially now that Bedwetter had called him out in *The New York Times*. He couldn't imagine a scenario where he let go of the vines. Otis could feel the dipshit stewing in his penthouse downtown.

Meanwhile, Rebecca and Otis would go a long time without talking about their feud with Lloyd. Otis's mother visited for two weeks, and they barely mentioned it. Rebecca was still dealing with her family, coming to grips with her crushed relationship with her brother. She still hadn't spoken to any of them, though they were still happily cashing her checks.

"You need to go see Carmine," Bec suggested while chatting about the future. "When's the last time you talked to him?" The television played the latest news on the LA riots.

"It's been a while."

"Go check in on him. Tell him what you're going through."

Considering Rebecca was always right, Otis did just that. It was June, and the vines were alive and well, working their way toward pushing out grapes. The whole valley was stunning. He pulled back the gate and descended the hill into Carmine's oasis.

Otis heard the whisper as always, that ever-present energy that came only when one was so incredibly connected to his place. Otis thought he'd found it on some level on his own land, but Carmine would always be the master.

The old man sat at a table in the shade, drinking a bottle of white and smoking a cigarette. He looked like he'd aged a decade. His dog, Antonio, sat at his feet. "There he is, the Grape Messiah."

Otis knelt and let Antonio lick his hand. Carmine kicked out a smile. "I remember the first time you came to see me. When was that? Twenty years ago?"

"Right about that."

Carmine sucked in smoke and let it out with another grin. "Such a shy kid, but you had that look in your eye. You've really done it now, haven't you? What'd you pull up in? A BMW?"

"Just the work truck."

"I'm giving you a hard time." With great effort, he pushed up from the table. They embraced, and Otis could feel how weak his mentor had become. "It's good to see you, Otis. How's the family?"

"They're well, you know. Mike's doing better, got his first girlfriend. She's been good for him. He's fourteen now. Can you believe that? Cam's loving Colorado. And Bec's punching above her weight, trying to keep the farm straight. Keep me straight."

Carmine sat back down. "I heard you picked in July last year." His grin was all-knowing, and they shared a chuckle.

"There was more to it than that."

"Yeah, I've heard. You're a celebrity now. I can't go anywhere without someone asking me about the great Otis Till. You've got what it takes, that's for sure."

"Until Lloyd takes it away."

Carmine poured Otis a glass. "Yeah, what are you going to do? He's not one I'd like to pick a fight with."

"He's about to win, one way or another."

"So let him. There's more than one good piece of land out here."

Otis sat and took a long sip of an absolutely mesmerizing chardonnay, a bottling with stunning vibrancy. "Yeah, but I'm . . . I'm tired. I don't want to start over. We raised our boys there. Planted and replanted so many of those vines. It's where I started to find that whisper, you know."

"Oh, I know."

"Imagine if you had to say goodbye to this place," Otis said.

"I am saying goodbye." Carmine looked at the closest vineyard block, a hodgepodge of varieties that had made some of the best and truest wines Otis had ever tasted. "I know you see it. Blackberry bushes taking over, more oak trees coming right out of the rows. The vineyards overgrown and starting to swallow me. I suppose I'll die doing this thing, pulled right back into the earth, swallowed up by my terroir."

A pain hit Otis, thinking about how he hadn't been there for Carmine since the whole mess with Heartbreak. "I'm sorry I've been so distant lately. I've been busy. Not only lately but for years."

Carmine stubbed out his cigarette in an ashtray full of butts. "Don't worry about me, but it is nice to see you. How are the wines? How's this early pick?" Another grin came. He clearly enjoyed what Otis had done.

"It's drinkable."

He slapped his leg. "You son of a bitch. You fell in love with her, didn't you, the wine life? That's the only way. You have clusters swinging between your legs, *ragazzo*. Whatever happens, don't let it eat you up. You fought the good fight."

Otis stared into the wine, scents of apricot and green apple wafting up out of the glass. "Would you sell if you were me?"

"Take the money and run? I might. Some people you can't fight. Lloyd Bramhall's one of them."

"I wonder if I ought to step away from wine. We'll have some money. It's been a lot, all-consuming. Maybe it would be better that way."

Carmine lit up another one, contributing with each puff to the yellow of his beard. "I suspect a man knows when he's farmed his last vintage. Is that how you feel?"

Otis took a moment to ponder the question. "Not by a long shot. I just don't know what to do."

"Go back to where it all began. Find the fun again. Somewhere along the line you got pulled in by distractions. Who could blame you? The money you've made doesn't come by most winemakers. You read the trends. Broke some hearts with that Heartbreaker."

"Nearly killed myself in the process."

"But you're alive." His words came out with smoke. "You're alive, Otis. Start again. Shake Lloyd loose. He's been eating at you way too long."

Otis reached for a cigarette. "You mind?"

"You smoke now?"

"No, but it seems like a good time to pick it up." He didn't wait for approval. Popped one into his mouth and lit it. "I hate letting him get the best of me."

Carmine leaned forward. "You're still doing it, letting that ego sneak in. If I'm being honest, I still taste it in your wines. They're good, Otis. Miles ahead of most out there, but I still taste you trying to make something of yourself. Even after all you've done, you've still got something to prove. I know it's coming off as you being a martyr, but all this rebellion. Warring with Lloyd. What about *love*? This thing we're doing, communicating with the earth, breaking bread with the divine, it can't be done while we're at war. What do I know? I'm shriveling up like a forgotten cluster on the ground, but the recipe for that celestial sauce, the holy muck we bottle . . . the best is always done when we're at peace with ourselves and others."

The man's words fell heavy in Otis's heart. "If it were only that easy, Carmine. I guess you're right. I still do have something to prove."

"You got nothing left to prove, which means you can go make the wine you're meant to make now."

"With the farm I'm about to lose."

"The place I grew up in Italy, an island off of Naples called Ischia. Only reached by boat. There was a saying. *C'è sempre un altro traghetto.* There's always another ferry. Same goes for wine; there's always another piece of land."

—

What could better sum up the wonder and beauty of the wine business than a long lunch on the farm? Otis had dined in some of the finest restaurants in the world, but there was nothing like joining Bec in the kitchen, putting together a meal amid the sounds of Crosby, Stills, Nash, and Young, then spreading it out on a long table and throwing anchor for an hour or three.

Otis wore his shades and looked at his bride across the table. "Tell me about you."

Her eyes grew wide. She cupped her glass in two hands, the way only she did, and she sniffed into it, and he wished he could slip into her mind and see what she was thinking.

"Oh, I don't know. I'm with Carmine. I'm tired of the fight. I feel like we have our heads in the guillotine, waiting for the blade to drop."

Otis breathed in his chardonnay. The citrusy spine rose gracefully into the floral overtones. Notes of guava and mango danced on the tongue. Only the slightest hint of vanilla smoothed out the tremendously wonderful acidity. He fell back through the years, landing squarely in the time when they were celebrating how they'd come upon this land, this ranch that had changed their lives.

He clinked her glass. "Ah, my love. So long as I'm always close to you, nothing else matters."

"Do you mean that?"

"You know I do."

The phone rang inside.

"Let it ring," Otis said, soaking in the beauty of Rebecca Till. "I think I could let it go, too, Bec. Perhaps we buy a simple place, a three-bedroom, two-bath, in a neighborhood. Take a break from farming. Maybe it would be better for Mike, to have some other kids around. You have a little garden with a few tomatoes and carrots. We don't need any more kale. In fact, I'd be good if I never had kale the rest of my life."

"Oh, I am perfectly aware that you'd be fine on the bacon-only diet."

He laughed. "If only there were bacon plants; that would be heaven." He took a long sip, thinking how he'd nailed the picking date that year, how the balance of this wine could be studied at Davis.

"I think we go travel for a while after Mike goes to school," Otis continued. "Let's go live in Beaune for a year, or Alba. Or take a Viking cruise through the canals or the Norwegian fjords."

Bec suppressed an I'm-trying-not-to-get-too-excited look. "Could you really give up making wine?"

"I nearly have," Otis proclaimed.

She looked marvelously happy. "I guess so. The grand overcorrection of Otis Till. That's the name of your book. You went from absolute obsession to redefining minimalism."

Otis spread his lips wide. "It's been nice."

"Only you could get away with it."

He cast a glance up the hill to the trellised vines. "It breaks my heart, Bec, to think of saying goodbye, but we can't keep going on like this. Do we really let go of the dream we carved out twenty years ago? Just when the new vines are starting to sing?"

Bec stabbed a marinated *giganté* bean with her fork. "Like Carmine said, there's always another piece of land. Let's talk to a Realtor, get them looking. We could find something better."

He let his thoughts wander. "I'd need one last vintage to say goodbye. One last Lost Souls." Otis circled the table and sat beside her. He slipped his arm around her and then raised a glass.

"One last vintage," he said. "Who knows from there?"

She sealed the toast with a kiss. "There's something nice about the idea, the unknown. Just like all those years ago on the purple bus."

"I think the answer's out there. Let's be open to—"

The phone rang again.

"I should get that," Bec said.

"No," Otis pleaded. "I don't want this lunch to end. Whatever it is, reality is on the other line. Leave it alone."

"What if it's about the boys?" As soon as she said that, he knew lunch was over.

Rebecca stood and kissed the top of his head and disappeared inside. Minutes later, she came back out onto the terrace and yelled, "Otis, get in the truck!"

"Why didn't you tell us?" Bec asked Mike with a poor attempt at hiding her frustration. They'd picked him up from the police station where he'd been booked for truancy.

"Why would I tell you?" He spoke with all the teenage attitude in the world.

"Because we're your parents," Otis said, one hand on the wheel, the other on Bec's lap.

"I don't want to bother you."

"Oh, my God. Teenagers." Bec turned to the back seat to face her son. "When did she do it? How did she do it?"

"She had a friend tell me."

"What?" Otis said, turning down NPR. "Annette broke up with you through a friend?"

"She said we didn't have anything in common."

"When was this?"

"Last week."

The pitch of Rebecca's voice rose. "And you didn't tell us. You just start skipping school. You haven't been once since then?"

Through the rearview mirror, Otis saw his son shake his head.

Otis and Rebecca knew that getting angry wasn't the answer; they'd agreed on their approach on the way over.

"I still don't know why the school didn't call," Rebecca said.

"I called in and said I was sick."

"They believed you? For four days in a row?"

Mike shrugged.

Otis jumped in. "Mike, you have to let us guide you. You can't always bear this stuff on your own."

"But I knew how much you liked her. I knew you'd be mad at me."

"For her breaking up with you?" Rebecca asked. Nothing could hurt her heart more than her children struggling. "Honey, this is what happens. It's no reflection on you. You guys are young. It was bound to happen. She was a nice girl, but more than anything, we liked what she did to you. She helped you see how special you are."

Mike fell back against the seat. "Oh, that's right. So special. That's exactly how being dumped makes you feel."

⌒

The next morning Otis and Rebecca called their lawyer and asked to move forward with the sale of Lost Souls.

Chapter 21

HARVESTING SOULS

Mike spent the summer working with his parents and hiding from any activity that took him into town. Heartache hit him hard, and it was all Otis and Rebecca could do to draw a smile from him. Or even get him to eat.

It was Bec who suggested they take him to see a psychiatrist, a Dr. Cormier, who recommended after a couple of sessions that Michael might benefit from taking an antidepressant. Otis was taken aback by the idea, but Dr. Cormier's words rang true for both Rebecca and Otis.

"You're right, Rebecca," Dr. Cormier said from the chair in his office while Mike flipped through magazines in the waiting room, "it very well could be genetic. More to the point, I think we should recognize that this could be bigger than him, something that he can't quite battle on his own. You said your father always had this pull-yourself-up-by-your-bootstraps mentality with your brother. No offense to him, but that's an archaic way of thinking. Medicine can be the lift up a person needs. I think Michael could see wonderful benefit."

When Otis turned to Bec, she was glowing with hope. Otis committed to approaching the idea with an open mind, something he imagined neither his father nor his father-in-law would be able to do. Perhaps that meant it was exactly what Otis had to do.

In the following weeks, they tried not to ask Michael how he was feeling, if he noticed any change due to the medicine, but they couldn't help it every few days. About two months in, though, they didn't have to ask. The change wasn't night and day, but little by little, they could see a lightness come over him.

That summer, Mike showed an interest in farming, more than ever before. He'd get up early, just to see what his dad was doing. It wasn't about taking the machinery apart. He wanted to understand the vines, what led to good fruit. Otis couldn't name any feeling in the world better than looking up from his morning work on the farm to see Mike coming to join him. Needless to say, Bec was the happiest of all of them, knowing that their son was finding a way out of his darkness.

"You hear that?" Otis asked Mike in late August, days before they were to pick chardonnay.

"Hear what?" The young man had filled out, slightly less awkward in his body. His face had cleared up some.

"Sit down with me."

The sun had eased up over the hill, but it wasn't terribly hot yet. In fact, this vintage had been rather cool, a true blessing for their last run. Brushstrokes of a mellow vermilion swam through the otherwise nitid baby-blue sky. Birds chirped their morning melodies. The whispers of the vines sounded like a breeze, but there was no wind today, only the magic of this land.

Otis and Mike both sat on the earth between rows. It was such a wonderful world down there, a bed of earthworms and abundant life, surrounded by vines that were the true soldiers of terroir. Through the trunks, you could see the hills rising up around them. The hanging clusters gave off a wonderfully sweet and delectable scent.

Cross-legged, Otis gathered his hands together on his lap. "You've heard me talk about Carmine and how his farm has a whisper. You're old enough now to understand. We could spray glyphosate. We could kill all these weeds, make it look like Disney World, but then you're killing the life around the trunk. We don't exist in a vacuum, and nor do the vines. You can't focus on one piece of the farm. Well, you can, but then your wines—and for that matter—your life, will not be as rich. I've spent years with Carmine and on this farm trying to figure that out, trying to figure out how to make a farm harmonious. When you do, she starts to sing. It sounds almost like if you place your ear up to a conch shell, and it feels . . . I don't know, like when someone you love touches you. There's nothing more magical. I can hear her now, singing. That's how I know it will be the perfect vintage."

Mike pinched some grass and tore it from the earth, then tossed it. It was big talk for a teenager, but he was listening.

"We've given back every way we can. With compost, manure. We've never once sprayed a chemical. We work with the earth, not against her. In return, she gives us fruit that tastes like nowhere else on the planet. I know you're young, and I may sound like some crazy old man, but wine is much more than a beverage. I hope you see that. Wine is life. We are harvesting and bottling the soul of this land, and we are part of it, so we're putting our souls in there too. Every bottle I've made since you were born has a piece of you in it. Your energy. Your—"

"My pee?"

Otis allowed a moment of levity. "Well, that's right. You have certainly done your share of peeing in the vineyard, but let's not tell anyone that."

"I'm kidding."

After a proper chuckle, Otis put his hand on Mike's shoulder. "I know I haven't always been around, but I'm working to change that. Forgive me, son, for not doing better."

Mike's eyebrows crinkled. "You've been a great dad."

"Thank you."

"Seriously. You're an inspiration. I don't think it's such a bad thing to show your kids how to work hard."

"Yeah, but there's a point." Otis wouldn't dare break eye contact.

"I know. Mom talks about it."

"She does?"

"She says you overcorrected. The Great Overcorrection of Otis Till."

Otis chuckled. "Maybe a little."

"I don't think you should quit. Look at you. You're happy. Your farm whispers to you."

"Are you making fun of me?"

Mike shook his head, a smirk playing on his face. "I'm okay with your delusions."

"You really don't hear that?"

They listened intently for a while.

"Maybe."

"You'll get there. It's like any language; you must immerse yourself."

Mike lay back against the mustards, clover, and buckwheat and put his arms behind his head. "What if we went somewhere else?"

Otis lay back as well, cushioned by the earth. "What do you mean?"

"I mean, like if I changed schools. We could go move somewhere, start over. Somewhere with vines, of course. I really don't want to see you living in a neighborhood. We all know how badly that would go."

Otis was so blindsided, he couldn't even smile at Mike's humor. "Did your mother put you up to this?"

"No, I've just been thinking. I don't love my school. I mean, I don't hate it, but I just . . . I wouldn't mind starting over somewhere. Now that I'm feeling better. I do hate seeing Annette. I don't really have any serious friends. I'd be fine if we left. Where else can you grow vines in the US?"

It was true: Mike was feeling better. The medicine had breathed new life into him. For a father, what could be better than knowing that your child is turning a corner, figuring things out, breaking through.

To Mike's question, Otis felt the flurries of youth in his chest. "Well, there are a few places on the East Coast. Charlottesville, Virginia. The Finger Lakes in New York. Not that this is even an idea."

"Where else?"

"Plenty of spots in California. Oregon. Washington State."

Mike perked up. "Washington State?"

"That's right, home to all your musical heroes."

"What do they grow?"

Otis kept his excitement at bay. "I've never actually been up there, but I've tried some of the wines. It's a hot climate. High desert."

"I thought it was wet."

Otis shook his head. "Seattle is. Not wine country. The Cascades run to the east of Seattle, turning the other half of the state into a rain shadow. It's a different world, on the east side. Hot days and cold nights, a diurnal shift that swings even more than here. The cold nights extend the growing season and allow the berries to develop more flavonoids and other compounds while still retaining . . ." Otis realized he was rambling.

"Listen to you go."

"It is what I do for a living." Mike encouraged him to keep going. "Back in the Ice Age," Otis said, "ice dams not too far from Bozeman, actually, would burst and release these massive floods that poured over the land, carving it out, tearing up whatever was there. In its place, the floods left all this alluvial silt." Otis scratched his head, thinking of some of the wines he'd tried at trade shows over the years. "Quite nice Bordeaux-style wines. Wonderful syrah too."

"You do talk about syrah a lot. What about Oregon?"

It was true. He'd fallen in love with syrah lately, with its versatility and its way of adapting to every nuance of the vintage. You didn't have to fight with syrah; it was an easygoing conversation all the way through harvest.

Even if this was only conversation, Otis found nothing more invigorating than talking wine with one of his boys.

"Oregon vineyards are near the ocean, so it's closer to a Seattle climate. Wet and cool, slow to ripen. It's pinot noir country. And some nice chardonnay and pinot gris. You could think of Oregon as Burgundy and Washington as Bordeaux. People would fry me for saying so, but I'm speaking from a climate perspective."

"Do you hear yourself? Going on and on . . . it's funny to imagine you quitting the wine business. You'd be a wreck."

"You might be right." Otis wondered what Bec might say about relocating. They'd not even considered the possibility of pulling Mike from his school.

That night, as they sat outside and shared a meal, Mike brought it up again. "Seriously, Mom. I know you don't want to go move into some suburb in Santa Rosa. You guys are farmers. Quit kidding yourselves."

"This isn't about us," Rebecca said. "It's about you and making sure you have a stable environment. You can't run every time a girl breaks up with you."

"It's so much more than that, and you know it. I guess the medicine's helping, and I kind of want to delete who I was before it."

Bec grabbed his hand. "Don't say that, honey."

"That's not what I mean. It's just . . . people know me a certain way here. A fresh start wouldn't be so bad. An adventure."

"For the record," Bec said, "the medicine hasn't changed who you are. You're still our Michael. It's just helped your brain process things in a different way."

"I know, I know. You've told me. Whatever it does, it's working. And this isn't about running from what happened with Annette. I'm saying that the idea is really exciting."

Bec looked at him for a while, then slid fearful yet excited eyes to Otis. "Where would we go?"

Otis rubbed his stubble, trying his best to temper his elation. "We'd have to do some research after harvest, wouldn't we?"

"Look at him, Mom. He's glowing."

Bec laughed at that. "He is, isn't he?"

"I can't deny that a new adventure sounds delightful," Otis said, noticing his upright posture and the happy tingling on his skin. "Trying to re-create what we have here feels like a dull second act, but maybe it's not about re-creating at all. Maybe it's about doing something new. Only if you're really on board. We'd have to talk to Cam too. It's important for a college student to have a home to return to."

"Dad, Cam's not coming home. Are you kidding me? As for me, it was my idea."

"Fair point, but women make us do crazy things." Otis looked over at Rebecca and winked.

"I want to walk into a new school and not know anyone, and no one have any opinions of me. Here, I'm the weird kid with a face covered in zits who finally had a girlfriend, then got dumped and then didn't go to school for a week. Here, I'm Otis's kid."

"Oh, come now. You're more than that," Bec said.

"Let's hope so," Otis said. "Mike, you're more than I'll ever be."

Mike gave a kind smile. "Anyway, I don't need to sleep on it. Nothing's tying me down here. What about your parents, Mom? And Jed?"

Rebecca paused and drew in a slow breath. The question had obviously been top of mind. "I can't take care of them forever. Maybe it would be good for all of us."

Otis swelled with pride when he heard her say that.

He took the bottle next to him and poured Mike a glass. "By God, let's toast to the idea of setting sail, fam."

Mike and Rebecca and Otis clinked their glasses, and Otis couldn't remember a time when everything felt more right.

～

"You're taking our daughter from us? And our last grandchild?" Marshall sat in his trusty recliner in the living room. They still hadn't painted over the scarlet-red walls—still hadn't put much effort into cleaning up the place.

"Dad, that's not what this is about." Rebecca had stayed incredibly strong since Jed had lashed out at her. In fact, that night had been good for her. She seemed to have finally found peace with all that had happened. Her decision to leave them verified it.

"You sure that's not what it's about?" Marshall asked. "That's what it feels like. Don't you think, Olivia?" He looked over at his wife, who sat in her go-to chair where she typically knitted as they watched their favorite news channel. There was no knitting today. She looked exhausted already, and Bec had only just told them.

"I don't know what to say. Why would you leave?" Her voice was caked in desperation.

"Because we want a new adventure."

"Where?" Olivia asked. "Why don't you move to Napa? Then we can still see you."

"We're not moving to Napa. We want to find something new, something fresh."

Marshall groaned. "Rebecca, you've always run from things. I don't know what you're running from now. Lloyd Bramhall. Us. Your brother. I was raised not to abandon my family, and I'd hoped I'd raised you the same way."

Sitting by his wife on the couch, Otis waited for her to dig her nails into his thigh, but she held strong. Dammit, he was proud of her.

"Dad, I have given you guys my everything. It's time I look out for my family. It's time I go live my life. We'll get some good money from the sale. We can help you out, but we're leaving, and I don't know where. That's the exciting part."

Marshall inclined his eyebrows. "The exciting part, yeah. I'm sure your brother will think so."

"He has to do his own growing; I can't carry him. If you want my opinion, which I know you don't, stop pandering to him. Quit picking him up every time he falls. I know that I'm done doing that."

"We're not asking for your opinion," Olivia said, showing rare backbone.

"Oh, I know." Bec centered herself. "I love you guys so much and can't wait for you to visit us. And I'd love to know you support us."

Olivia whimpered. "What happens when we can't take care of Jed any longer? What happens when we can't take care of ourselves?"

It was a hell of a question, a sharp blade of one.

"Mom, we'll always be there for you, however we can. Hopefully, you guys have a lot of years left anyway."

Marshall laughed. "Oh, joy."

"Look, guys. I have to live my life. Mike will be in college soon. Otis and I have new adventures ahead."

Silence. Absolute silence.

Bec didn't look devastated; she looked like she'd expected nothing less. Hell, she looked more at peace than he'd ever seen her.

⁓

Harvest was everything Otis had hoped, and he felt like they'd captured the whisper of the ranch like never before. Once the wines were in tanks and fermenting without issue, the three of them started taking research trips. They drove down to Paso Robles and up to the Russian River Valley. They flew to Charlottesville for a few days and tasted interesting cab francs and viogniers, then shot up to the Finger Lakes for riesling. Nothing quite hit home yet, but the journey couldn't have been more fun. Otis had never seen Mike happier. Something about this being his idea revved his engines.

The moving parts locked into place when they landed in Portland, Oregon. It felt different from California, but the West Coast vibe was still there and terribly appealing. Otis didn't know the first thing about growing pinot noir. He'd thought about trying some back in Sonoma but had never quite gotten around to it. Like riesling, a variety like that took all your focus. It wasn't something you could dabble in.

His suspicions proved to be true as they toured the Willamette Valley and met with growers over the course of a week. He couldn't imagine a prettier place in the country. Could they get used to the cold and wet? The food was extraordinary, and the people seemed like the good kind. They tasted pinot after pinot, and Otis would close his eyes and imagine a world where he devoted himself to a new grape.

Still, they had yet to see Washington State. They drove along the Columbia River in a rented Jeep, and when they finally crossed over the bridge, Otis's world shifted. He had never seen anything like this landscape in his life. It wasn't far from Montana, and yet it was a world away. When the vineyards came into view, he gasped. They were these beautiful stretches of green tucked onto desert hills. Oases in the desert. But that big wide river surely gave a nice cooling effect, not to mention an endless supply of irrigation water.

They stayed three nights in Walla Walla and met with folks that Otis had heard about over the years, the likes of Leonetti and Woodward Canyon. Everyone knew of Otis and treated him with almost too much respect. Not one let him go without asking about the early-pick vintage. He had done so much with his life, made some amazing vintages, but they'd likely put *He picked reds in early July one year* on his tombstone.

The wines.

Of.

Washington.

Otis wasn't sure what to make of them. Some were far from polished. He could tell quickly that many of the winemakers were former cherry farmers trying to figure things out. They lacked a proper education in wine, including ample time spent in the Old World. The potential of this fruit and land, however, could not be denied. In the right hands, Washington State could produce wines that could disrupt the world order.

There are moments that define a life. The day you meet your soulmate. The day you marry her. The day your children come into the world. The day you find your purpose. In a winemaker's life, the day you find your land.

If you're lucky, you might find a second plot.

Otis knew even as they came around the bend on the highway that he'd found a place that would be as important to him as a Stradivarius might be to the right violinist.

This land was a petite blonde stopping a bus, climbing on, walking down the aisle, and connecting eyes as if drawing coordinates in the stars. She was the first breaths of two baby boys as they curled into their mother's arms. She was a mirror of the piece of land that would become Lost Souls Ranch. She, this mountain, was as much destiny as Rebecca and the boys and the passion that had nearly consumed him.

Yes, she was a she.

Red Mountain exuded femininity. There were no formal signs, no tasting rooms. This wasn't Sonoma. Certainly not Napa. This wasn't even Walla Walla. This was the wild frontier.

She was just a blip on the map.

And yet she was everything.

Everything.

A southwest-facing slope, the sun showering warm, ripening rays over the vines that had already been picked of their bounty. Their leaves had changed to the colors of a campfire, and together those shades were a painting on a canvas of virgin soil.

Never had Otis seen a piece of land that called out more to him.

This wasn't California; it didn't even feel American. The land almost looked martian, some foreign plot on a hill on a planet millions of miles away. Who ever thought that grapes could grow here? Who was crazy enough to plant first? Yet it was perfect. Of course it was. The slope of this tiny mountain could only have been designed by a higher power. Just the right pitch to keep the spring freezes from settling in too long. The Yakima River running alongside evoked memories of the Mosel.

He couldn't believe that it was undiscovered, composition paper waiting for musical notes.

"Otis?"

"Huh?"

"I'm glad I'm driving."

"What?" Otis turned to Rebecca, who had slowed in the right lane of the highway so that they could all enjoy their first look of Red Mountain on full display, a woman stretched out on the sand, soaking up rays.

"Bec, it's . . . never in my . . . I'm . . ." He lost his breath.

"I know."

Otis's eyes grew misty. "I thought that . . ."

"Dad, what's happening up there?"

Otis turned back to find Mike grinning. "Reminds me of the first time I saw your mother, Mike." He turned back to this little mountain that was more a hill than anything, with a few experimental vineyards. Otherwise, a clean slate.

He was about to say more but caught himself. This decision wasn't his alone. Dialing it way back, he said, "It's a nice spot. I look forward to walking around."

Rebecca laughed because she could always read his mind.

Always.

Taking the exit, they passed a gas station and then began to climb up a winding road that led to their destination. Even on the approach, there were no signs—not even an indication that they had entered wine country. Red Mountain was nothing more than a hill in a sea of hills in the Columbia Valley, but a few men and women had seen potential. As told by a winemaker in Walla Walla, John Williams and Jim Holmes had planted the first vines back in 1975. The *exact* same year Otis and Bec had bought their ranch. If that wasn't a sign . . .

Then others had come: the Hedges family, Blackwood Canyon, Sandhill, Seth Ryan, and Terra Blanca, among others.

Otis had heard their names and stories, pioneers looking for something different.

Walla Walla was wonderful for so many reasons, but many of the winemakers bought their fruit elsewhere—as the colder climate brought intense challenges. Otis couldn't imagine making his wines in a place far from where the grapes were harvested. It would compromise the essence of the terroir. It would dilute the concentration.

They took a left onto Sunset Road and drove through a small village of sorts, dusty roads and double-wide trailers. Sagebrush rolled across the road. Desert grasses blew in the wind. A pickup truck passed by, the driver lifting his hand in a wave. What kind of bird was that overhead? Otis imagined how different the wildlife might be. The valley floor stretched for a long time, and Sunset Road followed the contours, revealing ample land that was entirely plantable. Tiny micro slopes that curved like the body of a voluptuous woman offered subtly different angles to the sun and endless possibilities.

Off in the west stood Mount Adams, a tall peak capped with snow that dominated the horizon and evoked an extraordinary sense of awe.

As the vineyards came into view, Otis sat on the edge of his seat, studying the trellises, the canopies, wondering what they were planting. "It would be like learning an entirely new trade, farming up here. I can't imagine. New pests, new weeds. An entirely different world."

"I want to go up there," Mike said, pointing to the top ridgeline.

"I'm up for it," Otis agreed. "Can you keep up with your old man?"

Mike put a hand on Otis's shoulder. "Maybe I should carry you."

"Just hold a slice of bacon out ahead of him," Bec said. "Then he'll keep up."

"Wifey," Otis said, "be kind. I'm having an out-of-body experience, and here you are attacking me."

They parked on the side of the road. Otis carried a backpack with sandwiches and water. There was no path, so they cut through tall grass, avoiding coyote dens and snake holes and stepping past boulders the size of cars. They paused on occasion to look out over the Columbia Valley, but the vision made sense only once they'd reached the top thirty minutes later. It was cold up there, another microclimate revealing itself. As the wind caused chill bumps to rise on his arms, Otis spun in every direction, taking in eastern Washington State in all its glory.

To the west, past the Yakima River, lay the small town of Benton City. Beyond, Mount Adams stood tall and mighty, all the other hills and mountains bowing to it. Farms dotted the martian landscape, more blocks of green swallowed by high desert.

"What do you think?" Otis asked.

Rebecca slipped her arm into his. "It's like nothing I've ever seen."

"I know. I'd love to track down some wines."

Mike spoke up. "I wonder what the schools are like here. The people."

"Good questions." Otis held his arm out, and Mike joined them. They looked down over the southwest slope of Red Mountain. "I wonder what life would be like down there. I'd take a plot closer to the river, where that second slope starts to slip down." He pointed.

"Maybe we should see if there's any land for sale." He looked at Bec and Mike while attempting to stifle his excitement. "Just to price it. We have to do our research."

The truth was that Otis knew the same thing Mike and Bec did.

This was home now. They all knew it in their bones.

Part II

THE RED MOUNTAIN YEARS

Chapter 22
(Interlude)

HOWLING AGAIN

Red Mountain, Washington State
April 2011

The man I loved found wings on that day. Never had I seen him so full of hope. It was dangerous, actually. Mike and I looked at each other, and we knew that Otis had been reborn. We knew we better hold on tight, because the Otis rocket ship was ready for its second launch.

Once we hiked back down the mountain, we ran into Tom and Anne-Marie Hedges, who had bought fifty stunning acres in prime position in the center of the mountain. They didn't have the beautiful château that they do now, but they invited us to a picnic table where they uncorked several sensational wines. In fact, I'll never forget Otis, charging up from the table and pacing as he kept jamming his nose into the glass and rambling on. "Brilliant, just brilliant! What's your oak treatment? What were the Brix when you picked? Do you drop fruit? How many tons per acre? How deep did you say your well is again? Absolutely brilliant!"

Tom, a mustachioed and debonaire Washingtonian, had grown up nearby in Richland and had only recently returned to his home state to try his hand in the wine business. He'd met Anne-Marie, an elegant redhead from Champagne, on a rooftop in Guadalajara while they were both studying Spanish and quenching their thirst to see the world. From that first moment, we became fast friends, as we saw eye to eye on so many things, including our wine philosophies.

We sat with slack jaws as Tom and Anne-Marie told us the tales of how the area had been a crucial site of the Manhattan Project during World War II and how an influx of scientists and engineers, along with their families, had led to an incredible population boom.

"It's a good place to raise a family," Tom said, swirling a velvety merlot. "Good people here. I can only imagine the future. One day Sunset Road will be a long line of tasting rooms. They'll be speaking about Washington State all over the world. The Columbia Valley. Maybe even this place, Red Mountain. I'd love for it to become an AVA one day. That's our dream."

Otis smiled. AVAs, or American Viticultural Areas, were legally designated regions recognized for their unique climatic and geographic characteristics. The status came with a certain clout and allowed its wineries to put the region on the label, as we'd done with Glen Ellen for all those years.

"Ah, what a dream that is," my husband said.

I'll never forget that smile. I could see him almost drooling at the idea of joining the Hedgeses and the other pioneers in making something unique and wonderful.

"There's only so much available land permitted with water rights," Anne-Marie said, "as the aquifers have to be protected from going dry, but there's a nice piece for sale on the other side down there."

They all looked to the southwest, across Sunset Road to exactly where Otis had pointed earlier.

Anne-Marie patted my arm, a smile rising on her face. Such a friendly soul. "We might let you beat us to buying it, if you're interested.

Let me put you in contact with the owner. He mentioned he might let go of the property if he found someone interested in planting a vineyard."

Otis bit his tongue, and I knew he was waiting on me to answer. Truth was, Mike and I were equally excited. I said yes, and we all walked down there together, dizzy with the promise of what was to come.

The plot had grand potential, a perfect slope, multiple microclimates, a front-row view of Mount Adams, a short walk to the Yakima River.

Otis threw himself onto the earth and didn't move for a long time. But when he stood, he looked like he could take over the world. He hugged Mike and me and then he hugged the Hedgeses and said maybe ten times in a row, "I'm home."

In writing this whatever-he-wants-to-call-it, he's certainly recalling the thirst he once had. I can see it in the way his back arches when he writes, the way he starts writing faster, talking to himself. The way he pauses and starts yapping with Amigo as if he were a writing partner. Like now.

—

"That first day, Amigo," Otis said, "I knew we'd found our Mecca. Climbing up the mountain. It was in the air, all this possibility. In my mind's palate, I could taste wines from grapes that hadn't even been grown yet. More than anything, I felt hopeful."

Otis gave Amigo a pat on the head and chewed on his pen for a moment. He stood and sat and stood and sat again. Finally, he found stillness. Desperate to relive those first years on the mountain, a smile spread across his face.

It was like having sex for the first time, stumbling and fumbling around, unsure of what to do or how to do it, but craving it all the same. Of course, I'm talking about figuring our way through the new terroir. I suspected that I'd have to learn a few new tricks, but I didn't know what it would require.

Amazingly, I thought I was on an easy glide for the rest of my life with regards to wine. I'd found my passion and made money from it, didn't have to keep learning.

That's what was so special about Red Mountain. She turned me into a kid again, lost and alive all at the same time.

Truthfully, all was well until . . .

Otis slapped his pen onto the desk. "For God's sake. If this isn't the mark of a bad writer, Amigo. *All was well until . . .* let's hope no one ever reads this namby-pamby. How else do I say it? I had the tools, the skills, the experience. Lloyd had disappeared in the rearview mirror. I was ready. The world was my oyster. Shit, another cliché."

Otis dragged a line over much of what he'd written.

"Can you imagine what Graham Greene would say? I suppose it means I should leave the writing to the pros. Don't worry, I'm almost done, but maybe I should back up a hair."

Chapter 23

The Elder Vine

They returned to Glen Ellen to finish what they'd started all those years ago. Otis moved the wines to barrel. Rebecca began working on both selling the winery and building a new one on Red Mountain.

While the land was under contract, they flew up a few more times to meet with a soil scientist and other experts, ensuring that their particular site would suit them well. They had many discussions on which varieties would thrive and how they should be planted to best take advantage of the slope and sun.

"This is a place for syrah," Otis finally said, after digesting everyone's opinions. He felt it in his bones. He'd learned the magic of syrah traveling through the Rhône Valley in France over the years, and he'd played with it down in Sonoma, but he had by no means learned to harness it.

"I don't care that the Aussies have butchered it. I don't care that it's trendy. It won't be forever. All I know is that I want to dedicate this place to syrah. We can dabble with others, but we must master syrah."

They toured the local high school and visited the nearby restaurants. Aside from some lovely Mexican food, it was a far cry from the culinary boom happening in the Sonoma Valley. Nevertheless, Red Mountain's time would come; Otis knew it with a curious yet confident certainty.

Cam flew in from Denver to join them on the day of closing. After signing the papers in Richland, they drove to the property and met with an architect from Seattle. They knew what they wanted, a place that evoked feelings of the Old World, a slice of Europe, the beginnings of a new chapter.

As Otis had learned, it was nearly impossible to get a construction loan from a bank, so the solution was mobile homes. That was why there were so many, including the two he could see from his property. Sonoma had once been that way too. It was pure farm country, nothing more. They were grateful that the good fortune of Lost Souls had armed them with the cash it took to build their dream house.

After the architect left, Otis stood in the center of where they would build the winery, and he raised his arms to the sky.

Taking in a deep breath of new beginnings, Otis howled like he hadn't howled in many moons. *"Ahhhwoooo! Ahhwoooooo!"* The energy rose from his toes and up his spine, shooting out toward the heavens.

Bec, Michael, and Camden joined him, smiles stretching wide, all of them shaking out the past, shaking out everything but this moment.

A series of coyote calls came back from somewhere up the hill.

Otis lost his breath. "You hear that, guys? A welcome call."

His every cell shimmered with delight, and Otis knew he would dedicate the rest of his life to this new terroir. Not by working his tail off but by finding the balance. By being the man he was meant to be, by becoming the man Rebecca deserved, a man his kids could look up to. Like Mike had said more than once, Red Mountain would be a second chance.

He would not mess it up.

꩜

So that Mike could get started with the second semester of his junior year in his new school and so Bec could manage construction of the new house and winery, they rented a house in Benton City, and Bec and Mike preceded Otis to their new state. They bought an old Chevy farm truck with limited miles but unlimited dents and scuffs and put a REDMTN license plate on the back. Eloise and Aunt Morgan made the eight-hour drive from Bozeman and stayed for a while. Otis sneaked up there as much as he could. His constant goodbyes began to break the connection between him and Lost Souls.

On Mother's Day, Rebecca and Otis planted their first vines, a syrah block that would be their new baby. A coyote appeared in the broad daylight and watched them for three days straight. They took turns with the posthole digger, the other plopping the baby vines into the earth and covering them back up with the dusty soil of this new promised land. They planted hundreds of vines per day, watching as each carefully selected block of land came to life. Along with syrah, cabernet, and merlot, they planted a few test rows of other varieties to see which thrived. They'd have to wait two to three years before they'd get enough fruit to make wine, but that was okay.

Otis was tired of rushing.

⌐

Almost a year later, in March 1995, Rebecca, Otis, and Mike moved into their new abode. It was everything they'd hoped, a stone cottage with three bedrooms in the center of thirty acres. From the looks of it, one might not know she was in the New World at all, and that was the point. This home and the stone winery up the hill were a nod to his European upbringing and to the great master vintners of long ago.

The back deck looked over the Yakima River to Mount Adams. Fencing lined the entire property to accommodate the sheep and chickens they'd brought up from Sonoma. After losing a couple of chickens to coyotes, they adopted a Great Pyrenees named Rosco from a local animal shelter. He slept outside to protect the livestock and poultry.

The winery featured their first tasting room, and they'd allowed the architect to give it a look of modernity with walls of thick glass, creating an immersive tasting experience offering a near-360-degree view of the Columbia Valley. When a visitor posted up to the concrete bar, illuminated by the naked Edison bulbs dangling above, Otis wanted them to feel the vines surrounding them.

They planned to keep the wine production small and to eventually go mailing-list only, but they wanted people to know that they could visit Red Mountain to taste the latest vintages. This was how a growing region was built, with an invitation for drinkers to come walk the land and see what they'd tasted in the bottle. One day there would be bed-and-breakfasts, dinner spots, performances, cultural celebrations. Rebecca and Otis would host their own events at the winery: harvest parties, concerts, book readings. For Otis, the definition of *terroir* continued to evolve. It wasn't only about the climate and soil; it was composed of the people and the culture, the energy buzzing around.

A stunning and well-over-budget underground cellar accommodated their growing wine collection. Beyond a thick wooden door and down a set of stone steps, large columns propped up arched brick ceilings. Wall sconces and candles were the only source of light. Concrete shelves held thousands of bottles of wines from all over the world, dating back to the 1940s, including several special bottles of Burgundy that had been hidden behind false walls by winemakers who refused to let the Nazis take their wines from them.

In the climate-controlled barrel room, a fancy bottling machine took over one corner. A new forklift waited to move barrels and bins. For fun, they'd imported some clay amphorae, which were alternative fermenting and aging vessels that had been used in other parts of the world since ancient times.

The garage doors opened to the crush pad, where a new crusher/destemmer and fancy bladder press waited. He'd decided he'd buy some fruit from the older vineyards on Red Mountain this year, to test the equipment and begin to understand this new frontier.

With careful water management, their baby vines took root. Otis said it was the Puccini and Ravel he'd been playing for them in the mornings. The animals seemed happy too. Chickens were easy, but sheep could be finicky. They seemed to take to the new land and had grown extra wool to get through the more aggressive eastern Washington State winters. Though they let Rosco come inside on occasion, he spent most of his time out with the animals and seemed perfectly content.

Mike excelled in this new community and his new school, nearly claiming valedictorian senior year, an impressive feat despite it being a small-town school. Otis elicited countless eye rolls when he'd say, "Thank God he got his mother's looks, but he did get my brains."

Several schools offered Michael a full ride; he chose UW in Seattle. Otis and Rebecca would sit out on their new deck looking west and clink their glasses and agree that it had all worked out. They were grateful to have found a medicine that helped Michael get out of his own way. Sure, he still had some bumps, but that was life.

—

A few days after graduation, Otis and Mike were changing the oil in the new Kubota tractor, both covered in grease, when Mike said timidly, "I don't know if I want to come back and farm, make wine." He still wore black jeans and a white T-shirt, only these were his more raggedy ones. His arms finally had some muscle to them, and all the Washington sun had tanned his pale skin. What's more, a certain confidence had sunk into him since moving.

Otis pulled his head up from the engine and wiped the grease off his fingers with a rag. An involuntary tightness twisted his insides, the leftovers of an overbearing father. "No?"

"I've been thinking about law school."

Right then, Otis let go of his hopes of passing the torch to his sons, but he told himself it was okay. He would not be his father. "You're telling me like you're worried I'll get mad at you."

"I know you want someone to take this place over, to carry on the tradition. I wish that it was me, but I don't feel the call."

Otis took his arm. "Hey, you have to find your own destiny. If this isn't it, so be it. Find your true north, son. That's all that matters."

It was the best gift Otis could have ever given his son, a far cry from the expectations Addison had held over him, and he knew bone deep that he'd done something good. As if getting confirmation from on high, the same coyote who'd been showing up appeared atop a rocky perch.

Otis pointed. "You see him, Mike? He's part of the pack that howled with us that night we all howled together. He's my good luck charm."

Mike cracked a grin as they both looked to the curious desert dog. "You're one of them, aren't you?"

Otis turned to his son. "For better or worse. Don't lose your connection to the magic out there, Mike. Whatever you do, open yourself up to the signs. Once you see them, you'll find they're enough to guide the way. Throughout your whole life. No matter where you go, what you do, find your coyote."

"Don't worry about me, Dad. I'll find it."

He pulled him into a hug. "I know you will."

⌐

Gifting Rebecca a break from her husband, Otis took his boys on a father-son trip to Germany, and they hit the sites of Munich, including a day trip to Hitler's Eagle's Nest, then shot up to Berlin to experience the amazing cultural renaissance that was washing away its ugly past. They'd ended the trip staying in Bernkastel-Kues on the Mosel River. He'd never taken the boys, and as they sat in a German beer hall over grand steins of pilsner, he reminded them to find their compasses and not to compromise.

Cam was taller than Otis and had grown his shaggy blond hair long. Having spent the last four years skiing and hiking in Boulder, he was in the best shape of his life. He was currently waiting to hear about a job with the National Park Service.

Mike glowed when he spoke about his future in Seattle and figuring out law school. He'd always been the sheriff of the family, always stood up for what was right, and Otis knew he would one day make a great difference once he found a cause that struck his heart.

Then, just like that, Otis and Rebecca had an empty nest. You can prepare for it all you like, but you can't know how it will feel until you're in the thick of it.

Even though Mike wasn't far away, his absence screamed into the quiet space of Rebecca's and Otis's lives. A few weeks after saying goodbye, Bec repeated something that she'd read: "By the time your kids leave for college, you will have spent 90 percent of your time with them."

The idea crushed Otis, and he cried on and off for two days. It was hard not to think about all the times he'd left Cam and Mike to go sell wine, all the times he'd been absent in mind even when his body was present. He wished he could do it differently, that he could have learned his lessons earlier, but all he could do was promise that he would spend the rest of his life making up for it, living a life that would allow him to pursue his passion in a way that afforded him plenty of time for family and friends.

Of course, that was an easy promise to make before his new neighbors came to town.

⌇

Ninety-five was an exceptional vintage, nice and cool, making for grapes that weren't ready to pick till well into October. Otis made wines from several tons of purchased fruit and also picked what he could from their virgin vines and made twenty cases of a fruity Beaujolais-style quaffer, for fun. He even bottled it before it had finished secondary, so that it had a bit of *pétillance*. The new guard years later would tell him excitedly that he was one of the first to make natural wine. He'd respond: "Natural wine was the original way, kids. Only in the last century did we muck up the tradition with our pesticides and insecticides and our homogeneous factory-farmed mentality."

An early evening in November they cracked the first bottle of their sessionable field blend, the inaugural effort under the new label of Till Vineyards. The nights had turned chilly, and Bec and Otis both wore sweaters as they enjoyed the warmth of the falling sun on the back deck overlooking Mount Adams, that dominant beast of a peak that watched over this side of the world. A Stephen Stills solo record played on the turntable inside. Down below, Rosco chased the sheep, making them scatter. The baby vines had shed their leaves and started to move toward hibernation, preparing themselves for winter.

"You know, Bec, I suppose I might admit that life is not that bad." He pulled out the cork and poured them each a glass. "How nice to have figured this thing out. We're here. The vines are in the ground. The boys are taking over the world. You and me, we have a whole new journey ahead of us."

Otis took in the woman who meant everything to him. She'd entered her mid-forties with all the grace in the world. A part of her was still that young hippie princess he'd met on the purple bus. Certainly the same warm eyes, though more wisdom shone through them now. Her jewelry was of a more sophisticated nature, as was her attire. She smelled of the rosemary mint soap she'd recently made from their sheep's milk. Her curly hair was still the same sandy blond with golden hues.

He raised a glass. "I wouldn't have made it without you, my love. Somehow you brought me back from the abyss. More than a time or two. I hope this next chapter is more about you than me."

"About that," she said. "I've been thinking the same thing—"

"Now hold on. Let's not get carried away. I'm not saying that you're not needed, or that I'm suddenly healed from my inner strife." He almost said more but held back. "Sorry, okay. Finish, please. What is going on with you?"

She crossed one leg over the other and clasped her fingers atop a knee. Her wise eyes twinkled with excitement as she directed them toward the splash of colors melting into the horizon. "I want to travel."

Otis seized up. One thing was true for farmers, especially those who had a new farm to tend: Travel is a recipe for disaster. She knew that as well as him.

"Don't worry," she said, throwing up a hand decorated with several rings. "I'm not going to pull you away from your new vines. I'm talking about just me. Maybe go to India, or even Bali. I'd love to do a yoga retreat. Or even a silent retreat."

"A silent retreat?" He said it like she'd suggested they abstain from alcohol for the holidays.

"Where you don't talk for a week or two."

"Dear God."

"It might be good for you, if you wanted to join?"

"You're, ugh, I . . . that sounds like . . . um."

She finally let him off the hook. "I'm joking. Of course you're welcome, but I would assume it sounds like your version of hell."

Otis breathed a sigh of relief. "Very close to it. All you'd have to do is invite Lloyd and restrict alcohol, and my hell it would be."

She sat back up, reached for her glass, and took a sip. "You've traveled so much for work while I've been at home, focusing on the boys. I want to get out and see places. It's my turn."

The sheep baaed below; crickets chirped.

"I don't love hearing that you feel like you've been trapped."

"Not trapped. I didn't say that. I wouldn't trade what I've done for the world, but I do have things that I want to do. We've done Europe plenty, but I want to see more of this world. And not just vineyards, no offense."

"No offense taken," he said. "There's no point in visiting anywhere in the world that doesn't put wine in the highest regard, but I suppose you'll have to learn that the hard way," he said with an annoying grin.

"There is more to life than wine, Otis."

"I know that," he said defensively. "Cheese is nearly as paramount . . . pork. Don't get me started."

She let out one of her famous *ughs* but in a playful way. "Believe it or not, there is more to the world than things that you put into your mouth. What about a surf or ski trip, or even skydiving, something extreme to get the adrenaline going?"

"Deary, my idea of extreme is a seven-hour gastronomic tour through Bologna. Nothing gets the adrenaline going like an all-day culinary romp that starts with a bottle of Pignoletto paired with a chunk of forty-month-aged Parmigiano-Reggiano and a stack of finely shaved *prosciutto di parma.*" The hair on his arms stood up as he delighted in even the idea of such an adventure.

Bec rolled her eyes, but Otis fought back with an all-knowing chuckle. "We'll have to agree to disagree, dear one. But again, just as the boys had to learn the hard way, so will you. Go take your trek to Machu Picchu and sleep on the hard ground and eat goat arepas and drink Peruvian lagers. Go sleep in a tent in the jungles of Zimbabwe whilst gurgling fermented elephant urine, then peer through your little binoculars for a leaping gazelle. Or—"

"Here we go," she said.

"Fine, fine. Just know that while you're sitting in a hut in Bali munching on bamboo during your silent retreat, you'll recall our visits to Paris, the exquisite satin sheets of the Hotel d'Angleterre, the selection of Bordeaux at Le Grand Véfour. Or you might recall setting our eyes on the vines of Romanée-Conti for the first time, quite surely our first brush with God. You will know, my dear, that I am sometimes right."

"I should record you. People should hear your ridiculousness."

"Isn't this why you love me?"

She laughed.

He threw up his hands. "What?" With a sigh, he spun his glass. "Fine, let's return to you. Tonight. No. *This year* is about you."

She paused, likely gauging his sincerity. "It's nice when your husband asks about you. Kind of rare. Has someone been coaching you?"

"Oh, dear. I feel like I'm teetering on being exiled to the doghouse. Believe it or not, I am capable of seeing outside of myself."

She grinned at him, showing both surprise and appreciation. "I do feel forgotten sometimes, just another vine down a row."

That one hurt. "You know that's not how I feel."

"I know."

Otis topped off their glasses. "Do whatever it is that fills your cup, but don't move on without me. I want us to grow together, you know?"

"We will. I'm in love with Red Mountain, too, and I want to be a part of its evolution, to help grow this community. I share in that dream with you, and I'm excited about getting into the tasting room. Can you believe we've never had one?"

"It will be a new—"

Gravel crunched in the distance, a foreign sound at this time of night. Headlights followed, a vehicle driving up the shared road past their farm. More headlights, another car—no, two more. All moving in the same direction.

"What's going on?" Otis asked, standing up and approaching the railing. He imagined his feeling was similar to that of the Romans when the Visigoths invaded their land.

The cars came to a stop outside the single-wide trailer on the orchard land that abutted the northern side of the Till property. Otis had briefly met Henry Davidson and his family on the other side, but he'd not come in contact with anyone from this property.

Car doors shut. A few raucous voices rose into the night. Yellow lights illuminated the trailer.

"I have a bad feeling," Otis said, recognizing a tingling in his chest.

Rebecca didn't say anything, and he knew she felt the same way.

⌒

A racket rose out over the land the next evening while Otis and Rebecca were preparing dinner: coq au vin. Otis had never heard anything so excruciating in his life. A moment ago, pure bliss, the very marrow of the universe humming through his land. Then . . .

Thrashing metal.

After tearing off his apron and stomping through the house, Otis slid open the back door and poked his head out.

"What in God's name is going on over there?" Turning back to the house, he said, "Bec, I may lose my mind right now!"

"What's wrong?" She stopped cooking as she picked up the noise herself. Her shoulders slumped. If Otis was reading her correctly, it wasn't the sound that bothered her. It was that she could tell that trouble was imminent.

Bec followed him out onto the porch, the racket shaking the land, disturbing the baby vines working to take root. Otis took the binoculars off the hook and looked north to their neighboring property, a hodgepodge mess of cherry trees.

Near the single-wide trailer that had stood empty for so long, a fire blazed. Behind it, three men attempted to make music in what looked like a band practice of sorts, though it sounded more like their attempt to wake the dead. The drummer pounded on his instrument with rage. A bassist thumped a beat that vibrated the planks of the deck. The guitarist—clearly Beelzebub himself—played with so much distortion there was barely any separation between the notes. This wasn't music at all, this was . . . torture.

Tears pricking his eyes, Otis offered her the binoculars. "See for yourself. We've worked too hard to . . ." His words fell off.

Once she'd gotten a good look, she said, "They're playing some music. It'll be over before too long."

"Playing some music? That's not music, Bec. That is the symphony of the devil."

"God, you're dramatic, Otis. I bet Michael would love it."

Otis cringed at the memory of the Metallica poster Mike once had on his wall. What had Otis done wrong? *What had he done wrong?* The poster had hung beside another featuring an on-the-edge-of-risqué photograph of supermodel Carmen Forrester. He should have ripped them both off the wall, but Bec had insisted they choose their battles. Considering his difficulties, she'd always given their youngest more slack than Camden.

"Okay, I'll admit that I'm not up on the latest trends, but—"

"That's an understatement—"

"This is not music, Bec. More importantly, they are ruining our peace. They're disturbing our babies out there who are far too young to endure such racket. From Puccini yesterday to this?"

"I think your vines can handle it."

Her tone suggested he was being absurd, and he didn't like it one bit. "Can they, Bec? I'm going to call the police." He started inside.

"The police? Honey, we're in ag country. There aren't any noise ordinances."

"Then I'll take matters into my own hands."

She didn't laugh; she cackled. "What does that mean? Take matters into your own hands. Are you going to go beat them up?"

"I don't know, but you're making light of the situation."

Bec tugged his arm, forcing him to peel his stare away from the travesty. Holding his cheeks, not allowing his eyes to wander, she said, "Let them be. We're in a different land now."

He slumped in surrender. "I know we can't expect everyone out here to show respect for the wines and vines, but lines must be drawn."

"Maybe we should make them cookies and walk over there. Apparently they're going to be here for a while."

It was Otis's turn to cackle. "Cookies? By gods, woman, you're funny sometimes. Could we sneak a little rat poisoning in them? Now, there's an idea."

"In no way is that funny, Otis. And is it by God, or by gods, because you come off as not knowing whether you're exclusive to one or a polytheist?"

"Depends on the day, my dear. How about a scoop of laxative?"

The music stopped, and a soothing quiet washed over the mountain. A stillness rose up Otis's spine. "Ah, you hear that? I feel like someone was drowning me."

Otis drew in a deep breath, sucking in the oxygen of silence.

"There you go, Otis. Let it go."

Less than a minute later, the devil's orchestra started up again. Otis broke away from Rebecca and rubbed his face and then pulled at his hair. "I can't. I just can't. I'm too old for this shit."

"Too old? You're in your forties. Please stop being such a drama king."

"Drama king? I don't think you're hearing what I hear."

"I do but choose to be okay with it."

"Oh, here we go with the"—he gave air quotes—"*choosing.* You can't always *choose.* Well, maybe you can, but I can't choose to ignore this commotion. I can't choose to—"

Bec placed a hand on his chest. "I'm going to return to the kitchen to finish cooking."

"How could you possibly cook while they're tearing a hole in the sky?"

She ignored him. He turned back toward the neighbors, then raised his hands and stared up to the moon. "Are you enjoying yourself? Crushing my soul, torturing my vines. Am I not wanted here? Is that it? The coyotes beg to differ."

⌇

The following afternoon, Bec stood at the door with her ginger cookies—Otis's favorite—displayed on a tray and covered in plastic wrap.

"Don't give them all of those. Come on. Did you leave any for me?" He poked one. They were soft and warm.

"Yes, you have a couple on the counter in there."

"A couple? They get an entire batch?"

"*And* a bottle of wine. Go grab something nice from the rack."

His chest began to cave in. "They're not wine people. Please don't waste a bottle on them."

Rebecca stomped on the hardwood floor. Actually stomped! "Otis, they are our neighbors. You want community, it starts with neighbors. Not everyone can be like you. Find the common ground."

"Common ground? The only common ground is that we breathe air. It stops there."

She stared at him till he broke.

With the cheapest bottle he could find in hand—a twist-top, barely quaffable, savagely nonsustainable cabernet sauvignon from the grocery store, Otis reluctantly walked beside Rebecca through the neighbor's cherry trees to the trailer. Though they'd never met the owner, Otis had seen a team tend to the trees their first year. Strangely that same team hadn't come this year, and the cherry trees looked malnourished.

A Honda Accord with a dent in the door and a truck with a camper bed were parked crooked in the gravel drive. The trailer had seen better days. It was white with brown trim and raised up on concrete blocks. Several extension cords came from underneath, clearly how they powered their amplifiers. A rotting set of wooden stairs led up to a dirty door with a diamond-shaped window. A tarp hung off one side and connected to two poles, providing shelter for a cooler and grill. There was no landscaping whatsoever.

"Anyone home?" Bec called. They stood about twenty feet from the door.

A barefooted man in jeans and a sleeveless Megadeth shirt pulled back the door. Likely in his early twenties, he had short ash-black hair and gauges in his ears. A big wiry beard came down to his chest.

"You're trespassing," he said in an alpha voice.

"I told you," Otis muttered to Rebecca.

Brave Bec stepped forward. "We're your neighbors. The Tills. We haven't had the pleasure of meeting you before." She held up the tray. "We baked you cookies."

"We? I didn't bake them cookies," Otis said under his breath.

The burly man descended the steps. "That was nice of you."

"I'm Rebecca, and this is Otis."

"Vance Mason." He had a backwoods kind of accent, what you might expect from a rodeo rider. They all shook hands, and then Vance took the tray of cookies with another thanks and set them on the steps.

He crossed his thick arms. "By the looks of it, you're growing grapes."

"That's right," Bec said. "Moved up here last year from California."

Vance let a grin surface. "Coming to the promised land, aren't you? Everyone talks about the grapes. That's what my brother wanted to do. Rip out all these cherry trees and plant grapes."

"Wanted?" Otis asked.

Vance looked past them to the trees. "Yeah, he died last winter during a training exercise off the coast of Maine. He was a Navy SEAL, about to discharge. Wanted to learn how to make wine. He left me the place."

In that moment Otis couldn't have felt more like a jerk. Now he understood why the trees had been neglected. He lifted the bottle, wishing he'd grabbed something more substantial. "If you're a wine guy, we brought you a bottle. Plenty more where that came from . . . if you like it."

"I don't know the first thing about wine, but we'll find a good use for it. Thanks." He took the bottle from Otis's hands.

"Vance!" came a loud male voice from inside. "You're missing it."

"I'm coming!" Back to Bec and Otis, he said, "We're watching the WSU game. Anyway, good to meet you. Thanks for the gifts."

"You guys staying awhile?" Otis asked casually.

"Until it's too cold. We don't have heat in there."

Otis made a quick prayer for an early winter, as Rebecca said, "Let us know if you need anything."

Once they were out of earshot of the trailer, Otis said, "Don't say it, please."

"I'm not saying anything."

"Lesson learned, okay?"

Rebecca took his hand.

A week later, Otis and Rebecca hiked up to the Hedgeses' property. They sat around a table in front of a château that approached completion. Their view was unparalleled on the mountain, offering unimpeded looks at the treeless Rattlesnake Hills and the great Mount Adams off toward Seattle.

Anne-Marie expertly opened a bottle of Taittinger Champagne with a saber—a long-held tradition—and they toasted to the future of Red Mountain. Soon the conversation moved to wine and stayed there.

Buzzing now from the lovely bottle of Champagne, Otis couldn't help himself. "We met our new neighbors. You might have heard them partying last night. Up past midnight blaring metal music. Do you even know what metal is? I wish I didn't."

"Otis, please behave yourself," Rebecca said.

Anne-Marie laughed. "You sound like me reining Tom in."

"It's a full-time job, Anne-Marie. He wants this to be Burgundy yesterday."

"My kind of guy," Tom said. "We have work to do."

Another bottle of Champagne later, the discussion led to the infamous Mitch Green. Otis and Rebecca had heard the name, the Red Mountain hermit who made undrinkable wines, the man who would hold out a hand with dirty fingernails and offer you warm cheese from his pocket.

"He really exists?" Rebecca asked.

"Oh, does he."

"I was thinking I might keep avoiding him," Otis said. "I hear, once he gets to know you, he'll show up at your house uninvited."

"That's true," Tom said, "but visiting him is a rite of passage." Tom stood and filled their glasses. "Let's go find him."

They strolled down the Hedgeses' property, talking farming techniques, then crossed Sunset Road and descended down the hill for a while. Soon a patch of vines came into view, a slopy vineyard of ups and downs. After a few more minutes, they came upon Mitch's house, a single-story effort from the seventies. The man himself appeared, wobbling on a cane out from the garage door of the shed next to the house. He was bald and wore a flannel shirt rolled up at the sleeves, showing hairy arms.

"Tom Hedges! How the hell are you!" He coughed like he had emphysema.

"Mitch!" Tom looked over to Otis and Rebecca. "Brace yourselves."

After short greetings, Mitch invited them to sit. He did not pull cheese out of his pocket, but he did provide a rather warm Camembert to go with his cabernets. They tasted through the lineup and spoke about the good old days. He'd gone to Davis before "escaping" to the Pacific Northwest. Word was that his family had chased him out of California. The wines were on the edge of undrinkable, though Otis admired the man's passion. It was just that his palate was shot or that he'd suffered too much trauma in Vietnam. He spoke in often-incoherent sentences as he rambled about the sad state of the wine industry.

After he ran out of words, he said, "Anyway, I know you came to see the vine."

"The vine?" Otis asked, raising a curious eyebrow.

"I thought they might be ready," Tom said, grinning from ear to ear.

Mitch led them up a hill, taking his time with the cane. Otis's curiosity had certainly been piqued. They stopped before a healthy syrah block. Though Mitch had his shortcomings, the man knew how to farm. They followed him down a row, until he came to an abrupt stop and set his gaze on one particularly interesting vine.

Otis wasn't sure at first what they were witnessing, only that it was a sign of some sort, a miracle. There before them stood a vine that glowed with energy. The trunk was twice the thickness of the others and swirled in wild abandon. The vines around it leaned toward it, as if being pulled in.

Otis had a feeling not dissimilar from when he'd first walked the rows of riesling in the Mosel, this tingly sensation of being in the presence of God.

Finally, he was able to get out a word. "What are we looking at?"

"You tell me," Mitch said.

Otis stepped closer, amazed. "Either an experiment with a powerful fertilizer or something far more serious."

"It's not fertilizer."

Otis nodded. Then his suspicions had been correct. He'd stepped into the chapel of Red Mountain.

Before he could even move, Rebecca knelt down and touched the trunk. "How old is she?"

"No one knows. This is the oldest block on the mountain, as far as I know. Guy who sold this land to me said it had been here long before him. Even before Jim Holmes and John Williams planted."

Rebecca turned back and showed a twinkle in her eye as she connected with Otis. "She's beautiful."

"You see how the other vines grow toward her?" Mitch asked, pointing with his cane. "No matter how I prune, they go to her like sunlight."

Rebecca waved Otis over; he knelt next to her. She guided his hand to the trunk of the vine. The whisper he once detected in Carmine's vines was there, a steady buzz of absolute peace, both a feeling and a sound.

"This is the heart of Red Mountain right here," Tom said. "I'm not much of a mystic, but you tell me this land's not meant for something special."

Mitch jabbed his cane into the dust. "It's not only these vines that grow toward her. Every vine I've planted. She's the heartbeat."

"The heartbeat," Otis whispered, gliding his fingers up into the leaves. "Does she have a name?" Not all grape vines were feminine, but this one was as feminine as Aphrodite.

Mitch shook his head. "I never could name her. Didn't feel worthy of it. But she has a personality. Snaps at me if I don't pay attention."

Everyone laughed.

Otis turned to their new friends. "You're only now showing us?"

"You have to plant some roots first," Anne-Marie said, "before we show you her secrets."

"There are more secrets?"

"They're endless," Tom said. "You've found a place begging to be tended to, begging to be discovered. A place that will one day grow some of the most important grapes in the New World."

Otis could have damn near cried.

That night, the coyotes howled their songs and sent tremors through Otis's bones.

Chapter 24

Neighborly Disturbances

On February 2, 1996, the temperature on Red Mountain fell to negative sixteen degrees, and so many vineyards were lost. Planting on a five-to-seven-degree slope had been the Tills' salvation. The steady run of air descending down to the river kept the freeze from settling. After countless bud dissections, they determined they'd lost only 25 percent of their vines.

Otis weathered the news well and found gratitude that they didn't lose more. He and Bec expected to face new challenges, but he couldn't have imagined such a jarring winter. Nevertheless, the pruning went well, and the entire mountain celebrated when budbreak came in mid-April. This was a farmer's life, fighting from year to year.

Camden and Michael were both thriving. Cam had landed his dream job as a biologist for the National Park Service. Though he was based in Denver, he spent a lot of time on the road, visiting parks all across the US. On weekly calls from his University of Washington dorm, Michael told them he was exactly where he needed to be. His love of football had never died, and he always squeezed in some talk about the Huskies games.

"Have you met anyone?" Bec asked one day, failing to hide how important his answer was to her. "Not a girl, I just mean friends. Have you found your people?"

"Yeah, Simmons and I hang out. He's pretty cool." Simmons was his roommate. Otis and Bec had first met him when they'd moved Michael in.

"And classes?" Otis asked.

"Guys, I'm fine. I love it here. I gotta go, but I'll call soon, okay?"

⁓

In May, Rebecca went to Bali for a month of torture. Well, yoga and silent retreats, same difference in Otis's opinion. He began to replant the vines they'd lost with the help of his new crew. He hired Chaco, a man with a silver front tooth who admitted to having a sordid history back in Mexico working with cartels, but he'd cleaned up and tended vines for fifteen years in Washington State. Chaco brought with him his team of hard workers, who understood the land and were entirely open to farming without chemicals.

Otis invited all the employees to taste wines, and he'd talk about his latest philosophies, how this was far more than a cash crop, that wine was life, and that he expected them to treat the vines and wines with reverence. In return, he would pay them well.

It was after one of these meetings, one week into Rebecca's trip, when Otis saw Vance coming up the road. He hadn't seen him all year and had hoped that it might be a quiet vintage, sans the sounds of the band from hell.

"Shit," he said, scratching his head.

"*Quién es ese?*" Chaco could speak English but knew Otis could understand him in Spanish.

"*El diablo,*" Otis said.

That night Otis sat on the back deck, Rosco at his feet, and lit a pipe, something he'd recently taken up. He felt a certain need to have a little extra fun while Rebecca was gone. Usually he'd take Mondays through Wednesdays off drinking, but while she was away, he'd abandoned restraint and was drinking a handful of special bottles from deep in the cellar.

He'd already enjoyed two glasses of a 1975 Trocken riesling from *Egon Müller*, and he'd just poured himself a stellar glass of a pinot noir from Coche-Dury. By God, it had some panache. He smacked his lips in delight. Even Vance couldn't get in the way of the glory of a well-made Burgundian wine.

The second glass tasted even more delightful, and he stepped inside to grab some tasty treats. A neighbor had recently gifted Otis a cut of salmon that he'd caught and smoked himself. Turned out to pair wonderfully with the pinot noir, and Otis fell into a joyful state of bathing in the setting sun on the back deck. Later, he'd grill a steak the size of his head, because Rebecca had been threatening to go vegetarian again, so he better take advantage while she was away.

Then came the sound of approaching vehicles. Rosco raced to the rail and let out a deep bark. Coming up behind his dog, Otis saw several cars driving entirely too fast along the shared gravel road—a line of morons who wouldn't know Barolo if it rained down upon them.

"Slow down, you ingrates!" Otis yelled, tobacco smoke rising from his lungs.

Of course, they couldn't hear him; their ears were clogged with bad music and poor taste. More bozos arrived, and within thirty minutes it had turned into a full-blown party at Vance's. A fire roared, smoke rising high into the big sky. Forty bohemians partied like it was their last night on earth.

Let it be said that Otis enjoyed a good party. How many festivities had he supplied with wines over the years? Still, this was different; these hooligans were threatening the sacred terroir. What if they threw out cigarette butts or shat in the rows? They were all a bunch of rabid raccoons. They might as bloody well walk into the Sistine Chapel and shoot fireworks!

A good bottle and a half in, Otis decided to investigate further.

He was slightly wobbly, but it was a good buzz, one that only Burgundy could bring. "When done right," Otis asked as he meandered his way into Vance's property, "what would a Red Mountain wine do to a man? I suppose I don't quite know yet." By gods, Bec would kill him if she knew what he was doing now, slipping back to his old self, but it wasn't that . . . not exactly.

It was simply that this land would be their swan song, their last ode to life, and how could he do that with this blubbering fool and his band of weirdos arriving just as the vines began to reproduce?

One hundred yards from the bonfire, Otis became stealthier, sneaking from cherry tree to cherry tree, peering around trunks to get a better look. On the other side, a line of cars and trucks were parked along the gravel road. Everyone gathered around the giant fire. By God, it was May. They shouldn't be having a fire now. Warnings were already out. Besides, they were surely the kind of people who'd burn Styrofoam and plastic, zero respect for Mother Earth.

It was past midnight, but it seemed the party was in its infancy. The scantily clad ruffians held Solo cups in their hands and made a commotion worthy of Vikings pillaging a village.

Vance had a funny-shaped guitar strapped around his neck and was adjusting a microphone. The drummer tested the high hat. A bassist with hair that fell past his shoulders began to toy with a groove that shook the land.

"Dear Lord," Otis said at this aural travesty.

He watched in bewilderment as these beasts broke into a song with no discernable melody, barely a rhythm at all, only a smashing of notes at a volume unsuited for human ears. The other guests began to bob their heads, which turned into banging their heads and screaming as loudly as they could.

Otis clutched his chest, recalling the feeling of when he'd burned his phylloxera-infested vines so many years ago. What he should do was sneak over and yank out the plug that was feeding the electricity to these devilish noises. Before he could act on it, though, a dizziness came over him, and he leaned on one of the malnourished trees to steady himself.

From where did these people come? From Benton City? Or Richland? From the bloody depths of hell? They were surely the devil's outcasts, humans blinded to art, to humanity.

If only Bec could see. She would understand his indignation and the associated punitive thoughts.

The next morning Otis marched over to visit Vance. He barely noticed the colors of the sunrise, the birdsong, or the cool morning air. He was a man on a mission to defend his vines.

The leftovers of the party made Otis's own hangover even worse. Most of the guests had left at some point in the night, but a couple of men had passed out under the stars and were stirring as Otis approached. Smoke rose from the leftovers of the fire. Solo cups, cigarette butts, and liquor bottles littered the clearing. A keg that was surely empty lay on its side. A rabbit shot into the sagebrush.

"Hello?" Otis called, reminding himself to be affable—not in an I-brought-cookies sort of way, but more out of self-preservation. Vance was larger and younger and could wipe the floor with Otis's body.

He climbed the wobbly wooden steps and rapped on the trailer door. "Hey, Vance, you around?"

A minute later, the door pulled open, and a shirtless Vance stood there looking even more hungover than Otis felt. He didn't have a six-pack, but his physique suggested that he bench-pressed tree trunks and did burpees with small cars strapped to his back.

Otis cleared his throat. This wasn't about reprimanding the man; it was about appealing to him. *And* not getting knocked in the mouth. "I wondered if we might talk for a moment. Man to man, as they say."

"Man to man?"

"Neighbor to neighbor."

"It's early."

"It's late for ag country," Otis corrected. "I just need a few moments of your time."

Vance stepped down from the trailer, his heavy boots knocking up the dust from the ground. He stretched and looked out over the property. "I'm assuming we're bothering you?"

"Well, yes, I suppose so. You know, I'm a winemaker. No stranger to a good party, but . . . heavy metal music, vehicles coming in and out at all hours, guns shooting off . . . it's a bit much for me, especially after midnight."

Vance raked his fingers through his beard. "Isn't that why we live out in the middle of nowhere, so we can do what we want?" He fired up a cigarette and waved at one of the guys who'd slept outside.

Otis wondered how Thomas Jefferson, who had done wonders for the American wine market, might appeal to Vance. "You mentioned your brother was a wine guy."

"I don't know if he was a wine guy, but it was always his dream."

"Mine too. Mine too." Otis almost slipped through a time portal, thinking back to that first day he came upon Paul Murphy's ranch. "The thing is . . . I play Ravel to my vines."

"Ravel?"

"The French composer. And Puccini and even Pavarotti. I'm sure you know Pavarotti, right?"

Vance shook his head.

"Oh, my." Otis turned back toward his own property. "Those vines are my babies, and I know it's hard for someone who isn't into wine to understand. Growing grapes, fermenting them, it's my passion, one of the reasons I was put on this earth. The thing is . . . a good winegrower must create harmony in his vineyard, and the goings-on here disrupt the synergy. The young vines coming to life absorb everything around them. They want to realize their full potential with . . ."

Otis stopped, unsure of what else to say.

Vance looked at him like he belonged in a straitjacket. He shot smoke through his nostrils like a bull who'd seen red. "Look, neighbor, what's your name again?"

"Otis, Otis Till."

"Look, Otis Till. Are you trying to tell me I can't have my friends over? Can't play music? It's the one thing my brother left me, this land. You trying to run me off? He was here long before you. I imagine a lot of people were. I know the Davidsons, your other neighbors, have been here for generations. Then you come up and start telling people what to do?"

This isn't going well, Otis thought. He wondered what would happen if he stuck his fingers right into the gauges in Vance's ears, then tugged with all his might.

Likely not a good idea, he decided.

Otis recalibrated. "I'm not trying to tell you what to do. I suppose I'm trying to find some common ground, perhaps appeal to the artist in you, even." *Not that the shit you're playing has anything to do with art,* he thought to himself. "There are ordinances. That kind of noise late at night. I can't sleep. My vines . . ."

"Your vines can't sleep either? Look, Otis Till, I have a naked and lonely woman in that trailer. Your problems, they aren't mine. You want a quieter place? I'm sure there's another mountain with a plot of land available."

Vance couldn't have said anything more ignorant, but Otis pressed on with a level tone. "Ah, that's just it. There are indeed other mountains, but they're not like this place. The land you're standing on is holy ground. Your brother must have known it too. I can't quite explain it. This slope here, the way the sun falls. Soil ripe for planting. The river down there. Proximity to a town. People with ambition. Above all, wines that sing. The wines from Red Mountain vines sing, Vance."

The guy worked on his cigarette as if it were the only oxygen in the vicinity. "Are you trying to belittle me?"

"No, I'm not—"

"I'm feeling belittled."

"Belittled?"

"Don't patronize me. You go play your stupid music to your vines; I'm going to play my music to my land too. I'm sure you understand. Now get off my property." Vance grew taller, his chest puffing up. A sense of foreboding filled the air.

Otis worried he might not have another opportunity to speak with Vance, so he clamored for a solution. "No, please. I . . . look, what if I bought your property? What is it, ten acres? Would you allow me to purchase it from you? It's clear you have no intention of taking care of the trees or planting grapes. It's worth far more than what your brother paid. I'll pay handsomely."

Vance laughed. "You come up from California like you're Lewis and Clark, try to impose your laws. This isn't California. Besides, I figure this land'll be worth a whole lot more if I hold on."

"Let's talk numbers."

Vance pulled at his beard. "Let's not. Now get off my property before we have a problem."

Otis thought it would be a good time to say goodbye. He lifted his hand and bid him adieu.

On his way to pick Rebecca up from the airport, Otis decided not to complain to her about Vance. He would spare her all the worry and disgust that had penetrated his cerebral cortex. He'd learned that, no matter the offense, and despite her equal passion for their land, she didn't harbor anger at people—even terroir terrorists—the way he did. If he brought it up, she'd worry that he was slipping back to the man who'd gone to the Super Bowl without his family. The man who'd struck Lloyd in the mouth.

No, he wouldn't bring it up to her. He'd wait for her to form her own opinions of Vance Mason.

The kid hadn't hosted parties every night, only on the weekends, but come Friday nights, it had been debauchery. Otis had tried calling the cops, but the officer who drove up echoed what Bec had said, that this was ag land, and nothing could be done. There were no noise ordinances. "Move into the city if you're looking for quiet time."

Otis didn't point out the irony in that. "What about the fires?"

"Fire ban starts in June," said the officer.

Otis found Rebecca at baggage claim, standing there in a breezy button-down dress and sandals, looking radiant. For a moment his new struggles washed away. She kissed him as if they'd only just met. By gods, he didn't know why she loved him so, but dammit, she did.

"How was your trip?" he asked, already knowing the answer from the look on her face. Her hair was pulled back, showing a potentially new piercing high up on her ear—he'd lost count years ago.

While he'd been decaying, along with his young vines, at the sounds of metal music shaking the land, she'd been healing her soul and igniting her chakras.

As they waited for her bag, she spoke of Bali and the people and how she'd found a new tribe over there. "You have to come with me next time."

"Did you come upon any vineyards?"

"Vineyards in Bali?"

"How were the wine lists in the restaurants? Surely they drink wine. They're not heathens, are they?"

"I didn't drink."

"Didn't drink for a month?" Otis was repulsed. "Yeah, not quite my speed. I think this is one of those treasures of a vacation that should be for you alone. No talking either?" He wondered why anyone would impose such self-flagellation.

She smiled as if saying to herself, *It's back to the real world, Bec. Back to the man you married for some ungodly reason.*

Oh, just wait, Otis thought. *I'm in rare form.*

"No, we didn't go silent the entire time. We meditated and connected. Ate healthy food."

He touched her warm cheek. "In the most mindful of ways, I'm sure. Tiny little bites, imagining your food's origins, delighting in the textures."

"Naturally."

"Did you at least indulge in some Balinese hashish? Perhaps smuggle a tiny bit home for your handsome lover?"

"All sober, Otis."

"Oh, dear." He retracted his hand and felt suddenly guilty for the 1978 Château Latour he'd delighted in the other night—without her. At least they had a few more bottles.

"So you sat there, stewing in your thoughts, slowly picking at turtle food, and sharing in hypothetically soul-stirring conversation without a bottle of wine—or even a thimble full of a fine Sauternes? No, thank you. Not quite my speed, but I'm glad it made you happy. Do you feel recharged and ready to put up with your plagued artist of a husband for another fifty or so years?"

She chuckled in a way that meant the entire purpose of her trip had been exactly to prepare for another stint with her husband. "I don't know if it was *that* much of a recharge, but it should get me through the vintage."

He kissed her lips. "One vintage at a time, then. That's the best way to live, I suppose."

The people of the Tri-Cities were an interesting breed, and one could see the entire scope of them at the baggage claim: overalled farmers, wine people in business-casual dress, serious religious types in interesting costumes, traveling salesmen and scientists returning home to their families.

Bec slipped an arm around him. "So . . . tell me, what's new? Are all the plantings in?"

"All plantings accounted for. All's well save our neighbor." *Dammit, I wasn't going to bring it up.*

"Vance?"

A month of frustration rose up within him and surely showed on his face. "He's back. I offered to buy him out. No luck. Tried to appeal to his heart. He does not have one. It's been shot up and shriveled by that metal music and cheap booze."

Bec let go of Otis. "What happened?"

The light on the baggage carousel lit up, and the belt began to run.

"Vance is redefining what it means to be a bad neighbor." Otis ran his fingers through his sideburns. "And given me my first gray hairs. These parties, they're out of control. I called the cops. They won't do a thing. So I hope you're rested because you won't sleep a wink on weekends. It's really awful, Bec. A big deal. I . . . I don't . . ."

She drew in a breath. "Do you remember the serenity prayer? Grant me the power to know the difference?"

"Oh, I've heard you quote it a time or two."

"Maybe this is one of those things we can't change."

"I'm not ready for surrender yet."

"Surrender? This isn't war."

"Is it not?"

Her body slumped on an exhalation as she pointed and said, "There's my bag."

~

Otis was the only one who didn't sleep that next weekend. "You don't hear that?"

"The only reason I'm up is because you woke me. Let's sleep in tomorrow. It's Saturday."

"I can't. I have . . ."

She curled her naked body up next to him, her feet grazing his legs. "I dream of a day when we can lie in bed till noon on Saturdays."

"Doing what?"

She pulled him close. "I could think of a few things."

343

"A few? Oh, dear. But what about—"

"What? The vines and wines? Maybe I'll ride into town tomorrow and find a rodeo man. I imagine he'd be happy to skip work and lie in bed with me all day."

Otis gave her a loving squeeze and kissed the top of her head. "I recall a time in Germany when you said something similar. Yet it was a nice German man you wanted to find. I see things have barely changed."

"I'm just a woman who wants to be satisfied."

"Do I not satisfy you?"

"Very often you do. Not lately, though. I think Vance has all your attention."

"Fair enough. I'll try to forget Vance. Let's lie in bed till noon and I'll do nothing but satisfy you over and over. I'll provide you with things not a handsome German nor a rodeo man could ever muster."

"What would that be?"

"You'll see. I will make orgasms like I make wine."

⌐

Michael came home for the summer, and it was enough to keep Otis's frustration with Vance at bay. UW had been good for him. If anything, his biggest fault was that he was like his father, always needing to do something, never sitting still. What Otis and Rebecca loved most was how his heart had grown even more. How many nineteen-year-olds were eager to ask questions of their parents? How many were eager to get back into the fields and work with their dad?

With the faint sound of Vance's metal band creeping into the house one night, Otis asked, "What do they all do for work? Where do they come from? Where are their parents?"

"Dad," Mike said, "I can barely hear them."

"But they're there, and just knowing they're there is the problem."

Rebecca and Mike looked at each other and shook their heads. *Our Otis,* they seemed to say. *Always disturbed, forever pursuing the perfect vintage.*

It was barely July when Mike met a kind young brunette named Emily, who worked as a nurse in Richland. He brought her over to dinner a few times, and Otis and Bec would let them enjoy a glass of wine. Emily would gush over the food, saying that she'd never had better in her life. Michael would spend most of the meal asking Otis not to embarrass him anymore.

Rebecca also did some connecting on the mountain. She developed a few friendships, joining several like-minded women on morning walks, sharing gardening and cooking tips, and likely expressing their never-ending frustrations with their husbands.

Meanwhile, Otis was trying to wrangle his vines. He constantly wondered what he'd gotten himself into. Sure it got cold at night, but those July days were a level of hot he'd never known. Those first two or three years, it was all about getting the new plantings to take root, which meant overwatering them. Not an easy task in the desert. His well water would drip out of the tubes and either dissipate in the heat or drain right through the silty soil.

August made July look like a cool winter month in San Francisco. There wasn't a drop of humidity, such a far cry from the fog of the Bay Area. Otis's skin flaked. Dust clung to everything, even the sheets.

Cam had come home for a visit, though, and that was far better than even a rainstorm. He adored his new job. A content smile nearly always graced his face. He was still as handsome as ever, long thick wavy hair and skin always brown from being outside.

At the moment, the boys had gone into town, and Otis had just wrapped up for the day. He found Rebecca on the back deck, stretched out on a lawn chair, reading. A slice of lemon floated in a tall glass of ice water on the small table beside her.

"How does anyone even survive in this heat?" Otis asked, wiping his dusty eyes. The lavender they'd planted was in full bloom and wafted off a lovely scent that Otis might have enjoyed had he not felt like an overcooked steak.

"At least there's no humidity," Bec said, setting down her book. "Kind of reminds me of that sauna we visited in Copenhagen."

Otis wondered if it was only him struggling. Not only with the climate, but life in general. "What are you reading?"

She covered it up. "Nothing you would like."

"What is it?"

"A romance that I picked up at the grocery store."

"The grocery store? Hold on, did I marry a woman who reads the books found at the checkout aisle in the grocery store?"

"You did indeed. Is there a problem?"

Otis sighed. "I suppose not. You know, I think the world is moving on without me. That's what it feels like."

"Then you best catch up."

She sipped her water, then returned to her book.

Otis stared at her for a while. What a wonder it was that this woman could easily settle into this new life. Here he was fighting for his terroir, desperately learning, while she was reading a trashy romance novel, not caring at all that her tomatoes weren't nearly as good as they had been in Sonoma. "We'll get 'em next year," she'd said as she slid a plate of salt-and-peppered heirlooms into the trash the previous evening.

We'll get 'em next year. Had she really said that? As if they had all the time in the world.

Otis couldn't wait until next year, and no, it wasn't about the money. They had plenty. This was about conquering a new land, being part of something bigger than himself. Harnessing the wild beast that was Red Mountain and squeezing juice out of her that would knock the world off its axis.

There was no time to wait. What, could the Allied forces have waited another year to challenge Hitler? Could Monet have set down his brush for a fortnight to focus on his Pilates practice? Could Einstein have paused his work to learn how to fish?

The roar of a four-wheeler stole him from his daydreaming. He turned to find Chaco coming toward them. His vineyard manager leaped off the four-wheeler before it had even come to a stop.

He jogged up to the back deck and called up to Otis, *"Jefe, no hay agua."*

"Cómo?"

"No tenemos agua."

There was no water. Otis raced off the deck. *"Cuál es el problema?"*

Chaco switched to English, his silver tooth reflecting in the sun. "The aquifer ran dry. We're out of water for the season."

"Out of water? That happens?"

"Sometimes. It's been a hot year."

"What do we do?"

Chaco kissed the tip of his index finger and pointed it up to the sky. "Pray to God."

~

"I'm not a prayer, Bec." He kept his voice down so the boys, who were watching television in the living room, wouldn't hear his frustration. Nothing got under Rebecca's skin more than Mike and Cam seeing Otis have a meltdown.

Otis sat at his desk; Bec was in the recliner. "That's Chaco's answer. Say our prayers. I called Tom Hedges, Jim Holmes. Same thing. There's nothing we can do. I guess I'll go fill buckets up from the river tomorrow."

"That's silly, Otis."

"It's not. This is our livelihood. I swear, I wonder if we screwed up coming here. It's the Wild West. I don't know this land, these people. Had I any idea we might run out of water, I would have conserved, but we share the same aquifer with Vance, the profligate swine. He probably used it all up anyway, with his overhead irrigation. The guy sprays like he's at a waterpark. Probably leaves his taps running while he sleeps."

"He's really gotten to you, hasn't he?"

"That's what I've been trying to say all summer."

"He lost his brother, Otis. He's grieving. Maybe he doesn't have a father figure in his life. Give him some slack."

Otis sliced a hand through the air. "I don't do slack. That's your department. All I want to do is get these new vines online and make some good wine this year. But I can't because there is no water. Hottest place on earth. Hotter than the Sahara. Why do we even have an oven? I can roast you a chicken by setting it under the hood of my truck for ten minutes."

She smiled.

"What?" He hated it when she didn't take him seriously.

"I think you're sexy when you get all fired up."

"Only you wouldn't be bothered by drought."

"Otis, listen to the land. Vance has you so riled up. Be smarter. Connect. We're where we're supposed to be. You have to embrace it. Remember the mildew our first year? Remember how the water wouldn't drain, and it wouldn't stop raining?"

"It's the opposite problem here."

She sighed in defeat. Even the great Balinese princess known as Rebecca Bradshaw Till had her limits. "It's not a problem. You're learning a new language. We all are. Give it time."

Otis shoved his hands into his pockets. "Time? I'm almost forty-four. You see my gray hair. A man only has so many vintages."

"You're such an exaggerator. You might have lived half your life, and you have three gray hairs."

"Four." He stopped, weary of himself. "I know, I know, it's just . . . I want this place to be perfect."

"Sounds to me like you're setting yourself up for disappointment."

A knock saved Otis from a full-on therapy session.

"Yes?"

Cam pulled open the door. "Hey, Dad, you want to go fishing with Mike and me in the morning? We're driving east to the Snake."

"I can't. I have . . ." His unsaid words trailed off to oblivion.

Otis didn't even have to look at Rebecca to know he was being given a choice right now. This wasn't about being guilted into something, or about dealing with the vines, or even fishing, for that matter. This was an opportunity to go spend time with his boys.

Otis looked up at his oldest son. "Why, yes, Cam. I'd love to go. What time do we leave?"

Cam looked at Rebecca with golf balls for eyes. She shrugged her shoulders.

"What? I'm full of surprises."

Cam let loose a smile. "Yes, you are. Shall I wake you or do you want to set an alarm? We're leaving early."

"Son, farmers are the ones who wake fishermen. Not the other way around. I will have fed and watered the sheep and will be eating lunch by the time you wipe your sleepy little eyes."

"How do you put up with him, Mom?"

"They should give me a medal, shouldn't they?"

~~~

Sometimes small victories were all one needed to keep going.

The next evening, fillets of steelhead sizzled on the grill on the back deck. The dark clouds in the pink sky threatened what could possibly be rain, though that would be rare for August. Besides, Otis never got that lucky.

"How'd your dad do?" Rebecca asked, sipping on a kombucha that she'd fermented herself, something she'd learned to do in Bali.

Mike and Cam looked at each other and smiled. Was there anything better than having raised two men who still enjoyed each other's company?

"He's getting better," Cam said. "Still needs more patience. He has to let the line unwind behind him before he moves it forward again." He stood and demonstrated with a fake rod in his hands.

Otis could see Camden back on the water earlier. The man had a touch like no other with a fly rod. While Otis hacked away at it, constantly getting snagged by a tree behind him, Camden made his line dance. He could set a dry fly exactly where it needed to be with such a light touch it was as if the fly had a parachute. Needless to say, Cam had caught his limit.

"I'm afraid patience is my Achilles' heel," Otis said, feeding a bite of fish to Eosco, who had come up to visit with the humans for a while.

Rebecca showed her teeth.

"What? Do you have something to say, wifey?"

"Oh, I don't think so."

"I'm perfectly happy owning my lack of patience. I don't want rain now. I wanted it yesterday. I want Vance and his crew to be gone . . . yesterday. I want those vines out there to be thirty years old, not little saplings with their white britches on." He was referring to the white grow tubes that still protected the trunks of most of his vines, the sign of young vines in any vineyard.

Mike came up and threw an arm around Otis. "We give you a hard time, Dad, but you're pretty amazing."

Otis jutted out his bottom lip at Rebecca. "You hear that, doll?"

Mike stood back up and faced Otis. "Seriously, you're an inspiration. I brag to everyone that you're my dad, the great vintner Otis Till."

"Be careful, Mike. You're going to make an old man cry."

"Maybe you should. I don't tell you enough. You've shown Camden and me what it's like to go after something with unbridled passion. Not only that, but you've also raised two fine men, if I do say so myself."

"We both know the only reason you're *fine* is your mother."

"Oh, c'mon. Don't make a joke. I mean what I'm saying."

Otis felt the hairs on the nape of his neck stand up. "Michael, you perhaps give me more credit than I'm due, but your words fill my heart."

"Is that a raindrop?" Cam asked, extending a hand.

Otis looked to the sky and felt one land on his forehead. He closed his eyes and waited for another. Was this a dream? Many more came, wetting his face. Bec had always said it, so it was amazing that it had taken him this long to learn. The world had a way of making it easy on you when you quit fighting and let the current take you.

His fishing trip today—his choice to be with his boys over working—had been a rain dance.

He pushed himself up and held out his arms. "Come here, my family."

The four of them formed a circle, arms interweaved. The rain picked up and splattered upon them.

"Everything that I do," he said, finding their eyes, "it's all for you three. I don't know what I did to deserve you, but I will be forever grateful." With that, he pulled them in tighter, and never had he felt more on top of the world.

Chapter 25

NO COCAINE OR NEGRONIS

The young vines survived the lack of water in August 1996, and in the following months, they produced enough fruit to allow Otis to make their first true wines from Red Mountain. While the wines bubbled their way toward fermentation, and as Otis and his team executed the required punch downs and pump overs, Vance and his band of kooks departed the mountain.

"We made it," Otis said to Rebecca one day in the empty tasting room. "Another year in the books." Otis poured her a sample of one of the first syrahs to have gone through primary fermentation.

Rebecca swirled the glass and took a sniff, then took a sip and sucked in some oxygen. "Now that's different, isn't it?"

"Different? Not exactly the word I'd hoped for."

"You know what I mean. So different from Lost Souls. I adore it. It's robust, almost intimidating on the nose, but the body is . . ."

"Yes?"

"Not as thick as I expected."

"I know, I know. Thank God we harnessed her. It's like learning all over again. I could have picked a few days earlier, but I didn't want to . . . I was a bit afraid."

"What are you doing being afraid? Haven't you proven yourself?"

"I suppose so, but I feel the pressure. People know who I am up here. God knows why, but they look up to me. They're hoping that our wines will help us all get on the map. I don't want to screw up."

"That's adorable," Bec said, "but don't put that pressure on yourself. Keep doing what you're doing. Have fun. These wines don't have to be perfect. You say it all the time . . . no wine is perfect. Just capture the year. I think this is a solid start of the tale of our journey to Red Mountain. I can't wait to see where these wines go."

Otis sniffed his own glass and noted the bright and dark cherry notes evident in all the reds so far. "It's a special place, isn't it? Unique. I don't quite have her figured out, but you're right—it's fun trying. I can see the potential on the horizon, perhaps only a few vintages away."

"Isn't that nice, that your life is about the challenge of a new vintage, about learning and growing and seeing what comes. You know what I look forward to? Opening up this tasting room. I want to be behind this bar and welcome people, pour our wines."

"I suppose it will be nice to finally have something to pour into the eager mouths of the public. We could open next summer, if the wines are ready."

"Might need to figure out our label design then. Have you thought about it?"

Otis dipped his chin. She was making a joke. He'd thought about it endlessly.

"Simplicity is what I want. Red Mountain in big letters. Till Vineyards under it."

Otis and Bec shared a smile. How fun to be doing this again, but on their own terms. No investors, no money worries, hypothetically nothing to prove.

As planned, Rebecca opened the tasting room that next summer, and she took on her new role with bright joy. They hoped to one day eliminate their distribution network and sell every case on property. What a dream, but it would take a few years.

In the meantime, they'd have to rebuild a distribution network. Sadly, the distributors they'd used for Lost Souls and Heartache showed little interest. Otis had anticipated an uphill battle to push unknown terroir, but the more he heard and learned, the more he realized he'd underestimated the challenge.

He could see why, though. Forget promoting Red Mountain, which would eventually be paramount. He had to first convince people to give Washington State a try. Most people didn't even know that this state made wine. The winegrowers and makers needed to get out there and spread the word and preach the gospel. They needed to hit trade shows and present at general sales meetings and drag bottles around to every retailer and restaurant and wine bar in the country—and the world. But very few had any interest in doing that.

California had such a big head start. Oregon too. What Otis saw on the mountain was a lack of vision. Many winemakers didn't care whether or not Balthazar in Manhattan poured Washington wines, or whether, God forbid, Bedwetter wrote about them. As point of fact, Bedwetter had never written a word about Washington State. He'd certainly gone on and on about such wineries as Archery Summit and Domaine Drouhin and the like in the Willamette Valley—all their glorious pinot noirs stealing any potential Washington attention. Not that Otis wanted Bedwetter to write about his new venture, but he wanted him to recognize his new state.

With regards to Red Mountain, Otis saw many more problems. Arguments about water rights. Disagreements over insecticides and pesticides. Tension over whether they should pave Sunset Road and who should pay for it. Basin Disposal had stopped picking up trash from wineries on Sunset Road because the gravel was destroying their new trash trucks. That meant that each winery had to carry their trash out on a daily basis. How could Red Mountain take over the wine world when they couldn't even agree on paving their main thoroughfare? Otis's vote went to paving. He saw a region where the same enthusiasts who visited Napa would fly up and spend a day tasting the stunning wines of a new frontier. He saw a place where everyone even used the same branding. He wanted Red Mountain to be recognized as an American Viticultural Area, and have its own logo, its own glass, its own trade shows.

Don't get him started on the food. By gods, Rebecca hated it when he brought this up in public, but the people around there, their idea of a night out on the town was to go to the Cheesecake Factory. Or Applebee's. For God's sake, one winemaker mentioned his love affair with TGI Fridays, and Otis's heart had hurt for a week, thinking that a proper fine-dining restaurant in the Tri-Cities area might be decades away.

For now, when he took Rebecca out on a date, they'd have a piece of previously frozen flounder with I Can't Believe It's Not Butter! mashed potatoes and canned green beans ordered off a menu with over one trillion options, paired with a glass of flabby Sutter Home chardonnay marred with more oak in it than the entirety of the Cascades.

Ah, oak. The French talk about a kiss of oak, the slightest bit to round out the edges of a wine. Americans overdid it—to put it lightly. Forget a kiss, some of those American chardonnays had endured a proper *fuck* of oak, slathered in an overabundance of oak's secretions like an overly seasoned dish prepared by an amateur chef. To make it even worse, these wines weren't even aged in oak barrels. The winemaker would shake large bags of flavored oak chips into the tanks, letting them impart their aromas before yet another filtering. They might as well be making Doritos! It was enough to send a man like Otis to his knees.

The highest hopes at the moment were that the new Asian chain called P.F. Chang's might grace the Tri-Cities with its presence.

Let it be said, though, that Rebecca didn't share such distaste for the chains of the Tri-Cities. First of all, she was delighted when Otis took her anywhere, as there had been a time when he'd gone months without taking her on a date or bringing her flowers or even taking her on a stroll hand in hand. More to the point, she adored the Cheesecake

Factory and would run her finger along the four-thousand-page menu with delight. She had no qualms about Applebee's or TGI Fridays either. In fact, she looked forward to the potential arrival of P.F. Chang's.

Otis took it as a reminder that no one, not even Rebecca, was perfect. He'd tell her that, too, as she moaned with delight over a salad she'd put together from the buffet.

"You make everything a war of principle, Otis," she'd respond. "For once, let go and enjoy a few bites. The food's delicious."

He'd pinch the bridge of his nose, take a last look at the bland rice pilaf and the overcooked popcorn shrimp on his plate, and mumble a quick prayer.

She'd always get the last word with one of her favorite subtle, passive-aggressive jabs—one that she must have picked up from a psychotherapist over the years. In the Southern states, they might have patted your thigh and offered, "Bless your heart." Rebecca would say, "It must be hard to be in your skin sometimes."

"Well, it is, thank you for noticing."

The wines from Till Vineyards were bloody there, though. Nineteen ninety-seven was far cooler, a fine vintage from the start. Budbreak had been on time; the mild temperatures had allowed for even ripening. The young vines yielded nearly twice what they had the year before, and the resulting wines inched one step closer to bringing Otis the pleasure he desired.

"We're not there yet," he told Mike over the phone one day in early winter, "but we're getting closer. Zeroing in on the right picking date. Figuring out canopy management. I think we might even drop a little fruit. Some of the blocks yielded *six* tons an acre. Can you believe that? I'd be happier with four."

"How about Vance? Did he come back?"

"Barely saw him. He has a team that manages irrigation—horribly, if you're wondering—and then they picked their cherries in August, but no complaints. I think he got the message. You mess with Otis Till, you get the horns." Otis winked at Rebecca as she prepared a fresh bouquet of flowers for the kitchen table.

"That's great, Dad. Seems like you're really happy with the move."

"It was your idea, my boy, and a great one. It truly was a phenomenal year, and I'm happy things are going well for you too. A Seattle lifer, you say?"

"That's right. Everybody's talking about Amazon now, how they might go beyond books. And Starbucks is growing. Microsoft. It's crazy here."

"Your mother and I bought a little Amazon stock during the IPO."

"Really? Wouldn't it be cool if I could land a job with them? They'll need lawyers."

Otis pulled at the cord of the phone. "I'd love it if you stayed in Seattle. Your mother wants to buy a place there soon anyway. Now that we have some wine to sell, it's probably time."

"I have two roommates who would love to be taken out to dinner."

"It would be our pleasure." Otis didn't mention that they hadn't eaten out since TGI Fridays had burned their jalapeño poppers. *It will all be okay,* Otis kept telling himself. Red Mountain would grow. There was a time like this back in Sonoma and Napa. Perhaps there had even been a Red Lobster in Burgundy at one time.

Wait, no.

Definitely not.

⌒

After the blistering harvest of '98, Otis hit the road. Rebecca was okay with his forthcoming departure this time, probably even excited about him leaving the house, as he hadn't traveled much in years. If he was being honest, he was excited too. It would be nice to get out there and share their new project with old friends.

He had a different mindset this time and was determined to travel in a health-minded way. Not only for Rebecca, but for himself.

Water. That was key. Drink lots of water and go find the bloody gym in the hotel. All those years of travel, and he'd always opted for a bacon omelet over the gym to start his day.

Midnight was the rule. Not a minute later, he had to get back to his room. This meant some of his old friends would get upset with him. No matter, he had to look out for himself.

Salads. That was another biggie. Sure, maybe some prosciutto and Manchego from time to time, perhaps a bagel with schmear or a slice or five of pizza when he reached New York, but he would focus on ordering a salad with protein on top.

Mindful drinking too. It was a concept he'd learned from Rebecca's incredible ability to eat mindfully. Whereas he could shove a rib eye into his mouth without even noticing, she would pause to consider all the people and animals and plants that had contributed to the plate before her, and she had the extraordinary ability to savor each bite as if it were her last. He would do the same thing with wine. He would cherish every sip, not only delighting in the bouquet and structure, but searching deep into the tertiary dimensions of the wine to find the essence of her—the land and climate and men and women behind it.

No Negronis, period. He needed to get that one tattooed on his hand. *No Negronis.* It went without saying that cocaine wasn't even an option. A *No cocaine or Negronis* tattoo would be a hell of a conversation starter, though.

As this new Otis, the reinvented and reinvigorated soldier of his land, arrived in each state to spread the Gospel of Red Mountain, his distribution network wouldn't know what hit them.

One of his first stops was right back where it all began in San Francisco. He arrived a day early to visit with a few old wine-biz friends. On the second night, he slipped up and stumbled into his hotel an hour past midnight, but he accepted that he was a work in progress. The next morning he peeled himself out of bed, hit the treadmill for thirty minutes, then enjoyed—no, not enjoyed—*survived* a green drink poisoned with wheatgrass. Rebecca wouldn't believe him when he told her.

That Tuesday, a young wine rep picked Otis up and spent the drive to Beltramo's gushing over him. An enormous case stack of Heartbreak cabernet sauvignon greeted them at the front of the store. Since white zin had fallen out of fashion, the new owner of his former property and brands was now trying out other varieties. Otis couldn't imagine what the wines tasted like, and he had no intention of finding out. A little harder to swallow was when he set his eyes on the new vintage of Lost Souls.

They'd fancied up the label. The glass was far heavier, heavy enough to make a good weapon. He glanced at the alcohol content. *Seventeen percent.* "Dear God," he said to the rep, who was barely old enough to drink, "they've really sold themselves out, haven't they? They must have picked on Christmas Day."

"It's selling like you wouldn't believe," Howard said, coming down the aisle in an apron. Gray whiskers spun like birds' nests around his ears. Their handshake turned into a hug, and they caught up for a while.

"How's the new project?" Howard asked, clearing his throat. "I'm excited to taste it."

Otis and the rep prepared the wines on an empty wine barrel in the back room. When Howard joined them, Otis took over and began to tell the tale of Red Mountain while extracting from his man bag a jar of Red Mountain soil. He twisted the lid, and a cloud of dust rose into the air like magic.

"Look at that," Howard said, grinning bird's nest to bird's nest.

"Alluvial silt," Otis said. "Several feet of this before reaching a hardpan floor of high-pH calcium carbonate that the roots rarely penetrate. So they don't go deep, they go wide."

After a few minutes of weaving together Red Mountain prose, he stopped himself. Howard was getting fidgety. "Let me back up. Let's talk Washington State." He told Howard of the Missoula floods and how they had carved out the Columbia Valley. He talked about the heat units, the amazing drainage of the soil, then backed up even further to talk about Seattle, just to set the stage.

Unlike Otis and the young rep, Howard didn't spit, and his cheeks turned red and his speech jolly as he caught his morning buzz.

Howard set down his empty glass on the barrel. "They're exceptional, Otis, but I can't sell them."

"What do you mean? They're a third of the price of Lost Souls." He could hear the frustration in his own voice.

"I know. The juice is as good too. Still, it's Washington. No one knows Washington makes wine. I'll take a couple of cases, for old times' sake, but I'll probably have to close it out by the end of the year. I'm just telling you the truth."

Otis exited Beltramo's with his head down.

~

It only grew worse on the East Coast. On a sales trip in Tampa, Otis dined by himself, a salad with a piece of roasted chicken. He'd skipped the white Negroni that he'd drooled over and gone straight for one single glass of Rioja and a large bottle of Pellegrino.

At the table next to him sat a chatty couple who lit up when he mentioned that he was in the wine business, but when he'd told them he made wines in Washington, their eager eyes turned shallow.

"I didn't know they make wines in Washington," the lad said. "We were there recently, did the whole White House tour, Museum of Natural History. Which side of the Potomac are you on?"

Otis lifted his glass of Rioja and stared into it, feeling like maybe he'd bitten off more than he could chew with his latest venture. Perhaps they should have bought a ranch house in Sonoma and traded in his tractor and shears for a Cadillac and golf clubs.

"No, not that Washington. I mean Washington State, on the other side of the country."

The guy's girlfriend hit him in the head. "And you call yourself a wine person, honey."

Otis raised a hand in calm understanding. "No, it's perfectly okay. It's an up-and-coming wine area. Truly lovely Bordeaux varieties, but without the price tag." *Did I just say that? I sound like I'm selling Corvettes, not liquid poetry. Rebecca would be so much better out here on the road.*

"What are the Bordeaux varieties?" she asked.

Otis spent the next thirty minutes giving them an education, and during their conversation he realized something. This was part of being a pioneer. It was a battle that would be fought one person, one palate at a time. What he knew as he paid their bill and bid them good night was that they would drink Washington State wines for the rest of their lives.

⌁

The experience of that evening lingered with Otis, and a renewed optimism came over him in the fall of 1999. He'd successfully navigated a rather heavy year of travel, something he hadn't expected, but spreading the word was absolutely required. If many of the others in the region wouldn't do it, then he'd do it on his own.

Rebecca was on board too. While he collected miles up high in the sky, she spent her days bettering Red Mountain in her own special ways, growing the nearly perfect tomato, planting flower beds, and tending to the sheep and chickens. She started a book club with many of the women on the mountain.

She ran the tasting room better than anyone Otis had ever seen. She had become so passionate about Washington State and Red Mountain, and when a new guest walked in, she pulled them into her and Otis's world, giving them tours of the land and facilities—sometimes even their home, God forbid—and then she'd taste them through the wines with all the patience in the world.

"Don't hold the bulb, hold the stem. There you go. Now give it a nice swirl and press your nose in. Don't be afraid. Close your eyes and see where it takes you." She could have sold grapes to a vineyard.

This was what it required, the second act of their lives, digging in and doing whatever it took to spread the Gospel of Red Mountain.

It was just that every time they found their stride, dark clouds came galloping in.

Otis was preparing a carne asada marinade for dinner when his phone rang on the counter. It was Aunt Morgan, who more often wrote letters than phoned. He quickly wiped his hands and accepted the call. "Everything okay?"

The long beat of silence confirmed bad news was coming. "Morgan?" he said. "What's wrong?"

"Your mother, Otis. She's in the hospital."

His pulse froze. "What . . . what happened?"

"They're doing tests now, no one knows. She complained of a headache this morning; then I found her on the floor in the living room an hour ago. She was barely breathing."

Otis pinched closed his eyes and drew in a long breath. "I'll be there as soon as I can."

It was too late to catch a flight, so they made the eight-hour drive and reached the hospital in Bozeman a little after midnight. In the hallway, they embraced Aunt Morgan, who told them that Eloise had had a heart attack and that she was in rough shape.

Otis entered the room to find his pale-faced mother staring back at him. A smile graced her face. "My son."

"Mum." He took her cold hand and kissed her forehead.

Eloise died two days later. Otis had barely left her side, and he was there when she closed her eyes for the last time. He wished he'd had more time with her, but life had gotten in the way. At least he had been there when she was issued her wings, and what he'd never forget was the strength and grace she'd showed all the way to the end. There'd been a time when he'd thought his father was the hero of the family, but by the time they laid her in the ground, he knew it was his mother who'd been the rock.

—

Vance hadn't shown up in a long time, which Otis had interpreted as divine intervention, perhaps even a gift from his mother from heaven. A hired team continued to work Vance's land, poorly if Otis was judging, but those men and women were the only signs of life over there. Clearly God had deemed this land too holy for Vance or his heavy metal music and his disrespect for the sacred.

Or so he thought. Otis was enjoying a nice afternoon. He'd hired a few interns from Washington State University to work with him in the cellar, and they'd spent the day cleaning. Otis found incredible joy in the sparkle of a spick-and-span winery. They were nearly ready to bring in fruit, and Otis was sure this was his year, the year he made a wine that would set the world on fire, a wine they would talk about from San Francisco to Tokyo.

He'd poured himself a finger—maybe two, maybe three—of a properly aged and particularly peaty Laphroaig and was about to peruse the newspaper when the familiar sound of vehicular invaders came from the vineyard road. As Rosco began to bark, Otis's body seized up. Vance was back.

Things had been better lately. He'd found peace with his mother's passing. Red Mountain was on the upswing.

And yet the darkest nights always followed the brightest days, especially in his world, as he spent his life under a ladder, his eyes on the black cat crossing in front of him.

Otis called for Rebecca and pulled back the curtains. She came into his office and looked out the window with him.

With his eyes on the cars kicking up dust as they moved through the cherry trees toward the trailer, Otis said, "If you tell me it's time to bake cookies, I will jump right out this window."

"Don't you have a new parlor trick yet? Besides, this window is a little high. It might hurt."

"Fine, then I'll stab myself in the jugular with a pen."

Rebecca reached for his forehead, his third eye, and made a spreading motion with her fingers. "Don't let him get in your way."

After her feeble attempt at pacifying him, Otis took her arm and pulled her in. "I know, I know. It's just . . . everything was so nice. So quiet. Now this vintage will be the one when Vance returned: 1999, the return of Vance Mason and his band of hooligans."

"Only if you let him define your vintage."

Otis gestured out the window. "He's there, dear. I'm looking at him with my own eyes. Are you saying it's my fault he returned?"

"I'm saying we have no control over him. Let's do what we do. This will be our best vintage yet. You and I both know it."

"I hope so," he said, his tone caked in dread.

"There's no room for hope," she said. "I know so."

Otis sighed. She was right. He'd done well, shedding the skin of the man who used to get plagued by these troubles. He was being tested; that was all.

—

Apparently Vance hadn't changed much. In the coming days, Otis watched with a sad heart as the man had his parties and band practices, wrecking the terroir with his ignorant ways.

Otis was a different man, though. Losing his mother had reminded him of the fragility of life and of the promises he'd made to himself and to Bec. He swallowed what he wanted to say, sparing Bec another rant.

He put earplugs in when the sounds crept into their bedroom late at night. He faced the deck chairs more southwest, so they couldn't see the trailer in his view.

"You know, Bec, if they were giving out medals, I'd get one for sure. Haven't you seen my patience?" It was Saturday afternoon. Late October, and autumn had painted the leaves. Otis and Rebecca sipped on a vermouth and soda with a spear of orange and olive and watched the sun melt into Mount Adams. Django Reinhardt played from the portable jam box the boys had given them.

"You certainly get your credit," she said. "I'm impressed."

"You say that like you doubted me."

"I have never doubted you, that's for sure. It's just that you still continue to surprise me. Look at you, healthier than I've ever seen you, despite a few challenges."

"A few? Had someone told me what farming a new land would be like, I'd be sitting in a rocking chair on our porch in Sonoma, chatting with you about which push lawn mower would be the best for our quarter acre of land."

"That is the one life I don't think you could have handled. What would you do all day?" Rebecca slid the olive off the toothpick with her teeth.

"Sleep a good bit. Listen to Chet Baker and take long naps." Otis changed to his best American accent. "Play poker with the fellas. Grill burgers in the cul-de-sac. Shoot hoops. Nine-to-five it every day. Go to the cinema. Watch ball games."

"Yeah, that's not you."

He laughed and returned to his natural tongue. "You love to pretend like this is all my dream, but it's yours too."

"Absolutely," she said. "I love what we've done. I love where we are."

He absorbed the beauty of his wife, the way the sun shone down upon her blond hair and golden skin. "I'm trying to imagine my Rebecca in that life we almost lived. Buying a tiny plot where you could hang a wreath on the front door, have a tulip garden—nothing more. An entire property set up with irrigation on timers. A yard service, so that we don't have to dirty our nails. Perhaps adopt a Labrador retriever."

Otis chuckled and kept going. "You'd be the prettiest lass on the cul-de-sac, that's for sure. Imagine waking up without a rooster, easing into the day, barely a stress in the world. Walk to the market for our vegetables. No need to go pick our own. If you want jam, you don't need to make it. They sell it at the store. Maybe we'd buy a second home in Palm Springs, a place to get away. You read your Nora Roberts, and I'll read the latest Grisham or Silva. Make sure we have a guesthouse for Cam and Mike and their kids. It actually doesn't sound that bad."

"It's not our life, though, is it?"

Otis took a long sip of the wonderfully bitter drink and smacked his lips. "My dear, for some reason, we chose the road less traveled. The gravel road that leads to life in the vines." He raised his glass to her. "To the wine life."

As their glasses clinked, a gunshot ripped through the air. Laughter followed, then a string of curses. Another gunshot. *Fwap, fwap!*

"What the hell?" He grabbed the binoculars from the hook by the door and rushed to the railing. Through the cherry trees, he saw Vance pointing a rifle into the sagebrush. A few people stood behind him, and their laughter drifted out over the land.

Otis directed his gaze to whatever it was Vance was aiming at. A target, maybe a bucket . . . or a rabbit.

Another gunshot. Smoke rose from the rifle.

Then he saw it, a coyote clamoring for a hiding place. It looked like it had been hit.

There are times when a man calculates. When he sees a problem and considers the best way to eliminate it. When he pauses to wonder if the risk is worth the reward, if chasing after a man with a gun is a good idea.

This was not one of those times.

Otis raced down the steps of the deck, sprinted along the fence line, then crossed over the gravel road into Vance's cherry farm.

Another gunshot only put more fire under Otis's feet.

Ignoring the pain, he weaved through the cherry trees like a skier slaloming down a double-black diamond. Fury rose out of him from the great depths of his soul.

As he drew close, he saw Vance chasing after the coyote, pausing to shoot and then taking off again.

"Put the gun down!" Otis called, spit spraying from his mouth, his breathing broken and desperate.

Vance turned back but only for a second. He continued to stalk the coyote.

Otis didn't slow at all. Racing as fast as he could, his heart roaring, his lungs heaving, he shouted with everything he had, ordering Vance to stop.

In the distance, the poor coyote—sand colored with patch fur— was racing away.

Vance looked like he had a clean shot on him. His finger was on the trigger when Otis plowed into him. They both hit the dust in a collision that knocked Otis's breath out of him. The gun landed five feet away with a *thwack!*

Vance rose to his knees, shouting, "What the . . . ?"

"Who do you think you are?" Otis roared.

Only then did he remember that Vance was fifteen years younger with biceps nearly double the size of Otis's. The coyote, in the meantime, raced farther up the hill.

"You don't shoot the animals here!"

"He's trespassing, just like you." Vance eyed the gun on the ground and worked his way over.

Otis mustered all the energy he had to barrel into the man, knocking him onto his side. Vance easily tossed Otis off him. Then he landed several punches onto Otis's face, knocking his head back, splattering blood onto his shirt.

This made Otis only more furious, and he threw punches back, striking Vance in the stomach several times, making him fold into a ball.

They tumbled over one another, pulling, punching, kicking. "You don't shoot a coyote!" Otis yelled as his knuckles met Vance's teeth.

Vance's friends had reached them, and one of them grabbed the gun. He shot it into the air.

Otis and Vance froze, and both fell back into the dirt, gasping for breath. Silence fell over the cherry farm. Otis felt dizzy enough to pass out. Blood dripped from Vance's chin and ran down his beard.

"You don't shoot coyotes on this mountain," Otis said. "You ever do it again, I'll kill you."

Vance dragged himself up and took the gun from his friend. "I'm the one with the gun."

Rebecca's voice came from somewhere around them, shouting to stop. She raced up to the scene. "Otis, let's go home."

Fear shone in her eyes. She looked to Vance. "The cops are on the way. I'm going to take my husband. You don't shoot animals around here."

"Whose land is this? According to the law, on my land I can shoot any animal I see fit."

"It's the unwritten law of this mountain," Otis said, pushing himself up with bloody knuckles.

A police siren sounded in the distance.

Vance pointed the gun at Otis's chest. "I'm sure the police will be happy to straighten things out. You ever come on my property again, I will put a bullet in you and let those dogs tear you apart. You understand?"

Otis didn't respond. Had Vance not had the gun, he'd go after him again, tear those gauges from his ears. But there Bec was at his side, tugging him away.

He kept his eyes locked on the enemy. This mountain was too small for both of them. Something had to give.

"Let's go," Rebecca whispered, pulling at his arm.

Otis nodded and finally turned away.

As they reached the gravel road, Otis limping in pain, a police car rolled to a stop in front of them. The officer climbed out, set his hat on his head, and frowned. "I guess you're going to bleed all over the back seat, aren't you?" His voice had a scratch to it, like he'd swallowed sawdust.

"I was trying to stop the man from shooting a coyote."

Rebecca stepped forward. "I'm the one who called you, Officer."

Another police car pulled off Sunset Road, headed in their direction.

Otis wobbled without Rebecca holding him up. "His name's Vance. He pointed a gun at me."

"That's his property?"

Otis nodded.

"I'm going to put you in the back of my car, go sort this out, all right?"

Bec jumped in. "He was trying to—"

"Lady, I'm in charge here. Why don't you return to your house? The other officer and I will assess the situation."

~

Otis had never been inside the police station in Kennewick. He'd never been behind bars before. It was a clean place, he'd give them that. A series of cells lined up along a sparkling tile floor. They'd strip-searched him, then thrown him in here an hour earlier.

Only problem was that Vance was in the cell next to him, huffing and puffing about how Otis had been the one to trespass. There had been a warrant out for Vance's arrest, which was why they'd dragged him in too.

"This is exactly the problem with you outsiders coming up here," Vance said.

The two men couldn't see each other. Through the barred window of Otis's cell, the half-moon glowed. One singular light bulb burned directly overhead.

Otis crouched on the hard floor, his arms around his legs, his eyes on the white wall above the toilet. "You were shooting at a bloody coyote."

"The damn thing cleaned out an entire cooler of deer meat. It's my right to protect my belongings on *my* land."

"He's a defenseless animal. Don't leave a cooler of meat out in the desert. What did you expect? What are you even doing out here anyway?" Otis couldn't contain himself. "You show up every once in a while to the land you've inherited and do nothing but disrespect it. You won't sell it to me. You certainly don't know how to take care of your orchard. What's the end game here? You keep holding on?"

"Why not? You say you're up here for a reason. That Red Mountain is special. I'm guessing a decade from now, it'll be even more special."

Otis wasn't getting anywhere. What was the point in even talking to him?

An hour must have gone by. Otis had calmed down. He moved to sit on the edge of the single bed. "What is it you're doing with your life, Vance? Tell me that."

"Why the hell do you care?"

"I want to understand, that's all. You don't know how difficult you're making mine, coming out, playing your music, having your friends over, shooting guns, destroying the stillness that my young vines require right now."

A long laugh. "Do you hear yourself? There are people out there like my brother fighting wars, and you're worried about your young vines."

"Yeah, okay. You're right. I'm no Navy SEAL. I'm not protecting people. I'm an artist, a winemaker. It might not seem important, but it's what I'm meant to do. I've known it for a long time. I'm not saving people, protecting people, but I'm creating something that maybe makes a little difference. How about you?"

Otis studied the shadow that his head cast on the concrete as he waited in the silence.

"Is it music?" Otis finally asked, imagining how Bec would see things. "Is that what you want to do? You an artist too?"

No response.

"If that's it, why are you out here in the middle of nowhere?"

"Life's not always simple."

"What does that mean?"

Time passed before Vance answered. "My mom, she has dementia. I can't leave her."

A spark of sympathy lit behind Otis's rib cage. "I'm sorry to hear that. You would, otherwise?"

"I'm a painter, paint houses, but you're damn right. I'd love to go down to LA and see if I could make something of myself."

"Where's your dad?"

"Never had one."

"What'd you do? What's the warrant for?"

"Got pulled over with a bunch of weed and then skipped my court date."

"I see."

A rattling of locks sounded and a clean-shaven officer about Vance's age slid open Otis's door. "You're out on bail." He clicked handcuffs around Otis's wrists and escorted him into the lobby.

Rebecca stood there, red-eyed.

"Hey, I'm fine. Don't worry."

"It's not that."

Otis felt his inside turn watery. "What is it? The boys okay?"

"Sparrow called." She squinted. "Carmine's dead. One of the workers found him in the vines."

Otis sought an explanation in her eyes, wishing it were a joke, or a . . . misunderstanding. "Carmine Coraggio?"

She took his hand and nodded.

Otis wasn't ready.

He just wasn't ready.

Chapter 26

Otis Rising

Paul and Sparrow threw their arms in the air as Otis and Rebecca descended the escalator at SFO. A whole lot of years came pouring over Otis, reminding him of exactly where it had all begun.

Their old friends were now into their fifties. Paul still had long hair, but it had thinned some and showed a few strands of gray. He wore a shirt that read: *When I die, you better ferment me.* The evidence of a lifetime of hippiedom still showed in Sparrow's jewelry and dress. She radiated calm, as if she'd been steeped in stillness, and as she hugged Otis, his pulse slowed.

"I'm sorry about your mom and Carmine," Paul said, squeezing Otis the way he always had, like they were saying goodbye forever. Dammit, it was nice to have friends like these, and Otis wished he could have talked them into joining them on Red Mountain.

"It's almost enough to make a man numb," Otis said. He rested his hand on Paul's shoulder. "They both lived big lives. I suppose that's all you can hope for."

"For sure, man." A beat eased by. "How's the harvest up there? You figured out what you're doing yet?"

"Not at all, but it was a nice year. Balanced. Still trying to find my way, though."

"Aren't we all?"

Otis rode shotgun and caught up with Paul, while Rebecca and Sparrow chatted nonstop all the way back to Sonoma. Paul drove them by Lost Souls. As they'd heard, the new owners had built a fancy tasting room, and the lawn where Otis and the boys had once thrown the football was now a parking lot packed tight with cars and two buses.

They chose not to go inside. Some parts of the past were best left buried.

At Paul and Sparrow's place, where they were spending the next two nights, Otis and Rebecca unpacked in the guest room, then went downstairs to pull corks and catch up.

By sunfall, fifty people had gathered in the back of the red barn to celebrate the life of Carmine Coraggio and to welcome back the Tills. All the winemakers brought their latest vintages, including Otis, and he felt proud to set a couple of his latest Red Mountain efforts onto the table.

"Look at you now, Otis Till," Paul said, clapping him on the back. The two men sat across from each other at one of the picnic tables overlooking the vines. "To think you stomped your first grapes here, what was it? Twenty years ago?"

"Thirty."

"Thirty? God, we're old."

Otis raised his glass. "*À ta santé*, my friend. With age comes beauty."

"*À ta santé*," Paul said. Without breaking eye contact, he asked, "You heard about Lloyd, didn't you?"

"Oh, boy. No, I haven't heard a thing of him lately."

"I think he might be going to jail."

"*What?*" Otis said, hoping his inner joy didn't sprout into a smile. "When did this happen?"

"The last few weeks. Tax problems. He tried to cut some corners. Thank God we bought him out last year."

Otis kept what he wanted to say lodged in his throat. Instead, he let out, "Then I'm glad we've both washed our hands of that mess." He lowered his voice. "Speaking of jail, did I mention I spent last night in a cell?"

Paul's mouth fell agape. "Otis Till."

Otis searched for Rebecca among the crowd and found her sitting in the grass with Sparrow. "*Shhh*, keep your voice down. I promised Bec I wouldn't bring it up." His filter had fallen off about three glasses of wine ago, and he told Paul the tale.

"How'd you get to leave the state?" Paul asked.

"I had an attorney get permission." Otis stretched his arms. "I feel bad, honestly. Vance didn't grow up the way I did. My dad may have pushed me too hard, but at least he was there. Both my parents. This kid . . . never had a father. Brother died in a Navy SEALs training accident. Mom has dementia. Is it any wonder he's struggling?"

"Life, man," Paul said.

"That's right," Otis agreed. "Life." He recalled the night so many years ago when Paul, Sparrow, and Bec had danced naked on this table. A gentle urge nearly pushed him to do what he had been too afraid to do back then, but he paused. He wasn't the same man he used to be, and he no longer had anything to prove.

~

The next morning, properly hungover and short on sleep, Otis and Rebecca grabbed a breakfast burrito and drove up to Santa Rosa to see the in-laws. He would have far preferred to have a kidney removed—even if the kidney were destined for either Lloyd the Beardsplitter or Bedwetter the Fopdoodle—but he knew he didn't have a choice.

On the drive Otis didn't complain. Didn't even grumble under his breath. This visit home wasn't about him. It was about supporting Rebecca as she worked to patch her broken relationship with her parents. It had been two years since they'd last seen them, as the Bradshaws hadn't been able to travel to Bozeman for Eloise's funeral due to all three of them fighting health issues.

Marshall pulled back the door. Old age was getting the best of him. His back hunched more than it used to. Red blood vessels collected around his nose. He looked worn out in the way that a good night of sleep couldn't fix.

He tried his best to smile. "I'm sorry about your mentor."

Otis thanked him and shook his hand, then moved inside to greet Olivia and Jed. Olivia's liberal application of makeup failed to mask what the years had done to her. Jed had cut his hair short but still had a scraggly beard. His frail frame seemed too small for his new motorized wheelchair. Things had never been the same between Jed and Rebecca since Jed exploded in the backyard. Rebecca hugged her brother, but warmth was missing.

They sat in the living room. The ugly red paint on the walls was cracking.

"So . . ." Rebecca started. "What's new?"

Her family didn't have to say it, but they still held her departure from California over her, as if she were the reason they were miserable.

Leave it to Olivia to try to brighten up the conversation—even if it was a weak attempt. "Jed's working at Friedman's in Sonoma."

"That's exciting," Rebecca said, genuinely upbeat. She'd told Otis on the way over that she didn't want to get dragged down by them, and she was doing a good job so far.

"If we don't have it, you don't need it," Otis offered, referring to the hardware store's motto.

A round of nervous laughter followed.

"Beats sitting around here all day," Jed said.

Dear God, Otis prayed, *please deliver me from this place.*

"What else?" Rebecca asked.

"We're getting old, Rebecca," Marshall said. "That's what's new. Your mom needs knee surgery. Needs to stop eating all that sugar. Doc's got me on a statin." He raised his hand, then dropped it on his lap. "I'm sorry we don't have anything worth celebrating to bring up."

"I understand," Rebecca said. "No need to apologize." She diverted the conversation to Camden and Mike, catching everybody up.

Jed seemed to want to repair his relationship with Rebecca. He didn't speak as much as usual, but when he did, he was kind and gentle.

"That went well," Otis said sarcastically, as they pulled away in Paul's car.

"What can be done?" Bec asked. "They choose to live this way. It reminds me why I left, you know?"

Otis took her hand. "They love you. You know that, right?"

She looked over at him. "I do."

"And I couldn't be prouder of you."

"Thank you."

They held Carmine's funeral in the only place that made sense: in his vineyard. As Otis listened to the whisper of the farm Carmine had tended to for most of his life, he recalled the sense of wonder he'd felt the first time he'd come through those gates.

By the time the preacher said his words, the farm was packed with people from all over California. Otis recognized and said hello to maybe fifty winemakers, including one of Carmine's best friends, renowned organic farmer Amigo Bob Cantisano, and also the Drapers, the Coturris, the Sangiacomos, the Grgiches, the Mondavis, the Petersons, and the Martinis.

Carmine's brother, Sal, had the final word. Though they bore a physical resemblance, Sal had taken a route that had led him to Wall Street. The gold watch and bespoke shirt and blazer indicated he'd done well for himself. Carrying the ashes in a bag in his hand, he said through a microphone, "I worried no one would show up."

Laughter rose over the quiet whisper of the vines.

"My brother, he was polarizing, but he did what he was meant to do. All of you are here because he did it the right way. His wines spoke of a place. This place. He was a hard man to get to know, challenging to love at times, but those of you who broke down his walls learned what I knew . . . he had a big heart and took care of those who worked with him."

After the ashes were spread, people started to leave. Otis told Rebecca he'd find her in a little while and then meandered into the depths of the vineyard and slipped down one of the rows. He sat on the ground, amid the red leaves that had begun to fall. He and Carmine had sat in the rows like this so many times, talking about wines and life, which were always one and the same to Carmine.

Tears welled up in Otis's eyes as he pictured the old man grabbing the trunk of a vine and guiding Otis toward the energy of his farm. He'd died out here doing what he loved, spent a lifetime doing it. In an instant, Otis felt old and wondered when his time would come.

Had he done enough?

He could dwell on the years he'd screwed it all up, the years he missed out on his family, but he would not do that today. Today he'd focus on the years to come. Because there were plenty left.

It wasn't about the fight anyway, was it? Carmine had told him that. Otis wiped his eyes, thinking that he'd been such a lost soul when he'd stepped onto this property and first introduced himself. If it weren't for this man, Otis wasn't sure whether he ever would have found his way.

Everyone needs someone like that, he thought.

Everyone.

Back in Washington State, Otis drove the farm truck with the REDMTN license plate to the police station in Kennewick and posted bail for Vance Mason. When the kid came walking out into the lobby, he said, "*You* sprang me? What for?"

"Can I give you a ride home? I'll tell you on the way."

Vance reluctantly climbed in and told Otis that his house was over on the Pasco side. Otis drove slowly as he spoke. "My mentor died this week. The same day you and I went to jail. It made me do a lot of thinking. I want to apologize for how I've treated you. You don't deserve it. Not that I condone you shooting at coyotes. That happens again, we're going to be right back to having a problem. But I didn't give you a chance from the outset. Maybe you're right. My wife listens to a lot of Pink Floyd, and there's that song 'Us and Them.' You were a 'them' to me. That's not right."

"What's your point?"

"I had an idea. Feel free to tell me to go fuck off, but I was thinking about your situation, losing your brother, inheriting that land. I don't want to run you off, Vance. I want to help. Let me help you plant your land. I could teach you to farm vines. Give you the tools you need to make a living—if you're tired of painting houses. I don't know that I'm much of a role model, but I had a few in my life, and maybe I could be there for you."

Otis felt embarrassed and wholly inadequate, but he stood firm. "Why don't we start over? We're neighbors. Let me help you bring to life what your brother wanted. Maybe there's something in that. I don't know if the wine bug will bite you like it did me, but you could give it a go. I'd be happy to teach you what I know. It's a nice way to make a living. Even that ten acres you have is a great start."

It was a long time before Vance said anything. "How much would it cost me to tear down the trees and plant grapes?"

"I'd pay for it."

"You kidding?"

Otis shook his head, hoping Rebecca would be on board with the plan. Knowing her, she would.

"You did what?" Rebecca asked as she polished glasses in preparation to open the tasting room for the day.

Otis leaned on the other side of the concrete bar. "We don't have to pay for it. I just thought . . . I don't know, Bec. I see a lost soul in Vance. Maybe instead of going to war with him, perhaps I—*we*—could make a difference in his life. Give him something to believe in."

Rebecca held a glass up to the light. Satisfied, she slid it into the rack, then turned to her husband. "I think you've found your way, my love."

"I don't know about that, but it feels good to get outside of myself. Maybe that's the secret to this life."

Her smirk said it all.

"I know, I know. I'm late to the party. You figured this out a long time ago."

"No, that's not why I smiled. I have my issues. I spent a lot of years not taking care of myself. That's equally important. I smiled because I fall in love with you more and more every single day."

"I'm right there with you, wifey." He leaned over the bar and planted one on her lips. "How about we go to dinner tonight? Try that new spot by the river?"

"Here I was thinking you'd forgotten about me."

"Not a chance."

⌐⌐

Otis invited Vance over for Christmas Eve dinner. He wore a pressed shirt tucked into khakis, and he brought a bouquet of flowers. Flecks of paint from the day's work lingered on his hands. After a few awkward moments, he loosened up and handled all the questions with grace.

Turned out his band was good—at least to the ears of some. They'd played gigs all over the country. Otis would have never known. Making it big was indeed Vance's dream. "Maybe one day after my mom's gone, I'll take a chance." Otis had invited her for Christmas as well, but Vance said she didn't leave her nursing home anymore. Her condition was too extreme. She didn't even know who Vance was.

Halfway through the dinner, Otis said, "Vance, we'd like to hire you, if you'd be interested. We need some help around the cellar. Be a good way for you to cut your teeth, get ready for your own vines."

He grabbed hold of his beard. "Really?"

"Otis doesn't joke when it comes to wine."

"Oh, that's not true."

"I'd be honored," Vance said, allowing a rare grin.

In May, Otis's team planted two thousand vines on Vance's property, mostly syrah and cabernet, with a smattering of chenin blanc for fun. Vance was out there the entire time, getting his hands dirty, and when they finished, Otis and Vance went down to the taco truck in Benton City.

While they waited for their orders, Vance said, "I want to thank you, Otis."

"You already have."

"I know, but . . . no one has ever cut me a break like you. I'll make you proud, try to grow good grapes."

"Hey, I'm proud right now. You'll be a great farmer if you stick with it."

"I hope so."

"By the way, I've called a meeting. Everyone on the mountain. Would you come?"

"Sure."

⌒

A week later, out front of the Till Vineyards tasting room, Otis stood in front of nearly every winegrower and winemaker on Red Mountain. They'd come up from the riverside and down from the hill. Many of them wore jeans and boots, but another set wore fancier clothes, as if they'd walked right out of a boardroom.

"I know we're all so different," Otis started, speaking loudly, "but I suspect we're all here for a reason. I won't get too mystical on you, but maybe there is some sort of design. Maybe it's our place to lift Red Mountain to new heights. I've tasted a lot of wine from around the world, and what I know is that this little blip of land makes wines something beautiful. It's a challenge. By God, it's a challenge, but isn't that what growing good fruit is all about?"

Otis paused, wondering if they really could all come together.

"Look, I'm an outsider, but I've been doing this a long time. Maybe we all want the same things. If that's the case, would you let me offer you my spin? Tom and Anne-Marie Hedges have a vision of Red Mountain one day becoming its own AVA. When I first heard that, I nearly fell from my chair. I'm convinced it's exactly the way we must forge ahead. As a collective."

Otis heard the urgency in his voice. "I hear talk of workers not being paid. That can't happen. I see some of our wines out there on shelves with the pricing slashed. Or retail pricing close to eight dollars. Lower sometimes. And the labels . . . they look like you printed them at home. Even the choice of glass matters. We don't want our wines in cheap glass . . . we don't want cheap corks. I don't even want to spray chemicals, but that's a fight I'll wage down the line. These are things we have to talk about. Especially as we work to make Red Mountain its own AVA."

He held up a finger, reminded of the first hard lesson he'd learned. "But first, as you know, we must sell Washington State. When I was on the road, someone bloody asked me which side of the Potomac we planted on."

Trickles of laughter blended with the skepticism in the air.

"How many times has someone said to you, 'I thought it always rained in Washington State'? Then you have to tell them that's in Seattle and explain how the Cascades stop the weather from moving our way. That's just fine. We're on virgin land. We are settlers, *pioneers*. Along with making the finest wines we can muster, ones that taste only of this place, we must work together to spread the word. That means we all have to devote marketing dollars to getting out there and pouring the wines. We can't wait for drinkers to come here. We have to go to them. We have to pour our wines down their gullets and show them that we have something extraordinary to offer."

He wondered whether he was getting through to anyone. A few eyes had glazed over. "Some of you might want to tell me to go back to California, but I'm here to ride the wave with you, to become a soldier of our terroir. I will give everything I have to this land for the rest of my life, and when the time comes, when my body starts to fade, I will let the vines wrap around me and take me back into the earth. My dying breath will be of this place, of Red Mountain."

His heart charged forward. "To some, it's a small thing. To me, the land, this land. The vines. What we're doing. It matters. It's the way I shine my light on the world. I'd like to offer an idea. I'd like everyone to have a voice and a way for us to communicate. So I propose we create a consortium. Anyone who has a foot in this land can join. A Red Mountain Round Table, if you like. No leaders, simply a united voice. We may not always see eye to eye, but we can find our common ground. We can work together to solve issues both in the fields and in the cellar. We can learn from each other."

Otis looked at Vance. "We must pave the way for the next generation. It took Burgundy hundreds of years to achieve its status, but it started somewhere. Like this, a collective of people willing to work together, wanting to change the world."

He searched the crowd for supporters. "What say you? Will you take a seat at the Red Mountain Round Table?"

A silence hovered in the air. Otis wasn't expecting cheering, but he thought he'd spoken some inspiring words.

"Not even a clap?" he asked.

A few nodded. The hermit Mitch Green raised an arm in solidarity.

Then a man in the back, one of the old guard, a cherry farmer named Bill Sussex, called out, "You're right, Otis. I think you need to go back to California. We don't need your hippie beliefs here."

Otis's first idea was to spray a round of insults right back. *Hippie beliefs? Have you ever set foot in Europe? Have you ever walked the rows of Romanée-Conti? Have you ever taken a sip from the holy grail of a first growth? Hippie beliefs. This isn't cherries, dear sir. You're in the big leagues now.*

Otis only smiled as he held back these thoughts. Instead, he looked at his wife, then said, "I'm not trying to get in the way of your dreams. I know they're all different, but . . . don't you want to go to bed at night knowing you're doing something that matters? Don't you want to meet your maker with your head held high, knowing that you gave your all to something?"

A rush of emotions came over him, and he had to collect himself. He bent down and took a handful of the Red Mountain dust, then he let it sift through his fingers. "I'm no good at a lot of things, but I understand wine, and I know that we can only lift this place up together. The wines will only sing at their finest when we as a people find harmony. Can we do that? Can we meet and listen to each other? Can we collect as artists and choose to do something that's beyond average? Something to make our families proud. Something worthy of giving back to God, to your maker, to the universe, to whomever you pray to at night."

Otis slammed a fist into his palm. "We're here only a short amount of time, my brothers and sisters. This mountain has brought us together. Let us make wines that transport, that inspire, that ignite!"

He stopped and looked around. Silence.

A few nods.

Then a clap.

A slow clap, but still a clap.

It was Rebecca, smacking her hands together.

Another clap, then another. Otis saw the Hedges family out there, Jim Holmes, John Williams and his sons, JJ and Tyler, all starting to put their hands together.

Not everyone was on board, but there were a few. That's where it all begins.

⌒

The thrashing of heavy metal guitar chords and the hammering of drums shook the ground, as Otis crossed into Vance's land. It was the early afternoon, a fine June day in the year 2000. Instead of letting the music bother him, he strolled through Vance's young vineyard with an open mind.

The vines barely peeked out of their white grow tubes. A steady drip from the recently installed irrigation gave them the power to extend their roots into this treacherous soil. The metal music played like a hellish lullaby to these younglings.

As opposed to trying to shut it out, Otis breathed it in. He opened his ears and listened like he never had before. No, he didn't hear a whisper. How could he? This was a scream.

And yet, he heard soul in it. A cry of three men desperate to find their way, to make their mark. Otis drew closer, until he could see Vance and his friends performing together. A few others sat in the grass, listening. The band stopped and started a few times, then found their groove again. Vance slammed his guitar pick down onto the strings as he yelled out indecipherable lyrics into the microphone. Admittedly, the drummer and bassist held the beat together incredibly well. Like it or not, the good people miles away in Richland could likely hear every note.

Otis sat down in the rows, among the baby vines. He lay on his back and let the earth rumble underneath him. No, it wasn't Puccini or Ravel, but this was passion, just the same. They were breaking bread with a higher power, making music that mattered to them.

How dare Otis ever claim to be more of an artist?

How dare he claim to know what the vines wanted to hear?

Otis focused on the sound and realized the music they were making was as pure as the wines he sought to make. A naked display of soul, a communion of their own church.

How dare he think that he knew the only way to free the soul.

⌒

A growing region is only as good as the people who inhabit it. It can only reach its perfect pitch if the people get out of their own way.

A month after that first all-hands meeting at Till Vineyards, the inaugural meeting of the Red Mountain Round Table was held. Twenty-one people collected in Otis's tasting room. They argued and shouted but worked their way toward a shared vision.

They met again a month later. Their numbers grew.

Members of the Round Table met with the Washington State Wine Commission to assist in promoting the state as a whole.

They sent formal invitations to wine critics and wine buyers, offering to host them on the mountain. Many showed interest. Though Bedwetter and *The New York Times* ignored them, many publications did not. *Decanter* and *Wines and Vines* and *Wine Spectator* began to mention Washington State wines. Wine buyers from the likes of Costco and Tesco visited. Canada's Liquor Control Board of Ontario and Sweden's Systembolaget worked their way through tasting rooms, buying out entire vintages.

The Round Table began to host their own wine tables at trade shows around the world. Otis and other Red Mountain soldiers flew to the likes of Beijing, Seoul, London, Copenhagen, and Stockholm, preaching about the land and introducing eager drinkers to the nectar of a new terroir.

It was subtle, but Otis could taste the difference in the wines in the coming years. He could see in the eyes of his neighbors the change brewing in the air. Everyone could feel it. The tasting rooms began to fill. People from the East Coast started to show up. They'd go to Walla Walla and then stop by Red Mountain on the way back to Seattle to see what the fuss was all about.

The Round Table began discussing building the infrastructure needed to support tourism. They needed to help steer the path before chain restaurants and motels took over. They envisioned farm-to-table, family-owned establishments, bed-and-breakfasts, local grocers, farmers' markets, and art shows.

Changes that they didn't think they'd see in their lifetime took root. A poet arrived, staking claim to a small property at the end of Sunset. A painter soon bought the land next to him. There was talk that Jake Forrester, the front man for Folkwhore, was looking at property.

On June 11, 2001, Red Mountain was recognized as the eleventh AVA in Washington State. The Hedgeses hosted a party that didn't end for two days, every person celebrating the hard work they'd put in for their land. Now they could all put Red Mountain as the official growing region on their bottles. Finally, Red Mountain was validated as a place that mattered.

Chapter 27

THE RIVER RUSHES BY

It wasn't for three more years that Sam Ledbetter reached out to Otis. "It's been a long time," Otis said through his first cell phone. He'd finally succumbed to the new technology a month prior.

"Yes, yes, it has." Otis cringed as he recalled the one and only time he'd seen Bedwetter in person, when he'd raced out of the steakhouse in Sonoma.

"Listen, I wanted to see if I could visit Red Mountain. I'll be in Portland next week and want to come see what all the fuss is about."

"I think I could squeeze you in," Otis said with a sly grin.

When the day came, the third Tuesday in June, Otis greeted him at the front door of the tasting room. Rebecca was there, too, thank God. At the very least he could rely on her charm.

"Welcome to Red Mountain," Otis said to Ledbetter.

"It's like nothing I've ever seen," the mediocre journalist said. He wore khakis and loafers. A thin scarf wrapped around his neck.

"Have you tried any Red Mountain wines?"

"No, not yet. I've tried the usual Washington State suspects, L'Ecole No. 41 and Leonetti, but I'm afraid my knowledge is limited."

Otis led him into the tasting room, and Rebecca poured the wines while Otis talked.

"It's like exploring an entirely new medium, working this land. What I love is that it's such an arid place. Mildew isn't a problem. Phylloxera would have a hard time surviving. We're the gods of water, situated by the river as we are. It doesn't rain, there's no humidity, so we don't suffer like Burgundy from bad years in that regard. We can fine-tune our water use with the drip irrigation."

"Oh, this one is nice. A syrah?"

"From the first block Bec and I planted."

Ledbetter spent a long time pondering the wine, then: "I see the appeal. You know, I suppose I owe you an apology, Otis. I've had friends tell me that you think I have something against you. It was never that, it's that . . . I suppose it seemed like you were trying too hard. I'm not sure how to put a finger on it, but your wines didn't resonate with me. Not like they do now. Maybe you were right when you told me that context is everything. I should have tasted with you."

"Well, here we are."

"Yes, indeed."

Ledbetter's article in *The New York Times* did more for Red Mountain than anything up until then. The only problem, if there was one, was that he coined a new nickname for Otis.

Several paragraphs into the article, he wrote:

> I've been following Otis Till since the beginning, and though I was well aware of his pedigree, his wines lacked something.
>
> They lack no more. I believe Otis Till has found his place. He is no doubt the Grapefather of Red Mountain, a man leading that small piece of land to stardom. The wines he's making now remind me why I fell in love with wine in the first place. I'm not tasting juice with

an agenda. I'm not tasting wines that are designed for any particular palate. I am tasting wines that speak of a place, and nothing more. That, my dear readers, is all that is required. If only it were that easy. In the meantime, go find Red Mountain, in a store, on a restaurant list. Know that you're tasting a region that will soon dominate our great country.

"The Grapefather," Rebecca said, after listening to Otis read it out loud.

Otis set down the page. "For the record, he said it. Not me."

"I think it's adorable. Sure is better than the vine messiah."

"I liked that one."

"So . . . how does it feel to finally have Bedwetter write about you?"

"You mean Ledbetter?"

They both chuckled. "It feels nice, Bec. What's funny is that it doesn't change a thing. I'm still just a farmer trying to make wine. Though there was a time when I would have thought differently, his words don't validate me as a man. I suppose the best part is they do lift up Red Mountain."

She petted his face. "My love, how you've grown since that young boy on the bus."

"Please, if you don't mind, you must refer to me as the Grapefather going forward. Capitalized, mind you."

"Okay, maybe you haven't grown that much."

⌒

If anyone else told Otis that he needed to go see the movie *Sideways* when it hit the theaters during harvest of 2004, he worried he'd attack them with his shears. Everyone told him that Paul Giamatti was a fictional version of Otis, a grump with unbridled passion. Some even claimed that the writer, Rex Pickett, had based the character in his novel on Otis.

"I'm not a grump," Otis would reply. Then he'd snidely ask how anyone involved with wine had time to go see a movie during harvest.

It became nearly annoying. Every person he saw, be it at the grocery store, the hardware store, the taco truck: "Did you see *Sideways* yet?"

Turned out Vance was the one who convinced him to see the film. He'd recently lost his mother, so Otis was trying to spend as much time with him as he could. They'd been working nonstop all harvest, and they'd finally brought in the last of the syrah. It had been a hell of a year, perhaps the best on record. Otis had never achieved such balance. Vance had proved to be a superb grower and promising winemaker. His wines were currently fermenting in the Till Vineyards winery.

They walked out of the theater that night, and Otis had nothing left. He'd never laughed so much in his entire life. Hopefully he wasn't too much like Miles, but by God, what a movie.

"He drank from the spit bucket!" Otis said. "And 'I'm not drinking any fucking merlot.' That man is funny."

"What was his deal with merlot?" Vance asked. "He hated it, didn't he?"

"Not at all." Otis wagged a finger. "That bottle at the end, the Château Cheval Blanc, most of the juice is *actually* merlot. It's not that he didn't like the variety. It's that it reminded him of his wife. But I can only imagine what this will do to the merlot market. The old me would start grafting all our merlot to cabernet." Otis slapped Vance on the back. "Actually, I have a few bottles of Cheval Blanc in the cellar. Shall we go dig one up?"

Down in the depths of the cellar, Otis uncorked an '81 Cheval Blanc and sat across from Vance in one of the small tables covered in melted wax.

A half glass in, Vance said, "I've been doing a lot of thinking since Mom died. It's been such an honor working with you. You've become a father to me, but I have to go. I want this to be my dream, but it's not.

I'm going to move to Los Angeles with the band, see if we can make something of ourselves. I'm hoping that I might sell my land to you."

In the last few weeks, Otis had detected that Vance had something brewing, and he raised a glass to him. "The honor has always been mine, Vance. By gods, yes, go live your dream."

After they'd finished the last drop of the bottle, they embraced. Otis kissed his neck and told him he'd always be there for him.

~

July of 2005, Otis flew out to Colorado to spend some time with Camden. He got out there at least once a year, but it never felt like enough. Otis took Cam and a few of his friends out to dinner that night; then they retired early so they could make the morning drive toward Breckenridge to the Blue River.

"How's the love life?" Otis asked on the drive. It was always a touchy subject.

"You know, steady."

"Steady? What does that mean?"

Cam wore a plaid shirt rolled up at the sleeves. He ran a hand through his long shaggy hair and gave a grin. "Nothing that makes me want to settle down."

"Fair enough. No doubt you have to wait for the right one."

"How about you guys? How's Vance working out?"

"He's leaving, taking the band to LA, see if they can make it."

"Good for him."

"You know his mom died. We're about to close on his ten acres. I gave him a fair price."

They stopped for pastries and coffee halfway there. They sat outside overlooking Grays Peak. A jet contrail striped the mostly blue sky. Cam had polarized glasses on, so it was hard to see his eyes, and Otis wondered what he was thinking.

"Tell me," Otis said, "are you happy?"

"Am I happy?" Cam smiled. "You know I am. What does that mean?"

"I'm just asking. We don't see you as much, and I want to know."

He held out his hands. "What's not to be happy about? Great job, plenty of time to get outside. I have good friends. Healthy fam. Life's good."

Otis set down his drink. "That's all I want to hear. It's hard when your kids leave. Whether you two are happy or not, I sometimes feel something missing. If I could do it all over again, I would have made more time for you growing up. Mikey got to see me more. You got the worst of me."

Cam removed his glasses. "Dad, really? You get so sentimental lately. On the phone too."

"You wait, son. Once you have kids, you'll see. I beat myself up sometimes, wishing I could have done better."

Cam placed a hand on Otis's arm. "You being right here now is all that matters. There's nothing that means more to me than your visits, just you and me. I know you don't love fishing like I do, but you come anyway. And I get it. You had to figure out a way to make the wine thing work when you were young. I came as a surprise. You figured it out, though. We didn't starve. You gave us a great life. Come to think of it, where I am now. My love for the outdoors. It comes from you. I might not have been interested in farming, but I'm like you in so many ways."

Otis patted his son's hand and offered a smile.

"Seriously, I'd rather throw myself out a window than work behind a desk. You and me, we belong out here." Cam lit up as he looked out over the mountain. "This is where we shine." Cam gave a quiet *"Ahhhwoooo."*

Otis echoed him back, a little louder: *"Ahhwwooooo."*

They held eye contact for a long time, and Otis would remember this moment with Camden above all others for always.

They were on the river an hour later, both in waders and vests loaded with gear. Cam told Otis the river was higher than usual, a result of recent heavy rains, so the fish might be a little harder to find. Though he only fished with Cam, Otis had improved over the years. He had a hell of a good teacher.

The Blue River rushed with tremendous force past the boulders poking out of it. The air was much cooler than Red Mountain, seventy-one or seventy-two. There were no signs of humans. This place must have looked exactly the same as it had thousands of years ago. Hills rose straight up from the water and worked their way toward taller mountains in the distance. Spruce and pines reached up toward the clouds. An eagle circled over its nest in the tallest of trees.

There was a summer hatch of bugs, so they both were using dry flies, casting upriver and watching the flies drift down with the current. Cam stood about fifty yards upriver from Otis, and Otis watched his son. Cam made his line dance in a way Otis had never seen elsewhere. Three casts in, he reeled in his first fish, capturing it in his net. A bright grin on his face, he held up the trout for Otis to see, then lowered it down into the water, letting it go with a splash.

Otis worked his section of river as best as he could. Cam had a way of knowing where the fish were. Otis could only guess. He found a solid place to stand, maybe twenty feet into the river. It was a lovely feeling, the cool water rushing by his legs.

It took him a while to get the hang of things. Cam had reminded him once again to let the line finish its path behind him before he brought it forward again. "Patience, Dad. Patience." Over and over, Otis set the fly in the same place and watched it drift down.

Twenty minutes in, a trout shot out of the water and nabbed his fly. Seeing that trout hit his fly was something magical.

"Look at that, Cam!" Otis yelled, tugging on his fish and reeling him in.

Cam raised his hands up in the air, a victory indeed.

Otis brought in the fish and was careful not to harm him. Cam had taught him exactly how to extract the barbless hook and get the fish back into the water so it could go on living.

It didn't take him long to hook a tree that hung out over the water. Cam noticed and climbed out and walked down to help. "I think that's the longest you've ever made it without getting snagged." He took over and followed the line into the leaves with his hand.

"I'm a fish in. Did you see that trout?" Otis asked.

"I did."

"How many have you caught?"

"A few."

"Good for you."

Cam had to break the line; then he went about tying on a new leader and fly. Otis held the reel in his hand and watched his son. Camden truly was content. Somehow he hadn't been burdened like Otis with a desperate need to prove himself. It was as if he'd already achieved all his goals, and now he was along for the ride. His son lived like a sailor who had caught the perfect wind, soaring by, unaffected by all the troubles out there.

"Okay," Cam said, looking over at Otis after finishing up the knot, "you're all set. Go get 'em, Dad."

Those were the last words Camden ever spoke.

Go get 'em, Dad.

He flashed a smile and then was gone, going back to what he enjoyed more than anything else on earth.

A while later, Otis looked upriver in time to see a fish tear into Cam's fly, the silver flapping out of the water. His son set the hook like a master, fully present. He stepped up onto a rock to bring it the rest of the way in, and as the fish surfaced again, Cam slipped.

In an instant, his feet flew above his head, and he came down hard on a neighboring rock, headfirst.

Otis's chest tightened. "Cam, you okay?"

Cam's body folded into itself and began to drift down the river, his fishing pole still in the water, tugged by the fish.

Otis dropped his rod and reel. Heart roaring, he started upriver, but it would take him forever wading through the water, so he cut a hard right straight to the shore. He slipped a few times as he fought the current, but he finally reached a flat path and raced out of the water.

On shore, dripping wet and slowed by the waders and boots, he ran as fast as he could, peeling off his vest, keeping one eye on Camden, who still hadn't raised his head out of the water. The rod and reel floated by.

Otis called Camden's name, but he was out of breath and terrified, so it barely came out. He navigated the rocky shore, climbed over several tree trunks, and once he was close enough, he splashed back into the river.

Blood rushed from a gap in Cam's head and swirled in the water. Otis wrapped his arms around his son's trunk and dragged him to a large flat rock.

Otis wasn't trained in CPR, and later, it would be one of the million things that would eat him up. How had he not been prepared?

He didn't know what to do; he didn't fucking know!

Following his instincts, he knelt and pressed his clasped hands against Cam's chest and pushed. He pushed again, not knowing whether it was the right spot, but there had to be water in his lungs, and he had to get it out.

"Cam, tell me what to do," he pleaded.

The gash spread blood all over the rock; the water was red.

Otis kept pushing down on his son's chest, waiting for water to come rushing out of his mouth, but nothing happened. He looked around, utterly lost. They were a long way from the car, a thirty-minute walk. He'd glanced at his phone before shoving it into the glove compartment; he had no service.

He was Cam's only hope.

He pulled Cam up onto his lap and continued to try to get the water out of him. When it didn't come, he laid his son back down and tried CPR, in and out, pushing his breath into him.

Tears washed over Otis's face as the reality of the situation became clear.

His son was dead.

Cam was dead.

"Don't take him from me," Otis begged.

He put his hand on Cam's chest; there was no heartbeat. He felt for a pulse. Nothing. He wept and begged for someone to help as he held his fingers over Cam's mouth, hoping for breath.

Nothing.

Finally, he decided he had to get him out of the water. He tore the vest off; a hook from a fly clinging to a patch of wool embedded itself in Otis's hand. He ripped it from his skin, ignoring the searing pain.

Grabbing hold of Cam under the arms, he dragged him through the water, past the rocks, and up onto the shore. He placed him in the grass and turned him to his side again. He hit his back, wondering what else he could do.

"Help!" he screamed.

Otis couldn't leave him, but he was out of options. He tried CPR again, and Cam's chest rose with Otis's breath, but he wouldn't come back to life. He tried again and again, but nothing.

Nothing.

"Help!" he screamed, pushing up from his knees and looking toward the trail. "Help!"

Nothing came back, only the silence of a forest and the rush of a river that carried on like nothing had happened.

It would take him an hour or more to get help, getting back to the car and then either driving to a place with cell service or finding an establishment with a landline. He had to keep trying. He performed the Heimlich maneuver harder and harder, and he heard one of Cam's ribs crack. Still, his son didn't come back to him. Otis fell to the ground and tried CPR again, watching Cam's chest rise and fall, up and down. Nothing.

It had been ten minutes. Camden wasn't coming back.

Otis pulled the body onto his lap and wept, his tears falling onto Cam's face. He brushed back his boy's hair. "I'm sorry, I'm so sorry. I don't know what happened. I don't know what to do."

The boy who'd grown into a man, the man who had inspired Otis in countless ways. He was dead and gone.

Otis didn't want to leave him, yet he had to. But what about the animals? They'd go after the body.

He thought of dragging him back out to a rock on the river, but he might wash away. Instead, Otis dragged Cam to the highest boulder along the shore. He kissed his cheeks and forehead and promised him he'd be right back.

With one last look at his son, he tore off toward the trail and ran at a dead sprint back to the car, his entire life running away from him.

～

In Cam's vehicle, Otis sped along Highway 9 toward Breckenridge with his cell phone in his hand, waiting to get reception. Finally, he came upon a whitewater rafting shop situated on the banks of the river. He slid into the parking lot next to several stacks of kayaks and inflatable boats. He was out before the SUV had stopped, and he raced into the entrance of the simply built wooden building. Fishing gear lined the walls. Bluegrass played from the speakers.

"Help!" Otis called, racing toward the counter in the back.

A man in his seventies sitting in a chair with his feet propped up next to the cash register slowly lowered his book. "Can I . . . ?" He clearly saw Otis's distress and moved quicker, standing up. "What's going on?"

"My son . . ." Otis was still out of breath. "My son . . . he's . . ." He pointed back from where he'd come. "He's dead." His voice cracked as his knees grew wobbly. Tears spilled from his eyes.

The old man rounded the counter and put a hand on Otis's shoulder. "Should I call the police? What happened?"

Otis could barely speak. Maybe there was a chance, maybe there was still a chance. "My son fell in the river. He's out there. A few miles back. I'm not getting any service. Please . . . please call an ambulance."

As the man raced toward his phone, Otis fell to his knees. Loss washed over him, stripping away all the good in the world.

"Oh, God, no," he said, crying into his hands. How could he tell Rebecca? It would crush her.

The man on the other side of the counter had reached the 911 operator and was filling them in. Otis summoned enough strength to stand again. "Tell them to come here, and then I'll lead them. They have to hurry. He might still have a chance, but he's not breathing."

The man relayed the message as Otis stared at him, watching his lips move, hearing the words that were impossible to believe leaving his mouth.

～

Camden's body rested cold and still in a hospital morgue in Frisco, about twenty minutes from where he'd died. Otis sat in the office of a kind man who had offered him privacy to call Rebecca. Dried tears stained his face. The digital clock on the wall read 2:32 p.m.

Otis held his cell phone in his hand, his fingers poised over the buttons, but he couldn't bring himself to call, to break the news to Rebecca that their son was dead. In an instant, he would destroy her life, and he wanted to let her keep on living this innocent existence for a little while longer. He couldn't bear the idea of her being alone when she learned what had happened. He thought of calling Michael in Seattle, but Otis didn't want Mike to know either. He wanted to keep them in a cocoon of safety, where the ones you loved didn't die. Where a young man who burst with life hadn't had it extinguished doing the thing he loved most. A high river, a wrong step, and the whole world shattered.

He set down the phone and fell back into the chair, letting his eyes rise to the ceiling. The hollowness in his chest echoed with loss. The last images of his son on the river, that gorgeous smile, that beautiful cast, slid by in his mind.

"How could you take him away?" Otis whispered, time moving so desperately slow.

After a while, he sat back up and reached for the phone. He would call Chaco and have him collect their friends to be there for her. Then Otis would break the news.

"Hola, boss," Chaco said.

Otis started to speak, but no words left his mouth. He pulled the phone from his ear and stared at it, then ended the call. His hands shook as he set the phone back down.

Standing, Otis found the nice man who had lent him his office. "I need help. Can you help me book a flight to the Tri-Cities? My brain's not working, my fingers. I'll drive to Denver, can be there in a . . ."

"It's about a two-hour drive. Yes, let me help you."

Determined to break the news to Rebecca face-to-face, Otis said, "If I can't get to the Tri-Cities, get me to Seattle." He fumbled for his wallet and slid out a credit card. "Thank you."

◦—

It was midnight when he reached Red Mountain. The stars shimmered in the clear black sky. A cool breeze slipped through the desert landscape. A tumbleweed rolled by him as Otis drove along Sunset Road toward his house.

She'd tried to call him several times, leaving messages that grew more desperate. "Everything okay? What's going on, Otis? Please call me."

He had to be there when she found out. He had to hold her in his arms.

The truck bumped along the driveway, ticking down the clock to Bec's devastation. She was a strong woman, but could any mother handle such loss? The lights came on as his boots hit the gravel. The clasp unlatched, and Rebecca pulled open the door in her nightgown.

Otis bit back more tears as he walked toward her. She clutched her chest and began to melt. "No," she said. "No."

Not a word from Otis, and she knew. Her cry filled the night with agony. Otis cried, too, as he pulled her in, and they slid down onto the welcome mat.

Nothing would ever be the same.

Chapter 28
(Interlude)

THE EMPTINESS INSIDE

Red Mountain, Washington
April 2011

I was absolutely shattered. There is nothing worse than losing a child. Nothing.

It's often only when you lose someone you love that you realize exactly what matters in life. I think everyone who came for Camden's funeral shared the same feeling: that no matter their differences, they had to look past them and remember that life is fragile and often far too short, and that they needed to love those around them with all they had.

We called Michael's friend Marcus and asked him to drive Michael home, as we didn't want him driving over those mountain roads right after he'd learned the news. Turned out Mike was the strongest of us, taking charge. Telling people what to do. Helping with funeral arrangements, getting organized, and making sure we notified everyone.

When I set eyes on Jed, as he rolled his chair around the corner to baggage claim at the Tri-Cities airport, all I felt was love. There was no harboring of blame, no guilt, no room for grievances. I smiled and ran to him, and he wheeled to me just as fast. I threw my arms around him, and an apology fell from his mouth.

My parents, both struggling with mobility issues by then, joined us, and we embraced and cried together, right there in the middle of the airport.

We held the service in the grass in front of the tasting room. Cam had been cremated, and the box with his ashes rested on a table below a cross. Our friends from Sonoma came up. Wine people from all over the country flew in. Cam's friends flew in. It was the biggest funeral I'd ever attended, and though I barely had anything left, I felt proud to have such great people in our life.

Afterward, Otis and I took Cam's ashes to Colorado and spread them in Boulder Creek, where he'd loved to fish since he'd first gone to college. Otis offered to take me to the Blue River, but I simply shook my head. I couldn't see where my son had breathed his last breaths.

Back home, we both looked brittle. I would peek into the mirror and see a woman who looked thirty years older. Otis was the same. We cried and cried and cried, holding each other on the couch, unsure of where to go from there.

Kind of like Otis now.

I've never seen him so brittle.

I watch him set down the pen after writing about the loss of our son, and I see him fading away. He walks into the living room and collapses onto his knees. He cries like the loss is fresh. Amigo sits on his haunches and looks up at Otis with bewildered eyes.

His toes curling on the hardwood floor, Otis looks down at him. "Why couldn't I have been the one to go? What did he do to deserve that?" Otis wipes the saliva that has dripped down his chin. "I don't know if I can go on. I don't know that I have what it takes."

Otis finally stands, and I watch from my place so close yet so far away, wishing I could comfort him. I wonder whether giving him that journal years ago, then urging it on him these last few weeks, was the right thing to do.

Perhaps I've meddled more than I should.

Otis enters our bedroom and pulls open the closet door. I know what he's doing, and I scramble to figure out how to stop him. He pulls a shoebox from the top shelf and removes the gun that we bought back in Sonoma years ago, one that Otis fired only to scare away bobcats and other predators.

"No," I say, but no words actually rise into the air. Otis doesn't hear me.

He sits down on the bed and stares at the gun. Amigo has followed him and looks at him quizzically. Otis pushes a bullet into the chamber, then closes it. He places his finger on the trigger and explores the feel, twisting the gun as if to examine it.

His face is dry. No more tears. His eyes are shallow.

I swipe my hands through the air, trying to slap him, to wake him up, but my hands pass through his flesh, drawing nothing more than a slight stir in the air. I am not of this earth. I don't have a body, though I can feel. I can feel my worry and pain, and in this moment I can feel how desperately I want him to keep fighting, to keep living.

He raises the gun to his head, sticks the barrel against his temple. He stares down at the rug. He doesn't see Amigo. Or he's chosen to ignore him.

I swipe at the air again, but nothing happens. I go for the gun. Nothing.

I get the sense that this is not my business, not my fight.

Pulling back, I find some modicum of relief in washing my hands of it. Only from this place where I am now could I know any sort of peace while I watch the love of my life hold a gun to his head.

He moves the gun about, sticking it in his mouth, then under his chin. I can't look away; I must stay with him until the end.

"I'm sorry," he whispers, and I brace myself for a gunshot.

The following silence is like none I've ever known.

Otis closes his eyes.

I have always been there for him. This doesn't change now.

All the while, Amigo wags his tail. He thinks Otis has a toy for him.

I can't know what Otis is thinking. I can only imagine the loss that has overwhelmed him, not only since Mikey and I perished, but since that day on the river with Cam. He'd fought so hard. We had fought so hard to overcome, only to be pulled right back into the mire.

Otis pulled the gun away from under his chin, exposing a mark from where the steel had pressed into flesh. His bottom lip fell open, and he set the gun down and clutched his chest.

Then he scooped up Amigo and brought him onto his lap. He did not speak, he barely breathed, as he ran his fingers over the coyote's fur.

Ten minutes later he removed the bullet and returned the gun to its place, then walked into the kitchen and made himself a tuna salad sandwich. He gave Amigo the remains of tuna in the can, then ate in his recliner while he watched the news. From a gun to his head to a tuna fish sandwich.

Once he polished off the sandwich, he went to the bar and started to pour a scotch, but then stopped. Instead, he hiked up to the winery, the first time he'd entered since losing them, and he descended into the cellar and went straight for his older vintages. He found a 2005, Cam's year, and returned to the house to pull the cork. The wine was just starting to find its stride, still a long way from having any proper age on it, but as he took the first sips, he found some sort of peace in the memories of how things lay out after Cam's passing.

With a fresh glass poured, he returned to his desk and picked up the pen. Without much hesitation, he began to write.

This journal. I should have known it would come into my life. I remember the day you handed it to me, assuring me it's the process, not the finished product. When I rolled my eyes at the idea, you said, "Don't call it a journal then. Call it a memoir. Or a grocery list. I don't care. Quit taking yourself so seriously and just write." You told me that you'd be okay, that we both had to find our own way back.

Well, here I am, Bec, focused on the process, ripping my heart out as I lose my oldest son for the second time. The gun is back in the closet, and I'm here, writing, because it's all that I know to do, the only way that I can keep you all alive, to write you back to life.

Chapter 29

Specks of Hope

Otis almost let the fruit hang on the vines in the harvest following Camden's passing. He'd thought long and hard about it, torn between not wanting to ever remember this year but also wanting to commemorate it, a way to never forget.

It was late October when Otis left Red Mountain for the first time since the funeral. He was in no shape to do so, but he'd given his word that he'd participate in a James Beard wine dinner in New York with a chef friend.

It had been four years since 9/11, but *Never Forget* T-shirts were still being sold on the street. He passed by a stand of them the morning after the dinner, while he killed time before his noon flight back home. Had he had room in his heart, he might have given more attention to the color of the leaves, the crispness in the air, the way in which fall brought Manhattan to life more than any other season.

Otis was trying, though. Trying to clear his head and find an ounce of joy amid the wreckage of loss.

He wound into Central Park, wandering to nowhere, stretching his legs, perhaps walking away from something more than anything.

His grief was such that he couldn't stop reliving the memories, couldn't stop falling into the regret of the countless ways he could have done better.

Something about the man who smoked a cigarette on the bench in front of him caught his eye. He looked a lot like Cam in a way, despite having brown hair and being unhealthily skinny and stamped with tattoos. He was no doubt homeless, considering his appearance, including the torn pants and sweater, the raggedy beard and hair.

Out of curiosity, Otis drew closer. A heady smell assaulted his nostrils. He hadn't known a smell like that since rubbing up against the ripe hippies at the Woodstock festival.

No judgment, though. That was not what he was doing. Actually, he wasn't sure what he was doing, but he felt compelled to say something. His heart broke for the man; maybe that was it, especially considering his likeness to Cam.

This wasn't something Otis did, but he did it—he sat down next to the man, the pungent smell growing even stronger.

"Good morning," Otis said.

"Mornin'." The young man didn't even turn his head. In fact, he seemed paranoid about the intrusion. Or perhaps shocked that someone was engaging with him.

"How's your day going?"

The young man smiled to himself, his shoulders shifting. "You're looking at it."

"I don't mean to intrude. I'm not looking for anything." Otis also didn't normally open up to people, but he did then. "You look a lot like my son, that's all."

"I see." The guy turned away and rubbed his four- or five-day-old beard.

"I lost him a few months back."

It took a while, but the man finally said, "I'm sorry."

"Never have I known pain like that. Here I was wandering the park, going nowhere in particular, then happen upon his likeness. I felt compelled to take a seat, say hello to you."

The man tugged on the last nib of the cigarette; smoke swirled around his head.

"What's your name?" Otis asked, still shaken by how much he looked like Cam.

"Brooks."

Otis offered a shake. "I'm Otis, it's nice to meet you. My son's name was Camden. He died right in front of me. Looked a lot like you. I guess I already said that."

"How'd he die?" Brooks asked, taking his time but eventually shaking Otis's hand.

"Lost his balance on a rock. We were fishing in Colorado. Fly-fishing. Where are you from? You look hungry, can I buy you something to eat?" Otis nodded to the food cart about thirty feet in front of him.

"I'm from California. And sure."

Otis stood. "I'm a West Coaster too. I might get myself a pretzel, that sound good? Mustard?"

"Sure, thanks."

Otis came back with two hot pretzels. Brooks took a fast bite, and Otis could almost hear his body thanking him.

They made shallow conversation as they ate, then: "Anyway, I know what it's like to be down and out. I don't know your story, but it looks like you need a hand up." Otis searched his wallet for a business card. "I'm a winemaker in Washington State and always looking for good men to help me."

Brooks made a quick attempt at eye contact. "I don't know shit about wine."

"That's the one thing I know about, and I'm an okay teacher. It's good, honest work, a way to work with your hands and make something that matters. If you have a drinking problem, probably not the best idea, but otherwise, it's a good way to spend a life. I could teach you, if you wanted."

"Because I look like your son?"

"There's that. Maybe the only way I feel like I can heal is by helping those around me. I could put you up, show you how to work the vines, teach you how to make wine. Where I live, Red Mountain, it's in the middle of nowhere. It's hard to find help. Maybe you're different, maybe you have something. There's a reason I'm on this bench right now."

Feeling like his best version of himself, Otis handed him the card. "There's my number. You need a second chance, I got one for you. Nothing in it for me, other than trying to find a way through my own grief, and I'm trying to build something special on this little mountain out there. So clean yourself up. I don't know if you're doing drugs, but that's not welcome. The cigarettes don't help your palate, but that didn't stop the man who taught me. Either way, call me and I'll get you out there, get you set up. But don't bother unless you're ready."

Brooks stared at the card.

Otis rose and started to go, but Brooks stopped him. "Your son was a lucky guy, having a dad like you. I didn't grow up like that."

"Maybe luck found you now. A pleasure to meet you, Brooks." He offered a wave and turned to go.

~

That night, back on Red Mountain, Otis lay in bed with Rebecca. Her head rested on his bare chest. "I don't want to leave you again," he said. "It's too hard."

"I know."

He glided his hand down her lotioned arm. "Do you think it ever stops hurting?"

"I doubt it, but I think we'll learn to live with it, learn to sit with the pain. I can't stop seeing him, reliving all the moments we had together."

410

He felt her pain blend into his, their hearts beating to the same agonizing rhythm. "I saw a guy today, a homeless man in the park, looked a lot like him. Same age. I sat down and talked to him for a while, gave him my card." Otis elaborated. "I don't know where to go from here, Bec. I've lost my passion for life. I want to keep lying in bed with you, holding you, not ever letting you go. I want Mike to move back home, and we just be together, the three of us." He shrugged his shoulder. "I don't even know that I have what it takes to keep growing wine."

Rebecca pressed up and brushed away his tears. "I've been writing in my journal, trying to make sense of it all. Trying to find a way through. All I can come up with is that it means we need to live our lives even brighter. We need to live enough to make up for the huge hole Camden left in this goddamn world."

She was right. He knew something else too. It was time to give Bec a break. She'd been carrying him and the boys since the beginning, and it was time that he carry the weight for a while.

﹏

Otis returned to the cellar and took the helm with the strength he found in Rebecca's words. He set out to make wine, because that's what he did best, and he would do it for Cam. This year would not be one that went down as a failure, as a year of grief and sadness. It would be a year of joy, a vintage celebrating a young man who was taken too early but who had figured out life, nonetheless.

He would never forget the day Cam died, the way his son looked at him with that confident smirk. He'd figured things out, and maybe that was why he'd been taken away. Otis, on the other hand, had a lot of work to do, and he would no longer do it by letting life beat him. He would do it on the wings of his amazing son, who would expect nothing less of his parents and younger brother than for them to give their all.

Taking a weekend off, Otis and Rebecca stayed in their place in Capitol Hill in Seattle. Michael was supposed to meet them for dinner at the Pink Door but had to cancel at the last minute due to work. He'd taken a job as a criminal defense attorney and was deep in the middle of a case.

Otis and Rebecca consumed far too much fresh pasta, and Otis convinced the owner to bring in one of his Red Mountain wines. Then they walked through town, holding hands, two broken pieces trying to find a way back together again.

In the morning they met Michael for coffee at the original Starbucks at Pike Place Market. He was a mess, clearly already a cup or two ahead of them. "Sorry about last night, guys," he said, kissing his mother's head. "This job . . . it's insane."

Otis straightened his son's tie, then pulled him in for a hug. He might not have been much of a hugger back in the old days, but he was like a dog with separation anxiety now. Even if he hadn't seen his family in five minutes, he'd race over for a hug and kiss.

They caught up while they stood in line, and Otis could see clearly that his son was struggling, despite trying to hide it. Or maybe he didn't even know it. Last they'd spoken, Mike had told them he was still taking his medicine.

"You wouldn't believe how much work we're taking on," he said. "The staff shortages are crazy, and prosecutions are at an all-time high."

"Are they all guilty?" Rebecca asked.

"No, not at all. I have my fair share of guilty clients, but some of them haven't done a thing. Without a good attorney, they have no hope." He tapped his fingers on his leg, a rhythm only he knew.

"Then they're awfully lucky," Otis said, wondering what he could do for Michael. "Are you coming home for Christmas?"

"I hope to. We'll see."

"You need to. The first Christmas without Cam. Make some time for us."

"I'll try."

Otis stood silently and waited for Michael to actually look at him. "Michael, you have a lot of me in you. Don't work your way through your grief. Don't forget what matters. Take a girl out. Go sailing. Come home for Christmas."

"I know, I know."

Otis felt like he was looking at his younger self, the one who'd lost his way.

~

Michael ended up having to work on Christmas Eve, so Otis and Rebecca spent the holidays in Seattle, which wasn't so bad. They enjoyed more than one meal at Mistral, experienced a wonderful Pat Metheny performance at Jazz Alley, and ate their weight in sushi at Shiro's. When they could, they spent time with Michael. Otis tried not to force his teachings on him, but sneaked in some advice when Michael would allow it. Talk about hardheaded. The man was likely a wonderful lawyer, because he had an answer for everything.

They were enjoying a glass of wine at a spot called Place Pigalle, which had been pouring Till Vineyards for a while now, when Otis's cell phone rang.

He looked to his wife and son. "Sorry, I need to take this. It's a New York number." Stepping outside, he pressed the phone to his ear. "Otis here."

"Otis, it's Brooks Baker. We met in Central Park last fall."

Otis's mouth hit the pavement. "Brooks! Hello."

Brooks didn't match his enthusiasm. "I've been thinking about what you said, your offer. I don't know anything about wine, but I need a job. Like you mentioned, I could use a hand up. So here I am."

A dazzling amount of energy rushed through Otis's body. "Yes, great, Brooks. Can I call you later? I'm having lunch with my—"

"This is a borrowed phone. I don't have a . . ."

Otis scrambled for a solution. "Tell you what. Call me tomorrow at noon, my time. Let me work out some details. I'll book you a flight."

"Really?"

"Absolutely. Do you have a place to stay tonight?"

"I can figure it out."

Perhaps the first real smile since Colorado graced Otis's face.

Brooks called at noon on the nose. Otis picked up from his living room in Seattle. "Okay, I'll need your full name, date of birth. You have a license, right?"

"Yes, I do."

"Good." Otis had been working on details all morning. He was glad he hadn't gotten rid of Vance's trailer. It wasn't much, but he didn't imagine Brooks was too picky.

When Otis hung up, he looked over at Rebecca, who had her feet up on the couch, reading. "I can't believe he's coming. Do you think I'm crazy?"

She set the book down. "No, I think this is . . . beautiful."

The rich feeling of knowing he was doing something right filled his chest. "You'll like him. Not that I know him that much, but he has this fire in his eyes."

"Like you and Michael?"

"That's right. It feels good to help somebody in need. Maybe it works out, maybe it doesn't."

A day later, Otis drove the farm truck to the Tri-Cities airport with equal parts trepidation and hope. What in the hell had he done, inviting a random stranger off the street to step into his world? It felt right, though. He'd spent a lifetime focused on number one—or mostly so—and it was time to look outside himself and see what good he could do.

Brooks came around the corner with a backpack slung over his shoulder. He'd shaved and looked quite handsome—a far cry from the man he'd met in the park. Perhaps the only way he surely knew it was him, other than the fire in his eyes, was the tattoos creeping out of his sleeves.

Otis opened his arms. "Welcome to Washington State."

Brooks accepted the hug, but he went about it as if he'd never been hugged before. He barely put any pressure into it, but Otis didn't mind. He squeezed him hard, patted his back a couple of times.

"How was the flight?"

"Fine. First time I've flown in my life."

"What?"

Brooks nodded and looked away, a move he apparently often resorted to.

Otis felt for him. "I think there will be a lot of firsts coming up. You've never seen anything like Red Mountain in your life. Have you been to the Pacific Northwest?"

"I spent time in Portland."

"Did you try the pinot noirs?"

His eyebrows curled nervously. "Nah. My experience in Portland probably wasn't like yours."

"Hey, there's no judgment here. I had some good men in my day who went out of their way for me. I'm trying to pay it forward. There was a time when I also knew nothing of wine."

Once they were in the truck, Otis apologized for the broken heater. He needed to find time to fix it soon. It had snowed a week back, and piles of it lined the highway. Otis gave him the tour, showing him Pasco, then Kennewick and Richland.

"I got you a place to live. Furnished. It's nothing fancy, but it has a hell of a view."

"I'm grateful. What is it we're going to be doing?"

"That's a good question. I'll show you some things in the cellar till it warms up. Then it's pruning time, the start of a new vintage."

An angry and icy wind forced its way through the door when Rebecca and Otis greeted Brooks that night. They both did their best to smile, trying to work muscles that had nearly atrophied. The last days of a devastating year were breaking away like pieces of a dying star, lingering in the air of their Red Mountain home, often making it hard to breathe.

Once Brooks had hung his jacket, Bec offered him a hug. "I'm happy you're here."

His face was red from the cold. He glanced at her before putting his eyes on the floor. "I appreciate you having me, though I'm still trying to figure it all out, why you're doing this for me."

She touched his arm. "As Otis told you, we lost our son earlier this year. He was about your age. It's been hard. What we're finding is the more we give to others, the less it hurts inside. Otis said he saw a bit of himself in you. Besides, he's been looking for a new assistant winemaker. Maybe you'll like it and want to stick around."

Otis stepped forward and shook Brooks's hand. "Did you get settled?"

"Oh, yeah. It's a nice place. Thank you."

They gave the young man a tour, ending in the living room with pictures and stories of the boys.

"If you feel like it, I'd love to hear your tale," Otis said, checking in on his tone, making sure there was some life in it. "We're going to spend a lot of time together coming up. No worries if you want to keep it to yourself. We get it. Like I said, there's no judgment here. Red Mountain has become a place that means a lot to us, and we're simply trying to bring in more people, people who want to make a difference. Is that you, Brooks?"

"I don't know, but so far, since I landed, it's better than anything I've known for a long time."

Otis clapped his back. "That's where we start then, and it only gets better. Wait till you try Rebecca's cooking. Do you have any dietary restrictions? I guess we should have asked earlier."

"Dietary restrictions?" Brooks laughed. It was the first time Otis had heard it, and it was a good laugh, a kind one. "No, I'll eat anything you put in front of me."

"Good, and wine? You like wine?"

"What I've had of it."

"Don't worry. By the time I'm done with you, should you accept the challenge, you'll know more than most."

Otis cracked a bottle of Red Mountain syrah and poured everyone a glass. "Hold it by the stem," he said in the way Rebecca would, a teaching voice, not the condescending one he might have employed in the past. "There you go. Now stick your nose in there, don't be afraid. That's the smell of where you live now, that bing cherry mixed with the gamy flavor. Take a sip, hold it on your tongue, then suck up some air. Like this." Otis demonstrated.

Brooks gave it a go. Some spilled onto his chin.

"Yep, that happens to everybody in the beginning. Don't worry. Taste that fruit, the balance. You know that zing you get when biting into a lemon? That's the acid. You don't pucker with these wines, but when you pick the grapes right off the vine, the acid is enough to make them tingle in your mouth. That same acid helps preserve the wine's aromatics as it ages. I know it's a lot, but bear with me for a while. You never know, you might fall in love."

Brooks took another sip. "It's good . . . really good. Sorry, I'm just out of my element."

"Not for long, Brooks. Not for long."

Otis and Rebecca shared a smile.

After dinner Brooks helped with the dishes, and then they returned to the table. Rebecca had made a pound cake. Otis pulled everyone espressos from his new machine.

Out of nowhere, Brooks started talking. "I don't know who my parents are. I grew up in the foster-care system, juggled by different homes in California. Then I ran away as a teenager, escaped a pretty ugly situation. Spent the last ten years bouncing around the country, bumming rides, hopping trains. Moving from one place to the next. I haven't been good at keeping jobs, but they haven't meant much to me. I hope that changes with this one. Seems like a damn fine place to be. I'm tired of sleeping on the ground or in a shelter. I'd like a life. I just don't know how to get one. I guess that's why I called, because it seemed like you'd given me something no one ever has before."

Brooks raised his eyes to Otis, then to Rebecca. "I don't want to disappoint you."

"You won't," Otis said.

Rebecca reached across the table and took his hand. "You're a good man. I can see that. Sometimes we all need a break. Let's make this one yours."

꩜

The next morning Jed called Rebecca to tell her that their mother had passed away from a stroke. Olivia had been diagnosed with diabetes a year prior and had done nothing to manage it. They met Mike later that afternoon at SFO and drove up to Santa Rosa together. How sad that it was always death that brought people together.

Otis and Rebecca paid for the funeral and bought two burial plots next to each other in a nearby cemetery, so that Marshall could join her when his time came. They'd offered to include Jed, but like Bec, he wanted to be cremated.

After people started to leave, Jed wheeled outside to speak with Otis and Rebecca. He wore a VIETNAM WAR VETERAN hat over his graying hair. "I know apologies only go so far, so I won't drown you in them, but I'm sorry. To both of you. Otis, I never gave you a chance. Bec, you have nothing to do with what happened." He gestured to his legs. "I'm sorry I ever said that. Maybe it's what was supposed to happen. Maybe it was the kick in the ass I needed. You were right—right about a lot of things. I should have gotten into computers way back when." He smiled warmly. "It's never too late, though. The VA is going to help me get into school, hopefully Sonoma State. I'm going to major in computer science, if this old brain can do it."

Bec's mouth fell open; her eyes reddened. "Really?"

Jed set his hands on the wheels of his chair. "I gotta do something. Just to get out of the house. Dad's driving me crazy, and now that Mom's gone . . . I don't want to abandon him, but I have to start looking out for myself."

Lowering, Bec put her hands on Jed's temples, and peered into his eyes. "I love you, brother."

"I love you, too, sis."

Brooks settled in and proved to be a hell of a hard worker. After dabbling for a month with the fermenting wines, Otis let Chaco teach Brooks how to prune and drive a tractor. Otis would often grab him for lunch, though, and they'd eat tacos on the back of the truck and talk about what makes a great wine, about permaculture, and how the sacred soil must be treated with reverence.

At night he'd take Brooks down into the cellar and open bottles of wine, sometimes spitting, sometimes not, but they'd always pay the wines respect. Otis could see the glimmer in Brooks's eyes, and though the young man didn't speak much, certainly not about inner feelings, he showed an enthusiasm that Otis recognized from his own experience.

They took a glass out into the vines one night. Rosco walked alongside them. Otis could feel Carmine in the chilly air. A full moon cast a warm glow over the land. Recalling his most valuable lesson, Otis reached for a handful of soil and dropped it into his glass, then knocked it back. "That's what we're doing here."

Brooks smiled, but not like he thought Otis was crazy. More like he got it; he understood.

Then Otis spoke of balance. "That's the key, Brooks. Not only in wine, but in life. You might have to learn the hard way like I did. Maybe you already have. This life, this wine life, can consume you. Just as the wines must strike the balance of its constituents, including the acidity, the alcohol, and the tannins, we must find our own. We must be at harmony with ourselves, with those around us, and the ones we've lost and found. Only then will our wines sing."

Otis sipped his wine and ran a hand through Rosco's thick coat of fur. "I don't know if I've ever made the wine I want to make, but I've tried. Sometimes tried too hard. I'm finally on the right path. I have found the terroir that sings to my soul, and I have come to peace with so much of the pain inside. Now, all I can do is wait for the vintage like a surfer waits for a wave. They always come, but not always when you need them to. Do I make sense?"

"You do."

Otis collected the glasses and stood. "On that note, I'm cooking my wife dinner tonight."

"How's she doing?" Brooks asked. "Since her mother . . ."

"She's working her way through it, as best she can. If I could take away her pain, I would, but I know she has what it takes to pull through. All I can do is be there for her, hold her when she wants holding, listen when she needs to talk." He sighed. "What I hope for you is that you find a woman like I have, and when you do, Brooks, you give her more than you give anything. Because she matters most. Don't ever forget that."

Brooks nodded and stood. "I want to thank you. For everything. I feel . . . I've been running all my life, and, maybe for the first time, I don't feel like running anymore."

Otis's chest filled. "I'll tell you what my father never told me. You have nothing to prove, Brooks Baker. Just chase your passions and love your people like you might never see them again. The rest will all work out."

⌒

Never had Otis left his land days before harvest, but things had changed. He'd corrected his overcorrection. Naturally, he planned on returning with plenty of time left to harvest grapes, but it was the right time to take Brooks to the Mosel in Germany. He asked Michael to go too. It took some arm twisting due to his son's tendency to lose himself in work, but he finally caved.

Otis flew them first class. Brooks had never been to Europe and stumbled around in wide-eyed awe at everything. When they started taking their appointments to taste, Brooks visibly became emotional. Otis could see that the wine bug had him, the toothy bastards sinking in their fangs.

The only thing he worried about was Michael. He hoped there wasn't any jealousy.

Brooks explored on his own one day, and Otis and Michael went for a long walk along the river. Two hours in, they got hungry and found a traditional restaurant for lunch.

Over sausage and potatoes and cabbage, Otis said, "I'm going to ask Brooks to become my assistant winemaker, but I wanted to run it by you first."

"You don't have to do that." Michael tapped his foot under the table, always on the go. He looked the part, a pressed shirt and chinos. A tight hairdo. On his wrist he wore Addison's Rolex. Otis had given it to him shortly after Camden had died.

"I know," Otis said, talking with his fork in his hand, "but I want to. I don't want you to think I'm leaving you out. I know you don't want to be a part of the business, but you're always welcome. You know I'll leave it to you. Maybe you'll sell. Hopefully to the right person. But I'd like you to be involved with the big decisions. More importantly, I don't want you to think Brooks matters more to me than you."

Michael slid his stein of beer closer to him. "Oh, c'mon."

"I'm serious. He does feel like a son to me, but—"

"Dad, stop. I think you have enough love to go around. It's amazing that you're mentoring him. Look at him. He's doing great, working hard. Keep doing that for him. You've done that for me all my life."

"I've tried."

"And succeeded. Look at what you did for Vance too. He never had that. I'm happy to share my dad with good men who didn't have a father."

Chills rose up Otis's back. He leaned forward, waiting for Michael to lock eyes with him. "I don't know what I did to deserve you."

—

Upon their return, Otis took Brooks to meet Mitch Green, the hermit. Brooks ate warm cheese from Mitch's pocket, cut from a dirty knife, and they drank several efforts from the previous vintage, all of them heavy with Brettanomyces, a yeast that makes a wine smell like the underside of a horse saddle.

"I hear the Round Table is becoming formalized," Mitch said.

"That's right," Otis said. "We're changing the name to the Red Mountain AVA Alliance, turning it into a nonprofit trade association, with a board of directors, the whole thing."

"Good God," Mitch said.

"I know. We're growing up."

Mitch led them to the vine that was the heartbeat of their land, and Otis could see that whatever road had led Brooks to Red Mountain, it might be that he would never leave. He burst with life out here and being around that vine seemed to heal him even more. Maybe he would one day take the helm of Till Vineyards, possibly even steer the ship that was Red Mountain.

In the months to come, Otis taught Brooks everything he could in the cellar, and when they were done, he said, "Take a couple of weeks off. Then we'll do it all over again. We put one vintage in front of the other—that's how you build a life in wine. That is, if you're hooked."

Brooks had turned less timid. He held Otis's gaze. "I think I've found my calling."

Otis's cheeks swelled. "I think you have too."

Chapter 30

Teaching Moments

"Who would have known that the 2009 vintage would be the one?" Otis had finally done it, made the wine he'd been going for all these years.

"What was your first vintage again?" Brooks asked. His confidence continued to grow, and he even seemed relaxed at the table, with one leg over the other.

Rebecca held out a hand. "Oh, don't encourage him. He'll race off to the—"

It was too late. Otis rose from the table where he, Brooks, Rebecca, and Mike sat in the living room. It was February 2011, and the '09 vintage had shipped out into the world today, and so they'd pulled the cork on a bottle to see how it had fared.

Of course, they already knew. They'd been tasting the wine for almost a year and a half now. From day one, the land had worked with them. The pests were manageable, the spring rains not too harsh. They had their obstacles, but that was fine, that was always the way. It was just that Otis had found renewed spirit in working with and teaching Brooks. They faced their challenges with optimism and curiosity. They tasted the grapes every morning till the balance was right. Then they picked.

Otis jogged up to the winery in the cold, then stuck the iron key in the lock and pulled open the great wooden door that protected their entire wine collection. Down below, he lit the sconces and found what he sought: the first vintage of Lost Souls, not counting the wine he'd poured out.

Back at the table, Otis extracted the cork and took a sniff. The old label had nearly peeled off. "Can you believe it, Bec? Nineteen seventy-five is considered old now. I haven't tasted this in years. There's not much left. Actually, it's a good thing Bec made me hold back a few cases."

"That's right," she said. "He wanted to sell every last drop."

Brooks set down a round of fresh glasses. "I'm glad you didn't."

Tasting the wine brought back a thousand memories, most of them not cringeworthy, though it was hard not to think of Lloyd for a moment. The man had successfully avoided jail so far, but he'd destroyed his reputation. Perhaps that was worse than jail for him.

"This could be your first hundred pointer," Michael said, referring to the '09 vintage.

For a moment Otis thought his son was serious. Hadn't he taught him better than that? "Oh, I hope not. Please, dear God. Finally, I'm satisfied with a vintage, and I don't want the critics to ruin it for me."

"It would be nice, though, wouldn't it?" Brooks asked, unawares.

"To get one hundred points?" Otis dramatically dropped his head into his hands. "Have I taught you nothing, boys?"

"Here we go," Bec said, grins all around.

Brooks spun the wine in his glass like a sommelier. Oh, how far he'd come. "I get it," he said. "Wine is subjective, but still . . . you admitted yourself that you were chasing a review from Sam Ledbetter all those years."

"Yeah, that's when I was making wine for all the wrong reasons. He was doing the far more admirable job of actually writing about the wine. A number is entirely different. Besides, my poor choices, my hope to be written about—those are mistakes I hope you don't make.

One-hundred-point wines can be fine, but they're no more special than any wine that captures its terroir with a degree of fine balance."

"Have you had that many?" Brooks asked, excitement radiating from him. Otis knew that no matter what he said, he couldn't unpolish the sheen of curiosity in the young lad's mind.

"I have a few one hundred pointers in the cellar," Otis said. "Gifts, mind you. I don't buy one-hundred-point wine. On principle."

Silence.

Otis could read the room. "Shall we drink one?"

Brooks failed to conceal his elation. "I wouldn't say no."

Otis looked at Rebecca. "I guess he does have to learn his own lessons."

Michael ran up to the cellar this time and returned with a bottle of wine they'd received five years earlier from a California winemaker who'd achieved his first "perfect" wine. Brooks set yet another round of glasses on the table.

Otis watched Brooks take his first sips of "perfection." Brooks looked around and then gave a smile. Otis held back his own opinion, waiting.

"Well . . ." Rebecca said.

"Ours is better," Brooks said.

Otis smacked the table, jarring the bottles. "You're damn right ours is better. I'm telling you, Brooks. The point system makes winemakers compromise their craft. They're competing in a game of making Hollywood-action-movie wines. You know the ones, the movies with no plot but plenty of explosions. It's a car chase that lasts thirty minutes on the screen. Rotten Tomatoes gives it a fresh score 100! No, no, no. What we have done . . ."

Otis lifted the glass of the '09. "She's a movie that grows on you, one you show your kids when you're older. One that makes you think. One that makes you *feel*." He kissed the glass. "This is the finest wine I've ever been a part of making. I don't know that I'll ever say it again, but this was our vintage. This is what Bec and I have been going after for forty years. Can you believe that? I think we finally did it, deary."

Bec was sitting back, watching it all with amusement. "You finally caught your wave, didn't you, Otis Pennington Till?"

"Our wave, my dear. None of this exists without you."

He kissed her on the lips, then went back to the one-hundred-point wine. "You know what this is good for?"

"Oh, God," Rebecca said. "Don't get all riled up, Otis."

"What? Seriously. I can't handle this system. How is it that we let a few people tell us what is good in wine? Even worse than attempting to sum up Mother Earth's greatest gift with a number . . . is that people believe it. They open their little magazines and see a score by a label and don't realize the score came from just one person, a person who might not even know the context of the wine, making their best guess at a rating."

"Now we've opened the can of worms," Mike said to Brooks. "He won't stop all night now."

Brooks folded over in laughter as Otis kept going. He ranted for five more minutes, then walked into the kitchen and grabbed an empty pitcher. He filled it with ice, then chopped up an apple and diced an orange, dropping it in.

"What are you doing?" Rebecca asked with exasperation.

"One minute, please."

At the bar, he grabbed a bottle of brandy, then set it all down on the table.

"Don't you dare," his lovely, patient, and charming wife warned.

Brooks and Michael stared at him in bewilderment.

Otis poured a proper amount of brandy over the ice, then took the one-hundred-point wine and turned it upside down, dumping it over his mixture. After a good stir, he poured a serving into an empty glass. "You see that. It's perfect sangria wine. We don't even need sugar!"

He looked up at Bec, Mike, and Brooks. "I give this one hundred and seven points."

"You're really five years old still."

428

"Always will be, my dear. Now let's get back to the 2009, our magnum opus. Or should I say, magnum Otis."

The eye rolls weren't enough to dent his pride.

—

After Brooks and Mike had left, Rebecca and Otis were finishing up the dishes when Otis pulled her toward him. "I'm happy, Bec."

"I can see that. You finally got your vintage, didn't you?"

"I guess so." He kissed her softly, touched her stomach with his finger. "I'm craving you right now."

"It's always that way when you like your wine," she whispered.

"Let's not beat Otis up tonight. I'm on top of the world."

"Oh, are you? Then I wouldn't dare do anything to knock you down."

She kissed *him* this time. "Can we take this to the bedroom, or are we doing it in the kitchen again?"

"I'll take it wherever you want it."

—

The sky dumped snow the next day. Otis and Brooks were racking wines. It was about two when they broke for lunch. Otis glanced at his phone and saw that Rebecca had texted.

> The lean-to fell onto one of the sheep, bad break, bone popping out. Michael and I are driving him to the vet.

Otis dialed her back.

No answer.

He called again.

No answer.

He texted: Please don't drive. Let me handle it.

He tried several more times, then raced down to the house. They'd already left. He saw the tire marks in the snow, and a lump formed in his throat.

It wasn't safe out there. He fished his phone out of his pocket and tried her one more time.

Chapter 31 (Interlude)

AFTER WE SAID GOODBYE

Red Mountain, Washington State
April 2011

Otis set down his pen and wiped his eyes, knowing he had finished. He'd told the story, no sense writing about the police showing up, his drive down to the morgue to identify the bodies, the days of terror that followed. The funeral that flooded him with tears. The spreading of Mike's ashes in the same place where they'd spread Cam's.

And yet there was more to say, wasn't there? Perhaps there was another page to be written, perhaps another chapter.

"It can't end here," he said, his voice cracking. He could feel his family's presence, as if they were in the room, and he looked up into the middle distance between him and the ceiling, wondering whether they were there.

And he knew.

Camden.

Michael.

Rebecca.

Together they had formed the keystone to his life. Without them, life never would have meant a thing.

There was something else, though. They were still here. Yes, they existed as memories, but it was more than that. They were in the air. They were in every breath he would ever take. They were in the wines and in the vines . . . and in his heart.

Otis felt his chest and closed his eyes. He could almost touch them. They were here now and would be here forever, both in memory and in spirit.

Perhaps there was no place for regret. He couldn't change the choices he'd made. He couldn't go back and polish those rough years, but he could see them in a different light. He could accept that he'd had his own growing to do, and by God, he'd done his fair share of it. Stepping out of the ashes of his demise, Otis had found his way back to his family. Returning from Miami, he'd found a way to continue their love story. He'd done what his father had never done.

It couldn't end now.

If he was gone from this earth, who would say their names? Who would raise their glasses and call upon a fond memory?

By God, who would make sure they weren't forgotten?

Amigo followed him as he reached for the urn on the mantel. He set his hands on the curve of it, sensing her even more.

"I am here, my love . . . and I will forge ahead because it is what we have always done. I will not mar the memory of you and the boys by giving up now. But I need you. If you're out there, if you can feel me, give me the strength I need to carry on."

He pulled his hand from the urn. For a moment he thought that maybe he would take her ashes today and spread them in the vineyard, but he wasn't ready. He kissed his fingers and touched the urn again. "I love you."

Otis watched the vet work the saw to remove Amigo's cast. As it broke free, Amigo went for his leg, licking it like a lollipop.

"There you go, little guy," the nice vet said. He was half Otis's age, wore a white coat with his name on it, and smelled of cologne. To Otis, he said, "Good as new."

"Now what do I do? Is he ready?"

"As ready as he can be."

"How do I do it?"

"Otis, you're the first coyote rescuer in my career. I don't know. So long as he's not completely domesticated, you get him to his family and see what happens."

Otis carried Amigo out to the truck and drove back to Red Mountain in a sharp silence. Otis took the little desert dog inside, gave him milk, and then sat with him a long time, stroking his fur. "I don't know what I'm going to do without you. You've become a part of this farm, but it's time. We can't wait another night."

Amigo looked at him curiously, tilting his head.

Otis touched his nose. "You must be brave tonight. I can't go with you."

The howls that night were wild, desperate calls, coming from all directions. Otis stepped out the front door, Amigo in hand. The moon wasn't quite full, but it shone like a lantern in a cave, showing the way.

Otis followed his heart, deciding he'd return Amigo to the same place where he'd found him. He hiked up the hill to his oldest syrah block and could feel Rebecca's presence as if she walked beside him. Off in the distance, the coyotes continued to howl.

Were they still looking for Amigo? Was it even the same pack?

All he could do was have faith.

They stepped down the row. Scents of desert sage filled the air. The vines had come alive and begun to push out leaves. Another vintage was upon them. No matter what happened, another vintage always came. A lot like those ferries that Carmine spoke about going to Ischia.

There was always another vintage.

How many did he have left?

"I hope to see you again, Amigo. You saved my life." He kissed the coyote on the side of the nose and held him up to meet his eyes. Forever they would be connected.

Emptiness hollowed out his heart. How many more goodbyes could he handle?

But he had to get better at letting go.

He set Amigo down, and the wild dog perked up his ears when the coyotes howled again.

"Howl back, my friend. I must leave you now."

Amigo stared up into Otis's eyes, lost and alone.

"You have to howl. Call to them. They'll come for you."

With those words, he nearly buckled to the ground. His family gone.

Gone for now, though. They were his forever family, out there in some cellular composition of their own, be it in heaven or scattered like dust in a celestial cloud. They were here in his heart and on this land that he would farm in their honor till the day the vines pulled him back into the earth.

Another howl, then a song from them, the wild dogs singing into the night. *Ahwwoooo!*

Amigo twisted his head, then walked a few feet toward the sound. His leg worked wonderfully, and should he find his family, he'd be okay.

At the next call, Amigo attempted to respond, but no sound came from his mouth.

Otis knelt next to him. "You must call them back, Amigo. Please. They will come to you. They will guide you home."

Amigo looked like he might cry, if it were possible.

Fear of finding Amigo dead in the morning rose over him. Could he take care of himself through the night? Perhaps it was Otis's job to shelter him, to raise him.

No.

Otis had to let go. He had to trust that the world always lined up in the end, that the grand design would lay out like a road hidden in the darkness.

"Let's try together," Otis said. On all fours, he made a soft sound, howling gently, easily, letting the coyote know that it was okay.

Amigo looked like he might start laughing at him.

"Okay, wise guy, show me how it's done."

Amigo kept watching Otis.

Otis tried again, this time slightly louder. *"Ahhhhwwooooooo!"*

The wild dog shuffled his feet and let out a meager bark.

"There you go." Otis felt the night then, the power it had.

"Again, do it again." Otis drew in a deep breath, and then: *"Ahwwwwooooooo!"*

Amigo lit up, his eyes glowing in the darkness.

Then came the calls from the night back to them, a collective howl of the desert dogs. They were drawing closer.

This time, Otis didn't hold back. *"Ahhhwwooooo! Ahhhwwoooooooo!"* He felt the power of the universe soar through him. *"Aaaahhhhhwwwwooooo!"*

The padding of paws sounded in the distance. He felt no fear, only the desperate hope that Amigo's family was coming for him.

Then it happened.

Amigo let out his first howl. *"Ahhwwwwwwooooo!"*

It came out like a baby speaking for the first time, testing the ability of the tongue.

He tried again and again. Otis joined in, two lost lonely souls out there calling to their loved ones.

Otis howled like he never had before, and he felt the call of the wild dogs and the presence of Rebecca and Cam and Mike, and he howled to them from his core, telling them that he wasn't done with this life, that he would give it all that he had, that he would do it all for them, in their honor. He would attempt to live this life with the grace that his family taught him, and when his time came, he would drift away from this body and find them in the hereafter.

A proud dog appeared at the end of a row, a beautiful beast of a coyote. The moon cast a shadow of him onto the ground.

"There he is," Otis said, then noticed the other dogs behind him.

Otis slowly rose and backed away. Amigo stood between him and the others. The coyote pup let loose another howl, this time far bigger, one that cut through the mountain air, showing the world that he, this little guy, had found his family.

He took several steps toward them, sniffing the air. The other dogs made light calls, singing lullabies to him. Amigo grew braver by the minute, moving closer.

Ten feet away, five feet away, and then he leaped toward them, and they all buried their snouts into him, knocking him to the ground. Belly up, he cried with delight, and the other dogs surrounded him in a way only family could.

Though there would always be those pieces of his heart that belonged to those he lost, Otis had never felt fuller in his heart, and he knew that his family was out there too.

When the excitement of the reunion dissipated, the alpha coyote looked at Otis and stared for a long time, eyes on eyes, soul on soul. One alpha to another.

A million things were said between those two, none of them requiring words.

Otis finally gave a nod, and the coyote backed away. He turned his attention to Amigo, who seemed to be smiling beyond those eyes that glowed in the dark.

Otis touched his heart; tears pricked his eyes. "Goodbye, my friend. Don't go too far."

He couldn't know what Amigo was thinking, but they shared something wonderful in that last moment before the alpha gently grabbed Amigo's fur with his teeth and urged him to follow.

Otis watched as the pack of dogs, Amigo's pack, meandered off into the night, the moon casting their shadows down as they went. He raised a hand in one last wave, bidding them farewell.

Returning to the house, Otis grabbed a beer from the fridge, because it takes a lot of good beer to make great wine, and he walked into his office and thumbed through his CDs. Finding Crosby, Stills, and Nash's first album, he set it onto the player and skipped to the song he needed to hear.

"Guinevere," the song they'd sung at Woodstock when Otis had knelt down into the mud and proposed to his forever girl, filled the air.

Otis sat in the chair he'd been sleeping in since they'd left him, and he wept big tears of loss and finding. He peered up at the urn, hoping and praying that there was more left to life than the ashes that we all became.

A purple bus. Two lovers making a promise in a sea of people. A life spent among the vines, raising two fine boys who lived boldly and beautifully and became damn fine men before they were taken away far too early.

That couldn't be the end, though. Not even close.

Otis pressed up from the recliner and went to the desk. He took the journal and closed it, its work completed. The rest of what he'd write wouldn't require a pen. He'd finish this journey out there in the vines, out there making something with what he had left.

Carrying the journal and a pack of matches, he walked to the fireplace and set it down on the grate, splayed open.

This was the way it should be, memories captured in ink but burned into the heart.

Otis struck the match; the flame came to life.

He held the flame under the words that had saved him, the words that Rebecca had urged him to write, the words that only barely scraped the surface of their love story.

As the flame drew near the page, a gust of wind pushed through, blowing out the match.

"What in the . . . ?" He held it in his hand, watching it smoke with a curious puzzlement.

He drew out another match and dragged it along the side of the box, bringing a second flame to life.

As he held it underneath the journal, another gust of wind, perhaps sucked from the flue, came rushing through and extinguished it.

"Are you there?" Otis asked. "Rebecca?"

Only stillness responded. But it was not a lonely stillness. It was the kind that allowed all the room in the world for faith and hope. Perhaps even more, perhaps knowingness.

Yes, indeed, she was there.

~

I know that it's time to go.

What is it like to say goodbye to your love, your best friend, your keystone, as he called me? What is it like to let go of this life? What is it like to hold on to hope that I might see him again one day?

It's a warm sensation that engulfs me.

I watch my Otis sleep, wishing I could stroke his hair. I watch him rise in the morning one last time. With NPR playing in the background, he makes fresh coffee and bacon and eggs.

Thoughts of him finding someone new come over me. We didn't talk about it, but I wish we had. I don't want him to be alone. Otis is not a man who should be alone. So I watch him eat his breakfast in solitude and hope that he might find someone one day. He has so much more life to live, so much more love to give.

After he shaves and dresses, I follow him up to the winery. Brooks is already there, perusing the newspaper in the tasting room.

He nearly spits his coffee out at the sight of my Otis stepping through the door. "Good morning," Brooks says, joy washing over him. His mentor is back.

Otis waves him off. "Now don't get all excited. I know it's been a while. Let's not make a big deal about it. How are our wines?"

He's back, and he's the same Otis he always was.

Brooks plays it calm, returns his eyes to the newspaper. "They're hanging in there. Could use some help from the Grapefather?"

"I'll do what I can." Otis takes a seat, looks around, likely taking inventory of everything that needs to be done.

Brooks peers over the paper. "Just like that, you're back?"

Otis crosses his arms. "Unless you want to have a parade."

I laugh, because this is exactly why I love him. I'm going to miss the ol' grump with every last bit of me.

Brooks folds the paper and extends his hand across the table. "Welcome back, maestro."

Otis shakes his hand and locks eyes with him, two lost and found souls amid a sea of lost and found souls, all fighting to carve out a life worth living.

Ours wasn't a perfect story, but I doubt many of them are. What I know now is that this life we shared, it's only a small chapter in a vast volume of books. It's time for me to see what lies ahead, to continue my own story. To reunite with my boys.

Without even thinking it, without even turning away from my forever man, a lightness washes over me . . .

. . . and off I go.

A Note to Readers

Let me set the record straight.

It goes without saying that a writer must take certain liberties when writing fiction, especially historical fiction, but I've taken the idea to an entirely new level. I've intentionally broken rules. Not everything in this book is historically accurate. I've made up the names of people and places and have even inserted real people into fake scenarios. In both Sonoma and Red Mountain, I have fused fact and fiction into a strange amalgam, such as Carmine's funeral scene attended by various real people, or the real-life Tom and Anne-Marie Hedges becoming friends with the Tills. Oh, and thank you to real-life Joe Montana for the HUGE cameo!

In truth, Jim Holmes of Ciel du Cheval and John Williams of Kiona Vineyards planted the first grapes on Red Mountain in 1975; then the Hedges family spearheaded the AVA process. But Otis is the Grapefather of Red Mountain, so I had to squeeze his contributions in there. With all respect to Jim and John, I also chose to make Red Mountain's spirit vine and that vineyard the first planted on Red Mountain.

I recently read *Dark Matter*, a sci-fi novel by Blake Crouch, which explores the idea of different dimensions—subtly different realities in which things look the same save some minor details. In one dimension, a man's front door is flanked by two shrubs. In another dimension, the shrubs are missing. In one dimension, that man is a barber. In another dimension, a series of small decisions has made that same man a banker.

Crouch's book captured exactly how I see the settings of my worlds lately. When you step into my novels, you are stepping into a dimension of my creating. Though I have done my research, I have chosen to put the world I see on the page, not exactly the one that you and I currently inhabit.

For example, if I want phylloxera to show up in Sonoma in '83, a couple of years earlier than most reported cases in California, then guess what: I can do that. If I want Otis to be one of the first to bring back the use of clay pots known as amphorae for fermenting and aging, nothing is stopping me. If I want to create a steak house in Sonoma that didn't exist, then I'm doing it. Or if I want to make 1992 the hottest year on record in Sonoma, so be it. Because this is a fictional world, and this book and all my books going forward will not be set in exact replicas of our world. My characters live in a dimension that differs in slight or even giant ways.

All this is to say, especially to my fellow winos out there who are hounds for wine history, I'm sorry I didn't get all facts right. Had I attempted, I likely would have failed. What I've offered here is the dimension Otis inhabits.

There is pure bliss in having found this freedom, and if you'll agree to suspend your disbelief, then I'll offer you the absolute truth of this particular world and all future worlds from which I'll pull tales.

Acknowledgments

Here I am today, January 8, 2025, in my home in Cape Elizabeth, Maine, wrapping this baby up and feeling all kinds of emotions. Especially gratitude. What a ride this novel has been. I've never deleted more words or been more frustrated, but those struggles are often evidence of my best work.

How could I have ever known when Otis first came alive on the page in my novel *Red Mountain* that he'd end up steering so much of my life, making it possible for me to write for a living? He led the cast in two more books in the Red Mountain Chronicles and now has his own origin story, one that feels bigger than any tale I've ever told. I suppose I should thank him, wherever he is now, imaginary or not, as he is no doubt the character who led me to find my voice. He's so alive in my head that it does make me wonder whether he's out there somewhere, in another dimension, perhaps, true flesh and bone. I raise my glass to you, Otis.

When I first broke away from writing thrillers and took a chance on this kind of fiction, it felt like something fell into place. My readers appeared, and a wonderful team of professionals began to support me. I *never* could have done this on my own. Many of you reading this note gave me the courage to chase my dreams. You read my books, spread the word, wrote me kind notes, lifted me up, taught me lessons, and helped me shatter the doubt that plagues all writers—or, at least, helped me keep it at bay long enough to stab out a first draft, which is the hardest part for me. You know who you are, the people who have made this thing I do possible. I'm tearing up right now as my heart swells.

I'd like to name a few folks in particular.

Jodi Warshaw, it was such a pleasure to work with you for the first time. Thank you for understanding me and my manuscript and giving me the courage to plow ahead. I love all your suggestions, especially regarding Mike and Bec, and it's clear that we see eye to eye. I hope this is the first of many projects I have the pleasure of working with you on.

Danielle Marshall, you're simply wonderful. Thank you for your guidance and belief. You did wonders for me and countless others at Lake Union, and I look forward to watching you soar in the next chapter of your career.

To everyone at Lake Union: huge appreesh for being amazing partners and bringing my books to life.

Andrea Hurst, thank you for suggesting I tell Otis's story and for inspiring so many ideas. I hope you enjoy it. You've taught me so much over the years, and I'm forever grateful. We did some wonderful things together.

My beta readers silently work in the background and do so much to help me polish my manuscripts. I'm beyond grateful to y'all. You make me a better writer and help me take each book to the next level. Lauren Cormier, you have been by my side since the day I decided to write Otis's origin story. You're a dream come true, and I'm ever grateful to have you in my life.

Romo, Romo, Romo, the wine Romo, not football Romo; a.k.a. Robert Morrison . . . what a blessing you are. You show me all the time what being a good friend means. Thank you for championing my work, reading every single story, caring about me and my family, and with this one, stomaching a very early draft and contributing big-time with your wine expertise. You're one of a kind, my man.

Sarah Hedges Goedhart, you and Brent were there from the start of my wine journey. Thank you for being such an awesome teacher and friend. Your help with the winemaking details of this book was invaluable. You make me look like I know what I'm doing. Though we're divided by a lot of miles, y'all are still very much in our hearts. Every time I drink one of your exquisite bottles, I am taken back to my time on Red Mountain. What a special and wonderfully raucous chapter.

To all of the Hedges family: I'm grateful to know you and to have learned from you. Our years together were some of the best of my life. You're such grand people who do amazing, inspiring things. Maggie and Christophe, you're one of a kind, and I'm not sure what I'd do without our often-absurd text thread that's been entertaining me for more than a decade. I don't think anyone could keep up with the amount of food pics we share with each other. Tom and Anne-Marie, my West Coast parents: You are two of my heroes. I hope you enjoyed your cameos.

Thank you to my friends in the beautifully irreverent Wine Knerds Facebook Group for guiding me on this one. Special thanks to Melissa Smith and Amy Troutmiller for introducing me to some of your wine friends.

Jacque Martini, a million gold bars of gratitude for hosting my family at your extraordinary house in Dillon Beach. I'll never forget our inspiring conversations, the pizza and wine, your stunning home, or Michael's guitar collection. My goodness, when can we do it again? Oh, and the sourdough starter you passed along is alive and well!

Tony Coturri, you're my kind of winemaker. Thank you for letting me spend time with you on your special property. I adore your vision and passion. So much of this book was inspired by our morning together. When I think of Otis's mentor, Carmine, I think of you.

David Ramey, I adored our visit together. You taught me so much, and your wines knocked me to my knees. Thanks for going out of your way and making the whole morning extra special.

Joel Peterson, thank you for our wonderful conversations and the tasting you set up at Bedrock. My wife and I were floored by the lineup, and what a special honor to taste them alongside Morgan's. Your descriptions of California wine country back in the old days sent my imagination reeling.

Thanks to Morgan Twain-Peterson and Chris Cottrell and Grant Wood at Bedrock Wine Co. for a killer tasting. Your wines are sensational and gave me a damn fine glimpse into what California is capable of. I have one bottle left, and I'm saving it for something special.

Clay Mauritson, you did so much for this book by simply answering one question: What drama has come up in the last forty years in Sonoma? I'm glad we were able to reconnect after all these years. Keep fighting the good fight.

Howard, the legendary wine buyer of San Francisco, thank you for letting me use your name and completely make stuff up about you. I hope it brought a smile to your face.

Thank you to Kahryn at Anelare on Red Mountain for slinging my books for all these years, spreading the word. It means more than you know.

To everyone on Red Mountain: Though I'm a long way away now, your terroir is still in my heart. Thank you for doing what you do to elevate your special appellation. I hope you enjoy my imaginary spin on life out there. As you can see, I still can't let go. Please accept my apologies if I left you out or got something wrong.

I'm incredibly lucky to belong to a small but mighty writers' group called the Tiki Bar Pals. It started out as an occasional chat about word stuff but has become far more. Nathan, James, Lucy, and Cecelia, you guys mean a tremendous amount to me, and I look forward to our first Guinness together in Ireland next summer.

Thank you as always to my friends and family, who put up with me, support me, and let me steal all the drama from their lives so that I can put it on the page.

Mikella and Riggs, we did it. Two books in one year. That's enough of that. Thank you for supporting me in this ambitious undertaking. I wish I could say this is getting easier, but it's not, which means I'm still a pain in the arse under deadline. Come to think of it, I'm probably a pain in the arse year-round, which means you both deserve medals. Infinite gratitude for your love. You teach me every day how to live, how to smile, how to let go. Y'all are *everything* to me, and I can't wait to turn the page and see what's next.

To the readers, bookstores, bloggers, and book clubs: You're the ones making this happen. If I could, I'd wrap my arms around all of you. Thank you for your support and allowing me to make art for a living.

My love and gratitude to all of you.

Book Club Questions

1. Have you read other books in the Red Mountain series? How does this story fit and compare with them? Do similar themes run through the other books?

2. Throughout Otis's journey, he has trouble getting out of his own way. Discuss his struggles. Could you show the same patience as Rebecca?

3. Looking at Otis's and Bec's parents, how did they affect their children? How do your parents affect you? (I know, that's a big one! Everyone grab their wine.)

4. What did Woodstock mean to you? Who were your favorite musicians of the sixties and seventies?

5. Did you know anyone who went to Vietnam? How did the war change them? How did it affect you?

6. Has this book altered how you feel about wine? Have you ever traveled to wine country?

7. Who were your favorite and least favorite characters? Discuss.

8. Otis learned a great deal from Carmine and then passed those skills to Vance and Brooks, among others. Discuss the importance of mentorship. Did you have a mentor?

9. How did you feel about Boo's employment of Bec's ghost as a narrator in the story?

10. Coyotes are a recurring symbol throughout the book. What do they symbolize? What other symbols did you notice?

11. Rebecca believed heavily in manifestation, the idea that you have a hand in creating your reality. What's your take on it? How much do you think Otis's and Bec's success was due to manifestation and how much to hard work?

12. Do you believe that we have a soulmate? Or soulmates? Does love transcend the grave?

About the Author

Photo © 2018 Brandi Morris

Boo Walker is the bestselling author of *An Echo in Time, The Stars Don't Lie, A Spanish Sunrise, The Singing Trees, An Unfinished Story,* and the Red Mountain Chronicles, among other novels. Boo initially tapped his creative muse as a songwriter and banjoist in Nashville before working his way west to Washington State, where he bought a gentleman's farm on the Yakima River. It was there, among the grapevines and wine barrels, that he fell in love with telling high-impact stories that now resonate with book clubs around the world. Rich with colorful characters and boundless soul, his novels will leave you with an open heart and a lifted spirit. Always a wanderer, Boo currently lives in Cape Elizabeth, Maine, with his wife and son. He also writes thrillers under the pen name Benjamin Blackmore. For more information, visit www.boowalker.com.